GUY DEVERELL

THE QUARREL.

(*See* Chap. 23.)

GUY DEVERELL

by

J. SHERIDAN LE FANU

DOVER PUBLICATIONS, INC.

NEW YORK

Published in Canada by General Publishing Company,
Ltd., 30 Lesmill Road, Don Mills, Toronto, Ontario.

Published in the United Kingdom by Constable and
Company, Ltd., 10 Orange Street, London WC2H 7EG.

This Dover edition, first published in 1984, is an unabridged republication of the edition published by Richard
Bentley, London, 1866 (first edition: 1865; the work
appeared in *The Dublin University Magazine* also in
1865).

Manufactured in the United States of America
Dover Publications, Inc., 31 East 2nd Street, Mineola,
N.Y. 11501

Library of Congress Cataloging in Publication Data

Le Fanu, J. Sheridan (Joseph Sheridan), 1814–1873.
  Guy Deverell.

  Reprint. Originally published: London : R. Bentley,
1866.
  I. Title.
PR4879.L7G8   1984   823'.8   83-20655
ISBN 0-486-24618-3

CONTENTS.

GUY DEVERELL

SIR JEKYL MARLOWE AT THE PLOUGH INN.

GUY DEVERELL.

CHAPTER I.

SIR JEKYL MARLOWE AT THE PLOUGH INN.

THE pretty little posting station, known as the Plough Inn, on the Old London Road, where the Sterndale Road crosses it, was in a state of fuss and awe, at about five o'clock on a fine sharp October evening, for Sir Jekyl Marlowe, a man of many thousand acres, and M.P. for the county, was standing with his back to the fire, in the parlour, whose bow-window looks out on the ancient thoroughfare I have mentioned, over the row of scarlet geraniums which beautify the window-stone.

'Hollo!' cried the Baronet, as the bell-rope came down in answer to an energetic but not angry pull, and he received Mrs. Jones, his hostess, who entered at the moment, with the dismantled bell-handle still in his hand. 'At my old tricks, you see. I've been doing you a mischief, hey? but we'll set it right in the bill, you know. How devilish well you look! wonderful girl, by Jove! Come in, my dear, and shut the door. Not afraid of me. I want to talk of ducks and mutton-chops. I've had no luncheon, and I'm awfully hungry,' said the comely Baronet in a continued chuckle.

The Baronet was, by that awful red-bound volume of dates, which is one of the melancholy drawbacks of aristocracy, set down just then, and by all whom it might concern, ascertainable to be precisely forty-nine years and three months old; but so well had he worn, and so cleverly was he got up, that he might have passed for little more than forty.

He was smiling, with very white teeth, and a gay leer on pretty Mrs. Jones, an old friend, with black eyes and tresses, and pink cheeks, who bore her five-and-thirty years as well almost as he did his own burthen. The slanting autumnal sun became her, and she simpered and courtesied and blushed the best she could.

'Well, you pretty little devil, what can you do for me—hey? You know we're old friends—hey? What have you got for a hungry fellow? and don't stand at the door there, hang it—come in, can't yon? and let me hear what you say.'

So Mrs. Jones, with a simpering bashfulness, delivered her bill of fare off book.

The Baronet was a gallant English gentleman, and came of a healthy race, though there were a 'beau' and an archbishop in the family; he could rough it good-humouredly on beefsteak and port, and had an accommodating appetite as to hours.

'That will do very nicely, my dear, thank you. You're just the same dear hospitable little rogue I remember you—how long is it, by Jove, since I stopped here that day, and the awful thunder-storm at night, don't you recollect? and the whole house in such a devil of a row, egad!' And the Baronet chuckled and leered, with his hands in his pockets.

'Three years, by Jove, I think—eh?'

'Four years in August last, Sir Jekyl,' she answered, with a little toss of her head and a courtesy.

'Four years, my dear—four devils! Is it possible? why upon my life it has positively improved you.' And he tapped her cheek playfully with his finger. 'And what o'clock is it?' he continued, looking at his watch, 'just five. Well, I suppose you'll be ready in half-an-hour—eh, my dear?'

'Sooner, if you wish, Sir Jekyl.'

'No, thank you, dear, that will do very nicely; and stay,' he added, with a pluck at her pink ribbon, as she retreated: 'you've some devilish good port here, unless it's all out—old Lord Hog-wood's stock—eh?'

'More than two dozen left, Sir Jekyl; would you please some ?'

'You've hit it, you wicked little conjurer—a bottle; and you must give me a few minutes after dinner, and a cup of coffee, and tell me all the news—eh ?'

The Baronet, standing on the threadbare hearthrug, looked waggishly, as it were, through the pannels of the shut door, after the fluttering cap of his pretty landlady. Then he turned about and reviewed himself in the sea-green mirror over the chimney-piece, adjusted his curls and whiskers with a touch or two of his finger's ends, and plucked a little at his ample silk necktie, and shook out his tresses, with his chin a little up, and a saucy simper.

But a man tires even of that prospect; and he turned on his heel, and whistled at the smoky mezzotint of George III. on the opposite wall. Then he turned his head, and looked out through the bow-window, and his whistling stopped in the middle of a bar, at the sight of a young man whom he espied, only a yard or two before the covered porch of the little inn.

This young gentleman was, it seemed, giving a parting direction to some one in the doorway. He was tall, slender, rather dark, and decidedly handsome. There were, indeed, in his air, face, and costume, that indescribable elegance and superiority which constitute a man 'distinguished looking.'

When Sir Jekyl beheld this particularly handsome young man, it was with a disagreeable shock, like the tap on a big drum, upon his diaphragm. If anyone had been there he would have witnessed an odd and grizzly change in the pleasant Baronet's countenance. For a few seconds he did not move. Then he drew back a pace or two, and stood at the further side of the fire, with the mantelpiece partially between him and the young gentleman who spoke his parting directions, all unconscious of the haggard stare which made Sir Jekyl look a great deal less young and good-natured than was his wont.

This handsome young stranger, smiling, signalled with his cane, as it seemed, to a companion, who had preceded him, and ran in pursuit.

For a time Sir Jekyl did not move a muscle, and then, with a sudden pound on the chimneypiece, and a great oath, he exclaimed—

'I could not have believed it! What the devil can it mean?'

Then the Baronet bethought him—'What confounded stuff one does talk and think, sometimes! Half the matter dropt out of my mind. Twenty years ago, by Jove, too. *More* than that, egad! How could I be such an ass?'

And he countermarched, and twirled on his heel into his old place, with his back to the fire, and chuckled and asked again—

'How the plague *could* I be such a fool?'

'And after some more of this sort of catechism he began to ruminate oddly once more, and, said he—

'It's plaguy *odd*, for all that.'

And he walked to the window, and, with his face close to the glass, tried in vain to see the stranger again. The bow-window did not command the road far enough to enable him to see any distance; and he stuck his hat on his head, and marched by the bar, through the porch, and, standing upon the road itself, looked shrewdly in the same direction.

But the road makes a bend about there, and between the hedgerows of that wooded country the vista was not far.

With a cheerful air of carelessness, Sir Jekyl returned and tapped on the bar window.

'I say, Mrs. Jones, who's that good-looking young fellow that went out just now?'

'The gentleman in the low-crowned hat, sir, with the gold-headed cane, please?'

'Yes, a tall young fellow, with large dark eyes, and brown hair.'

'That will be Mr. Strangers, Sir Jekyl.'

'Does he sleep here to-night?'

'Yes, sir, please.'

'And what's his business?'

'Oh, dear! No business, Sir Jekyl, please. He's a real gentleman, and no end of money.'

'I mean, how does he amuse himself?'

'A looking after prospects, and old places, and such like, Sir Jekyl. Sometimes riding and sometimes a fly. Every day some place or other.'

'Oh! pencils and paint-boxes—eh?'

'I aven't seen none, sir. I can't say how that will be?'

'Well, and what is he about; where is he gone; where is he now?' demanded the Baronet.

'What way did Mr. Strangers go, Bill, just now?' the lady demanded of boots, who appeared at the moment.

'The Abbey, ma'am.'

'The Abbey, please, Sir Jekyl.'

'The Abbey—that's Wail Abbey—eh? How far is it?'

'How far will it be, Bill?'

''Taint a mile all out, ma'am.'

'Not quite a mile, Sir Jekyl.'

'A good ruin—isn't it?' asked the Baronet.

'Well, they do say it's *very* much out of repair; but I never saw it myself, Sir Jekyl.'

'Neither did I,' said Sir Jekyl. 'I say, my good fellow, you can point it out, I dare say, from the steps here?'

'Aye, please, Sir Jekyl.'

'You'll have dinner put back, Sir—please, Sir Jekyl?' asked Mrs. Jones.

'Back or forward, *any* way, my dear child. Only I'll have my walk first.'

And kissing and waving the tips of his fingers, with a smile to Mrs. Jones, who courtesied and simpered, though her heart was perplexed with culinary solicitudes 'how to keep the water from getting into the trout, and prevent the ducks of over-roasting,' the worthy Baronet, followed by Bill, stepped through the porch, and on the ridge of the old highroad, his own heart being oddly disturbed with certain cares which had given him a long respite; there he received Bill's directions as to the route to the Abbey.

It was a clear frosty evening. The red round sun by this time,. near the horizon, looked as if a tall man on the summit of the western hill might have touched its edge with his finger. The Baronet looked on the declining luminary as he buttoned his loose coat across his throat, till his eyes were almost dazzled, thinking all the time of nothing but that handsome young man; and as he walked on briskly toward the Abbey, he saw little pale green suns dancing along the road and wherever else his eyes were turned.

'I'll see this fellow face to face, and talk a bit with him. I dare say if one were near he's not at all so like.. It *is* devilish odd though; twenty-five years and not a relation on earth—and dead—hang him! Egad, its like the wandering Jew, and the what do you call 'em, *vitæ*. Ay, here it is.'

He paused for a moment, looking at the pretty stile which led a little pathway across the fields to the wooded hollow by the river, where the ruin stands. Two old white stone, fluted piers, once a doorway, now tufted with grass, and stained and worn by time, and the stile built up between.

'I know, of course, there's nothing in it; but it's so odd—it *is* so *devilish* odd. I'd like to know all about it,' said the Baronet, picking the dust from the fluting with the point of his walking-cane. 'Where has he got, I wonder, by this time?' So he mounted the stile, and paused near the summit to obtain a commanding view.

'Well, I suppose he's got among the old walls and rubbish by this time. I'll make him out; he'll break cover.'

And he skipped down the stile on the. other side, and whistled a little, cutting gaily in the air with his cane as he went.

But for all he could do the same intensely uncomfortable curiosity pressed upon him as he advanced. The sun sank behind the distant hills, leaving the heavens flooded with a discoloured crimson, and the faint silver of the moon in the eastern sky glimmered coldly over the fading landscape, as he suddenly emerged from the hedged pathway on the rich meadow level by the slow river's brink, on which, surrounded by lofty timber, the ruined Abbey stands.

The birds had come home. Their vesper song had sunk with the setting sun, and in the sad solitude of twilight the grey ruins rose dimly before him.

'A devilish good spot for a picnic!' said he, making an effort to recover his usual agreeable vein of thought and spirits.

So he looked up and about him, and jauntily marched over the sward, and walked along the line of the grey walls until he found a doorway, and began his explorations.

Through dark passages, up broken stairs, over grass-grown piles of rubbish, he peeped into all sorts of roofless chambers. Everything was silent and settling down into night. At last, by that narrow doorway, which in such buildings so oddly gives entrance here and there into vast apartments, he turned into that grand chamber, whose stone floor rests on the vaults beneath ; and there the Baronet paused for a moment with a little start, for at the far end, looking towards him, but a little upward, with the faint reflected glow that entered through the tall row of windows, on the side of his face and figure, stood the handsome young man of whom he was in pursuit.

The Baronet being himself only a step or two from the screw stairs, and still under the shadow of the overhanging arch in the corner, the stranger saw nothing of him and to announce his approach, though not much of a musician, he hummed a bar or two briskly as he entered, and marched across and about as if thinking of nothing but architecture or the picturesque.

'Charming ruin this, sir,' exclaimed he, raising his hat, so soon as he had approached the stranger sufficiently near to make the address natural. 'Although I'm a resident of this part of the world, I'm ashamed to say I never saw it before.'

The young man raised his hat too, and bowed with a ceremonious grace, which, as well as his accent, had something foreign in it.

'While I, though a stranger, have been unable to resist its fascination, and have already visited it three times. You have reason to be proud of your county, sir, it is full of beauties.'

The stranger's sweet, but peculiar, voice thrilled the Baronet

with a recollection as vivid and detested. In fact this well-sea-
soned man of the world was so much shocked that he answered
only with a bow, and cleared his voice, and chuckled after
his fashion, but all the time felt a chill creeping over his
back.

There was a broad bar of a foggy red light falling through the
ivy-girt window, but the young man happened to stand at that
moment in the shadow beside it, and when the Baronet's quick
glance, instead of detecting some reassuring distinction of feature
or expression, encountered only the ambiguous and obscure, he
recoiled inwardly as from something abominable.

' Beautiful effect—beautiful sky!' exclaimed Sir Jekyl, not
knowing very well what he was saying, and waving his cane
upwards towards the fading tints of the sky.

The stranger emerged from his shadow and stood beside him,
and such light as there was fell full upon his features, and as the
Baronet beheld he felt as if he were in a dream.

CHAPTER II.

THE BARONET VISITS WARDLOCK MANOR.

IN fact Sir Jekyl would have been puzzled to know exactly what
to say next, so odd were his sensations, and his mind so pre-oc-
cupied with a chain of extremely uncomfortable conjecture, had
not the handsome young gentleman who stood beside him at the
gaping window with its melancholy folds of ivy, said—

' I have often tried to analyse the peculiar interest of ruins like
these—the mixture of melancholy and curiosity. I have seen
very many monasteries abroad—perhaps as old as this, even older
—still peopled with their monks, with very little interest indeed,
and no sympathy ; and yet here I feel a yearning after the bygone
age of English monasticism, an anxiety to learn all about their
ways and doings, and a sort of reverence and sadness I can't
account for, unless it be an expression of that profound sympathy

which mortals feel with every expression of decay and dissolution.'

The Baronet fancied that he saw a lurking smile in the young man's face, and recoiled from psychologic talk about mortality.

' I dare say you're right, sir, but I am the worst metaphysician in the world.' He thought the young man smiled again. ' In your liking for the picturesque, however, I quite go with you. Do you intend extending your tour to Wales and Scotland ?'

' I can hardly call this little excursion a tour. The fact is, my curiosity is pretty much limited to this county ; there are old reasons which make me feel a very particular interest in it,' said the young man, with a very pointed carelessness and a smile, which caused the Baronet inwardly to wince.

' I should be very happy,' said Sir Jekyl, ' if you would take Marlowe in your way : there are some pictures there, as well as some views you might like to see. I am Sir Jekyl Marlowe, and own two or three places in this county, which are thought pretty —and, may I give you my card ?'

The snowy parallelogram was here presented and accepted with a mutual bow. The stranger was smiling oddly as Sir Jekyl introduced himself, with an expression which he fancied he could read in spite of the dark, as implying ' rather old news you tell me.'

' And—and—what was I going to say ?—oh !—yes—if I can be of any use to you in procuring access to any house or place you wish to see, I shall be very happy. You are at present staying at my occasional quarters, the " Plough." I'm afraid you'll think me very impertinent and intrusive ; but I should like to be able to mention your name to some of my friends, who don't usually allow strangers to see their places.'

This was more like American than English politeness ; but the Baronet was determined to know all about the stranger, commencing with his name, and the laws of good breeding, though he knew them very well, were not likely to stand long in his way when he had made up his mind to accomplish an object.

' My name is Guy Strangways,' said the stranger.

'O—ho—it's very odd!' exclaimed the Baronet, in a sharp snarl, quite unlike his previous talk. I think the distance between them was a little increased, and he was looking askance upon the young gentleman, who made him a very low foreign bow.

There was a silence, and just then a deep metallic voice from below called, ' Guy—hollo!'

'Excuse me—just a moment,' and the young man was gone. The Baronet waited.

' He'll be back,' muttered Sir Jekyl, ' in a minute.'

But the Baronet was mistaken. He waited at that open window, whistling out upon the deepening twilight, till the edges of the ivy began to glitter in the moonbeams, and the bats to trace their zigzags in the air; and at last he gave over expecting.

He looked back into the gloomy void of that great chamber, and listened, and felt rather angry at his queer sensations. He had not turned about when the stranger withdrew, and did not know the process of his vanishing, and for the first time it struck him, ' who the plague could the fellow who *called* him be ?'

On the whole he wished himself away, and he lighted a cigar for the sake of its vulgar associations, and made his way out of the ruins, and swiftly through darkened fields toward the Old London Road; and was more comfortable than he cared to say, when he stepped through the porch into the open hall of the ' Plough,' and stopped before the light at the bar, to ask his hostess once more, quite in his old way, whether Mr. Strangways had returned.

' No, not yet; always uncertain; his dinner mostly overdone.'

' Has he a friend with him ?'

' Yes, sir, sure.'

' And what is he like ?'

' Older man, Sir Jekyl, a long way than young Mr. Guy Strangways; some relation I do think.'

' When do they leave you ?'

' To-morrow evening, with a chaise and pair for Awkworth.'

' Awkworth ? why, that's another of my properties !—ha, ha, ha, by Jove! Does he know the Abbey here is mine ?'

'I rayther think not, Sir Jekyl. Would you please to wish dinner?'

'To be sure, you dear little quiz, dinner by all means; and let them get my horses to in half-an-hour; and if Mr. Strangways should return before I go, I'd like to see him, and don't fail to let me know—do ye see?'

Dinner came and went, but Mr. Strangways did not return, which rather vexed Sir Jekyl, who, however, left his card for that gentleman, together with an extremely polite note, which he wrote at the bar with his hat on, inviting him and his companion to Marlowe, where he would be at home any time for the next two months, and trusted they would give him a week before they left the country.

It was now dark, and Sir Jekyl loitered under the lamplight of his chaise for a while, in the hope that Mr. Strangways would turn up. But he did not; and the Baronet jumped into the vehicle, which was forthwith in motion.

He sat in the corner, with one foot on the cushion, and lighted a cigar. His chuckling was all over, and his quizzing, for the present. Mrs. Jones had not a notion that he was in the least uneasy, or on any but hospitable thoughts intent. But anyone who now looked in his face would have seen at a glance how suddenly it had become overcast with black care.

'Guy Strangways!' he thought; 'those two names, and his wonderful likeness! Prowling about this county! Why this more than another? He seemed to take a triumphant pleasure in telling me of his special fancy for this county. And his voice—a tenor they call it—I hate that sweet sort of voice. Those d—— singing fellows. I dare say he sings. They never do a bit of good. It's very odd. It's the same voice. I forgot that odd silvery sound. The *same*, by Jove! I'll come to the bottom of the whole thing. D—— me, I will!'

Then the Baronet puffed away fast and earnestly at his cigar, and then lighted another, and after that a third. They steadied him, I dare say, and helped to oil the mechanism of thought. But he had not recovered his wonted cheer of mind when the

chaise drew up at a pair of time-worn fluted piers, with the gable
of an old-fashioned dwelling-house overlooking the road at one
side. An iron gate admitted to a court-yard, and the hall door of
the house was opened by an old-fashioned footman, with some
flour on the top of his head.

Sir Jekyl jumped down.

'Your mistress quite well, hey? My daughter ready?' inquired the Baronet. 'Where are they? No, I'll not go up, thank
you; I'll stay here,' and he entered the parlour. 'And, do you
see, you just go up and ask your mistress if she wishes to see me.'

By this time Sir Jekyl was poking up the fire and frowning
down on the bars, with the flickering glare shooting over his face.

'Can the old woman have anything to do with it? Pooh! no.
I'd like to see her. But who knows what sort of a temper she's
in?'

As he thus ruminated, the domestic with the old-fashioned
livery and floured head returned to say that his mistress would be
happy to see him.

The servant conducted him up a broad stair with a great oak
banister, and opening a drawing-room door, announced—

'Sir Jekyl Marlowe.'

He was instantly in the room, and a tall, thin old lady, with a
sad and stately mien, rose up to greet him.

'How is little mamma?' cried the Baronet, with his old
chuckle. 'An age since we met, hey? How well you look!'

The old lady gave her thin mittened hand to her son-in-law,
and looked a grim and dubious sort of welcome upon him.

'Yes, Jekyl, an age; and only that Beatrix is here, I suppose
another age would have passed without my seeing you. And an
old woman at my years has not many ages between her and the
grave.'

The old lady spoke not playfully, but sternly, like one who had
suffered long and horribly, and who associated her sufferings with
her visitor; and in her oblique glance was something of deep-
seated antipathy.

'Egad! you're younger than I, though you count more years.

You live by clock and rule, and you show it. You're as fresh as
that bunch of flowers there ; while I am literally knocking myself
to pieces—and I know it—by late hours, and all sorts of nonsense.
So you must not be coming the old woman over me, you know,
unless you want to frighten me. And how is Beatrix ? How do,
Beatrix ? All ready, I see. Good child.'

Beatrix at this moment was entering. She was tall and slightly
formed, with large dark eyes, hair of soft shadowy black, and
those tints of pure white and rich clear blush, scarlet lips, and
pearly teeth, and long eyelashes, which are so beautiful in contrast and in harmony. She had the prettiest little white nose,
and her face was formed in that decided oval which so heightens
the charms of the features. She was not a tragic heroine. Her
smile was girlish and natural—and the little ring of pearls between her lips laughed beautifully—and her dimples played on
chin and cheek as she smiled.

Her father kissed her, and looked at her with a look of gratifi-
cation, as he might on a good picture that belonged to him ; and
turning her smiling face, with his finger and thumb upon her
little dimpled chin, toward Lady Alice, he said—

' Pretty well, this girl, hey ?'

' I dare say, Jekyl, she'll do very well ; she's not formed yet,
you know,'—was stately Lady Alice's qualified assent. She was one
of that school who are more afraid of spoiling people than desirous
of pleasing them by admiration. ' She promises to be like her darling mother ; and that is a melancholy satisfaction to me, and, of
course, to you. You'll have some tea, Jekyl ?'

The Baronet was standing, hat in hand, with his outside coat on,
and his back to the fire, and a cashmere muffler loosely about his
throat.

' Well, as it is here, I don't mind.'

' May I run down, grandmamma, and say good-bye to Ellen and
old Mrs. Mason ?'

' Surely—you mean, of course to the parlour ? You may have
them there.'

'And you must not be all night about it, Beatrix. We'll be going in a few minutes. D'ye mind?'

'I'm quite ready, papa,' said she; and as she glided from the room she stole a glance at her bright reflection in the mirror.

'You are always in a hurry, Jekyl, to leave me when you chance to come here. I should be sorry, however, to interfere with the pleasanter disposition of your time.'

"Now, little mother, you musn't be huffed with me. I have a hundred and fifty things to look after at Marlowe when I get there. I have not had a great deal of time, you know—first the session, then three months knocking about the world.'

'You never wrote to me since you left Paris,' said the old lady, grimly.

'Didn't I? That was very wrong! But you knew those were my holidays, and I detest writing; and you knew I could take care of myself; and it is so much better to tell one's adventures than to put them into letters, don't you think?'

'If one could tell them all in five minutes,' replied the old lady, drily.

"Well, but you'll come over to Marlowe—you really must—and I'll tell you everything there—the truth, the whole truth, and as much more as you like.'

This invitation was repeated every year, but, like Don Juan's to the statue, was not expected to lead to a literal visit.

'You have haunted rooms there, Jekyl,' she said, with an unpleasant smile and a nod. You have not kept house in Marlowe for ten years, I think. Why do you go there now?'

'Caprice, whim, what you will,' said the Baronet, combing out his favourite whisker with the tips of his fingers, while he smiled on himself in the glass upon the chimney-piece, 'I wish *you'd* tell me, for *I* really don't know, except that I'm tired of Warton and Dartbroke, as I am of all monotony. I like change, you know.'

'Yes; you *like change*,' said the old lady, with a dignified sarcasm.

'I'm afraid it's a true bill,' admitted Sir Jekyl, with a chuckle. 'So you'll come to Marlowe and see us there—won't you?'

'No, Jekyl—certainly *not*,' said the old lady, with intense emphasis.

A little pause ensued, during which the Baronet twiddled at his whisker, and continued to smile amusedly at himself in the glass.

'I wonder you could think of asking me to Marlowe, considering all that has happened there. I sometimes wonder at myself that I can endure to see you at all, Jekyl Marlowe; and I don't think, if it were not for that dear girl, who is so like her sainted mother, I should ever set eyes on you again.'

'I'm glad we have that link. You make me love Beatrix better,' he replied. He was now arranging the elaborate breastpin with its tiny chain, which was at that date in vogue.

'And so you are going to keep house at Marlowe?' resumed the lady, stiffly, not heeding the sentiment of his little speech.

'Well, so I propose.'

'I don't like that house,' said the old lady, with a subdued fierceness.

'Sorry it does not please you, little mother,' replied Sir Jekyl.

'You know I don't like it,' she repeated.

'In that case you need not have told me,' he said.

'I choose to tell you. I'll say so as often as I see you—as often as I like.'

It was an odd conference—back to back—the old lady stiff and high—staring pale and grimly at the opposite wall. The Baronet looking with a quizzical smile on his handsome face in the mirror —now plucking at a whisker—now poking at a curl with his finger-tip—and now in the same light way arranging the silken fall of his necktie.

'There's nothing my dear little mamma can say, I'll not listen to with pleasure.'

'There is much I might say you could not listen to with pleasure.' The cold was growing more intense, and bitter in tone and emphasis, as she addressed the Italian picture of Adonis and his two dogs hanging on the distant wall.

'Well, with *respect, not* with pleasure—no,' said he, and tapped his white upper teeth with the nail of his middle finger.

'Assuming, then, that you speak truth, it is high time, Jekyl Marlowe, that you should alter your courses—here's your daughter, just come out. It is ridiculous, your affecting the vices of youth. Make up as you will—you're past the middle age—you're an elderly man now.'

'You can't vex me that way, you dear old mamma,' he said, with a chuckle, which looked for the first time a little vicious in the glass. 'We baronets, you know, are all booked, and all the world can read our ages; but you women manage better—you and your two dear sisters, Winifred and Georgiana.'

'They are *dead*,' interrupted Lady Alice, with more asperity than pathos.

'Yes, I know, poor old souls—to be sure, peers' daughters die like other people, I'm afraid.'

'And when they do, are mentioned, if not with sorrow, at least with decent respect, by persons, that is, who know how to behave themselves.'

'There was a slight quiver in Lady Alice's lofty tone that pleased Sir Jekyl, as you might have remarked had you looked over his shoulder into the glass.

'Well, you know, I was speaking not of deaths but births, and only going to say if you look in the peerage you'll find all the men, poor devils, pinned to their birthdays, and the women left at large, to exercise their veracity on the point; but you need not care—you have not pretended to youth for the last ten years I think.'

'You are excessively impertinent, sir.'

'I *know* it,' answered Sir Jekyl, with a jubilant chuckle.

A very little more, the Baronet knew, and Lady Alice Redcliffe would have risen gray and grim, and sailed out of the room. Their partings were often after this sort.

But he did not wish matters to go quite that length at present. So he said, in a sprightly way, as if a sudden thought had struck him—

'By Jove, I believe I *am devilish* impertinent, without knowing it though—and you have forgiven me so often, I'm sure you *will* once more, and I am really so much obliged for your kindness to Beatrix. I am, indeed.'

So he took her hand, and kissed it.

<hr>

CHAPTER III.

CONCERNING TWO REMARKABLE PERSONS WHO APPEARED IN WARDLOCK CHURCH.

LADY ALICE carried her thin Roman nose some degrees higher; but she said—

'If I say anything disagreeable, it is not for the pleasure of giving you pain, Jekyl Marlowe; but I understand that you mean to have old General Lennox and his artful wife to stay at your house, and if so, I think it an arrangement that had better be dispensed with. I don't think her an eligible acquaintance for Beatrix, and you know very well she's *not*—and it is not a respectable or creditable kind of thing.'

'Now, what d——d fool. I beg pardon—but who the plague has been filling your mind with those ridiculous stories—my dear little mamma? You know how ready I am to confess; you *might* at least; I tell you everything; and I do assure you I *never* admired her. She's good looking, I know; but so are fifty pictures and statues I've seen, that don't please me.'

'Then it's true, the General and his wife are going on a visit to Marlowe?' insisted Lady Alice, drily.

'No, they are not. D—— me, I'm not thinking of the General and his wife, nor of any such d——d trumpery. I'd give something to know who the devil's taking these cursed liberties with my name.'

'Pray, Jekyl Marlowe, command your language. It can't the least signify who tells me; but you see I do sometimes get a letter.'

'Yes, and a precious letter too. Such a pack of lies did any

human being ever hear fired off in a sentence before? I'm *épris*
of Mrs. General Lennox. Thumper number one! She's a lady
of—I beg pardon—easy virtue. Thumper number two! and I invite her and her husband down to Marlowe, to make love of
course to her, and to fight the old General. Thumper number
three!'

And the Baronet chuckled over the three 'thumpers' merrily.

'Don't talk slang, if you please—gentlemen don't, at least in
addressing ladies.'

'Well, then, I won't; I'll speak just as you like, only you
must not blow me up any more; for really there is no cause, and
we here only two or three minutes together, you now; and I
want to tell you something, or rather to ask you—do you ever hear
anything of those *Deverells*, you know?'

Lady Alice looked quite startled, and turned quickly half round
in her chair, with her eyes on Sir Jekyl's face. The Baronet's
smile subsided, and he looked with a dark curiosity in hers. A
short but dismal silence followed.

'You've heard from them?'

'No!' said the lady, with little change in the expression of her
face.

'Well, *of* them?'

'No,' she repeated; 'but *why* do you ask? It's *very* strange!'

'*What's* strange? Come, now, you *have* something to say;
tell me what it is.'

'I wonder, Jekyl, you ask for them, in the first place.'

'Well—well, of course; but what next?' murmured the
Baronet, eagerly; 'why is it so strange?'

'Only because I've been thinking of them—a great deal—for
the last few days; and it seemed very odd your asking; and in
fact I fancy the same thing has happened to us both.'

'Well, may be; but what *is* it?' demanded the Baronet, with
a sinister smile.

'I have been startled; most painfully and powerfully affected;
I have seen the most extraordinary resemblance to my beautiful,
murdered Guy.'

She rose, and wept passionately, standing with her face buried in her handkerchief.

Sir Jekyl frowned with closed eyes and upturned face, waiting like a patient man bored to death, for the subsidence of the storm which he had conjured up. Very pale, too, was that countenance, and contracted for a few moments with intense annoyance.

'I saw the same fellow,' said the Baronet, in a subdued tone, as soon as there was a subsidence, 'this evening; he's at that little inn on the Sterndale Road. Guy Strangways he calls himself; I talked with him for a few minutes; a gentlemanly young man; and I don't know what to make of it. So I thought I'd ask you whether *you* could help me to a guess; and that's all.'

The old lady shook her head.

'And I don't think you need employ quite such hard terms,' he said.

'I don't want to speak of it at all,' said she; 'but if I do I can't say less; nor I won't—no, never!'

'You see it's very odd, those two names,' said Sir Jekyl, not minding; 'and as you say, the likeness so astonishing—I—I—what do *you* think of it?'

'Of course it's an accident,' said the old lady.

'I'm glad you think so,' said he, abruptly.

'Why, what could it be? you don't believe in apparitions?' she replied, with an odd sort of dryness.

'I rather think not,' said he; 'I meant he left no very near relation, and I fancied those Deverell people might have contrived some trick, or intended some personation, or something, and I thought that you, perhaps, had heard something of their movements.'

'Nothing—what could they have done, or why should they have sought to make any such impression? I don't understand it. It is very extraordinary. But the likeness in church amazed and shocked me, and made me ill.'

'In church, you say?' repeated Sir Jekyl.

'Yes, in church,' and she told him in her own way, what I shall tell in mine, as follows :—

Last Sunday she had driven, in her accustomed state, with
Beatrix, to Wardlock church. The church was hardly five hundred yards away, and the day bright and dry. But Lady Alice
always arrived and departed in the coach, and sat in the Redcliffe
seat, in the centre of the gallery. She and Beatrix sat face to face
at opposite sides of the pew.

As Lady Alice looked with her cold and steady glance over the
congregation in the aisle, during the interval of silence that
precedes the commencement of the service, a tall and graceful
young man, with an air of semi-foreign fashion, entered the church,
accompanied by an elderly gentleman, of whom she took comparatively little note.

The young man and his friend were ushered into a seat confronting the gallery. Lady Alice gazed and gazed transfixed with
astonishment and horror. The enamelled miniature on her bosom
was like; but there, in that clear, melancholy face, with its large
eyes and wavy hair, was a resurrection. In that animated
sculpture were delicate tracings and touches of nature's chisel,
which the artist had failed to represent, which even memory had
neglected to fix, but which all now returned with the startling
sense of identity in a moment.

She had put on her gold spectacles, as she always did on taking
her seat, and opened her 'Morning Service,' bound in purple
Russia, with its golden clasp and long ribbons fringed with the
same precious metal, with the intent to mark the proper psalms
and lessons at her haughty leisure. She therefore saw the moving
image of her dead son before her, with an agonizing distinctness
that told like a blight of palsy on her face.

She saw his elderly companion also distinctly. A round-
shouldered man, with his short caped cloak still on. A grave man,
with a large, high, bald forehead, a heavy, hooked nose, and great
hanging moustache and beard. A dead and ominous face enough,
except from the piercing glance of his full eyes, under very thick
brows, and just the one you would have chosen out of a thousand
portraits, for a plotting high-priest or an old magician.

This magnus fixed his gaze on Lady Alice, not with an osten--

tation of staring, but sternly from behind the dark embrasure of his brows; and leaning a little sideways, whispered something in the ear of his young companion, whose glance at the same moment was turned with a dark and fixed interest upon the old lady.

It was a very determined stare on both sides, and of course ill-bred, but mellowed by distance. The congregation were otherwise like other country congregations, awaiting the offices of their pastor, decent, listless, while this great stare was going on, so little becoming the higher associations and solemn aspect of the place. It was, with all its conventional screening, a fierce, desperate scrutiny, cutting the dim air with a steady congreve fire that crossed and glared unintermittent by the ears of deceased gentlemen in ruffs and grimy doublets, at their posthumous devotions, and brazen knights praying on their backs, and under the eyes of all the gorgeous saints, with glories round their foreheads, in attitudes of benediction or meekness, who edified believers from the eastern window.

Lady Alice drew back in her pew. Beatrix was in a young-lady reverie, and did not observe what was going on. There was nothing indeed to make it very conspicuous. But when she looked at Lady Alice, she was shocked at her appearance, and instantly crossed, and said—

'I am afraid you are ill, grandmamma; shall we come away?'

The old lady made no answer, but got up and took the girl's arm, and left the seat very quietly. She got down the gallery stairs, and halted at the old window on the landing, and sate there a little, ghastly and still mute.

The cold air circulating upward from the porch revived her.

'I am better, child,' said she, faintly.

'Thank Heaven,' said the girl, whose terror at her state proved how intensely agitated the old lady must have been.

Mrs. Wrattles, the sextoness, emerging at that moment with repeated courtesies, and whispered condolence and inquiries, Lady Alice, with a stiff condescension, prayed her to call her woman, Mason, to her.

So Lady Alice, leaning slenderly on Mason's stout arm, insisted

that Beatrix should return and sit out the service; and she herself, for the first time within the memory of man, returned from
Wardlock church on foot, instead of in her coach.   Beatrix waited
until the congregation had nearly disgorged itself and dispersed,
before making her solitary descent.

When she came down, without a chaperon, at the close of the
rector's discourse, the floured footman in livery, with his gold-
headed cane, stood as usual at the coach-door only to receive her,
and convey the order to the coachman, 'home.'

The churchyard gate, as is usual, I believe, in old places of that
kind, opens at the south side, and the road to Wardlock manor
leads along the churchyard wall and round the corner of it at a
sharp angle just at the point where the clumsy old stone mauso-
leum or vault of the Deverell family overlooks the road, with its
worn pilasters and beetle-browed cornice.

Now that was a Sunday of wonders.   It had witnessed Lady
Alice's pedestrian return from church, an act of humiliation,
almost of penance, such as the memory of Wardlock could furnish
no parallel to; and now it was to see another portent, for her
ladyship's own gray horses, fat and tranquil beasts, who had
pulled her to and from church for I know not how many years,
under the ministration of the careful coachman, with exemplary
sedateness, on this abnormal Sabbath took fright at a musical
performance of two boys, one playing the Jew's harp and the other
drumming tambourine-wise on his hat, and *suadente diabolo* and
so forth, set off at a gallop, to the terror of all concerned, toward
home.   Making the sharp turn of the road, where the tomb of the
Deverells overhangs it from the churchyard, the near-gray came
down, and his off-neighbour reared and plunged frightfully.

The young lady did not scream, but, very much terrified, she
made voluble inquiries of the air and hedges from the window,
while the purple coachman pulled hard from the box, and spoke
comfortably to his horses, and the footman, standing out of reach
of danger, talked also in his own vein.

Simultaneously with all this, as if emerging from the old mauso-
leum, there sprang over the churchyard fence, exactly under its

shadow, that young man who had excited emotions so various in the Baronet and in Lady Alice, and seized the horse by the head with both hands, and so co-operated that in less than a minute the two horses were removed from the carriage, and he standing, hat in hand, before the window, to assure the young lady that all was quite safe now.

So she descended, and the grave footman, with the Bible and Prayer-book, followed her steps with his gold-headed rod of office, while the lithe and handsome youth, his hat still in air which stirred his rich curls, walked beside her with something of that romantic deference which in one so elegant and handsome has an inexpressible sentiment of the tender in it.

He walked to the door of Wardlock Manor, and I purposely omit all he said, because I doubt whether it would look as well in this unexceptionable type as it sounded from his lips in Beatrix Marlowe's pretty ear.

If the speaker succeed with his audience, what more can oratory do for him? Well! he was gone. There remained in Beatrix's ear a music; in her fancy a heaven-like image—a combination of tint, and outline, and elegance, which made every room and scene without it lifeless, and every other object homely. These little untold impressions are of course liable to fade and vanish pretty quickly in absence, and to be superseded even sooner. Therefore it would be unwarranted to say that she was in love, although I can't deny that she was haunted by that slightly foreign young gentleman.

This latter portion of the adventure was not divulged by old Lady Alice, because Beatrix, I suppose, forgot to tell her, and she really knew nothing about it. All the rest, her own obser-vation and experience, she related with a grim and candid par-ticularity.

CHAPTER IV.

THE GREEN CHAMBER AT MARLOWE.

So the Baronet, with a rather dreary chuckle, said :—

'I don't think, to say truth, there is anything in it. I really can't see why the plague I should bore myself about it. You know your pew in the middle of the gallery, with that painted hatchment thing, you know . . . .'

'Respect the dead,' said Lady Alice, looking down with a dry severity on the table.

'Well, yes ; I mean, you know ,it is so confoundedly conspicuous, I can't wonder at the two fellows, the old and young, staring a bit at it, and, perhaps, at *you*, you know,' said Sir Jekyl, in his impertinent vein. 'But I agree with you they are no ghosts, and I really shan't trouble my head about them any more. I wonder I was such a fool—hey ? But, as you say, you know, it is un-pleasant to be reminded of—of those things ; it can't be helped now, though.'

'Now, nor ever,' said Lady Alice, grimly.

'Exactly ; neither now, nor ever,' repeated Sir Jekyl ; 'and we both know it can't possibly be poor—I mean any one con-cerned in that transaction ; so the likeness must be accidental, and therefore of no earthly significance—eh ?'

Lady Alice, with elevated brows, fiddled in silence with some crumbs on the table with the tip of her thin finger.

'I suppose Beatrix is ready ; may I ring the bell ?'

'Oh! here she is. Now bid grandmamma good night,' said the Baronet.

So slim and pretty Beatrix, in her cloak, stooped down and placed her arms about the neck of the old lady, over whose face came a faint flush of tender sunset, and her old grey eyes looked very kindly on the beautiful young face that stooped over her, as she said in a tone that, however, was stately—

'Good-bye, my dear child ; you are warm enough—you are certain ?'

'Oh, yes, dear grandmamma—my cloak and this Cashmere thing.'

'Well, darling, good-night. You'll not forget to write—you'll not fail? Good-night, Beatrix, dear—good-bye.'

'Good-night,' said the Baronet, taking the tips of her cold fingers together, and addressing himself to kiss her cheek, but she drew back in one of her whims, and said stiffly, 'There, not to-night. Good-bye, Jekyl.'

'Well,' chuckled he, after his wont, 'another time; but mind, you're to come to Marlowe.'

He did not care to listen to what she replied, but he called from the stairs, as he ran down after his daughter—

'Now mind, I won't let you off this time; you really must come. Good-night, *au revoir*—good-night.'

I really think that exemplary old lady hated the Baronet, who called her 'little mamma,' and invited her every year, without meaning it, most good-naturedly, to join his party under the ancestral roof-tree. He took a perverse sort of pleasure in these affectionate interviews, in fretting her not very placid temper—in patting her, as it were, wherever there was a raw, and in fondling her against the grain; so that his caresses were cruel, and their harmony, such as it was, amounted to no more than a flimsy deference to the scandalous world.

But Sir Jekyl knew that there was nothing in this quarter to be gained in love by a different tactique; there was a dreadful remembrance, which no poor lady has ostrich power to digest, in the way; it lay there, hard, cold, and irreducible; and the morbid sensation it produced was hatred. He knew that 'little mamma,' humanly speaking, ought to hate him. His mother, indeed, she was not; but only the step-mother of his deceased wife. Mother-in-law is not always a very sweet relation, but with the prefix 'step' the chances are, perhaps, worse.

There was, however, as you will by-and-by see, a terrible accident, or something, always remembered, gliding in and out of Wardlock Manor like the Baronet's double, walking in behind him when he visited her, like his evil genius, and when they met affectionately, standing by his shoulder, black and scowling, with clenched fist.

Now pretty Beatrix sat in the right corner of the chariot, and Sir Jekyl, her father, in the left. The lamps were lighted, and though there was moonlight, for they had a long stretch of road always dark, because densely embowered in the forest of Penlake. Tier over tier, file behind file, nodding together, the great trees bent over like plumed warriors, and made a solemn shadow always between their ranks.

Marlowe was quite new to Beatrix; but still too distant, twelve miles away, to tempt her to look out and make observations as she would on a nearer approach.

' You don't object to my smoking a cigar, Beatrix ? The smoke goes out of the window, you know,' said the Baronet, after they had driven about a mile in silence.

What young lady, so appealed to by a parent, ever did object ? The fact is, Sir Jekyl did not give himself the trouble to listen to her answer, but was manifestly thinking of something quite different, as he lighted his match.

When he threw his last stump out of the window they were driving through Penlake Forest, and the lamplight gleamed on broken rows of wrinkled trunks and ivy.

' I suppose she told you all about it ?' said he, suddenly pursuing his own train of thought.

' Who ?' inquired Beatrix.

' I never was a particular favourite of her's, you know—grandmamma's, I mean. She does not love me, poor old woman ! And she has a knack of making herself precious disagreeable, in which I try to imitate her, for peace' sake, you know; for, by George, if I was not uncivil now and then, we could never get on at all.'

Sir Jekyl chuckled after his wont, as it were, between the bars of this recitative, and he asked—

' What were the particulars—the adventure on Sunday—that young fellow, you know ?'

Miss Beatrix had heard no such interrogatory from her grandmamma, whose observations in the church-aisle were quite as unknown to her; and thus far the question of Sir Jekyl was a shock.

'Did not grandmamma tell you about it?' he pursued.

'About what, papa?' asked Beatrix, who was glad that it was dark.

'About her illness—a young fellow in a pew down in the aisle staring at her. By Jove! one would have fancied that sort of thing pretty well over. Tell me all about it.'

The fact was that this was the first she had heard of it.

'Grandmamma told me nothing of it,' said she.

'And did not you see what occurred? Did not you see him staring?' asked he.

Beatrix truly denied.

'You young ladies are always thinking of yourselves. So you saw nothing, and have nothing to tell? That will do,' said Sir Jekyl, drily; and silence returned.

Beatrix was relieved on discovering that her little adventure was unsuspected. Very little was there in it, and nothing to reflect blame upon her. From her exaggeration of its importance, and her quailing as she fancied her father was approaching it, I conclude that the young gentleman had interested her a little.

And now, as Sir Jekyl in one corner of the rolling chariot brooded in the dark over his disappointed conjectures, so did pretty Beatrix in the other speculate on the sentences which had just fallen from his lips, and long to inquire some further particulars, but somehow dared not.

Could that tall and handsome young man, who had come to her rescue so unaccountably—the gentleman with those large, soft, dark eyes, which properly belong to heroes—have been the individual whose gaze had so mysteriously affected her grandmamma? What could the associations have been that were painful enough so to overcome that grim, white woman? Was he a relation? Was he an outcast member of that proud family? Or, was he that heir-at-law, or embodied Nemesis, that the yawning sea or grave will sometimes yield up to plague the guilty or the usurper?

For all or any of these parts he seemed too young. Yet Beatrix fancied instinctively that he could be no other than the basilisk who had exercised so strange a spell over her grim, but withal kind old kinswoman.

Was there not, she thought, something peculiar in the look he threw across the windows of old stone-fronted Wardlock Manor—reserved, curious, half-smiling—as if he looked on an object which he had often heard described, and had somehow, from personal associations or otherwise, an interest in ? It was but a momentary glance just as he took his leave ; but there was, she thought, that odd character in it.

By this time the lamps were flashing on the village windows and shop-fronts ; and at the end of the old gabled street, under a canopy of dark trees, stood the great iron gate of Marlowe.

Sir Jekyl rubbed the glass and looked out when they halted at the gate. The structures of his fancy had amused him, rather fearfully, indeed, and he was surprised to find that they were entering the grounds of Marlowe so soon.

He did not mind looking out, or speaking to the old game-keeper, who pulled open the great barriers, but lay back in his corner sullenly, in the attitude of a gentleman taking a nap.

Beatrix, however, looked out inquisitively, and saw by the misty moonlight a broad level studded with majestic timber—singly, in clumps, and here and there in solemn masses ; and soon rose the broad-fronted gabled house before them, with its steep roofs and its hospitable clumps of twisted chimneys showing black against the dim sky.

Miss Marlowe's maid, to whom the scene was quite as new as to her mistress, descended from the back seat, in cloaks and mufflers, and stood by the hall-door steps, that shone white in the moonlight, before their summons had been answered.

Committing his daughter to her care, the Baronet—who was of a bustling temperament, and never drank tea except from motives of gallantry—called for Mrs. Gwynn, the housekeeper, who presently appeared.

She was an odd-looking woman—some years turned of fifty, thin, with a longish face and a fine, white, glazed skin. There was something queer about her eyes: you soon discovered it to arise from their light colour and something that did not quite match in their pupils.

On entering the hall, where the Baronet had lighted a candle, having thrown his hat on the table, and merely loosed his muffler and one or two buttons of his outside coat, she smiled a chill gleam of welcome with her pale lips, and dropped two sharp little courtesies.

'Well, old Donica, and how do ye do?' said the Baronet, smiling, with a hand on each thin grey silk shoulder. 'Long time since I saw you. But, egad! you grow younger and younger, you pretty old rogue;' and he gave her pale, thin cheek a playful tap with his fingers.

'Pretty well, please, Sir Jekyl, thank ye,' she replied, receding a little with dry dignity. 'Very welcome, sir, to Marlowe. Miss Beatrix looks very well, I am happy to see; and you, sir, also.'

'And you're glad to see us, I know?'

'Certainly, sir, glad to see you,' said Mrs. Gwynn, with another short courtesy.

'The servants not all come? No, nor Ridley with the plate. He'll arrive to-morrow; and—and we shall have the house full in little more than a week. Let us go up and look at the rooms; I forget them almost, by Jove—I really do—it's so long since. Light you another, and we'll do very well.'

'You'll see them better by daylight, sir. I kept everything well aired and clean. The house looks wonderful—it do,' replied Mrs. Gwynn, accompanying the Baronet up the broad oak stairs.

'If it looks as fresh as you, Donica, it's a miracle of a house— egad! you're a wonder. How you skip by my side, with your little taper, like a sylph in a ballet, egad!'

'You wear pretty well yourself, Sir Jekyl,' drily remarked the white-faced sylph, who had a sharp perpendicular line between her eyebrows, indicative of temper.

'So they tell me, by Jove. We're pretty well on through, Donnie—eh? Everyone knows my age—printed, you know, in the red book. You've the advantage of me there—eh, Don?'

'I'm just fifty-six, sir, and I don't care if all the world knewd it.'

'All the world's curious, I dare say, on the point; but I shan't tell them, old Gwynn,' said Sir Jekyl.

'Curious or no, sir, it's just the truth, and I don't care to hide it. Past that folly now, sir, and I don't care if I wor seventy and a steppin' like a——'

'Sylph,' supplied he.

'Yes—a sylph—into my grave. It's a bad world, and them that's suffered in it soon tires on it, sir.'

'*You* have not had a great deal to trouble you. Neither chick, nor child, nor husband, egad! So here we are.'

They were now standing on the gallery, at the head of the great staircase.

'These are the rooms your letter says are not furnished—eh? Let us come to the front gallery.'

So, first walking down the gallery in which they were, to the right, and then entering a passage by a turn on the left, they reached the front gallery which runs parallel to that at the head of the stairs.

'Where have you put Beatrix?'

'She wished the room next mine, please, sir, upstairs,' answered the housekeeper.

'Near the front—eh?'

'The left side, please, sir, as you look from the front,' replied she.

'*From* the front?' he repeated.

'From the front,' she reiterated.

'Over there, then?' he said, pointing upward to the left.

'That will be about it, sir,' she answered.

'How many rooms have we here in a row?' he asked, facing down the gallery, with its file of doors at each side.

'Four bed-rooms and three dressing-rooms at each side.'

'Ay, well now, I'll tell you who's coming, and how to dispose of them.'

So Sir Jekyl quartered his friends, as he listed, and then said he—

'And the large room at the other end, here to the right—come along.'

And Sir Jekyl marched briskly in the direction indicated.

'Please, sir,' said the slim, pale housekeeper, with the odd leer in her eye, overtaking him quietly.

'Ay, here it is,' said he, not minding her, and pushing open the door of a dressing-room at the end of the gallery. 'Inside this, I remember.'

'But that's the green chamber, sir,' continued Mrs. Gwynn, gliding beside him as he traversed the floor.

'The room we call Sir Harry's room, I know—capital room—eh?'

'I don't suppose,' began the pale lady, with a sinister sharpness.

'Well?' he demanded, looking down in her face a little grimly.

'It's the green chamber, sir,' she said, with a hard emphasis.

'You said so before, eh?' he replied.

'And I did not suppose, sir, you'd think of putting anyone there,' she continued.

'Then you're just as green as the chamber,' said Sir Jekyl, with a chuckle.

And he entered the room, holding the candle high in air, and looking about him a little curiously, the light tread and sharp pallid face of Donica Gwynn following him.

CHAPTER V.

SIR JEKYL BETHINKS HIM OF PELTER AND CROWE.

THE Baronet held his candle high in air, as I have said, as he gazed round him inquisitively. The thin housekeeper, with her pale lips closed, and her odd eyes dropped slantingly toward the floor, at the corner of the room, held hers demurely in her right finger and thumb, her arms being crossed.

The room was large, and the light insufficient. Still you could not help seeing at a glance that it must be, in daylight, a tolerably cheerful one. It was roomy and airy, with a great bow-window looking to the front of the building, of which it occupied the extreme left, reaching about ten feet from the level of the more ancient frontage of the house. The walls were covered with stamped leather, chiefly green and gold, and the whole air of the room, even in its unarranged state, though somewhat quaint and faded, was wonderfully gay and cozy.

'This is the green chamber, sir,' she repeated, with her brows raised and her eyes still lowered askance, and some queer wrinkles on her forehead, as she nodded a sharp bitter emphasis.

'To be sure it is, damme!—why not?' he said, testily, and then burst into a short laugh.

'You're not a going, I suppose, Sir Jekyl, to put anyone into it?' said she.

'I don't see, for the life of me, why I should not—eh? a devilish comfortable room.'

'Hem! I can't but suppose you are a joking me, Sir Jekyl,' persisted the gray silk phantom.

'Egad! you forget how old we're growing; why the plague should I quiz you! I want the room for old General Lennox, that's all—though I'm not bound to tell you for whom I want it—am I?'

'There's a plenty o' rooms without this one, Sir Jekyl,' persevered the lady, sternly.

'Plenty, of course; but none so good,' said he, carelessly.

'No one ever had luck that slept in it,' answered the oracle, lifting her odd eyes and fixing them on Sir Jekyl.

'I don't put them here for luck. We want to make them comfortable,' answered Sir Jekyl, poking at the furniture as he spoke.

'You know what was your father's wish about it, sir?' she insisted.

'My father's wish—egad, he did not leave many of his wishes unsatisfied—eh?' he answered, with another chuckle.

'And your poor lady's wish,' she said, a good deal more sharply.

'I don't know why the devil I'm talking to you, old Gwynn,' said the Baronet, turning a little fiercely about.

'*Dying* wishes,' emphasised she.

'It is time, Heaven knows, all that stuff should stop. You slept in it yourself, in my father's time. I remember you, here, Donica, and I don't think I ever heard that you saw a ghost—did I?' he said, with a sarcastic chuckle.

She darted a ghastly look to the far end of the chamber, and then, with a strange, half-frozen fury, she said—

'I wish you good night, Sir Jekyl,' and glided like a shadow out of the room.

'Saucy as ever, by Jupiter,' he ejaculated, following her with his glance, and trying to smile; and as the door shut, he looked again down the long apartment as she had just done, raising the candle again.

The light was not improved of course by the disappearance of Mrs. Gwynn's candle, and the end of the room was dim and unsatisfactory. The great four-poster, with dark curtains, and a plume at each corner, threw a vague shadow on the back wall and up to the ceiling, as he moved his candle, which at the distance gave him an uncomfortable sensation, and he stood for a few seconds sternly there, and then turned on his heel and quitted the room, saying aloud, as he did so—

'What a d—d fool that old woman is—always *was!*'

If there was a ghost there, the Baronet plainly did not wish it to make its exit from the green chamber by the door, for he locked it on the outside, and put the key in his pocket. Then, crossing the dressing-room I have mentioned, he entered the passage which crosses the gallery in which he and Mrs. Gwynn, a few minutes before, had planned their dispositions. The dressing-room door is placed close to the window which opens at the end of the corridor in the front of the house. Standing with his back to this, he looked down the long passage, and smiled.

For a man so little given to the melo-dramatic, it was a very well expressed smile of mystery—the smile of a man who knows something which others don't suspect, and would be surprised to learn.

It was the Baronet's fancy, as it had been his father's and his grandfather's before him, to occupy very remote quarters in this old house. Solitary birds, their roost was alone.

Candle in hand, Sir Jekyl descended the stairs, marched down the long gaunt passage, which strikes rearward so inflexibly, and at last reaches the foot of a back staircase, after a march of a hundred and forty feet, which I have measured.

At top of this was a door at his left, which he opened, and found himself in his own bed-room.

You would have said on looking about you that it was the bed-room of an old campaigner or of a natty gamekeeper—a fellow who rather liked roughing it, and had formed tastes in the matter like the great Duke of Wellington. The furniture was slight and plain, and looked like varnished deal; a French bed, narrow, with chintz curtains, and a plain white coverlet, like what one might expect in a barrack dormitory or an hospital; a little strip of carpet lying by the bed, and a small square of Turkey carpet under the table by the fire, hardly broke the shining uniformity of the dark oak floor; a pair of sporting prints decorated the sides of the chimney-piece, and an oil-portrait of a gray hunter hung in the middle. There were fishing-rods and gun-cases, I dare say the keys were lost of many, they looked so old and dingy.

The Baronet's luggage, relieved of its black japanned casings, lay on the floor, with his hat-case and travelling-desk. A pleasant fire burnt in the grate, and a curious abundance of wax-lights, without which Sir Jekyl, such was his peculiarity, could not exist, enlivened the chamber.

As he made his toilet at his homely little dressing-table, he bethought him suddenly, and rang the bell in his shirt-sleeves.

'My letters.'

'Yes, sir.'

And up came a salver well laden with letters, pamphlets, and newspapers, of all shapes and sizes.

'And tell Miss Beatrix I shan't have any tea, and get some brandy from Mrs. Gwynn, and cold water and a tumbler, and let them leave me alone—d'ye see?—and give me that.'

It was a dressing-gown which Tomlinson's care had already liberated from its valise, and expanded before the fire.

The Baronet's tastes, as we might see, were simple. He could dine on a bit of roast mutton, and few glasses of sherry. But his mutton was five years old, and came all the way from Dartbroke, and his sherry cost more than other men's Madeira, and he now lighted one of those priceless cigars, which so many fellows envied, and inhaled the disembodied aroma of a tobacco which perhaps, Jove smokes in his easy chair on Olympus, but which I have never smelt on earth, except when Sir Jekyl dispensed the inestimable treasures of his cigar-case.

Now, the Baronet stood over his table, with a weed between his lips, tall in his flowing silk dressing-gown, his open hands shoving apart the pile of letters, as a conjurer at an exhibition spreads his pack of cards.

'Ha! poor little thing!' he murmured, with a sly simper, in a petting tone, as he plucked an envelope, addressed in a lady's hand, between two fingers, caressingly, from the miscellaneous assortment.

He looked at it, but reserved it as a *bonne bouche* in his waistcoat pocket, and pursued his examination.

There were several from invited guests, who were either coming or not, with the customary expressions, and were tossed together in a little isolated litter for conference with Mrs. Gwynn in the morning.

'Not a line from Pelter and Crowe! the d——d fellows don't waste their ink upon me, except when they furnish their costs. It's a farce paying fellows to look after one's business—no one ever does it but yourself. If those fellows were worth their bread and butter, they'd have known all about this thing, whatever it is, and I'd have had it all *here*, d—— it, to-night.'

Sir Jekyl, it must be confessed, was not quite consistent about this affair of the mysterious young gentleman; for, as we have seen, he himself had a dozen times protested against the possibility of there being anything in it, and now he was seriously censuring his respectable London attorneys for not furnishing him with the solid contents of this 'wind-bag.'

But it was only his talk that was contradictory. Almost from the moment of his first seeing that young gentleman, on the open way under the sign of the 'Plough,' there lowered a fantastic and cyclopean picture, drawn in smoke or vapour, volcanic and thunderous, all over his horizon, like those prophetic and retrospective pageants with which Doree loves to paint his mystic skies. It was wonderful, and presaged unknown evil; and only cowed him the more that it baffled analysis and seemed to mock at reason.

'Pretty fellows to keep a look-out! It's well I can do it for myself—who knows where we're driving to, or what's coming? Signs enough—whatever they mean—he that runs may read, egad! Not that there's anything in it *necessarily*. But it's not about drawing and ruins and that stuff—those fellows have come down here. Bosh! looking after my property. I'd take my oath they are advised by some lawyer; and if Pelter and Crowe were sharp, they'd know by whom, and all about it by Jove!'

Sir Jekyl jerked the stump of his cigar over his shoulder into the grate as he muttered this, looking surlily down on the unprofitable papers that strewed the table.

He stood thinking, with his back to the fire, and looking rather cross and perplexed, and so he sat down and wrote a short letter. It was to Pelter and Crowe, but he began, as he did not care which got it, in his usual way—

'MY DEAR SIR,—I have reason to suspect that those ill-disposed people, who have often threatened annoyance, are at last seriously intent on mischief. You will be good enough, therefore, immediately to set on foot inquiries, here and at the other side of the water, respecting the movements of the D—— family, who, I fancy, are at the bottom of an absurd, though possibly troublesome, demonstration. I don't fear them, of course. But I think you will find that some members of that family are at present in this country, and disposed to be troublesome. You will see, therefore, the urgency of the affair, and will better know than I where and how to prosecute the necessary inquiries. I do not, of course, apprehend the least *danger* from their machinations; but you have always thought *annoyance* possible ; and if any be in store for me, I should rather not have to charge it upon our supineness. You will, therefore, exert your vigilance and activity on my behalf, and be so good as to let me know, at the earliest possible day—which, I think, need not be later than Wednesday next—the result of your enquiries through the old channels. I am a little disappointed, in fact, at not having heard from you before now on the subject.

‘ Yours, my dear sir, very sincerely,

‘ JEKYL M. MARLOWE.’

Sir Jekyl never swore on paper, and, as a rule, commanded his temper very creditably in that vehicle. But all people who had dealings with him knew very well that the rich Baronet was not to be trifled with. So, understanding that it was strong enough, he sealed it up for the post-office in the morning, and dropped it into the post-bag, and with it the unpleasant subject for the present.

And now, a little brandy and water, and the envelope in the well-known female hand ; and he laughed a little over it, and looked at himself in the glass with a vaunting complacency, and shook his head playfully at the envelope. It just crossed his sunshine like the shadow of a flying vapour—‘ that cross-grained old Gwynn would not venture to meddle ?’ But the envelope was honestly closed, and showed no signs of having been fiddled with.

He made a luxury of this little letter, and read it in his easy chair, with his left leg over the arm, with the fragrant accompaniment of a weed.

‘ Jealous, by Jove !’ he ejaculated, in high glee ; ‘ little fool, what’s put that in your head ?’

‘ Poor, little, fluttering, foolish thing !’ sang the Baronet, and then laughed, not cynically, but indulgently rather.

‘ How audacious the little fools are upon paper ! Egad, it’s a wonder there is not twice as much mischief in the world as actually happens. We must positively burn this little extravagance.’

But before doing so he read it over again ; then smiling still, he gallantly touched it to his lips, and re-perused it, as he drew another cigar from the treasury of incense which he carried about him. He lighted the note, but did not apply it to his cigar, I am bound to say—partly from a fine feeling, and partly, I am afraid, because he thought that paper spoiled the flavour of his tobacco. So, with a sentimental smile, a gentle shrug, and a sigh of the Laurence Sterne pattern, he converted that dangerous little scrawl into ashes—and he thought, as he inhaled his weed—

'It is well for you, poor little fanatics, that we men take better care of you than you do of yourselves, sometimes!'

No doubt; and Sir Jekyl supposed he was thinking only of his imprudent little correspondent, although there was another person in whom he was nearly interested, who might have been unpleasantly compromised also, if that document had fallen into other hands.

CHAPTER VI.

SIR JEKYL'S ROOM IS VISITED.

IT was near one o'clock. Sir Jekyl yawned and wound his watch, and looked at his bed as if he would like to be in it without the trouble of getting there; and at that moment there came a sharp knock at his door, which startled him, for he thought all his people were asleep by that time.

'Who's there?' he demanded in a loud key.

'It's me, sir, please,' said Donica Gwynn's voice.

'Come in, will you?' cried he; and she entered.

'Are you sick?' he asked.

'No, sir, thank you,' she replied, with a sharp courtesy.

'You look so plaguy pale. Well, I'm glad you're not. But what the deuce can you want of me at this hour of night? Eh?'

'It's only about that room, sir.'

'Oh, curse the room! Talk about it in the morning. You ought to have been in your bed an hour ago.'

'So I was, sir; but I could not sleep, sir, for thinking of it.'

'Well, go back and think of it, if you must. How can I stop you? Don't be a fool, old Gwynn.'

'No more I will, sir, please, if I can help, for fools we are, the most on us; but I could not sleep, as I said, for thinking o't; and so I thought I'd jist put on my things again, and come and try if you, sir, might be still up.'

'Well, you see I'm up; but I want to get to bed, Gwynn, and not to talk here about solemn bosh; and you must not bore me about that green chamber—do you see?—to-night, like a good old girl; it will do in the morning—won't it?'

'So it will, sir; only I could not rest in my bed, until I said, seeing as you mean to sleep in this room, it would never do. It won't. I can't stand it.'

'Stand what? Egad! it seems to me you're demented, my good old Donica.'

'No, Sir Jekyl' she persisted, with a grim resolution to say out her say. 'You know very well, sir, what's running in my head. You know it's for no good anyone sleeps there. General Lennox, ye say; well an' good. You know well what a loss Mr. Deverell met with in that room in Sir Harry, your father's time.'

'And you slept in it, did not you, and saw something? Eh?'

'Yes, I *did*,' she said, in a sudden fury, with a little stamp on the floor, and a pale, staring frown.

After a breathless pause of a second or two she resumed.

'And you know what your poor lady saw there, and never held up her head again. And well you know, sir, how your father, Sir Harry, on his death bed, desired it should be walled up, when you were no more than a boy; and your good lady did the same many a year after, when *she* was a dying. And I tell ye, Sir Jekyl, ye'll sup sorrow yourself yet if you don't. And take a fool's counsel, and shut up that door, and never let no one, friend or foe, sleep there; for well I know it's not for nothing, with your dead father's dying command, and your poor dear lady's dying entreaty against it, that you put anyone to sleep there. I don't know who this General Lennox may be—a good gentleman or a bad; but I'm sure it's for no righteous reason he's to lie there. You would not do it for nothing.'

This harangue was uttered with a volubility, which, as the phrase is, took Sir Jekyl aback. He was angry, but he was also perplexed and a little stunned by the unexpected vehemence of his old housekeeper's assault, and he stared at her with a rather bewildered countenance.

'You're devilish impertinent,' at last he said, with an effort. 'You rant there like a madwoman, just because I like you, and you've been in our family, I believe, since before I was born; you think you may say what you like. The house is mine, I believe, and I rather think I'll do what I think best in it while I'm here.'

'And you going to sleep in this room!' she broke in. 'What else can it be?'

'You mean—what the devil do you mean?' stammered the Baronet again, unconsciously assuming the defensive.

'I mean you know very well *what*, Sir Jekyl,' she replied.

'It was my father's room, hey?—when I was a boy, as you say. It's good enough for his son, I suppose; and I don't ask *you* to lie in the green chamber.'

'*I'll* be no party, sir, if you please, to anyone lying there,' she observed, with a stiff courtesy, and a sudden hectic in her cheek.

'Perhaps you mean because my door's a hundred and fifty feet away from the front of the house, if any mischief should happen, I'm too far away—as others were before me—to prevent it, eh?' said he, with a flurried sneer.

'What I mean, I mean, sir—you ought not; that's all. You won't take it amiss, Sir Jekyl—I'm an old servant—I'm sorry, sir; but I'a made up my mind what to do.'

'You're not thinking of any folly, surely? You seemed to me always too much afraid, or whatever you call it, of the remembrance, you know, of what you *saw* there—eh?—*I* don't know, of course, *what*—to speak of it to me. I never pressed you, because you seemed—you know you did—to have a horror; and surely you're not going now to talk among the servants or other people. You can't be far from five-and-thirty years in the family.'

' Four-and-thirty, Sir Jekyl, next April. It's a good while;
but I won't see no more o' that; and unless the green chamber be
locked up, at the least, and used no more for a bed-room, I'd
rather go, sir. Nothing may happen, of course, Sir Jekyl—it's a
hundred to one nothing *would* happen; but ye see, sir, I've a
feeling about it, sir; and there has been these things ordered by
your father that was, and by your poor lady, as makes me feel
queer. Nothing being done accordingly, and I could not rest upon
it, for sooner or later it would come to this, and stay I could not.
I judge no one—Heaven forbid, Sir Jekyl——oh, no ! my own
conscience is as much as I can look to ; so sir, if you please, so soon
as you can suit yourself I'll leave, sir.'

' Stuff! old Gwynn; don't mind talking to-night,' said the
Baronet, more kindly than he had spoken before ; ' we'll see about
it in the morning. Good-night. We must not quarrel about
nothing. I was only a schoolboy when you came to us, you know.'

But in the morning 'old Gwynn' was resolute. She was actually going, so soon as the master could suit himself. She was
not in a passion, nor in a panic, but in a state of gloomy and
ominous obstinacy.

' Well, you'll give me a little time, won't you, to look about me ?'
said the Baronet, peevishly.

' Such is my intention, sir.'

' And see, Gwynn, not a word about that—that green chamber,
you know, to Miss Beatrix.'

' As you please, sir.'

' Because if you begin to talk, they'll all think we are haunted.'

' Whatever you please to order, sir.'

' And it was not—it was my grandfather, you know, who
built it.'

' Ah, so it was, sir ;' and Gwynn looked astonished and shook
her head, as though cowed by the presence of a master-spirit of evil.

' One would fancy you saw his ghost, Gwynn; but he was not
such a devil as your looks would make him, only a bit wild, and a
favourite with the women, Gwynn—always the best judge of
merit—hey ? Beau Marlowe they called him—the best dressed

man of his day. How the devil could such a fellow have any
harm in him ?'

There is a fine picture, full length, of Beau Marlowe, over the
chimneypiece of the great hall of Marlowe. He has remarkably
gentlemanlike hands and legs; the gloss is on his silk stockings
still. His features are handsome, of that type which we conven-
tionally term aristocratic; high, and smiling with a Louis-
Quatorze insolence. He wears a very fine coat of cut velvet, of a
rich, dusky red, the technical name of which I forget. He was of
the gilded and powdered youth of his day.

He certainly was a handsome fellow, this builder of the 'green
chamber,' and he has not placed his candle under a bushel. He
shines in many parts of the old house, and has repeated himself in
all manner of becoming suits. You see him, three-quarter, in the
parlour, in blue and silver ; you meet him in crayon, and again in
small oil, oval ; and you have him in half a dozen miniatures.

We mention this ancestor chiefly because when his aunt, Lady
Mary, left him a legacy, he added the green chamber to the house.

It seems odd that Sir Jekyl, not fifty yet, should have had a
grandfather who was a fashionable and wicked notoriety of mature
years, and who had built an addition to the family mansion so
long as a hundred and thirty years ago. But this gentleman had
married late, as rakes sometimes do, and his son, Sir Harry, married still later—somewhere about seventy ; having been roused to
this uncomfortable exertion by the proprietorial airs of a nephew
who was next in succession. To this matrimonial explosion Sir
Jekyl owed his entrance and agreeable sojourn upon the earth.

' I won't ask you to stay now; you're in a state. I'll write to
town for Sinnott, as you insist on it; but you won't leave us in
confusion, and you'll make her *au fait*—won't you ? Give her any
hints she may require; and I know I shall have you back again
when you cool a little, or at all events when we go back to Dartbroke ; for I don't think I shall like this place.'

So Donica Gwynn declared herself willing to remain till Mrs.
Sinnott should arrive from London; and preparations for the reception of guests proceeded with energy.

CHAPTER VII.

THE BARONET PURSUES.

SIR JEKYL MARLOWE was vexed when the letters came, and none from Pelter and Crowe. There are people who expect miracles from their doctors and lawyers, and, in proportion to their accustomed health and prosperity, are unreasonable when anything goes wrong. The Baronet's notion was that the legal firm in question ought to think and even dream of nothing else than his business. It was an impertinence their expecting *him* to think about it. What were *they* there for? He knew that London was a pretty large place, and England still larger; and that it was not always easy to know what everybody was about in either, and still less what each man was doing on the Continent. Pelter and Crowe had some other clients too on their hands, and had hitherto done very satisfactorily. But here was a serious-looking ˌthing—the first really uncomfortable occurrence which had taken place under his reign—the first opportunity for exhibiting common vigilance—and he ventured to say those fellows did not know these Strangways people were in these kingdoms at all!

Sir Jekyl, though an idle fellow, was a man of action, so he ordered his horse, and rode nine miles to the 'Plough Inn,' where he hoped to see Mr. Strangways again, improve his intimacy, and prevail with the gentlemen to return with him to Marlowe, and spend a fortnight there, when, or the devil was in it, he should contrive to get at the bottom of their plans.

He looked shrewdly in at the open door as he rode up, and halloed for some one to take his horse. The little porch smiled pleasantly, and the two gables and weather-cock, in the sunlight; and the farmer on the broad and dingy panel, in his shirt-sleeves, low-crowned, broad-leafed hat, crimson waistcoat, canary-coloured shorts, and blue stockings, and flaxen wig, was driving his plump horses, and guiding his plough, undiscouraged, as when last he saw him.

Boots and Mrs. Jones came out. Sir Jekyl was too eager to wait to get down; so from the saddle he accosted his buxom hostess, in his usual affable style. The Baronet was not accustomed to be crossed and thwarted as much as, I have been told, men with less money sometimes are; and he showed his mortification in his face when he learned that the two gentlemen had left very early that morning.

'This morning! Why you said yesterday they would not go till *evening*. Hang it, I wish you could tell it right; and what the d—l do you mean by Strangers? Call him Strangways, can't you. It's odd people can't say names.'

He must have been very much vexed to speak so sharply; and he saw, perhaps, how much he had forgotten himself in the frightened look which good Mrs. Jones turned upon him.

'I don't mean you, my good little soul. It's *their* fault; and where are they gone to? I wanted to ask them both over to Marlowe. Have you a notion?'

'They took our horses as far as the "Bell and Horns," at Slowton.' She called shrilly to Boots, 'They're not stoppin' at the "Bell and Horns," sure. Come here, and tell Sir Jekyl Marlowe about Mr. Strangers.'

'You said last night they were going to Awkworth;' and Sir Jekyl chuckled scornfully, for he was vexed.

'They changed their minds, sir.'

'Well, we'll say so. You're a wonderful fascinating sex. Egad! if you could only carry anything right in your heads for ten minutes, you'd be too charming.' And at this point Boots emerged, and Sir Jekyl continued, addressing him—

'Well, where are the gentlemen who left this morning?' asked he.

'They'll be at the "Bell and Horns," sir.'

'Where's that?'

'Slowton, sir.'

'I know. What hour did they go?'

'Eight o'clock, sir.'

'Just seven miles. The Sterndale Road, isn't it?'

' Yes, sir.'

And that was all Boots had to tell.

' Will ye please to come in, sir ?' inquired Mrs. Jones.

' No, my good creature. I haven't time. The old gentleman—what's his name ?'

' I don't know, sir, please. He calls the young gentleman Guy, and the young gentleman calls him *sir.*'

' And both the same name ?'

' We calls 'em both Strangers, please, sir.'

' I know. Servants, had they ?'

' Yes, sir, please. But they sent 'em on.'

' Rich—don't want for money, I suppose. Eh ?'

' Oh ! plenty money, sir.'

' And the servants called the men Strangways, I suppose, eh ?'

' Yes, Sir Jekyl, please ; and so the letters came.'

' You never happened to hear any other name ?'

' No, Sir Jekyl.'

' *Think.*'

Mrs. Jones did think, but could recall nothing.

' Nothing with a D ?'

' D, sir ! What, sir ?'

' No matter what,' said the Baronet. ' No name beginning with D—, eh ?'

' No, sir. You don't think they're going by a false name ?' inquired the lady, curiously.

' What the devil puts that in your head ? Take care of the law ; you must not talk that way, you foolish little rogue.'

' I did not know, sir,' timidly answered Mrs. Jones, who saw in Sir Jekyl, the Parliament-man, Deputy-Lieutenant, and Grand Juror, a great oracle of the law.

' I only wanted to know whether you had happened to hear the name of the elder of the two gentlemen, and could recollect what letter it begins with.'

' No, sir, please.'

' So you've no more to tell me ?'

' Nothing, sir.'

'If they come back tell them I rode over to offer them some shooting, and to beg they'd remember to come to Marlowe. You won't forget?'

'No, sir.'

'Do they return here?'

'I think not, sir.'

'Well, I believe there's nothing else,' and the Baronet looked up reflectively, as if he expected to find a memorandum scribbled on the blue sky, leaning with his hand on the back of his horse. 'No, nothing. You won't forget my message, that's all. Good-bye, my dear.'

And touching the tips of his gloves to his lips, with a smile and a nod, he cantered down the Sterndale Road.

He pulled up at the 'Bell and Horns,' in the little town of Slowton, but was disappointed. The entire party, servants and all, had taken the train two hours before, at the station three miles away.

Now Sir Jekyl was blooded, and the spirit of the chase stirred within him. So he rode down in his jack-boots, and pulled up his steaming horse by the station, and he went in and made inquiry.

A man like him is received even at one of these cosmopolitan rallying-points within his own county with becoming awe. The station-master was awfully courteous, and the subaltern officials awfully active and obliging, and the resources of the establishment were at once placed at his sublime disposal. Unhappily, two branch lines converge at this point, causing the usual bustle, and there was consequently a conflict and confusion in the evidence; so that Sir Jekyl, who laughed and chatted agreeably amidst all the reverential zeal that surrounded him, could arrive at nothing conclusive, but leaned to the view that the party had actually gone to Awkworth, only by rail, instead of by road.

Sir Jekyl got on his horse and walked him through the town, uncertain what to do next. This check had cooled him; his horse had his long trot home still. It would not do to follow to Awkworth; to come in, after a four-and-twenty miles' ride, bespattered like a courier, merely to invite these gentlemen, *vivâ voce*, who had hardly had his note of invitation a score hours. It would be making too much of them with a vengeance.

As he found himself once more riding under the boughs of Marlowe, the early autumnal evening already closing in, Sir Jekyl experienced one of those qualms and sinkings of the heart, which overcome us with a vague anticipation of evil.

The point of the road which he had now gained, commands a view of the old hall of Marlowe, with that projecting addition, and its wide bow-window, every pane of which was now flaming in the sunset light, which indicated the green chamber.

The green chamber! Just at that moment the glare of its broad window flashed with a melancholy and vengeful light upon his brain, busied with painful retrospects and harassing conjecture.

Old Gwynn going away! It was an omen. Marlowe without old Gwynn. Troy without its palladium. Old Gwynn going with something like a denunciation on her lips! That stupid old woman at Wardlock, too, who really knew nothing about it, undertaking also to prophesy! Out of the mouths of babes and sucklings! There was no sense in it—scarcely articulation. Still it was the croak of the raven—the screech of the owl.

He looked across the gentle slope at the angle of the inauspicious room. Why should old General Lennox be placed within the unhallowed precincts of that chamber? The image of old Gwynn as she gabbled her grim protest on the preceding night, rose before him like a ghost. What business was it of hers, and how could she divine his motives? Still, if there was anything wrong, did not this vehement warning make the matter worse.

An old man he felt himself on a sudden that evening, and for the first time. There was some failure of the electric fire, and a subsidence of the system. His enterprise was gone. Why should he take guilt, if such it were, on his soul for vanity and vexation of spirit? If guilt it were, was it not of a kind inexcusably cold-blooded and long-headed. Old Gwynn, he did not like to lose you on those terms—just, too, as those unknown actors were hovering at the wing, and about to step upon the stage, this old man and young, who, instinctively he felt, were meditating mischief against him. Mischief—*what?* Such, perhaps, as might shatter the structure of his greatness, and strew its pinnacles in the dust. Perhaps all this gloom was but the depression of a long ride, and still longer fast. But he was accustomed to such occasional strains upon his strength without any such results. Ah, no! He had come within the edge of the shadow of judgment, and its darkness was stealing over him, and its chill touched his heart.

These were the dreamy surmisings with which he rode slowly toward the house, and a few good resolutions in a nebulous state hovered uncomfortably about him.

No letter of any interest had come by the early post, and Sir Jekyl sat down *téte-à-téte* with his pretty daughter, in very dismal spirits, to dinner.

CHAPTER VIII.

THE HOUSE BEGINS TO FILL.

BEATRIX was fond of her father, who was really a good-natured man, in the common acceptance of the term, that is to say, he had high animal spirits, and liked to see people pleasant about him, and was probably as kind as a tolerably selfish and vicious man can be, and had a liking, moreover, for old faces, which was one reason why he hated the idea of his housekeeper's leaving him. But Beatrix was also a little in awe of him, as girls often are of men of whom they see but little, especially if they have something of the masculine decision of temper.

'You may all go away now,' said the Baronet suddenly to the servants, who had waited at dinner; and when the liveried phantoms had withdrawn, and the door had closed on the handsome calves of tall and solemn Jenkins, he said—

'Nothing all day—no adventure, or visitor, Trixie—not a word of news or fun, I dare say?'

' Nothing—not a creature, papa; only the birds and dogs, and some new music.'

' Well, it is not much worse than Wardlock, I suppose; but we shall have a gay house soon—at all events plenty of people. Old General Lennox is coming. His nephew, Captain Drayton, is very rich; he will be Lord Tewkesbury—that is, if old Tewkesbury doesn't marry; and, at all events, he has a very nice property, and does not owe a guinea. You need not look modest, Trixie. You may do just as you please, only I'd be devilish glad you liked one another—there, don't be distressed, I say; I'll mention it no more if you don't like; but he'll be here in a few days, and you mayn't think him so bad.'

After this the Baronet drank two glasses of sherry in silence, slowly, and with a gloomy countenance, and then, said he—

' I think, Trixie, if you were happily placed, I should give the whole thing up. I'm tired of that cursed House of Commons. You can't imagine what a bore it is, when a fellow does not want anything from them, going down there for their d——d divisions. I'm not fit for the hounds either. I can't ride as I used—egad! I'm as stiff as a rusty hinge when I get up in the morning. And I don't much like this place, and I'm tired to death of the other two. When you marry I'll let them, or, at all events, let them alone. I'm tired of all those servants. I know they're robbing me, egad! You would not believe what my gardens cost me last year, and, by Jove, I don't believe all that came to my table was worth two hundred pounds. I'll have quite a different sort of life. I haven't any time to myself, looking after all those confounded people one must keep about them. Keepers, and gardeners, and devil knows who beside. I don't like London half as well as the Continent. I hate dinner-parties, and the season, and all the racket. It doesn't pay, and I'm growing old—you'll not mind if I smoke it?' (he held a cigar between his fingers)—'a complaint that doesn't mend by time, you know. Oh! yes, I *am* old, you little rogue. Everybody knows I'm just fifty; and the fact is I'm tired of the whole thing, stock, lock, and barrel; and I believe what little is to be got of life is best had—that is, if you know how to look for it—abroad.

A fellow like me who has got places and properties—egad! they expect him to live *pro bono publico*, and not to care or think two-pence about himself—at least it comes to that. How is old Gwynn?'

'Very well, I think.'

'And what has she to say for herself; what about things in general?'

'She's not very chatty, poor old Gwynn, and I think she seems a little—just ever so little—cross.'

'So she does—damnably cross. She was always a bit of a vixen, and she isn't improving, poor old thing; but don't be afraid, I like old Donnie for all that, though I don't think I ever quite under-stood her, and I don't expect either.' These observations concluded the conversation subsided, and a long silence supervened.

'I wonder who the devil he is,' said the Baronet abruptly, as he threw the stump of his cigar into the fire. If it's a fluke, it's as like a miracle as anything I ever saw.'

He recollected that he was talking without an interlocutor, and looked for a moment hesitatingly at his daughter.

'And your grandmamma told you nothing of her adventure in church?'

'No, papa—not a word.'

'It seems to me, women can hold their tongues sometimes, but always in the wrong places.'

Here he shook the ashes of his cigar into the grate.

'Old Granny's a fool—isn't she, Trixie, and a little bit vicious—he?'

Sir Jekyl put his question dreamily, in a reverie, and it plainly needed no answer. So Beatrix was spared the pain of making one; which she was glad of, for Lady Alice was good to her after her way, and she was fond of her.

'We must ask her to come, you know. You write. Say I thought *you* would have a better chance of prevailing. She won't, you know; and so much the better.'

So as the Baronet rose, and stood gloomily with his back to the fire; the young lady rose also, and ran away to the drawing-

room and her desk ; and almost at the same moment a servant
entered the room, with a letter, which had come by the late post.

Oddly enough, it had the Slowton post-mark.

'Devilish odd !' exclaimed Sir Jekyl, scowling eagerly on it ;
and seating himself hastily on the side of a chair, he broke it open
and read at the foot the autograph, ' Guy Strangways.'

It was with the Napoleonic thrill, ' I have them, then, these
English!' that Sir Jekyl read, in a gentlemanlike, rather foreign
hand, a ceremonious and complimentary acceptance of his invitation to Marlowe, on behalf both of the young man and of his
elder companion. His correspondent could not say exactly, as
their tour was a little desultory, where a note would find them ;
but as Sir Jekyl Marlowe had been so good as to permit them to
name a day for their visit, they would say so and so.

' Let me see—what day's this—why, that will be'—he was
counting with the tips of his fingers, pianowise, on the table—
' Wednesday week—eh ?' and he tried it over again with nature's
' Babbage's Machine,' and of course with an inflexible result.
' Wednesday week, Wednesday,' and he heaved a great sigh, like
a man with a load taken off him.

' Well, I'm devilish glad. I hope nothing will happen to stop
them now. It can't be a *ruse* to get quietly off the ground? No
—that would be doing it too fine.' He rang the bell.

' I want Mrs. Gwynn.'

The Baronet's spirit revived within him, and he stood erect, with
his back to the fire, and his hands behind him, and when the
housekeeper entered, he received her with his accustomed smile.

' Glad to see you, Donnie. Glass of sherry? No—well, sit
down—won't take a chair!—why's that? Well, we'll be on
pleasanter terms soon—you'll find it's really no choice of mine. I
can't help using that stupid green room. Here are two more
friends coming—not till Wednesday week though—two gentlemen.
You may put them in rooms beside one another—whereever you
like—only not in the garrets, of course. *Good* rooms, do ye see.'

' And what's the gentleman's names, please, Sir Jekyl,' inquired
Mrs. Gwynn.

'Mr. Strangways, the young gentleman; and the older, as well as I can read it, is Mr. Varbarriere.'

'Thank ye, sir.'

The housekeeper having again declined the kindly distinction of a glass of sherry, withdrew.

In less than a week guests began to assemble, and in a few days more old Marlowe Hall began to wear a hospitable and pleasant countenance.

The people were not, of course, themselves all marvels of agreeability. For instance, Sir Paul Blunket, the great agriculturist and eminent authority on liquid manures, might, as we all know, be a little livelier with advantage. He is short and stolid; he wears a pale blue muslin neck-handkerchief with a white stripe, carefully tied. His countenance, I am bound to say, is what some people would term heavy—it is frosty, painfully shaven, and shines with a glaze of transparent soap. He has small, very light blue round eyes, and never smiles. A joke always strikes him with unaffected amazement and suspicion. Laughter he knows may imply ridicule, and he may himself possibly be the subject of it. He waits till it subsides, and then talks on as before on subjects which interest him.

Lady Blunket, who accompanies him everywhere, though not tall, is stout. She is delicate, and requires nursing; and, for so confirmed an invalid, has a surprising appetite. John Blunket, the future baronet, is in the Diplomatic Service, I forget exactly where, and by no means young; and lean Miss Blunket, at Marlowe with her parents, though known to be older than her brother, is still quite a girl, and giggles with her partner at dinner, and is very *naïve* and animated, and sings arch little chansons discordantly to the guitar, making considerable play with her eyes, which are black and malignant.

This family, though neither decorative nor entertaining, being highly respectable and ancient, make the circuit of all the good houses in the county every year, and are wonderfully little complained of. Hither also they had brought in their train pretty little Mrs. Maberly, a cousin, whose husband, the Major, was in

India—a garrulous and good-humoured siren, who smiled with pearly little teeth, and blushed easily.

At Marlowe had already assembled several single gentlemen too. There was little Tom Linnett, with no end of money and spirits, very good-natured, addicted to sentiment, and with a taste for practical joking too, and a very popular character notwithstanding.

Old Dick Doocey was there also, a colonel long retired, and well known at several crack London clubs; tall, slight, courtly, agreeable, with a capital elderly wig, a little deaf, and his handsome high nose a little reddish. Billy Cobb—too, a gentleman who could handle a gun, and knew lots about horses and dogs—had arrived.

Captain Drayton had arrived: a swell, handsome, cleverish, and impertinent, and, as young men with less reason will be, egotistical. He would not have admitted that he had deigned to make either plan or exertion with that object, but so it happened that he was placed next to Miss Beatrix, whom he carelessly entertained with agreeable ironies, and anecdotes, and sentiments poetic and perhaps a little vapid. On the whole, a young gentleman of intellect, as well as wealth and expectations, and who felt, not unnaturally, that he was overpowering. Miss Beatrix, though not quite twenty, was *not* overpowered, however, neither was her heart preoccupied. There was, indeed, a shadow of another handsome young gentleman—only a shadow, in a different style—dark, and this one light; and she heart-whole, perhaps fancy-free, amused, delighted, the world still new and only begun to be explored. One London season she had partly seen, and also made her annual tour twice or thrice of all the best county-houses, and so was not nervous among her peers.

CHAPTER IX.

DINNER.

OF the two guests destined for the green chamber, we must be permitted to make special mention.

General and Lady Jane Lennox had come. The General, a tall,

soldierlike old gentleman, who held his bald and pink, but not very high forehead, erect, with great grey projecting moustache, twisted up at the corners, and bristling grey eyebrows to correspond, over his frank round grey eyes—a gentleman with a decidedly military bearing, imperious but kindly of aspect, good-natured, prompt, and perhaps a little stupid.

Lady Jane—everybody knows Lady Jane—the most admired of London belles for a whole season. Golden brown hair, and what young Thrumly of the Guards called, in those exquisite lines of his, 'slumbrous eyes of blue,' under very long lashes and exquisitely-traced eyebrows, such brilliant lips and teeth, and such a sweet oval face, and above all, so beautiful a figure and wonderful a waist, might have made one marvel how a lady so well qualified for a title, with noble blood, though but a small *dot*, should have wrecked herself on an old general, though with eight thousand a year. But there were stories and reasons why the simple old officer, just home from India, who knew nothing about London lies, and was sure of his knighthood, and it was said of a baronetage, did not come amiss.

There were people who chose to believe these stories, and people who chose to discredit them. But General Lennox never had even heard them; and certainly, it seemed nobody's business to tell him now. It might not have been quite pleasant to tell the General. He was somewhat muddled of apprehension, and slow in everything but fighting; and having all the old-fashioned notions about hair-triggers, and 'ten paces,' as the proper ordeal in a misunderstanding, people avoided uncomfortable topics in his company, and were for the most part disposed to let well alone.

Lady Jane had a will and a temper; but the General held his ground firmly. As brave men as he have been henpecked; but somehow he was not of the temperament which will submit to be bullied even by a lady; and as he was indulgent and easily managed, that tactique was the line she had adopted. Lady Jane was not a riant beauty. Luxurious, funeste, sullen, the mystery and melancholy of her face was a relief among the smirks and simpers of the ball-room, and the novelty of the style interested for a time even the *blazé* men of twenty seasons.

Several guests of lesser note there were; and the company had sat down to dinner, when the Reverend Dives Marlowe, rector of the succulent family living of Queen's Chorleigh, made his appearance in the parlour, a little to the surprise of his brother the Baronet, who did not expect him quite so soon.

The Rector was a tall man and stalwart, who had already acquired that convex curve which indicates incipient corpulence, and who, though younger than his brother, looked half-a-dozen years his senior. With a broad bald forehead, projecting eyebrows, a large coarse mouth, and with what I may term the rudiments of a double chin—altogether an ugly and even repulsive face, but with no lack of energy and decision—one looked with wonder from this gross, fierce, clerical countenance to the fine outlines and proportions of the Baronet's face, and wondered how the two men could really be brothers.

The cleric shook his brother's hand in passing, and smiled and nodded briefly here and there, right and left, and across the table his recognition, and chuckled a harsher chuckle than his brother's, as he took his place, extemporized with the quiet legerdemain of a consummate butler by Ridley; and answered in a brisk, abrupt voice the smiling inquiries of friends.

'Hope you have picked up an appetite on the way, Dives,' said the Baronet. Dives generally carried a pretty good one about with him. 'Good air on the way, and pretty good mutton here, too—my friends tell me.'

'Capital air—capital mutton—capital fish,' replied the ecclesiastic, in a brisk, business-like tone, while being a man of nerve, he got some fish, although that esculent had long vanished, and even the entrées had passed into history, and called over his shoulder for the special sauces which his soul loved, and talked, and compounded his condiments with energy and precision.

The Rector was a shrewd and gentleman-like, though not a very pretty, apostle, and had made a sufficient toilet before presenting himself, and snapped and gobbled his fish, in a glossy, single-

breasted coat, with standing collar; a ribbed silk waistcoat, cover-
ing his ample chest, almost like a cassock, and one of those transparent muslin dog-collars which High Churchmen affect.

'Well, Dives,' cried Sir Jekyl, 'how do the bells ring? I gave
them a chime, poor devils' (this was addressed to Lady Blunket at
his elbow), 'by way of compensation, when I sent them Dives.'

'Pretty well; they don't know how to pull 'em, I think, quite,'
answered Dives, dabbing a bit of fish in a pool of sauce, and
punching it into a shape with his bit of bread. 'And how is old
Parson Moulders?' continued the Baronet, pleasantly.

'I haven't heard,' said the Rector, and drank off half his glass
of hock.

'Can't believe it, Dives. Here's Lady Blunket knows. He's the
aged incumbent of Droughton. A devilish good living in my gift;
and of course you've been asking how the dear old fellow is.'

'I haven't, upon my word; not but I ought, though,' said the
Rev. Dives Marlowe, as if he did not see the joke.

'He's very severe on you,' simpered fat Lady Blunket, faintly,
across the table, and subsided with a little cough, as if the exertion hurt her.

'Is he? Egad! I never perceived it.' The expression was not
clerical, but the speaker did not seem aware he had uttered it.
'How dull I must be! Have you ever been in this part of the
world before, Lady Jane?' continued he, turning towards General
Lennox's wife, who sat beside him.

'I've been to Wardlock, a good many years ago; but that's a
long way from this, and I almost forget it,' answered Lady Jane,
in her languid, haughty way.

'In what direction is Wardlock,' she asked of Beatrix, raising
her handsome, unfathomable eyes for a moment.

'You can see it from the bow-window of your room—I mean
that oddly-shaped hill to the right.'

'That's from the green chamber,' said the Rector. 'I remember the view. Isn't it?'

'Yes. They have put Lady Jane in the haunted room,' said
Beatrix, smiling and nodding to Lady Jane.

'And what fool, pray, told you that?' said the Baronet, perhaps just a little sharply.

'Old Gwynn seems to think so,' answered Beatrix, with the surprised and frightened look of one who fancies she has made a blunder. 'I—of course we know it is all folly.'

'You must not say that—you shan't disenchant us,' said Lady Jane. 'There's nothing I should so like as a haunted room; it's a charming idea—isn't it, Arthur?' she inquired of the General.

'We had a haunted room in my quarters at Puttypoor,' observed the General, twiddling the point of one of his moustaches. 'It was the store-room where we kept pickles, and olives, and preserves, and plates, and jars, and glass bottles. And every night there was a confounded noise there; jars and bottles, and things tumbling about, made a devil of a row, you know. I got Smith, my servant Smith, you know, a very respectable man—uncommon steady fellow, Smith—to watch, and he did. We kept the door closed, and Smith outside. I gave him half-a-crown a night, and his supper—very well for Smith, you know. Sometimes he kept a light, and sometimes I made him sit in the dark with matches ready.'

'Was not he very much frightened?' asked Beatrix, who was deeply interested in the ghost.

'I hope you gave him a smelling-bottle?' inquired Tom Linnett, with a tender concern.

'Well, I don't suppose he was,' said the General, smiling good-humouredly on pretty Beatrix, while he loftily passed by the humorous inquiry of the young gentleman. 'He was, in fact, on dooty, you know; and there were occasional noises and damage done in the store-room—in fact, just the same as if Smith was not there.'

'Oh, possibly Smith himself among the bottles!' suggested Linnett.

'He always got in as quick as he could,' continued the General; 'but could not see anyone. Things were broken—bottles sometimes.'

'How very strange,' exclaimed Beatrix, charmed to hear the tale of wonder.

'We could not make it out; it was very odd, you know,' resumed the narrator.

'*You* weren't frightened, General?' inquired Linnett.

'*No*, sir,' replied the General, who held that a soldier's courage, like a lady's reputation, was no subject for jesting, and conveyed that sentiment by a slight pause, and a rather alarming stare from under his fierce grey eyebrows. 'No one was frightened, I suppose; we were all men in the house, sir.'

'At home, I think, we'd have suspected a rat or a cat,' threw in the Rector.

'Some did, sir,' replied the General; 'and we made a sort of search; but it wasn't. There was a capital tiled floor, not a hole you could put a ramrod in; and no cat, neither—high windows, grated; and the door always close; and every now and then something broken by night.'

'Delightful! That's what Mrs. Crowe, in that charming book, you know, "The Night Side of Nature," calls, I forget the name; but it's a German word, I think—the noisy ghost it means. Racket—something, isn't it, Beet?' (the short for Beatrix). 'I do so *devour* ghosts!' cried sharp old Miss Blunket, who thought Beatrix's enthusiasm became her; and chose to exhibit the same pretty fanaticism.

'I didn't *say* it was a ghost, mind ye,' interposed the General, with a grave regard for his veracity; 'only we were puzzled a bit. There *was* something there we all knew; and something that could reach up to the high shelves, and break things on the floor too, you see. We had been watching, off and on, I think, some three or four weeks, and I heard one night, early, a row in the store-room—a devil of a row it was; but Smith was on dooty, as we used to say, that night, so I left it to him; and he could have sung out, you know, if he wanted help—poor fellow! And in the morning my native fellow told me that poor Smith was dead in the store-room! and, egad! so he was, poor fellow!'

'How awful!' exclaimed Beatrix.

And Miss Blunket, in girlish horror, covered her fierce black eyes with her lank fingers.

'A bite of a cobra, by Jove! above the knee, and another on the hand. A fattish fellow, poor Smith, the natives say they go faster—that sort of man; but no one can stand a fair bite of a cobra—I defy you. We killed him after.'

'What! *Smith?*' whispered Linnett in his neighbour's ear.

'He lay in a basket; you never saw such a brute, continued the General; he was very near killing another of my people.'

'So *there* was your ghost?' said Doocey, archly.

'Worse than a ghost,' observed Sir Paul Blunket.

'A dooced deal,' acquiesced the General, gravely.

'You're very much annoyed with vermin out there in India?' remarked Sir Paul.

'So we are, sir,' agreed the General.

'It's very hard, you see, to meet with a genuine ghost, Miss Marlowe; they generally turn out impostors,' said Doocey.

'I should like to think my room was haunted,' said Lady Jane.

'Oh! *dear* Lady Jane, how *can* you be so *horribly* brave?' cried Miss Blunket.

'We have no cobras here, at all events,' said Sir Paul, nodding to Sir Jekyl, with the gravity becoming such a discovery.

'No,' said Sir Jekyl, gloomily. I suppose he was thinking of something else.

The ladies now floated away like summer clouds, many-tinted, golden, through the door, which Doocey held gracefully open; and the mere mortals of the party, the men, stood up in conventional adoration, while the divinities were translated, as it were, before their eyes, and hovered out of sight and hearing into the resplendent regions of candelabra and mirrors, nectar and ambrosia, tea and plum cake, and clouds of silken tapestry, and the musical tinkling of their own celestial small-talk.

CHAPTER X.

INQUIRIES HAVE BEEN MADE BY MESSRS. PELTER AND CROWE.

BEFORE repairing to bed, such fellows, young or old, as liked a talk and a cigar, and some sherry—or, by'r lady, brandy and water—were always invited to accompany Sir Jekyl to what he termed the back settlement, where he bivoacked among deal chairs and tables, with a little camp-bed, and plenty of wax candles and a brilliant little fire.

Here, as the baronet smoked in his homely little 'hut,' as he termed it, after his guests had dispersed to their bed-rooms, the Rev. Dives Marlowe that night knocked at the door, crying, 'May I come in, Jekyl?'

'Certainly, dear Dives.'

'You really mean it?'

'Never was parson so welcome.'

'By Jove!' said the Rector, 'it's later than I thought—you're sure I don't bore you.'

'Not sure, but you *may*, Dives,' said Sir Jekyl, observing his countenance, which was not quite pleasant. 'Come in, and say your say. Have a weed, old boy?'

'Well, well—a—we're alone. I don't mind—I don't generally—not that there's any harm; but some people, very good people, object—the weaker brethren, you know.'

'Consummate asses, we call them; but weaker brethren, as you say, does as well.'

The Rector was choosing and sniffing out a cigar to his heart's content

'Milk for babes, you know,' said the Rector, making his preparations. 'Strong meats'—

'And strong cigars; but you'll find these as mild as you please. Here's a match.'

The Rector sat down, with one foot on the fender, and puffed away steadily, looking into the fire; and his brother, at the opposite angle of the fender, employed himself similarly.

'Fine old soldier, General Lennox,' said the cleric, at last. 'What stay does he make with you?'

'As long as he pleases. Why?' said Sir Jekyl.

'Only he said something to-night in the drawing-room about having to go up to town to attend a Board of the East India Directors,' answered the parson.

'Oh, did he?'

'And I think he said the day after to-morrow. I thought he told you, perhaps.'

'Upon my life I can't say—perhaps he did,' said Sir Jekyl, carelessly. 'Lennox is a wonderful fine old fellow, as you say, but a little bit slow, you know; and his going or staying would not make very much difference to me.'

'I thought he told his story pretty well at dinner—that haunted room and the cobra, you remember,' said the Rector.

The Baronet grunted an assent, and nodded, without removing his cigar. The brothers conducted their conversation, not looking on one another, but each steadily into the grate.

'And, apropos of haunted rooms, Lady Jane mentioned they are in the green chamber,' continued the Rector.

'Did she? I forgot—so they are, I think,' answered the Baronet.

Here they puffed away in silence for some time.

'You know, Jekyl, about that room? Poor Amy, when she was dying, made you promise—and you did promise, you know—and she got me to promise to remind you to shut it up; and then, you know, my father wished the same,' said the Rector.

'Come, Dives, my boy, somebody has been poking you up about this. You have been hearing from my old mother-in-law, or talking to her, the goosey old shrew!'

'Upon my honour!' said the Rector, solemnly resting the wrist of his cigar-hand upon the black silk vest, and motioning his cheroot impressively, 'you are quite mistaken. One syllable I have not heard from Lady Alice upon the subject, nor, indeed, upon any other, for two months or more.'

'Come, come, Dives, old fellow, you'll not come the inspired preacher over me. Somebody's been at you, and if it was not poor old Lady Alice it was stupid old Gwynn. You need not deny it—ha! ha! ha! your speaking countenance proclaims it, my dear boy.'

' I'm not thinking of denying it. Old Donica Gwynn did write to me,' said the pastor.

' Let me see her note ?' said Sir Jekyl.

' I threw it in the fire; but I assure you there was nothing in it that would or could have vexed you. Nothing, in fact, but an appeal to me to urge you to carry out the request of poor Amy, and not particularly well spelt or written, and certainly not the sort of thing I should have liked anyone to see but ourselves, so I destroyed it as soon as I had read it.'

' I'd like to have known what the plague could make you come here two days—of course I'm glad to see you—two days before you intended, and what's running in your mind.'

' Nothing in particular—nothing, I assure you, but this. I'm certain it will be talked about—it will—the women will talk. You'll find there will be something very unpleasant; take my advice, my dear Jekyl, and just do as you promised. My poor father wished it, too—in fact, directed it, and—and it ought to be done—you know it ought.'

' Upon my soul I know no such thing. I'm to pull down my house, I suppose, for a sentiment ? What the plague harm does the room do anybody ? It doesn't hurt me, nor you.'

' It may hurt *you* very much, Jekyl.'

' I can't see it; but if it does, that's my affair,' said Sir Jekyl, sulkily.

' But, my dear Jekyl, surely you ought to consider your promise.'

' Come, Dives, no preaching. It's a very good trade, I know, and I'll do all I can for you in it; but I'm no more to be humbugged by a sermon than you are. Come! How does the dog I sent you get on ? Have you bottled the pipe of port yet, and how is old Moulders, as I asked you at dinner ? Talk of shooting, eating and drinking, and making merry, and getting up in your profession—by-the-bye, the Bishop is to be here in a fortnight, so manage to say and meet him. Talk of the port, and the old parson's death and the tithes small and great, and I'll hear you with respect, for I shall know you are speaking of things you understand, and take a real interest in; but pray don't talk any more about that stupid old room, and the stuff and nonsense these women connect with it; and, once for all, believe me when I say I have no notion of making a fool of myself by shutting up or pulling down a room which we want to use—I'll do no such thing,' and Sir Jekyl clenched the declaration with an oath, and chucking the stump of his cigar into the fire, stood up with his back to it, and looked down on his clerical Mentor, the very impersonation of ungodly obstinacy.

'I had some more to say, Jekyl, but I fancy you don't care to hear it.'

'Not a word of it,' replied the Baronet.

'That's enough for me,' said the parson, with a wave of his hand, like a man who has acquitted himself of a duty.

'And how soon do you say the Bishop is to be here?' he inquired, after a pause.

'About ten days, or *less*—egad! I forget,' answered Sir Jekyl, still a good deal ruffled.

The Rector stood up also, and hummed something like 'Rule Britannia' for a while. I am afraid he was thinking altogether of himself by this time, and suddenly recollecting that he was not in his own room, he wished his brother good-night, and departed.

Sir Jekyl was vexed. There are few things so annoying, when one has made up his mind to a certain course, as to have the unavowed misgivings and evil auguries of one's own soul aggravated by the vain but ominous dissuasions of others.

'I wish they'd keep their advice to themselves. What hurry need there be? Do they want me to blow up the room with old Lennox and his wife in it? I don't care two-pence about it. It's a gloomy place.' Sir Jekyl was charging the accidental state of his own spirits upon the aspect of the place, which was really handsome and cheerful, though antique.

'They're all in a story, the fools! What is it to me? I don't care if I never saw it again. They may pull it down after Christmas, if they like, for *me*. And Dives, too, the scamp, talking pulpit. He thinks of nothing but side-dishes and money. As worldly a dog as there is in England!'

Jekyl Marlowe could get angry enough on occasion, but he was not prone to sour tempers and peevish humours. There was, however, just now, something to render him uncomfortable and irritable, and that was that his expected guests, Mr. Guy Strangways and M. Varbarriere had not kept tryste. The day appointed for their visit had come and gone, and no appearance made. In an ordinary case a hundred and fifty accidents might account for such a miscarriage; but there was in this the unavowed specialty which excited and sickened his mind, and haunted his steps and his bed with suspicions; and he fancied he could understand a little how Herod felt when he was mocked of the wise men.

Next morning's post-bag brought Sir Jekyl two letters, one of which relieved, and the other rather vexed him, though not very profoundly. This latter was from his mother-in law, Lady Alice, in reply to his civil note, and much to his surprise, accepting his invitation to Marlowe.

'Cross-grained old woman! She's coming, for no reason on earth but to vex me. It shan't though. I'll make her most damnably welcome. We'll amuse her till she has not a leg to stand on; we'll take her an excursion every second day, and bivouac on the side of a mountain, or in the bottom of a wet valley. We'll put the young ponies to the phaeton, and Dutton shall run them away with her. I'll get up theatricals, and balls, and concerts; and I'll have breakfast at nine instead of ten. I'll entertain her with a vengeance, egad! We'll see who'll stand it longest.'

A glance at the foot of the next letter, which was a large document, on a bluish sheet of letter-paper, showed him what he expected, the official autograph of Messrs. Pelter and Crowe; it was thus expressed—

'MY DEAR SIR JEKYL MARLOWE,—

'Pursuant to your's of the —th, and in accordance with the in-

structions therein contained, we have made inquiries, as therein
directed, in all available quarters, and have received answers to
our letters, and trust that the copies thereof, and the general
summary of the correspondence, which we hope to forward by
this evening's post, will prove satisfactory to you. The result
seems to us clearly to indicate that your information has not been
well founded, and that there has been no movement in the quarter
to which your favour refers, and that no member—at all events no
prominent member—of that family is at present in England. In
further execution of your instructions, as conveyed in your favour as
above, we have, through a reliable channel, learned that Messrs.
Smith, Rumsey, and Snagg, have nothing in the matter of
Deverell at present in their office. Nor has there been, we are
assured, any correspondence from or on the part of any of those
clients for the last five terms or more. Notwithstanding, therefore, the coincidence of the date of your letter with the period to
which, on a former occasion, we invited your attention, as indicated by the deed of 1809——'

'What the plague is that?' interpolated Sir Jekyl. 'They
want me to write and ask, and pop it down in the costs;' and
after a vain endeavour to recall it, he read the passage over again
with deliberate emphasis.

'Notwithstanding, therefore, the coincidence of the date of your
letter with the period to which, on a former occasion, we invited
your attention, as indicated by the deed of 1809, we are clear upon
the evidence of the letters, copies of which will be before you as
above by next post, that there is no ground for supposing any unusual activity on the part or behalf of the party or parties to
whom you have referred. Awaiting your further directions,

'I have the honour to remain,
'My dear Sir Jekyl Marlowe,
'Your obedient servant,
'N. CROWE.
'For PELTER and CROWE.

'Sir Jekyl Marlowe, Bart.
'Marlowe, Old Swayton.'

When Sir Jekyl read this he felt all on a sudden a dozen years younger. He snapped his fingers, and smiled, in spite of himself. He could hardly bring himself to acknowledge, even in soliloquy, how immensely he was relieved. The sun shone delightfully: and his spirits returned quite brightly. He would have liked to cricket, to ride a steeple-chase—anything that would have breathed and worked him well, and given him a fair occasion for shouting and cheering.

CHAPTER XI.

OLD GRYSTON BRIDGE.

VERY merry was the Baronet at the social breakfast-table, and the whole party very gay, except those few whose natures were sedate or melancholic.

'A tremendous agreeable man, Sir Jekyl—don't you think so, Jennie?' said General Lennox to his wife, as he walked her slowly along the terrace at the side of the house.

'I think him intolerably noisy, and sometimes absolutely vulgar,' answered Lady Jane, with a languid disdain, which conveyed alike her estimate of her husband's discernment and of Sir Jekyl's merits.

'Well, I thought he was agreeable. Some of his jokes I think, indeed, had not much sense in them. But sometimes I don't see a witty thing as quick as cleverer fellows do, and they were all laughing, except you; and I don't think you like him, Jennie.'

'I don't dislike him. I dare say he's a very worthy soul; but he gives me a headache.'

'He *is* a little bit noisy, maybe. Yes, he certainly *is*,' acquiesced the honest General, who, in questions of taste and nice criticism, was diffident of his own judgment, and leaned to his wife's. 'But I thought he was rather a pleasant fellow. I'm no great judge; but I like to see fellows laughing, and that sort of thing. It looks good-humoured, don't you think?'

'I hate good-humour,' said Lady Jane.

The General, not knowing exactly what to say next, marched by her side in silence, till Lady Jane let go his arm, and sat down on the rustic seat which commands so fine a view, and, leaning back, eyed the landscape with a dreamy indolence, as if she was going to 'cut' it.

The General scanned it with a military eye, and his reconnoitring glance discerned, coming up the broad walk at his right, their host, with pretty Mrs. Maberly on his arm, doing the honours plainly very agreeably.

On seeing the General and Lady Jane, he smiled, quickened his pace, and raised his hat.

'So glad we have found you,' said he. 'Charming weather, isn't it? *You* must determine, Lady Jane, what's to be done to-day. There are two things you really ought to see—Gryston Bridge and Hazelden Castle. I assure you the great London artists visit both for studies. We'll take our luncheon there, it's such a warm, bright day—that is, if you like the plan—and, which do you say?'

'My husband always votes for me. What does Mrs. Maberly say?' and Lady Jane looked in her face with one of her winning smiles.

'Yes, what does Mrs. Maberly say?' echoed the General, gallantly.

'So you won't advise?' said the Baronet, leaning toward Lady Jane, a little reproachfully.

'I won't advise,' she echoed, in her indolent way.

'Which is the best?' inquired Mrs. Maberly, gleefully. 'What a charming idea!'

'For my part, I have a headache, you know, Arthur—I told you, dear; and I shall hardly venture a long excursion, I think. What do you advise to-day?'

'Well, I think it might do you good—hey? What do *you* say, Sir Jekyl?'

'So very sorry to hear Lady Jane is suffering; but I really think your advice, General Lennox—it's so very fine and mild—

and I think it might amuse Lady Jane;' and he glanced at the lady, who, however, wearing her bewitching smile, was conversing with Mrs. Maberly about a sweet little white dog, with long ears and a blue ribbon, which had accompanied her walk from the house.

'Well, dear, Sir Jekyl wants to know. What do you say?' inquired the General.

'Oh, pray arrange as you please. I dare say I can go. It's all the same,' answered Lady Jane, without raising her eyes from silvery little Bijou, on whom she bestowed her unwonted smiles and caresses.

'You belong to Beatrix, you charming little fairy—I'm sure you do; and is not it very wicked to go out with other people without leave, you naughty little truant.'

'You must not attack her so. She really loves Beatrix; and though she has come out to take the air with me, I don't think she cares twopence about me; and I know I don't about her.'

'What a cruel speech!' cried pretty Mrs. Maberly, with a laugh that showed her exquisite little teeth.

'The *fact* is cruel—if you will—not the speech—for she can't hear it,' said Sir Jekyl, patting Bijou.

'So they *act* love to your face, poor little dog, and say what they please of you behind your back,' murmured Lady Jane, soothingly to little Bijou, who wagged his tail and wriggled to her feet. 'Yes, they do, poor little dog!'

'Well, I shall venture—may I? I'll order the carriages at one. And we'll say Gryston Bridge,' said Sir Jekyl, hesitating notwithstanding, inquiry plainly in his countenance.

'Sir Jekyl's waiting, dear,' said General Lennox, a little imperiously.

'I really don't care. *Yes*, then,' she said, and getting up, she took the General's arm and walked away, leaving Mrs. Maberly and her host to their *tête-à-tête*.

Gryston Bridge is one of the prettiest scenes in that picturesque part of the country. A river slowly winds its silvery way through the level base of a beautifully irregular valley. No enclosure breaks the dimpling and undulating sward—for it is the common of Gryston—which rises in soft pastoral slopes at either side, forming the gentle barriers of the valley, which is closed in at the further end by a bold and Alpine hill, with a base rising purple and dome-like from the plain; and in this perspective the vale of Gryston diverges, and the two streams, which at its head unite to form the slow-flowing current of the Greet, are lost to sight. Trees of nature's planting here and there overhang its stream, and others, solitarily or in groups, stud the hill-sides and the soft green plain. A strange row of tall, grey stones, Druidic or monu-- mental, of a bygone Cyclopean age, stand up, time-worn and mysterious, on a gentle slope, with a few bending thorn and birch trees beside them, in the near distance; and in the foreground, the steep, Gothic bridge of Gretford, or Gryston, spans the river, with five tall arches, and a loop-holed gatehouse, which once guarded the pass, now roofless and ruined.

In this beautiful and sequestered scene the party from Marlowe had loitered away that charming afternoon. The early sunset had been rapidly succeeded by twilight, and the moon had surprised them. The servants were packing up hampers of plates and knives and forks, and getting the horses to for the return to Marlowe; while, in the early moonlight a group stood upon the bridge, overlooking from the battlement the sweet landscape in its changing light.

Sir Jekyl could see that Captain Drayton was by Beatrix's side, and concluded, rightly, I have no doubt, that his conversation was tinted by the tender lights of that romantic scenery.

'The look back on this old bridge from those Druidic stones there by moonlight is considered very fine. It is no distance— hardly four hundred steps from this—although it looks so misty,' said the Baronet to Lady Jane, who leaned on his arm. 'Suppose we make a little party, will you venture?'

I suppose the lady acquiesced, for Sir Jekyl ordered that the carriages should proceed round by the road, and take them up at the point where these Druidic remains stand.

The party who ventured this little romantic walk over the grass, were General Lennox, in charge of the mature Miss Blunket, who loved a frolic with all her girlish heart; Sir Jekyl, with Lady Jane upon his arm; and Captain Drayton, who escorted Beatrix. Marching gaily, in open column, as the General would have said, they crossed the intervening hollow, and reached the hillock, on which stand these ungainly relics of a bygone race; and up the steep bank they got, each couple as best they could. Sir Jekyl and Lady Jane, for he knew the ground, by an easy path, were first to reach the upper platform.

Sir Jekyl, I dare say, was not very learned about the Druids, and I can't say exactly what he was talking about, when on a sudden he arrested both his step and his sentence, for on one of these great prostrate stones which strew that summit, he saw standing, not a dozen steps away, well illuminated by the moon, the figure of that very Guy Strangways, whom he so wished and hated to see—whom he had never beheld without such strange sensations, and had not expected to see again.

The young man took no note of them apparently. He certainly did not recognise Sir Jekyl, whose position placed his face in the shade, while that of Mr. Strangways was full in the white light of the moon.

They had found him almost in the act of descending from his pedestal; and he was gone in a few moments, before the Baronet had recovered from his surprise.

The vivid likeness which he bore to a person whom the Baronet never wished to think of, and the suddenness of his appearance and his vanishing, had reimpressed him with just the same secret alarms and misgivings as when first he saw him; and the serene confidence induced by the letter of Messrs. Pelter and Crowe was for a moment demolished. He dropped Lady Jane's arm, and forgetting his chivalry, strode to the brow of the hillock, over which the mysterious young man had disappeared. He had lost sight of him, but he emerged in a few seconds, about fifty yards away, from behind a screen of thorn, walking swiftly toward the road close by, on which stood a chaise, sharp in the misty moonlight.

Just in time to prevent his shouting after the figure, now on the

point of re-entering the vehicle, he recollected and checked himself. Confound the fellows, if they did not appreciate his hospi-
talily, should he run after them; or who were they that he should
care a pin about them? Had he not Pelter and Crowe's letter?
And suppose he did overtake and engage the young rogue in talk,
what could he expect but a parcel of polite lies. Certainly, under
the circumstances, pursuit would have been specially undignified;
and the Baronet drew himself up on the edge of the eminence, and
cast a haughty half-angry look after the young gentleman, who
was now stepping into the carriage; and suddenly he recollected
how very ill he had treated Lady Jane, and he hastened to rejoin
her.

But Sir Jekyl, in that very short interval, had lost something of
his spirits. The sight of that young man had gone far to undo
the tranquillising effect of his attorney's letter. He would not
have cared had this unchanged phantom of the past and his hoary
mentor been still in England, provided it were at a distance. But
here they were, on the confines of his property, within a short
drive of Marlowe, yet affecting to forget his invitation, his house,
and himself, and detected prowling in its vicinity like spies or
poachers by moonlight. Was there not something insidious in
this? It was not for nothing that so well-bred a person as that
young man thus trampled on all the rules of courtesy for the
sake of maintaining his incognito, and avoiding the obligations of
hospitality.

So reasoned Sir Jekyl Marlowe, and felt himself rapidly relapsing into that dreamy and intense uneasiness, from which for a
few hours he had been relieved.

'A thousand apologies, Lady Jane,' cried he, as he ran back
and proffered his arm again. 'I was afraid that fellow might be
one of a gang—a very dangerous lot of rogues—poachers, I believe. There were people robbed here about a year ago, and I
quite forgot when I asked you to come. I should never have
forgiven myself—so selfishly forgetful—never, had you been
frightened.'

Sir Jekyl could, of course, tell fibs, especially by way of apology,

as plausibly as other men of the world. He had here turned a
negligence skilfully into a gallantry, and I suppose the lady for-
gave him.

The carriages had now arrived at the bend of this pretty road;
and our Marlowe friends got in, and the whole cortège swept away
merrily towards that old mansion. Sir Jekyl had been, with an
effort, very lively all the way home, and assisted Lady Jane to
the ground, smiling, and had a joke for General Lennox as he
followed; and a very merry party mustered in the hall, prattling,
laughing, and lighting their candles, to run up-stairs and dress
for a late dinner.

CHAPTER XII.

THE STRANGERS APPEAR AGAIN.

SIR JEKYL was the last of the party in the hall; and the last joke
and laugh had died away on the lobby above him, and away fled
his smiles like the liveries and brilliants of Cinderella to the region
of illusions, and black care laid her hand on his shoulder and
stood by him.

The bland butler, with a grave bow, accosted him in mild
accents—

'The two gentlemen, sir, as you spoke of to Mrs. Sinnott, has
arrived about five minutes before you, sir; and she has, please sir,
followed your directions, and had them put in the rooms in the
front, as you ordered, sir, should be kept for them, before Mrs.
Gwynn left.'

'*What* two gentlemen?' demanded Sir Jekyl, with a thrill.

'Mr. Strangways and M. Varbarriere?'

'Them, sir, I think, is the names—Strangways, leastways, I
am sure on, 'aving lived, when young, with a branch of the
Earl of Dilbury's family, if you please, sir—which Strangways is
the name.'

'A good-looking young gentleman, tall and slight, eh?'

'Yes, sir; and a heavy gentleman haccompanies him—something in years—a furriner, as I suppose, and speaking French or Jarmin; leastways, it is not English.'

'Dinner in twenty minutes,' said Sir Jekyl, with the decision of the Duke of Wellington in action; and away he strode to his dressing-room in the back settlements, with a quick step and a thoughtful face.

'I shan't want you, Tomlinson, you need not stay,' said he to his man; but before he let him go, he asked carelessly a word or two about the new guests, and learned, in addition to what he already knew, nothing but that they had brought a servant with them.

'So much the worse,' thought Sir Jekyl; 'those confounded fellows hear everything, and poke their noses everywhere. I sometimes think that rascal, Tomlinson, pries about here.'

And the Baronet, half-dressed, opened the door of his study, as he called it, at the further end of his homely bed-chamber, and looked round.

It is or might be a comfortable room, of some five-and-twenty feet square, surrounded by book-shelves, as homely as the style of the bed-room, stored with volumes of the 'Annual Register,' 'Gentleman's Magazine,' and 'Universal History' sort—long rows in dingy gilding—moved up here when the old library of Marlowe was broken up. The room had a dusty air of repose about it. A few faded pieces of old-fashioned furniture, which had probably been quartered here in genteel retirement, long ago, when the principal sitting-rooms were undergoing a more modern decoration.

Here Sir Jekyl stood with a sudden look of dejection, and stared listlessly round on the compact wall of books that surrounded him, except for the one door-case, that through which he had entered, and the two windows, on all sides. Sir Jekyl was in a sort of collapse of spirits. He stepped dreamily to the far shelf and took down a volume of Old Bailey Reports, and read the back of it several times, then looked round once more dejectedly, and blew the top of the volume, and wondered at the quantity of dust there, and replacing it, heaved a deep sigh. Dust and death are old associations, and his thoughts were running in a gloomy channel.

' Is it worth all this ?' he thought. ' I'm growing tired of it—utterly. I'm half sorry I came here ; perhaps they are right. It might be a devilish good thing for me if this rubbishy old house were burnt to the ground—and I in it, by Jove ! " Out, out, brief candle !" What's that Shakspeare speech ?—" A tale told by an idiot—a play played by an idiot"—egad ! I don't know why I do half the things I do.'

When he looked in the glass he did not like the reflection.

' Down in the mouth—hang it ! this will never do,' and he shook his curls, and smirked, and thought of the ladies, and bustled away over his toilet; and when it was completed, as he fixed in his jewelled wrist-buttons, the cold air and shadow of his good or evil angel's wing crossed him again, and he sighed. Capricious were his moods. Our wisdom is so frivolous, and our frivolities so sad. Is there time here to think out anything completely ? Is it possible to hold by our conclusions, or even to remember them long ? And this trifling and suffering are the woof and the warp of an eternal robe—wedding garment, let us hope—maybe winding-sheet, or—toga molesta.

Sir Jekyl, notwithstanding his somewhat interrupted toilet, was in the drawing-room before many of his guests had assembled. He hesitated for a moment at the door, and turned about with a sickening thrill, and walked to the table in the outer hall, or vestibule, where the postbag lay. He had no object in this countermarch, but to postpone for a second or two the meeting with the gentlemen whom, with, as he sometimes fancied, very questionable prudence, he had invited under his roof.

And now he entered, frank, gay, smiling. His eyes did not search, they were, as it were, smitten instantaneously with a sense of pain, by the image of the young man, so handsome, so peculiar, sad, and noble, the sight of whom had so moved him. He was conversing with old Colonel Doocey, at the further side of the fire-place In another moment Sir Jekyl was before him, his hand very kindly locked in his.

' Very happy to see you here, Mr. Strangways.'

' I am very much honoured, Sir Jekyl Marlowe,' returned the young gentleman, in that low sweet tone which he also hated. ' I have many apologies to make. We have arrived two days later than your note appointed ; but an accident'——

' Pray, not a word—your appearance here is the best compensation you can make me. Your friend, Monsieur Varbarriere, I hope——'

' My uncle—yes ; he, too, has the honour. Will you permit me to present him ? Monsieur Varbarriere,' said the young man, presenting his relative.

A gentleman at this summons turned suddenly from General Lennox, with whom he had been talking ; a high-shouldered, portly man, taller a good deal when you approached him than he looked at first ; his hair, ' all silvered,' brushed up like Louis Philippe's, conically from his forehead ; grey, heavily projecting eyebrows, long untrimmed moustache and beard ; altogether a head and face which seemed to indicate that combination of strong sense and sensuality which we see in some of the medals of Roman Emperors ; a forehead projecting at the brows, and keen dark eyes in shadow, observing all things from under their grizzled penthouse ; these points, and a hooked nose, and a certain weight and solemnity of countenance, gave to the large and rather pallid aspect, presented suddenly to the Baronet, something, as we have said, of the character of an old magician. Voluminous plaited black trousers, slanting in to the foot, foreshadowed the peg-top of more recent date ; a loose and long black velvet waistcoat, with more gold chain and jewellery generally than Englishmen are accustomed to wear, and a wide and clumsy black coat, added to the broad and thick-set character of his figure.

As Sir Jekyl made his complimentary speech to this gentleman, he saw that his steady and shrewd gaze was attentively considering him in a way that a little tried his patience ; and when the stranger spoke it was in French, and in that peculiar metallic diapason which we sometimes hear among the Hebrew community, and which brings the nasals of that tongue into sonorous and rather ugly relief.

'England is, I dare say, quite new to you, Monsieur Varbar-riere?' inquired Sir Jekyl.

'I have seen it a very long time ago, and admire your so fine country very much,' replied the pallid and bearded sage, speaking in French still, and in those bell-like tones which rang and buzzed unpleasantly in the ear.

'You find us the same foggy and tasteless islanders as before,' said the host. 'In art, indeed, we have made an advance; *there*, I think, we have capabilities, but we are as a people totally de-ficient in that fine decorative sense which expresses itself so grace-fully and universally in your charming part of the world.'

When Sir Jekyl talked of France, he was generally thinking of Paris.

'We have our barbarous regions, as you have; our vineyards are a dull sight after all, and our forest trees you, with your grand timber, would use for broom-sticks.'

'But your capital; why every time one looks out at the window it is a fillip to one's spirits. To me, preferring France so infi-nitely, as I do,' said Sir Jekyl, replying in his guest's language, 'it appears a mystery why any Frenchman, who can help it, ever visits our dismal region.'

The enchanter here shrugged slowly, with a solemn smile.

'No wonder our actions are mysterious to others, since they are so often so to ourselves.'

'You are best acquainted with the south of France?' said Sir Jekyl, without any data for such an assumption, and saying the reverse of what he suspected.

'Very well with the south; pretty well, indeed, with most parts.'

Just at this moment Mr. Ridley's bland and awful tones in-formed the company that dinner was on the table, and Sir Jekyl hastened to afford to Lady Blunket the support of his vigorous arm into the parlour.

It ought to have been given to Lady Jane; but the Blunket was a huffy old woman, and, on the score of a very decided seniority, was indulged.

Lady Blunket was not very interesting, and was of the Alderman's opinion, that conversation prevents one's tasting the green fat; Sir Jekyl had, therefore, time, with light and careless glances, to see pretty well, from time to time, what was going on among his guests. Monsieur Varbarriere had begun to interest him more than Mr. Guy Strangways, and his eye oftener reviewed that ponderous and solemn face and form than any other at the table. It seemed that he liked his dinner, and attended to his occupation. But though taciturn, his shrewd eyes glanced from time to time on the host and his guests with an air of reserved observation that showed his mind was anything but sluggish during the process. He looked wonderfully like some of those enchanters whom we have seen in illustrations of Don Quixote.

'A deep fellow,' he thought, 'an influential fellow. That gentleman knows what he's about; that young fellow is in his hands.'

CHAPTER XIII.

IN THE DRAWING-ROOM.

SIR JEKYL heard snatches of conversation, sometimes here, sometimes there.

Guy Strangways was talking to Beatrix, and the Baronet heard him say, smiling—

'But you don't, I'm sure, believe in the elixir of life; you only mean to mystify us.' He was looking more than ever—identical with that other person, whom it was not pleasant to Sir Jekyl to be reminded of—horribly like, in this white wax-like splendour.

'But there's another process, my uncle, Monsieur Varbarriere, says, by slow refrigeration; you are first put to sleep, and in that state frozen; and once frozen, without having suffered death, you may be kept in a state of suspended life for twenty or thirty years, neither conscious, nor growing old; arrested precisely at the point of your existence at which the process was applied, and at the same

point restored again whenever for any purpose it may be expedient
to recall you to consciousness and activity.'

One of those restless, searching glances which the solemn,
portly old gentleman in black directed, from time to time, as he
indulged his taciturn gulosity, lighted on the Baronet at this
moment, and Sir Jekyl felt that they exchanged an unintentional
glance of significance. Each averted his quickly ; and Sir Jekyl,
with one of his chuckles, for the sake merely of saying something,
remarked—

'I don't see how you can restore people to life by freezing them.'

'He did not speak, I think, of restoring life—did you, Guy ?'
said the bell-toned diapason of the old gentleman, speaking his
nasal French.

'Oh, no—suspended merely,' answered the young man.

'To restore life, you must have recourse, I fancy, to a higher
process,' continued the sage, with an ironical gravity, and his eye
this time fixed steadily on Sir Jekyl's; 'and I could conceive
none more embarrassing to the human race, *under certain circumstances*,' and he shrugged slowly and shook his head.

'How delightful!—no more death!' exclaimed enthusiastic
Miss Blunket.

'Embarrassing, of course, I mean, to certain of the survivors.'

This old gentleman was hitting his tenderest points rather hard
and often. Was it by chance or design ? Who was he ?

So thought the Baronet as he smiled and nodded.

'Do you know who that fat old personage is who dresses like an
undertaker and looks like a Jew ?' asked Captain Drayton of
Beatrix.

'I think he is a relative of Mr. Strangways.'

'And who *is* Mr. Strangways ?'

'He's at my right, next me,' answered she in a low tone, not
liking the very clear and distinct key in which the question was
put.

But Captain Drayton was not easily disconcerted, being a young
gentleman of a bold and rather impertinent temperament, and he

continued leaning back in his chair and looking dreamily into his hock-glass.

'Not a friend of yours, is he?'

'Oh, no.'

'Really—not a friend. You're *quite* certain.'

'Perfectly. We never saw either—that is, papa met them at some posting place on his way from London, and invited them; but I think he knows nothing more.'

'Well, I did not like to say till I knew, but I think him—the old fellow—I have not seen the young man—a most vulgar-looking old person. He's a wine-jobber, or manager of a factory, or something. You never saw—I know Paris by heart—you *never saw* such a thing in gentlemanly society there.'

And the young lady heard him say, *sotto voce*, 'Brute!' haughtily to himself, as an interjection, while he just raised the finger-tips of the hand which rested on the table, and let them descend again on the snowy napery. The subject deserved no more troublesome gesture.

'And where is the young gentleman?' asked Captain Drayton, after a little interval.

Beatrix told him again.

'Oh! *That's* he! Isn't his French very bad—did it strike you? Bad *accent*—I can tell in a moment. That's not an accent one hears anywhere.'

Oddly enough, Sir Jekyl at the same time, with such slight interruptions as his agreeable attentions to Lady Blunket imposed, was, in the indistinct way in which such discussions are mentally pursued, observing upon the peculiarities of his two new guests, and did not judge them amiss.

The elder was odd, take him for what country you pleased. Bearded like a German, speaking good French, with a good accent, but in the loud full tones of a Spaniard, and with a quality of voice which resounds in the synagogue, and a quietude of demeanour much more English than continental. His dress, such as I have described it, fine in material, but negligent and easy, though odd. Reserved and silent he was, a little sinister perhaps, but his bearing unconstrained and gracious when he spoke. There was, indeed, that odd, watchful glance from under his heavy eyebrows, which, however, had nothing sly, only observant, in it. Again he thought, ' Who could he be ?' On the whole, Sir Jekyl was in nowise disposed to pronounce upon him as Captain Drayton was doing a little way down the table; nor yet upon Guy Strangways, whom he thought, on the contrary, an elegant young man, according to French notions of the gentlemanly, and he knew the French people a good deal better than the youthful Captain did.

The principal drawing-room of Marlowe is a very large apartment, and people can talk of one another in it without any risk of detection.

' Well, Lady Jane,' said the Baronet, sitting down before that handsome woman, and her husband the General, so as to interrupt a conjugal *tête-à-tête*, probably a particularly affectionate one, for he was to leave for London next day. ' I saw you converse with Monsieur Varbarriere. What do you think of him ?'

' I don't think I conversed with him—did I ? He talked to me ; but I really did not take the trouble to think about him.'

The General laughed triumphantly, and glanced over his shoulder at the Baronet. He liked his wife's contempt for the rest of the sex, and her occasional—*only* occasional—enthusiasm for him.

' Now you are much too clever, Lady Jane, to be let off so. I really want to know something about him, which I don't at present; and if anyone can help me to a wise conjecture, you, I am certain, can.'

' And don't you really know who he is ?' inquired General Lennox, with a haughty military surprise.

' Upon my honour, I have not the faintest idea,' answered Sir Jekyl. ' He may be a cook or a rabbi, for anything I can tell.'

The General's white eyebrows went some wrinkles up the slanting ascent of his pink forehead, and he plainly looked his amazement that Lady Jane should have been subjected at Marlowe to the risk of being accosted on equal terms by a cook or a rabbi. His lips screwed themselves unconsciously into a small o, and his eyes went in search of the masquerading menial.

'We had a cook,' said the General, still eyeing M. Varbarriere, 'at Futtychur, a French fellow, fat like that, but shorter—a capital cook, by Jove! and a very gentlemanly man. He wore a white cap, and he had a very good way of stewing tomatas and turkeys, I think it was, and—yes it was—and a monstrous gentlemanlike fellow he was; rather too expensive though; he cost us a great deal,' and the General winked slily. 'I had to speak to him once or twice. But an uncommon gentlemanlike man.'

'He's not a cook, my dear. He may be a banker, perhaps,' said Lady Jane, languidly.

'You have exactly hit my idea,' said Sir Jekyl. 'It was his knowing all about French banking, General, when you mentioned that trick that was played you on the Bourse.'

At this moment the massive form and face of M. Varbarriere was seen approaching with Beatrix by his side. They were conversing, but the little group we have just been listening to dropped the discussion of M. Varbarriere, and the Baronet said that he hoped General Lennox would have a fine day for his journey, and that the moon looked particularly bright and clear.

'I want to show Monsieur Varbarriere the drawings of the house, papa; they are in this cabinet. He admires the architecture very much.'

The large enchanter in black made a solemn bow of acquiescence here, but said nothing; and Beatrix took from its nook a handsome red-leather portfolio, on the side of which, in tall golden letters, were the words—

VIEWS AND ELEVATIONS

OF

MARLOWE MANOR HOUSE.

PAULO ABRUZZI,

ARCHITECT.

1711.

'Capital drawing, I am told. He was a young man of great promise,' said Sir Jekyl, in French. 'But the style is quite English, and, I fear, will hardly interest an eye accustomed to the more graceful contour of southern continental architecture.'

'Your English style interests me very much. It is singular, and suggests hospitality, enjoyment, and mystery.'

Monsieur Varbarriere was turning over these tinted drawings carefully.

'Is not that very true, papa—hospitality, enjoyment, mystery?' repeated Beatrix. 'I think that faint character of mystery is so pleasant. We have a mysterious room here.' She had turned to M. Varbarriere.

'Oh, a dozen,' interrupted Sir Jekyl. 'No end of ghosts and devils, you know. But I really think you excel us in that article. I resided for five weeks in a haunted house once, near Havre, and the stories were capital, and there were some very good noises, too. We must get Dives to tell it by-and-by; he was younger than I, and more frightened.'

'And Mademoiselle says you have a haunted apartment here,' said the ponderous foreigner with the high forehead and projecting brows.

'Yes, of course. We are very much haunted. There is hardly a crooked passage or a dark room that has not a story,' said Sir Jekyl. 'Beatrix, why don't you sing us a song, by-the-bye?'

'May I beg one other favour first, before the crowning one of the song?' said M. Varbarriere, with an imposing playfulness. 'Mademoiselle, I am sure, tells a story well. Which, I entreat, is the particular room you speak of?'

'We call it the green chamber,' said Beatrix.

'The green chamber—what a romantic title!' exclaimed the large gentleman in black, graciously; 'and where is it situated?' he pursued.

'We must really put you into it,' said Sir Jekyl.

'Nothing I should like so well,' he observed, with a bow.

'That is, of course, whenever it is deserted. You have not been plagued with apparitions, General? Even Lady Jane—and there are no ghost-seers like ladies, I've observed—has failed to report anything horrible.'

His hand lay on the arm of her chair, and, as he spoke, for a moment pressed hers, which, not choosing to permit such accidents, she, turning carelessly and haughtily toward the other speakers, slipped away.

CHAPTER XIV.

MUSIC.

'AND pray, Mademoiselle Marlowe, in what part of the house is this so wonderful room situated?' persisted the grave and reverend signor.

'Quite out of the question to describe to one who does not already know the house,' interposed Sir Jekyl. 'It is next the six-sided dressing-room, which opens from the hatchment gallery —that is its exact situation; and I'm afraid I have failed to convey it,' said Sir Jekyl, with one of his playful chuckles.

The Druidic-looking Frenchman shrugged and lifted his fingers with a piteous expression of perplexity, and shook his head.

'Is there not among these drawings a view of the side of the house where this room lies?' he inquired.

'I was looking it out,' said Beatrix.

'I'll find it, Trixie. Go you and sing us a song,' said the Baronet.

'I've got them both, papa. Now, Monsieur Varbarriere, here they are. This is the front view—this is the side.'

'I am very much obliged,' said Monsieur, examining the drawings curiously. 'The room recedes. This large bow-window belongs to it. Is it not so?—wide room?—how long? You see I want to understand everything. Ah! yes, here is the side view. It projects from the side of the older building, I see. How charming! And this is the work of the Italian artist? The style is quite novel—a mixture partly Florentine—really very elegant. Did he build anything more here?'

'Yes, a very fine row of stables, and a temple in the grounds,' said Sir Jekyl. 'You shall see them to-morrow.'

'The chamber green. Yes, very clever, very pretty;' and having eyed them over again carefully, he said, laying them down—

'A curious as well as a handsome old house, no doubt. Ah! very curious, I dare say,' said the sage Monsieur Varbarriere. 'Are there here the ground plans?'

'We have them somewhere, I fancy, among the title-deeds, but none here,' said Sir Jekyl, a little stiffly, as if it struck him that his visitor's curiosity was a trifle less ceremonious than, all things considered, it might be.

Pretty Beatrix was singing now to her own accompaniment; and Captain Drayton, twisting the end of his light moustache, stood haughtily by her side. The music in his ear was but a half-heard noise. Indeed, although he had sat out operas innumerable, like other young gentlemen, who would sit out as many hours of a knife-grinder's performance, or of a railway whistle, if it were the fashion, had but an imperfect recollection of the airs he had paid so handsomely to hear, and was no authority on music of any sort.

Now Beatrix was pretty—more than pretty. Some people called her lovely. She sang in that rich and plaintive contralto—so rare and so inexplicably moving—the famous 'Come Gentil,' from Don Pasquale. When she ceased, the gentleman at her other side, Guy Strangways, sighed—not a complimentary—a real sigh.

'That is a wonderful song, the very spirit of a serenade. Such distance—such gaiety—such sadness. Your Irish poet, Thomas Moore, compares some spiritual music or kind voice to sunshine spoken. This is *moonlight*—moonlight *sung*, and *so* sung that I could dream away half a life in listening, and yet sigh when it ceases.'

Mr. Guy Strangways' strange, dark eyes looked full on her, as with an admiring enthusiasm he said these words.

The young lady smiled, looking up for a moment from the music-

stool, and then with lowered eyes again, and that smile of gratifi-
cation which is so beautiful in a lovely girl's face.

'It is quite charming, really. I'm no musician, you know;
but I enjoy good music extravagantly, especially singing,' said
Captain Drayton. 'I don't aspire to talk sentiment and that kind
of poetry.' He was, perhaps, near using a stronger term—' a mere
John Bull; but it *is*, honestly, charming.'

He had his glass in his eye, and turned back the leaf of the
song to the title-page.

'Don Pasquale—yes. Sweet opera that. How often I have
listened to Mario in it! But never, Miss Marlowe, with more real
pleasure than to the charming performance I have just heard.'

Captain Drayton was not making his compliment well, and felt
it somehow. It was clumsy—it was dull—it was meant to over-
ride the tribute offered by Guy Strangways, whose presence he
chose, in modern phrase, to ignore; and yet he felt that he had, as
he would have expressed it, rather 'put his foot in it;' and, with
just a little flush in his cheek and rather angry eyes, he stooped
over the piano and read the Italian words half aloud.

'By-the-bye,' he said, suddenly recollecting a topic, 'what a
sweet scene that is of Gryston Bridge? Have you ever been to see
it before?'

'Once since we came, we rode there, papa and I,' answered
Miss Marlowe. 'It looked particularly well this evening—quite
beautiful in the moonlight.'

'Is it possible, Miss Marlowe, that *you* were there this evening?
I and my uncle stopped on our way here to admire the exquisite
effect of the steep old bridge, with a wonderful foreground of
Druidic monuments, as they seemed to me.'

'Does your father preserve that river?' asked Captain Drayton,
coolly pretermitting Mr. Strangways altogether.

'I really don't know,' she replied, in a slight and hurried way
that nettled the Captain; and, turning to Guy Strangways, she
said, 'Did you see it *from* the bridge?'

'No, Mademoiselle; from the mound in which those curious
stones are raised,' answered Mr. Strangways.

Captain Drayton felt that Miss Marlowe's continuing to talk to Mr. Strangways, while *he* was present and willing to converse, was extremely offensive, choosing to entertain a low opinion in all respects of that person. He stooped a little forward, and stared at the stranger with that ill-bred gaze of insolent surprise which is the peculiar weapon of Englishmen, and which very distinctly expresses, ' who the devil are you?'

Perhaps it was fortunate for the harmony of the party that just at this moment, and before Captain Drayton could say anything specially impertinent, Sir Jekyl touched Drayton on the shoulder, saying—

' Are you for whist?'

' No, thanks—I'm no player.'

' Oh! Mr. Strangways—I did not see—do *you* play?'

Mr. Strangways smiled, bowed, and shook his head.

' Drayton, did I present you to Mr. Strangways?' and the Baronet made the two young gentlemen technically known to one another—though, of course, each knew the other already.

They bowed rather low, and a little haughtily, neither smiling. I suppose Sir Jekyl saw something a little dangerous in the countenance of one at least of the gentlemen as he approached, and chose to remind them, in that agreeable way, that he was present, and wished them acquainted, and of course friendly.

He had now secured old Colonel Doocey to make up his party—the sober old Frenchman and Sir Paul Blunket making the supplementary two; and before they had taken their chairs round the card-table, Captain Drayton said, with a kind of inclination rather insolent than polite—

' You are of the Dilbury family, of course? I never knew a Strangways yet—I mean, of course, a Strangways such as one would be likely to meet, you know—who was not.'

' You know one now, sir; for I am not connected ever so remotely with that distinguished family. My family are quite another Strangways.'

' No doubt quite as respectable,' said Captain Drayton, with a bow, a look and a tone that would have passed for deferential with many; but which, nevertheless, had the subtle flavour of an irony in it.

' Perhaps more so; my ancestors are the Strangways of Lynton; you are aware they had a peerage down to the reign of George II.'

Captain Drayton was not as deep as so fashionable and moneyed a man ought to have been in extinct peerages, and therefore he made a little short supercilious bow, and no answer. He looked drowsily toward the ceiling, and then—

' The Strangways of Lynton are on the Continent or something— one does not hear of them,' said Captain Drayton, slightly but grandly. ' We are the Draytons of Drayton Forest, in the same county.'

' Oh! then my uncle is misinformed. He thought that family was extinct, and lamented over it when we saw the house and place at a distance.'

Captain Drayton coloured a little above his light yellow mous- tache. He was no Drayton, but a remotely collateral Smithers, with a queen's letter constituting him a Drayton.

' Aw—yes—it is a fine old place—quite misinformed. I can show you our descent if you wish it.'

If Drayton had collected his ideas a little first he would not have made this condescension.

' Your descent is high and pure—*very* high, I assume—mine is only respectable—presentable, as you say, but by no means so high as to warrant my inquiring into that of other people.'

' Inquiry! of course. I did not say inquiry,' and with an effort Captain Drayton almost laughed.

' Nothing more dull,' acquiesced Mr. Strangways slightly.

Both gentlemen paused—each seemed to expect something from the other—each seemed rather angrily listening for it. The ostensible attack had all been on the part of the gallant Captain, who certainly had not been particularly well bred. The Captain, nevertheless, felt that Mr. Strangways knew perfectly all about Smithers, and that Smithers really had not one drop of the Drayton blood in his veins; and he felt in the sore and secret centre of his soul that the polished, handsome young gentleman, so easy, so graceful, with that suspicion of a foreign accent and of foreign gesture, had the best of the unavowed battle. He had never spoken a word or looked a look in the course of this little dialogue which could have suggested an idea of altercation, or any kind of mutual unpleasantness, to the beautiful young girl; who, with one hand on the keys of the piano, touched them so lightly with her fingers as to call forth a dream of an air rather than the air itself.

To her Guy Strangways turned, with his peculiar smile—so winning, yet so deep—an enigmatic smile that had in it a latent sadness and fierceness, and by its very ambiguousness interested one.

'I upbraid myself for losing these precious moments while you sit here, and might, perhaps, be persuaded to charm us with another song.'

So she was persuaded; Captain Drayton still keeping guard, and applauding, though with no special goodwill toward the un-offending stranger.

The party broke up early. The ladies trooped to their bed-room candles and ascended the great staircase, chatting harmo-niously, and bidding mutual sweet good-nights as in succession they reached their doors. The gentlemen, having sat for awhile lazily about the fire, or gathered round the tray whereon stood sherry and seltzer water, repaired also to the cluster of bedchamber candlesticks without, and helped themselves, talking together in like sociable manner.

'Would you like to come to my room and have a cigar, Mon-sieur Varbarriere?' asked the Baronet in French.

Monsieur was much obliged, and bowed very suavely, but declined.

'And you, Mr. Strangways?'

He also, with many thanks, a smile, and a bow, declined.

'My quarters are quite out of reach of the inhabited part of the house—not very far from two hundred feet from this spot, by Jove! right in the rear. You must really come to me there some night; you'll be amused at my deal furniture and rustic bar-

barism; we often make a party there and smoke for half an hour.'

So, as they were not to be persuaded, the Baronet hospitably accompanied them to their rooms, at the common dressing-room door of which stood little Jacque Duval with his thin, bronzed face, candle in hand, bowing, to receive his master.

CHAPTER XV.

M. VARBARRIERE CONVERSES WITH HIS NEPHEW.

HERE then Sir Jekyl bid them good night, and descended the great staircase, and navigated the long line of passage to the back stairs leading up to his own homely apartment.

The elder man nodded to Jacque, and moved the tips of his fingers towards the door—a silent intimation which the adroit valet perfectly understood; so, with a cheerful bow, he withdrew.

There was a gay little spluttering fire in the grate, which the sharpness of the night made very pleasant. The clumsy door was shut, and the room had an air of comfortable secrecy which invited a talk.

It was not to come, however, without preparation. He drew a chair before the fire, and sat down solemnly, taking a gigantic cigar from his case, and moistening it diligently between his lips before lighting it. Then he pointed to a chair beside the hearth, and presented his cigar-case to his young companion, who being well versed in his elder's ways, helped himself, and having, like him, foreign notions about smoking, had of course no remorse about a cigar or two in their present quarters.

Up the chimney chiefly whisked the narcotic smoke. Over the ponderous features and knotted forehead of the sage flushed the uncertain light of the fire, revealing all the crows' feet—all the lines which years, thought, passion, or suffering had traced on that large, sombre, and somewhat cadaverous countenance, reversing oddly some of its shadows, and glittering with a snake-like brightness on the eyes, which now gazed grimly into the bars under their heavy brows.

The large and rather flat foot, shining in French leather, of the portly gentleman in the ample black velvet waistcoat, rested on the fender, and he spoke not a word until his cigar was fairly smoked out and the stump of it in the fire. Abruptly he began, without altering his pose or the direction of his gaze.

'You need not make yourself more friendly with any person here than is absolutely necessary.'

He was speaking French, and in a low tone that sounded like the boom of a distant bell.

Young Strangways bowed acquiescence.

'Be on your guard with Sir Jekyl Marlowe. Tell him *nothing*. Don't let him be kind to you. He will have no kind motive in being so. Fence with his questions—don't answer them. Remember he is an artful man without any scruple. I know him and all about him.'

M. Varbarriere spoke each of these little sentences in an isolated way, as a smoker might, although he was no longer smoking, between his puffs. 'Therefore, not a word to him—no obligations—no intimacy. If he catches you by the hand, even by your little finger, in the way of friendship, he'll cling to it, so as to impede your *arm*, should it become necessary to exert it.'

'I don't understand you, sir,' said the young man, in a deferential tone, but looking very hard at him.

'You *partly* don't understand me; the nature of my direction, however, is clear. Observe it strictly.'

There was a short silence here.

'I don't understand, sir, what covert hostility can exist between us; that is, why I should, in your phrase, keep my hand free to exert it against him.'

'No, I don't suppose you do.'

'And I can't help regretting that, if such are our possible relations, I should find myself as a guest under his roof,' said the young man, with a pained and almost resentful look.

'You can't help regretting, and—you can't help the circumstance,' vibrated his Mentor, in a metallic murmur, his cadaverous features wearing the same odd character of deep thought and apathy.

'I don't know, with respect to *him*—I know, however, how it has affected me—that I have felt unhappy, and even guilty since this journey commenced, as if I were a traitor and an impostor,' said the young man, with a burst of impatience.

'Don't, sir, use phrases which reflect back upon *me*,' said the other, turning upon him with a sudden sternness. 'All you have done is by my direction.'

The ample black waistcoat heaved and subsided a little faster than before, and the imposing countenance was turned with pallid fierceness upon the young man.

'I am sorry, uncle.'

'So you should—you'll see one day how little it is to me, and how much to you.'

Here was a pause. The senior turned his face again toward the fire. The little flush that in wrath always touched his forehead subsided slowly. He replaced his foot on the fender, and chose another cigar.

'There's a great deal you don't see now that you will presently. I did not want to see Sir Jekyl Marlowe any more than you did or do; but I did want to see this place. You'll know hereafter why I'd rather not have met him. I'd rather not be his guest. Had he been as usual at Dartbroke, I should have seen all I wanted without that annoyance. It is an accident his being here— another, his having invited me; but no false ideas and no trifling chance shall regulate, much less stop, the action of the machine which I am constructing and will soon put in motion.'

And with these words he lighted his cigar, and after smoking for a while he lowered it, and said—

'Did Sir Jekyl put any questions to you, with a view to learn particulars about you or me?'

'I don't recollect that he did. I rather think not; but Captain Drayton did.'

'I know, *Smithers* ?'

'Yes, sir.'

'With an object ?' inquired the elder man.

'I think not—merely impertinence,' answered Guy Strangways.

'You are right—it is nothing to him.   I do not know that even Marlowe has a suspicion.   Absolutely impertinence.'

And upon this M. Varbarriere began to smoke again with resolution and energy.

'You understand, Guy ; you may be as polite as you please— but no friendship—nowhere—you must remain quite unembarrassed.'

Here followed some more smoke, and after it the question—

'What do you think of the young lady, Mademoiselle Marlowe ?'

'She sings charmingly, and for the rest, I believe she is agreeable ; but my opportunities have been very little.'

'What do you think of our fellow Jacque—is he trustworthy ?'

'Perfectly, so far as I know.'

'You never saw him peep into letters, or that kind of thing ?'

'Certainly not.'

'There is a theory which must be investigated, and I should like to employ him.   You know nothing against him, nor do I.'

'Suppose we go to our beds ?' resumed the old gentleman, after having finished his cigar.

A door at either side opened from the dressing-room, by whose fire they had been sitting.

'See which room is meant for me—Jacque will have placed my things there.'

The young man did as he was bid, and made his report.

'Well, get you to bed, Guy, and remember—no friendships and no follies.'

And so the old man rose, and shook his companion's hand, not smiling, but with a solemn and thoughtful countenance, and they separated for the night.

Next morning as the Rev. Dives Marlowe stood in his natty and unexceptionable clerical costume on the hall-door steps, looking with a pompous and, perhaps, a somewhat forbidding countenance upon the morning prospect before him, his brother joined him.

'Early bird, Dives, pick the worm—eh? Healthy and wise already, and wealthy to be. Slept well, eh?'

'Always well here,' answered the parson. He was less of a parson and more like himself with Jekyl than with anyone else. His brother was so uncomfortably amused with his clerical airs, knew him so well, and so undisguisedly esteemed him of the earth earthy, that the cleric, although the abler as well as the better read man, always felt invariably a little sheepish before him, in his silk vest and single-breasted coat with the standing collar, and the demi-shovel, which under other eyes he felt to be imposing properties.

'You look so like that exemplary young man in Watts' hymns, in the old-fashioned toggery, Dives—the fellow with the handsome round cheeks, you know, piously saluting the morning sun that's rising with a lot of spokes stuck out of it, don't you remember?'

'I look like something that's ugly, I dare say,' said the parson, who had not got up in a good temper. 'There never was a Marlowe yet who hadn't ugly points about him. But a young man, though never so ugly, is rather a bold comparison—eh? seeing I'm but two years your junior, Jekyl.'

'Bitterly true—every word—my dear boy. But let us be pleasant. I've had a line to say that old Moulders is very ill, and really dying this time. Just read this melancholy little bulletin.'

With an air which seemed to say, 'well, to please you,' he took the note and read it. It was from his steward, to mention that the Rev. Abraham Moulders was extremely ill of his old complaint, and that there was something even worse the matter, and that Doctor Winters had said that morning he could not possibly get over this attack.

'Well, Dives, there is a case of "sick and weak" for you; you'll have prayers for him at Queen's Chorleigh, eh?'

'Poor old man!' said Dives, solemnly, with his head thrown

back, and his thick eyebrows elevated a little, and looking straight before him as he returned the note, 'he's very ill, indeed, unless this reports much too unfavourably.'

'Too favourably, you mean,' suggested the Baronet.

'But you know, poor old man, it is only wonderful he has lived so long. The old people about there say he is eighty-seven. Upon my word, old Jenkins says he told him, two years ago, himself, he was eighty-five; and Doctor Winters, no chicken—just sixty—says his father was in the same college with him, at Cambridge, nearly sixty-seven years ago. You know, my dear Jekyl, when a man comes to that time of life, it's all idle—a mere pull against wind and tide, and everything. It is appointed unto all men once to die, you know, and the natural term is threescore years and ten. All idle—all in vain!'

And delivering this, the Rev. Dives Marlowe shook his head with a supercilious melancholy, as if the Rev. Abraham Moulders' holding out in that way against the inevitable was a piece of melancholy bravado, against which, on the part of modest mortality, it was his sad duty to protest.

Jekyl's cynicism was tickled, although there was care at his heart, and he chuckled.

'And how do you know you have any interest in the old fellow's demise?'

The Rector coughed a little, and flushed, and looked as careless as he could, while he answered—

'I said nothing of the kind; but you have always told me you meant the living for me. I've no reason, only your goodness, Jekyl.'

'No goodness at all,' said Jekyl, kindly. 'You shall have it, of course. I always meant it for you, Dives, and I wish it were better, and I'm very glad, for I'm fond of you, old fellow.'

Hereupon they both laughed a little, shaking hands very kindly.

'Come to the stable, Dives,' said the Baronet, taking his arm. 'You must choose a horse. You don't hunt now?'

'I have not been at a cover for *ten* years,' answered the reverend gentleman, speaking with a consciousness of the demi-shovel.

'Well, come along,' continued the Baronet. 'I want to ask you—let's be serious' (everybody likes to be serious over his own business). 'What do you think of these foreign personages?'

'The elder, I should say, an able man,' answered Dives; 'I dare say could be agreeable. It is not easy to assign his exact rank though, nor his profession or business. You remarked he seems to know something in detail and technically of nearly every business one mentions.'

'Yes; and about the young man—that Mr. Guy Strangways, with his foreign accent and manner—did anything strike you about him?'

'Yes, certainly, could not fail. The most powerful likeness, I think, I ever saw in my life.'

They both stopped, and exchanged a steady and anxious look, as if each expected the other to say more; and after a while the Rev. Dives Marlowe added, with an awful sort of nod—

'Guy Deverell.'

The Baronet nodded in reply.

'Well, in fact, he appeared to me something *more* than like—the same—identical.'

'And old Lady Alice saw him in Wardlock Church, and was made quite ill,' said the Baronet gloomily. 'But you know he's gone these thirty years; and there is no necromancy now-a-days; only I wish you would take any opportunity, and try and make out all about him, and what they want. I brought them here to pump them, by Jove; but that old fellow seems deuced reserved and wary. Only, like a good fellow, if you can find or make an opportunity, you must get the young fellow on the subject—for I don't care to tell you, Dives, I have been devilish uneasy about it. There are things that make me confoundedly uncomfortable; and I have a sort of foreboding it would have been better for me to have blown up this house than to have come here; but ten to one —a hundred to one—there's nothing, and I'm only a fool.'

As they thus talked they entered the gate of the stable-yard.

CHAPTER XVI.

CONTAINING A VARIETY OF THINGS.

' GUY DEVERELL left no issue,' said Dives.

' No ; none in the world ; neither chick nor child. I need not care a brass farthing about any that can't inherit, if there were any ; but there isn't one; there's no real danger, you see. In fact, there *can't* be *any*—eh ? *I* don't see it. Do *you ?* You were a sharp fellow always, Dives. *Can* you see anything threatening in it ?'

' *It ! What ?*' said the Rev. Dives Marlowe. ' I see *nothing— nothing whatever—absolutely* nothing. Surely you can't fancy that a mere resemblance, however strong, where there can't possibly be identity, and the fact that the young man's name is Guy, will make a case for alarm !'

' Guy *Strangways*, you know,' said Sir Jekyl.

' Well, what of Strangways ? I don't see.'

' Why, Strangways, you remember, or *don't* remember, was the name of the fellow that was always with—with—that cross-grained muff.'

' With Guy Deverell, you mean ?'

' Ay, with him that night, and constantly, and abroad I think at those German gaming-places where he played so much.'

' I forgot the name. I remember hearing there *was* a person in your company that unlucky night; but you never heard more of him ?'

' No, of course ; for he owed me a precious lot of money ;' and from habit he chuckled, but with something of a frown. ' He could have given me a lot of trouble, but so could I him. My lawyers said he could not seriously affect me, but he might have annoyed me ; and I did not care about the money, so I did not follow him ; and, as the lawyers say, we turned our backs on one another.'

' Strangways,' murmured the Rector, musingly.

'Do you remember him now?' asked Sir Jekyl.

'No; that is, I'm not sure. I was in orders then though, and could hardly have met him. I am sure I should recollect him if I had. What was he like?'

'A nasty-looking Scotch dog, with freckles—starved and tall —a hungry hound—large hands and feet—as ugly a looking cur as you ever beheld.'

'But Deverell, poor fellow, was a bit of a dandy—wasn't he? How did he come to choose such a companion?'

'Well, maybe he was not quite as bad as he describes, and his family was good, I believe; but there must have been something more, he hung about him so. Yes, he *was* a most objectionable-looking fellow—so awkward, and not particularly well dressed; but a canny rascal, and knew what he was about. I could not make out what use Deverell made of him, nor exactly what advantage he made of Deverell.'

'I can't, for the life of me, see, Jekyl, anything in it except a resemblance, and that is positively nothing, and a Christian name, that is all, and Guy is no such uncommon one. As for Strangways, he does not enter into it at all—a mere accidental association. Where is that Strangways—is he living?'

'I don't know now; ten years ago he was, and Pelter and Crowe thought he was going to do me some mischief, a prosecution or something, they thought, to extort money; but I knew they were wrong. I had a reason—at least it was unlikely, because I rather think he had repaid me that money about then. A year or so before a large sum of money was lodged to my account by Herbert Strangways, that was his name, at the International Bank in Lombard Street; in fact it was more than I thought he owed me—interest, I suppose, and that sort of thing. I put Pelter and Crowe in his track, but they could make out nothing. The bank people could not help us. Unluckily I was away at the time, and the lodgment was two months old when I heard of it. There were several raw Scotch-looking rascals, they said, making lodgments about then, and they could not tell exactly what sort of fellow

made this. I wanted to make out about him. What do you
think of it?'

'I don't see anything suspicious in it. He owed you the money
and chose to pay.'

'He was protected by the Statute of Limitations, my lawyer
said, and I could not have recovered it. Doesn't it look odd?'

'Those Scotch fellows.'

'He's not Scotch, though.'

'Well, whatever he is, if he has good blood he's proud, perhaps, and would rather pay what he owes than not.'

'Well, of course, a fellow's glad of the money; but I did not
like it; it looked as if he wanted to get rid of the only pull
I had on him, and was going to take steps to annoy me, you see.'

'That's ten years ago?'

'Yes.'

'Well, considering how short life is, I think he'd have moved
before now if he had ever thought of it. It is a quarter of a
century since poor Deverell's time. It's a good while, you know,
and the longer you wait in matters of that kind the less your
chance;' and with a brisk decision the Rector added, 'I'll stake,
I think, all I'm worth, these people have no more connection with
poor Deverell than Napoleon Bonaparte, and that Strangways has
no more notion of moving any matter connected with that unhappy business than he has of leading an Irish rebellion.'

'I'm glad you take that view—I know it's the sound one. I
knew you *would*. I think it's just a little flicker of gout. If I
had taken Vichy on my way back I'd never have thought of it.
I've no one to talk to. It's a comfort to see you, Dives. I wish
you'd come oftener.' And he placed his hand very kindly on his
brother's shoulder.

'So I will,' said Dives, not without kindness in his eyes, though
his mouth was forbidding still. ' You must not let chimeras take
of you. I'm very glad I was here.'

'Did you remark that fat, mountainous French fellow, in that
cursed suit of black, was very inquisitive about the green chamber?' asked Sir Jekyl, relapsing a little.

'No, I did not hear him mention it; what was it?' asked Dives.

'Well, not a great deal; only he seemed to want to know all about that particular room and its history, just as if there was already something in his head about it.'

'Well, I told you, Jekyl,' said Dives, in a subdued tone and looking away a little, 'you ought to do something decisive about that room, all things considered. If it were mine, I can tell you, I should pull it down—not, of course, in such a way as to make people talk and ask questions, but as a sort of improvement. I'd make a conservatory, or something; you *want* a conservatory, and the building is positively injured by it. It is not the same architecture. You might put something there twice as good. At all events I'd get rid of it.'

'So I will—I *intend*—I think you're right—I really do. But it was brought about by little Beatrix talking about haunted rooms, you know, and that sort of nonsense,' said Sir Jekyl.

'Oh! then she mentioned it? He only asked questions about what she told him. Surely you're not going to vex yourself about that?'

Sir Jekyl looked at him and laughed, but not quite comfortably.

'Well, I told you, you know, I do believe it's great; and whatever it is, I know, Dives, you've done me a great deal of good. Come, now, I've a horse I think you'll like, and you shall have him; try him to-day, and I'll send him home for you if he suits you.'

While the groom was putting up the horse, Sir Jekyl, who was quick and accurate of eye, recognised the dark-faced, intelligent little valet, whom he had seen for a moment, candle in hand, at the dressing-room door, last night, to receive his guests.

With a deferential smile, and shrug, and bow, all at once, this little gentleman lifted his cap with one hand, removing his German pipe with the other.

He had been a courier—clever, active, gay—a man who might be trusted with money, papers, diamonds. Besides his native French, he spoke English very well, and a little German. He could keep accounts, and write a neat little foreign hand with florid capitals. He could mend his own clothes, and even his shoes. He could play the flute a little, and very much the fiddle.

He was curious, and liked to know what was taking place. He liked a joke and the dance, and was prone to the tender passion, and liked, in an honest way, a little bit of intrigue, or even espionage. Such a man he was as I could fancy in a light company of that marvellous army of Italy, of which Napoleon I. always spoke with respect and delight.

In the stable-yard, as I have said, the Baronet found this dark sprite smoking a German pipe; and salutations having been exchanged, he bid him try instead two of his famous cigars, which he presented, and then he questioned him on tobacco, and on his family, the theatres, the railways, the hotels; and finally Sir Jekyl said—

'I wish you could recollect a man like yourself—I want one confoundedly. I shall be going abroad in August next year, and I'd give him five thousand francs a year, or more even, with pleasure, and keep him probably as long as he liked to stay with me. Try if you can remember such a fellow. Turn it over in your mind—do you see? and I don't care how soon he comes into my service.'

The man lifted his cap again, and bowed even lower, as he undertook to 'turn it over in his mind;' and though he smiled a great deal, it was plain his thoughts were already seriously employed in turning the subject over, as requested by the Baronet.

Next morning M. Varbarriere took a quiet opportunity, in the hall, of handing to his host two letters of introduction, as they are called—one from the Baronet's old friend, Charteris, attached to the embassy at Paris—a shrewd fellow, a man of the world, amphibious, both French and English, and equally at home on either soil—speaking unmistakably in high terms of M. Varbarriere as of a gentleman very much respected in very high quarters. The other was equally handsome. But Charteris was exactly the man whose letter in such a case was to be relied upon.

The Baronet glanced over these, and said he was very glad to hear from his friend Charteris—the date was not a week since—but laughed at the formality, regretting that he had not a note from Charteris to present in return, and then gracefully quoted an old French distich, the sentiment of which is that 'chivalry proclaims itself, and the gentleman is no more to be mistaken than the rose,' and proceeded to ask his guest, ' How is Charteris—he had hurt his wrist when I saw him last—and is there any truth in the report about his possible alliance with that rich widow ?' and so forth.

When Sir Jekyl got into his sanctum I am afraid he read both letters with a very microscopic scrutiny, and he resolved inwardly to write a very sifting note to Charteris, and put it upon him, as an act of friendship, to make out every detail of the past life and adventures of M. Varbarriere, and particularly whether he had any young kinsman, nephew or otherwise, answering a certain description, all the items of which he had by rote.

But writing of letters is to some people a very decided bore. The Baronet detested it, and his anxieties upon these points being intermittent, the interrogatories were not so soon despatched to his friend Charteris.

Old General Lennox was away for London this morning ; and his host took a seat beside him in the brougham that was to convey him to the station, and was dropped on the way at the keeper's lodge, when he bid a kind and courteous adieu to his guest, whom he charged to return safe and soon, and kissed his hand, and waved it after the florid smiling countenance and bushy white eyebrows that were protruded from the carriage-window as it glided away.

' You can manage it all in a day or two, can't you ?' said the Baronet, cordially, as he held the General's wrinkled hand, with its knobby and pink joints, in his genial grasp, ' We positively won't give you more than three days' leave. Capital shooting when you come back. I'm going to talk it over with the keeper here—that is, if you come back before we've shot them all.'

' Oh! yes, hang it, you must leave a bird or two for me,' laughed the General, and he bawled the conclusion of the joke as the vehicle drove away ; but Sir Jekyl lost it.

Sir Jekyl was all the happier for his morning's talk with his brother. An anxiety, if only avowed and discussed, is so immensely lightened ; but Dives had scouted the whole thing so peremptorily that the Baronet was positively grateful. Dives was a wise and clear-headed fellow. It was delightful his taking so decided a view. And was it not on reflection manifestly, even to him, the sound view ?

CHAPTER XVII.

THE MAGICIAN DRAWS A DIAGRAM.

THE Baronet approached Marlowe Manor on the side at which the stables and out-offices lie, leaving which to his left, he took his way by the path through the wood which leads to the terrace-walk that runs parallel to the side of the old house on which the green chamber lies.

On this side the lofty timber approaches the walks closely, and the green enclosure is but a darkened strip and very solitary. Here, when Sir Jekyl emerged, he saw M. Varbarriere standing on the grass, and gazing upward in absorbed contemplation of the building, which on the previous evening seemed to have excited his curiosity so unaccountably.

He did not hear the Baronet's approaching step on the grass. Sir Jekyl felt both alarmed and angry; for although it was but natural that his guest should have visited the spot and examined the building, it yet seemed to him, for the moment, like the act of a spy.

'Disappointed, I'm afraid,' said he. 'I told you that addition was the least worth looking at of all the parts of this otherwise ancient house.'

He spoke with a sort of sharpness that seemed quite uncalled for ; but it was unnoticed.

M. Varbarriere bowed low and graciously.

'I am much interested—every front of this curious and hand-some house interests me. This indeed, as you say, is a good deal spoiled by that Italian incongruity—still it is charming—the contrast is as beautiful frequently as the harmony—and I am perplexed.'

' Some of my friends tell me it spoils the house so much I ought to pull it down, and I have a great mind to do so. Have you seen the lake ? I should be happy to show it to you if you will permit me.'

The Baronet, as he spoke, was, from time to time, slyly searching the solemn and profound face of the stranger ; but could find there no clue to the spirit of his investigation. There was no shrinking—no embarrassment—no consciousness. He might as well have looked on the awful surface of the sea, in the expectation of discovering there the secrets of its depths.

M. Varbarriere, with a profusion of gratitude, regretted that he could not just then visit the lake, as he had several letters to write ; and so he and his host parted smiling at the hall-door ; and the Baronet, as he pursued his way, felt some stirrings of that mental dyspepsia which had troubled him of late.

' The old fellow had not been in the house two hours,' such was his train of thought, ' when he was on the subject of that green chamber, in the parlour and in the drawing-room—again and again recurring to it ; and here he was just now, alone, absorbed, and gazing up at its windows, as if he could think of nothing else !'

Sir Jekyl felt provoked, and almost as if he would like a crisis ; and half regretted that he had not asked him—' Pray can I give you any information ; is there anything you particularly want to know about that room ? question me as you please, you shall see the room—you shall sleep in it if you like, so soon as it is vacant. Pray declare yourself, and say what you want.'

But second thoughts are said to be best, if not always wisest ; and this brief re-hearing of the case against his repose ended in a ' dismiss,' as before. It was so natural, and indeed inevitable, that he should himself inspect the original of those views which he had examined the night before with interest, considering that, being a man who cared not for the gun or the fishing-rod, and plainly without sympathies with either georgics or bucolics, he had not many other ways of amusing himself in these country quarters.

M. Varbarriere, in the meantime, had entered his chamber. I suppose he was amused, for so soon as he closed the door he smiled with a meditative sneer. It was not a fiendish one, not even moderately wicked; but a sneer is in the countenance what irony is in the voice, and never pleasant.

If the Baronet had seen the expression of M. Varbarriere's countenance as he sat down in his easy-chair, he would probably have been much disquieted—perhaps not without reason.

M. Varbarriere was known in his own neighbourhood as a dark and inflexible man, but with these reservations kind; just in his dealings, bold in enterprise, and charitable, but not on impulse, with a due economy of resource, and a careful measurement of desert; on the whole, a man to be respected and a little feared, but a useful citizen.

Instead of writing letters as, of course, he had intended, M. Varbarriere amused himself by making a careful little sketch on a leaf of his pocket-book. It seemed hardly worth all the pains he bestowed upon it; for, after all, it was but a parallelogram with a projecting segment of a circle at one end, and a smaller one at the side, and he noted his diagram with figures, and pondered over it with a thoughtful countenance, and made, after a while, a little cross at one end of it, and then fell a-whistling thoughtfully, and nodded once or twice, as a thought struck him; and then he marked another cross at one of its sides, and reflected in like manner over this, and as he thought, fiddling with his pencil at the foot of the page, he scribbled the word 'hypothesis.' Then he put up his pocket-book, and stood listlessly with his hands in the pockets of his vast black trowsers, looking from the window, and whistled a little more, the air hurrying sometimes, and sometimes dragging a good deal, so as to come at times to an actual standstill.

On turning the corner of the mansion Sir Jekyl found himself on a sudden in the midst of the ladies of his party, just descending from the carriages which had driven them round the lake. He was of that gay and gallant temperament, as the reader is aware,

which is fired with an instantaneous inspiration at sight of this
sort of plumage and flutter.

'What a fortunate fellow am I!' exclaimed Sir Jekyl, forgetting
in a moment everything but the sunshine, the gay voices, and the
pretty sight before him. 'I had laid myself out for a solitary
walk, and lo! I'm in the midst of a paradise of graces, nymphs,
and what not!'

'We have had such a charming drive round the lake,' said gay
little Mrs. Maberly.

'The lake never looked so well before, I'm sure. So stocked,
at least, with fresh-water sirens and mermaids. Never did mirror
reflect so much beauty. An instinct, you see, drew me this way.
I assure you I was on my way to the lake: one of those enamoured
sprites who sing us tidings in such tiny voices, we can't distinguish
them from our own fancies, warbled a word in my ear, only a
little too late, I suppose.'

The Baronet was reciting his admiring nonsense to pretty Mrs.
Maberly, but his eye from time to time wandered to Lady Jane,
and rested for a moment on that haughty beauty, who, with downcast languid eyes, one would have thought neither heard nor saw
him.

This gallant Baronet was so well understood that every lady
expected to hear that kind of tender flattery whenever he addressed himself to the fair sex. It was quite inevitable, and
simply organic and constitutional as blackbird's whistle and kitten's
play, and in ninety-nine cases out of a hundred, I am sure, meant
absolutely nothing.

'But those sprites always come with a particular message; don't
they?' said old Miss Blunket, smiling archly from the corners of
her fierce eyes. 'Don't you think so, Mr. Linnett?'

'You are getting quite above me,' answered that sprightly gentleman, who was growing just a little tired of Miss Blunket's
attentions. 'I suppose it's spiritualism. I know nothing about
it. What do you say, Lady Jane?'

'I think it very heathen,' said Lady Jane, tired, I suppose, of
the subject.

'I like to be heathen, now and then,' said Sir Jekyl, in a lower key; he was by this time beside Lady Jane. 'I'd have been a most pious Pagan. As it is, I can't help worshipping in the Pantheon, and trying sometimes even to make a proselyte.'

'Oh! you wicked creature!' cried little Mrs. Maberly. 'I assure you, Lady Jane, his conversation is quite frightful.'

Lady Jane glanced a sweet, rather languid, sidelong smile at the little lady.

'You'll not get Lady Jane to believe all that mischief of me, Mrs. Maberly. I appeal for my character to the General.'

'But he's hundreds of miles away, and can't hear you,' laughed little Mrs. Maberly, who really meant nothing satirical.

'I forgot; but he'll be back to-morrow or next day,' replied Sir Jekyl, with rather a dry chuckle, 'and in the meantime I must do without one, I suppose. Here we are, Mr. Strangways, all talking nonsense, the pleasantest occupation on earth. Do come and help us.'

This was addressed to Guy Strangways, who, with his brother angler, Captain Doocey, in the picturesque negligence and black wide-awakes of fishermen, with baskets and rods, approached.

'Only too glad to be permitted to contribute,' said the young man, smiling, and raising his hat.

'And pray permit me also,' said courtly old Doocey. 'I could talk it, I assure you, before he was born. I've graduated in the best schools, and was a doctor of nonsense before *he* could speak even a word of sense.'

'Not a bad specimen to begin with. Leave your rods and baskets there; some one will bring them in. Now we are so large a party, you must come and look at my grapes. I am told my black Hamburgs are the finest in the world.'

So, chatting and laughing, and some in other moods, toward those splendid graperies they moved, from which, as Sir Jekyl used to calculate, he had the privilege of eating black Hamburgh and other grapes at about the rate of one shilling each.

'A grapery—how delightful!' cried little Mrs. Maberly.

'I quite agree with you,' exclaimed Miss Blunket, who effer-

vesced with a girlish enthusiasm upon even the most difficult subjects. 'It is not the grapes, though they are so pretty, and a—
bacchanalian—no, I don't mean that—why do you laugh at me
so?—but the atmosphere. Don't you love it? it is so like Lisbon
—at least what I fancy it, for I never was there; but at home, I
bring my book there, and enjoy it so. I call it mock Portugal.'

' It has helped to dry her,' whispered Linnett so loud in Doocey's
ear as to make that courteous old dandy very uneasy.

It was odd that Sir Jekyl showed no sort of discomfort at sight
of Guy Strangways on his sudden appearance; a thrill he felt indeed whenever he unexpectedly beheld that handsome and rather
singular-looking young man—a most unpleasant sensation—but
although he moved about him like a resurrection of the past, and
an omen of his fate, he yet grew in a sort of way accustomed to
this haunting enigma, and could laugh and talk apparently quite
carelessly in his presence. I have been told of men, the victims of
a spectral illusion, who could move about a saloon, and smile, and
talk, and listen, with their awful tormentor gliding always about
them and spying out all their ways.

Just about this hour the clumsy old carriage of Lady Alice
Redcliffe stood at her hall-door steps, in the small square court-
yard of Wardlock Manor, and the florid iron gates stood wide
open, resting on their piers. The coachman's purple visage looked
loweringly round; the footman, with his staff of office in hand,
leaning on the door-post, gazed with a peevish listlessness through
the open gateway across the road; the near horse had begun to
hang his head, and his off-companion had pawed a considerable
hole in Lady Alice's nattily-kept gravel enclosure. From these
signs one might have reasonably conjectured that these honest
retainers, brute and human, had been kept waiting for their mistress somewhat longer than usual.

CHAPTER XVIII.

ANOTHER GUEST PREPARES TO COME.

LADY ALICE was at that moment in her bonnet and ample black velvet cloak and ermines, and the rest of her travelling costume, seated in her stately parlour, which, like most parlours of tolerably old mansions in that part of the country, is wainscoted in very black oak. In her own way Lady Alice evinced at least as much impatience as her dependants out of doors; she tapped with her foot monotonously upon her carpet; she opened and shut her black shining leather bag, and plucked at and re-arranged its contents; she tattooed with her pale prolix fingers on the table; sometimes she sniffed a little; sometimes she muttered. As often as she fancied a sound, she raised her chin imperiously, and with a supercilious fixity, stared at the door until expectation had again expired in disappointment, when she would pluck out her watch, and glancing disdainfully upon it, exclaim—

' Upon my life!' or, ' Very pretty behaviour!'

At last, however, the sound of a vehicle—a ' fly' it was—unmistakably made itself heard at the hall-door, and her lady, with a preparatory shake of her head, as a pugnacious animal shakes its ears, and a ' hem,' and a severe and pallid countenance, sat up, very high and stiffly, in her chair.

The door opened, and the splendid footman inquired whether her ladyship would please to see Mrs. Gwynn.

' Show her in,' said Lady Alice, with a high look and an awful quietude.

And our old friend, Donica, just as thin, pallid, and, in her own way, self-possessed, entered the room.

' Well, Donica Gwynn, you've come at *last!* you have kept my horses standing at the door—a thing I never do myself—for three-quarters of an hour and four minutes!'

Donica Gwynn was sorry; but she could not help it. She explained how the delay had occurred, and, though respectful, her explanation was curt and dry in proportion to the sharpness and dryness of her reception.

'Sit down, Donica,' said the lady, relenting loftily. 'How do you do?'

'Pretty well, I thank your ladyship; and I hope I see *you* well, my lady.'

'As well as I can ever be, Donica, and that is but poorly. I'm going, you know, to Marlowe.'

'I'm rayther glad on it, my lady.'

'And I wish to know *why?*' said Lady Alice.

'I wrote the why and the wherefore, my lady, in my letter,' answered the ex-housekeeper, looking askance on the table, and closing her thin lips tightly when she had spoken.

'Your letter, my good Donica, it is next to impossible to read, and quite impossible to understand. What I want to know distinctly is, why you have urged me so vehemently to go to Marlowe?'

'Well, my lady, I thought I said pretty plain it was about my Lady Jane, the pretty creature you had on visits here, and liked so well, poor thing; an' it seemed to me she's like to be in danger where she is. I can't explain how exactly; but General Lennox is gone up to London, and I think, my lady, you ought to get her out of that unlucky room, where he has put her; and, at all events, to keep as near to her as you can yourself, at *all* times.'

'I've listened to you, Donica, and I can't comprehend you. I see you are hinting at something; but unless you are explicit, I don't see that I can be of any earthly use.'

'You can, my lady—that is, you *may*, if you only do as I say— I *can't* explain it more, nor I *won't*,' said Donica, peremptorily, perhaps bitterly.

'There can be no good reason, Donica, for reserve upon a point of so much moment as you describe this to be. Wherever reserve exists there is mystery, and wherever mystery—*guilt.*'

So said Lady Alice, who was gifted with a spirit of inquiry which was impatient of disappointment.

'Guilt, indeed!' repeated Gwynn, in an under-key, with a toss of her head and a very white face; 'there's secrets enough in the world, and no guilt along of 'em.'

'What room is it you speak of—the green chamber, is not it?'

'Yes, sure, my lady.'

'I think you are all crazed about ghosts and devils over there,' exclaimed Lady Alice.

'Not much of ghosts, but devils, maybe,' muttered Gwynn, oddly, looking sidelong over the floor.

'It is that room, you say,' repeated Lady Alice.

'Yes, my lady, the green chamber.'

'Well, what about it—come, woman, did not you sleep for years in that room?'

'Ay, my lady, a good while.'

'And what did you see there?'

'A deal.'

'*What*, I say?'

'Well, supposin' I was to say devils,' replied Donica.

Lady Alice sneered.

'What did poor Lady Marlowe see there?' demanded Donica, looking with her odd eyes askance at Lady Alice's carpet, and backing her question with a nod.

'Well, you know I never heard exactly; but my darling creature was, as you remember, dying of a consumption at the time, and miserably nervous, and fancied things, no doubt, as people do.'

'Well, she did; I knew it,' said Donica.

'You may have conjectured—every one can do that; but I rather think my poor dear Amy would have told *me*, had she cared to divulge it to any living being. I am persuaded she herself suspected it was an illusion—fancy; but I know she had a horror of the room, and I am sure my poor girl's dying request ought to have been respected.'

'So it ought, my lady,' said Donica, turning up her eyes, and raising her lean hands together, while she slowly shook her head. 'So I said to him, and in like manner his own father's dying *orders*, for such they was, my lady; and they may say what they will of Sir Harry, poor gentleman! But he was a kind man, and good to many that had not a good word for him after, though there may a' been many a little thing that was foolish or the like; but there is mercy above for all, and the bishop that is now, then he was the master of the great school where our young gentlemen used to go to, was with him.'

'When he was dying?' said Lady Alice.

'Ay, my lady, a beautiful summer it was, and the doctor, nor I, thought it would be nothing to speak of; but he was anxious in his mind from the first, and he wrote for Doctor Wyndale—it was the holidays then—asking him to come to him; and he did, but Sir Harry had took an unexpected turn for the worse, and not much did he ever say, the Lord a' mercy on us, after that good gentleman, he's the bishop now, came to Marlowe, and he prayed by his bed, and closed his eyes; and I, in and out, and wanted there every minute, could not but hear some of what he said, which it was not much.'

'He said something about that green chamber, as you call it, I always understood?' said Lady Alice, interrogatively.

'Yes, my lady, he wished it shut up, or taken down, or summut that way; "but man proposes and God disposes," and there's small affection and less gratitude to be met with now-a-days.'

'I think, Donica Gwynn, and I always thought, that you knew a good deal more than you chose to tell me. Some people are re-served and secret, and I suppose it is your way; but I don't think it could harm you to treat me more as your friend.'

Donica rose, and courtesied as she said—

'You have always treated me friendly, I'm sure, my lady, and I hope I am thankful; and this I know, I'll be a faithful servant to your ladyship so long as I continue in your ladyship's service.'

'I know that very well; but I wish you were franker with me, that's all—here are the keys.'

So Donica, with very little ceremony, assumed the keys of office.

'And pray what *do* you mean exactly?' said Lady Alice, rising and drawing on her glove, and not looking quite straight at the housekeeper as she spoke; 'do you mean to say that Lady Jane is giddy or imprudent? Come, be distinct.'

'I can't say what she is, my lady, but she may be brought into folly some way. I only know this much, please my lady, it will be good for her you should be nigh, and your eye and thoughts about her, at least till the General returns.'

'Well, Gwynn, I see you don't choose to trust me.'

'I have, my lady, spoke that free to you as I would not to any other, I think, alive.'

'No, Gwynn, you don't trust me; you have your reasons, I suppose; but I think you are a shrewd woman—shrewd and mean well. I don't suppose that you · could talk as you do without a reason; and though I can't see any myself, not believing in appar-itions or—or——'

She nearly lost the thread of her discourse at this point, for as she spoke the word apparition, the remembrance of the young gentleman whom she had seen in Wardlock Church rose in her memory—handsome, pale, with sealed lips, and great eyes—un-readable as night—the resurrection of another image. The old yearning and horror overpowered the train of her thoughts, and she floundered into silence, and coughed into her handkerchief, to hide her momentary confusion.

'What was I going to say?' she said, briskly, meaning to refer her break-down to that little fit of coughing, and throwing on Gwynn the onus of setting her speech in motion again.

'Oh! yes. I *don't* believe in those things not a bit. But Jennie, poor thing, though she has not treated me quite as she might, is a young wife, and very pretty; and the house is full of wicked young men from London; and her old fool of a husband chooses to go about his business and leave her to her devices—*that's* what you mean, Gwynn, and that's what I *understand*.'

'I have said all I can, my lady; you can help her, and be near her night and day,' said Donica.

'Sir Jekyl in his invitation bid me choose my own room—so I shall. I'll choose that oddly-shaped little room that opens into hers—if I remember rightly, the room that my poor dear Amy occupied in her last illness.'

'And, my lady, do you take the key of the door, and keep it in your bag, please.'

'Of the door of communication between the two room s ?'

' Yes, my lady.'

' *Why* should I take it ; you would not have me lock her up ?'

' Well, no, to be sure, my lady.'

' Then *why* ?'

' Because there is no bolt to her door, inside or out.   You will see what I mean, my lady, when you are there.'

' Because she can't secure her door without it, I'm to take possession of her key !' said Lady Alice, with a dignified sneer.

' Well, my lady, it may seem queer, but you'll see what I mean.'

Lady Alice tossed her stately head.

'Any commands in particular, please, my lady, before you leave ?' inquired Donica, with one of her dry little courtesies.

'No; and I must go.   Just hand this pillow and bag to the man ; and I suppose you wish your respects to Miss Beatrix ?'

' To all which, in her own way, Donica Gwynn assented ; and the old lady, assisted by her footman, got into the carriage, and nodded a pale and silent farewell to her housekeeper ; and away drove the old carriage at a brisk pace toward Marlowe Manor.

CHAPTER XIX.

LADY ALICE TAKES POSSESSION.

WHAT to the young would seem an age ; what, even in the arithmetic of the old, counts for something, about seventeen years had glided into the eternal past since last Lady Alice had beheld the antique front and noble timber of Marlowe Manor ; and memory was busy with her heart, and sweet and bitter fancies revisiting her old brain, as her saddened eyes gazed on that fair picture of the past.   Old faces gone, old times changed, and she, too, but the shadow of her former self, soon, like those whom she remembered there, to vanish quite, and be missed by no one.

' Where is Miss Beatrix ?' inquired the old lady, as she set her

long slim foot upon the oak flooring of the hall. 'I'll rest a
moment here.' And she sat down upon a carved bench, and looked
with sad and dreaming eyes through the open door upon the
autumnal landscape flushed with the setting sun, the season and
the hour harmonising regretfully with her thoughts.

Her maid came at the summons of the footman. 'Tell her that
granny has come,' said the old woman gently. '*You* are quite
well, Jones?'

Jones made her smirk and courtesy, and was quite well; and so
tripped up the great stair to apprise her young mistress.

'Tell the new housekeeper, please, that Lady Alice Redcliffe
wishes very much to see her for a moment in the hexagon dressing-
room at the end of the hatchment-gallery,' said the old lady,
names and localities coming back to her memory quite naturally in
the familiar old hall.

And as she spoke, being an active-minded old lady, she rose,
and before her first message had reached Beatrix, was ascending
the well-known stairs, with its broad shining steps of oak, and her
hand on its ponderous banister, feeling strangely, all in a moment,
how much more she now needed that support, and that the sum of
the seventeen years was something to her as to others.

On the lobby, just outside this dressing-room door, which stood
open, letting the dusky sunset radiance, so pleasant and so sad,
fall upon the floor and touch the edges of the distant banisters,
she was met by smiling Beatrix.

'Darling!' cried the girl, softly, as she threw her young arms
round the neck of the stately and thin old lady. 'Darling,
darling, I'm so glad!'

She had been living among strangers, and the sight and touch
of her true old friend was reassuring.

Granny's thin hands held her fondly. It was pretty to see this
embrace, in the glow of the evening sun, and the rich brown
tresses of the girl close to the ashen locks of old Lady Alice, who,
with unwonted tears in her eyes, was smiling on her very tenderly.
She was softened that evening. Perhaps it was her real nature,

disclosed for a few genial moments, generally hidden under films of reserve or pride—the veil of the flesh.

'I think she does like her old granny,' said Lady Alice, with a gentle little laugh; one thin hand on her shoulder, the other smoothing back her thick girlish tresses.

'I do love you, granny; you were always so good to me, and you are so—so *fond* of me. Now, you are tired, darling; you must take a little wine—here is Mrs. Sinnott coming—Mrs. Sinnott.'

'No, dear, no wine; I'm very well. I wish to see Mrs. Sinnott, though. She's your new housekeeper, is not she?'

'Yes; and I'm so glad poor, good old Donnie Gwynn is with you. You know she would not stay; but our new housekeeper is, I'm told, a very good creature too. Grandmamma wants to speak to you, Mrs. Sinnott.'

Lady Alice by this time had entered the dressing-room, three sides of which, projecting like a truncated bastion, formed a great window, which made it, for its size, the best lighted in the house. In the wall at the right, close to this entrance, is the door which admits to the green chamber; in the opposite wall, but nearer the window, a door leading across the end of the hatchment-gallery, with its large high window, by a little passage, screened off by a low oak partition, and admitting to a bed-room on the opposite side of the gallery.

In the middle of the Window dressing-room stood Lady Alice, and looked round regretfully, and said to herself, with a little shake of the head—

'Yes, yes, poor thing!'

She was thinking of poor Lady Marlowe, whom, with her usual perversity, although a step-daughter, she had loved very tenderly, and who in her last illness had tenanted these rooms, in which, seventeen years ago, this old lady had sat beside her and soothed her sickness, and by her tenderness, no doubt, softened those untold troubles which gathered about her bed as death drew near.

'How do you do, Mrs. Sinnott?' said stately Lady Alice, recovering her dry and lofty manner.

'Lady Alice Redcliffe, my grandmamma,' said Beatrix, in an undertoned introduction, in the housekeeper's ear.

Mrs. Sinnott made a fussy little courtesy.

'Your ladyship's apartments, which is at the other end of the gallery, please, is quite ready, my lady.'

'I don't mean to have those rooms, though—that's the reason I sent for you—please read this note, it is from Sir Jekyl Marlowe. By-the-bye, is your master at home ?'

'No, he was out.'

'Well, be so good as to read this.'

And Lady Alice placed Beatrix's note of invitation in Mrs. Sinnot's hand, and pointed to a passage in the autograph of Sir Jekyl, which spoke thus :—

'P.S.—Do come, dearest little mamma, and you shall command everything. Choose your own apartments and hours, and, in short, rule us all. With all my worldly goods I thee endow, and place Mrs. Sinnott at your orders.'

'Well, Mrs. Sinnott, I choose *these* apartments, if you please, said Lady Alice, sitting down stiffly, and thereby taking possession.

'Very well, my lady,' said Mrs. Sinnott, dropping another courtesy; but her sharp red nose and little black eyes looked sceptical and uneasy; 'and I suppose, Miss,' here she paused, looking at Beatrix.

'You are to do whatever Lady Alice directs,' said the young lady.

'This here room, you know, Miss, is the dressing-room properly of the green chamber.'

'Lady Jane does not use it, though ?' replied the new visitor.

'But the General, when he comes back,' insinuated Mrs. Sinnott.

'Of course, he shall have it. I'll remove then; but in the meantime, liking these rooms, from old remembrances, best of any, I will occupy them, Beatrix; *this* as a dressing-room, and the apartment *there* as bed-room. I hope I don't give you a great deal of trouble,' added Lady Alice, addressing the housekeeper, with an air that plainly said that she did not care a pin whether she did or not.

So this point was settled, and Lady Alice sent for her maid and her boxes ; and rising, she approached the door of the green chamber, and pointing to it, said to Beatrix—

' And so Lady Jane has this room.   Do you like her, Beatrix ?'

' I can't say I know her, grandmamma.'

' No, I dare say not.   It is a large room—too large for my notion of a cheerful bed-room.'

The old lady drew near, and knocked.

' She's not there ?'

' No, she's in the terrace-garden.'

Lady Alice pushed the door open, and looked in.

' A very long room.   That room is longer than my drawing-room at Wardlock, and that is five-and-thirty feet long.   Dismal, I - say—though so much light, and that portrait— Sir Harry smirking there.   What a look of duplicity in that face !   He was an old man when I can remember him ; an old beau ; a wicked old man, rouged and whitened ; he used to paint under his eye-lashes, and had, they said, nine or ten sets of false teeth, and always wore a black curled wig that made his contracted counte-nance more narrow.   There were such lines of cunning and mean-ness about his eyes, actually crossing one another.   Jekyl hated him, I think.   I don't think anybody but a fool could have really liked him ; he was so curiously selfish, and so contemptible ; he was attempting the life of a wicked young man at seventy !'

Lady Alice had been speaking as it were in soliloquy, staring drearily on the clever portrait in gold lace and ruffles, stricken by the spell of that painted canvas into a dream.

' Your grandpapa, my dear, was not a good man ; and I believe he injured my poor son irreparably, and your *father*.   Well—these things, though never forgotten, are best not spoken of when people happen to be connected.   For the sake of others we bear our pain in silence ; but the heart knoweth its own bitterness.'

And so saying, the old lady drew back from the threshold of Lady Jane's apartment, and closed the door with a stern countenance.

CHAPTER XX.

AN ALTERCATION.

ALMOST at the same moment Sir Jekyl entered the hexagon, or, as it was more pleasantly called, the Window dressing-room, from the lobby. He was quite radiant, and, in that warm evening light, struck Lady Alice as looking quite marvellously youthful.

'Well, Jekyl Marlowe, you see you have brought me here at last,' said the old lady, extending her hand stiffly, like a wooden marionette, her thin elbow making a right angle.

'So I have; and I shall always think the better of my eloquence for having prevailed. You're a thousand times welcome, and not tired, I hope; the journey is not much after all.'

'Thanks; no, the distance is not much, the fatigue nothing,' said Lady Alice, drawing her fingers horizontally back from his hospitable pressure. 'But it is not always distance that separates people, or fatigue that depresses one.'

'No, of course; fifty things; rheumatism, temper, hatred, affliction: and I am so delighted to see you! Trixie, dear, would not grandmamma like to see her room? Send for ——'

'Thank you, I mean to stay here,' said Lady Alice.

'*Here!*' echoed Sir Jekyl, with a rather bewildered smile.

'I avail myself of the privilege you give me; your postscript to Beatrix's note, you know. You tell me there to choose what rooms I like best,' said the old lady, drily, at the same time drawing her bag toward her, that she might be ready to put the documents in evidence, in case he should dispute it.

'Oh! did I?' said the Baronet, with the same faint smile.

Lady Alice nodded, and then threw back her head, challenging contradiction by a supercilious stare, her hand firmly upon the bag as before.

'But this room, you know; it's anything but a comfortable one —don't you think?' said Sir Jekyl.

'I like it,' said the inflexible old lady, sitting down.

'And I'm afraid there's a little difficulty,' he continued, not minding. 'For this is General Lennox's dressing-room. Don't you think it might be awkward?' and he chuckled agreeably.

'General Lennox is absent in London, on business,' said Lady Alice, grim as an old Diana; 'and Jane does not use it, and there *can* be no *intelligible* objection to my having it in his absence.'

There was a little smile, that yet was not a smile, and a slight play about Sir Jekyl's nostrils, as he listened to this speech. They came when he was vicious; but with a flush, he commanded himself, and only laughed slightly, and said—

'It is really hardly a concern of mine, provided my guests are happy. You don't mean to have your bed into this room, do you?'

'I mean to sleep *there*,' she replied drily, stabbing with her long forefinger toward the door on the opposite side of the room.

'Well, I can only say I'd have fancied, for other reasons, these the very last rooms in the house you would have chosen—particularly as this really belongs to the green chamber. However, you and Lady Jane can arrange that between you. You'd have been very comfortable where we would have put you, and you'll be very *un*comfortable here, I'm afraid; but perhaps I'm not making allowance for the affection you have for Lady Jane, the length of time that has passed since you've seen her, and the pleasure of being so near her.'

There was an agreeable irony in this; for the Baronet knew that they had never agreed very well together, and that neither spoke very handsomely of the other behind her back. At the same time, this was no conclusive proof of unkindness on Lady Alice's part, for her goodwill sometimes showed itself under strange and uncomfortable disguises.

'Beatrix, dear, I hope they are seeing to your grandmamma's room; and you'll want candles, it is growing dark. Altogether I'm afraid you're very uncomfortable, little mother; but if *you* prefer it, you know, of course I'm silent.'

With these words he kissed the old lady's chilly cheek, and vanished.

As he ran down the darkening stairs the Baronet was smiling
mischievously; and when, having made his long straight journey
to the foot of the back stairs, he reascended, and passing through
the two little ante-rooms, entered his own homely bed-chamber,
and looked at his handsome and wonderfully preserved face in the
glass, he [laughed outright two or three comfortable explosions
at intervals, and was evidently enjoying some fun in anticipation.

When, a few minutes later, that proud sad beauty, Lady Jane,
followed by her maid, sailed rustling into the Window dressing-
room—I call it so in preference—and there saw, by the light of a
pair of wax candles, a stately figure seated on the sofa at the
further end in grey silk draperies, with its feet on a boss, she
paused in an attitude of sublime surprise, with just a gleam of defiance in it.

'How d' y' do, Jennie, my dear?' said a voice, on which, as on
the tones of an old piano, a few years had told a good deal, but
which she recognised with some little surprise, for notwithstanding
Lady Alice's note accepting the Baronet's invitation, he had
talked and thought of her actually coming to Marlowe as a very
unlikely occurrence indeed.

'Oh! oh! Lady Alice Redcliffe!' exclaimed the young wife,
setting down her bed-room candle, and advancing with a transitory smile to her old kinswoman, who half rose from her throne
and kissed her on the cheek as she stooped to meet her salutation.
'You have only arrived a few minutes; I saw your carriage
going round from the door.'

'About forty minutes—hardly an hour. How you have filled
up, Jane; you're quite an imposing figure since I saw you. I
don't think it unbecoming; your *embonpoint* does very well; and
you're quite well?'

' *Very* well—and you?'

' I'm pretty well, dear, a good deal fatigued; and so you're a
wife, Jennie, and very happy, I hope.'

' I can't say I have anything to trouble me. I am quite happy,
that is, as happy as other people, I suppose.'

'I hear nothing but praises of your husband. I shall be so happy to make his acquaintance,' continued Lady Alice.

'He has had to go up to town about business this morning, but he's to return very soon.'

'How soon, dear?'

'In a day or two,' answered the young wife.

'To-morrow?' inquired Lady Alice, drily.

'Or next day,' rejoined Lady Jane, with a little stare.

'Do you *really*, my dear Jane, expect him here the day after to-morrow?'

'He said he should be detained only a day or two in town.'

Old Lady Alice shook her incredulous head, looking straight before her.

'I don't think he can have said that, Jane, for he wrote to a friend of mine, the day before yesterday, mentioning that he should be detained by business at least a week.'

'Oh! did he?'

'Yes, and Jekyl Marlowe, I dare say, thinks he will be kept there *longer*.'

'I should fancy *I* am a better opinion, rather, upon that point, than Sir Jekyl Marlowe,' said Lady Jane, loftily, and perhaps a little angrily.

The old lady, with closed lips, at this made a little nod, which might mean anything.

'And I can't conceive how it can concern Sir Jekyl, or even you, Lady Alice, what business my husband may have in town.'

It was odd how sharp they were growing upon this point.

'Well, Sir Jekyl's another thing; but *me*, of course, it does concern, because I shall have to give him up his room again when he returns.'

'What room?' inquired Lady Jane, honestly puzzled.

'*This* room,' answered the old lady, like one conscious that she drops, with the word, a gage of battle.

'But this is *my* room.'

'You don't use it, Lady Jane. *I* wish to occupy it. I shall, of

course, give it up on your husband's return; in the meantime I
deprive you of nothing by taking it. Do I?'

'That's not the question, Lady Alice. It is *my* room—it is *my*
dressing-room—and I don't mean to give it up to *any* one. You
are the last person on earth who would allow *me* to take such a
liberty with *you*. I don't *understand* it.'

'Don't be excited, my dear Jenny,' said Lady Alice—an ex-
hortation sometimes a little inconsistently administered by members of her admirable sex when they are themselves most exciting.

'I'm not in the least excited, Lady Alice; but I've had a note
from you,' said Lady Jane, in rather a choking key.

'You have,' acquiesced her senior.

'And I connect your extraordinary intrusion here, with it.'
Lady Alice nodded.

'I do, and—and I'm right. You mean to insult me. It is a
shame—an *outrage*. What do you mean, madam?'

'I'd have you to remember, Jane Chetwynd (the altercation
obliterated her newly-acquired name of Lennox), that I am your
relation and your senior.'

'Yes, you're my cousin, and my senior by fifty years; but an
old woman may be very impertinent to a young one.'

'*Compose* yourself, if you please, *compose* yourself,' said Lady
Alice, in the same philosophic vein, but with colour a little
heightened.

'I don't know what you mean—you're a disgraceful old woman.
I'll complain to my husband, and I'll tell Sir Jekyl Marlowe.
Either you or I must leave this house to-night,' declaimed Lady
Jane, with a most beautiful blush, and eyes flashing lurid light-
nings.

'You forget yourself, my dear,' said the old lady, rising grimly
and confronting her.

'No, I don't, but *you* do. It's perfectly disgusting and intolerable,' cried Lady Jane, with a stamp.

'One moment, if you please—you can afford to listen for one
moment, I suppose,' said the old lady, in a very low, dry tone,
laying two of her lean fingers upon the snowy arm of the beauti-

ful young lady, who, with a haughty contraction and an uplifted head, withdrew it fiercely from her touch. ' You forget your maid, I think. You had better tell her to withdraw, hadn't you ?'

' I don't care ; why should I ?' said Lady Jane, in a high key.

' Beatrix, dear, run into my bed-room for a moment,' said ' Granny' to that distressed and perplexed young lady, who, accustomed to obey, instantly withdrew.

CHAPTER XXI.

LADY ALICE IN BED.

' WE may be alone together, if *you* choose it ; if not, *I* can't help it,' said Lady Alice, in a very low and impressive key.

' Well, it's nothing to me,' said Lady Jane, more calmly and sullenly—'nothing at all—but as you insist—Cecile, you may go for a few minutes.'

This permission was communicated sulkily, in French.

' Now, Jane, you shall hear me,' said the old lady, so soon as the maid had disappeared and the doors were shut; ' you must hear me with patience, if not with respect—*that* I don't expect— but remember you have no mother, and I am an old woman and your kinswoman, and it is my duty to speak——'

' I'm rather tired standing,' interrupted Lady Jane, in a suppressed passion. ' Besides, you say you don't want to be overheard, and you can't know who may be on the *lobby there*,' and she pointed with her jewelled fingers at the door. ' I'll go into my bed room, if you please ; and I have not the slightest objection to hear everything you can possibly say. Don't fancy I'm the least afraid of you.'

Saying which Lady Jane, taking up her bed-room candle, rustled out of the room, without so much as looking over her shoulder to see whether the prophetess was following.

She did follow, and I dare say her lecture was not mitigated by

Lady Jane's rudeness. That young lady was lighting her candles on her dressing-table when her kinswoman entered and shut the door, without an invitation. She then seated herself serenely, and cleared her voice.

'I live very much out of the world—in fact, quite to myself; but I learn occasionally what my relations are doing; and I was grieved, Jane, to hear a great deal that was very unpleasant, to say the least, about you.'

Something between a smile and a laugh was her only answer.

'Yes, extremely foolish. I don't, of course, say there was anything wicked, but very foolish and reckless. I know perfectly how you were talked of; and I know also why you married that excellent but old man, General Lennox.'

'I don't think anyone talked about me. Everybody is talked about. There has been enough of this rubbish. I burnt your odious letter,' broke in Lady Jane, incoherently.

'And would, no doubt, burn the writer, if you could.'

As there was no disclaimer, Lady Alice resumed.

'Now, Jane, you have married a most respectable old gentleman; I dare say you have nothing on earth to conceal from him —remember I've said all along I don't suppose there is—but as the young wife of an old man, you ought to remember how very delicate your position is.'

'What do you mean?'

'I mean, *generally*,' answered the old lady, oracularly.

'I do declare this is perfectly insufferable! What's the meaning of this lecture? I'm as little likely, madam, as *you* are to disgrace myself. You'll please to walk out of my room.'

'And how dare you talk to me in that way, young lady; how dare you attempt to hector me like your maid there?' broke out old Lady Alice, suddenly losing her self-command. 'You know what I mean, and what's more, *I* do, too. We *both* know it— you a young bride—what does Jekyl Marlowe invite you down here for? Do you think I imagine he cares twopence about your stupid old husband, and that I don't know he was once making love to you? Of course I do; and I'll have nothing of the sort here—and that's the reason I've come, and that's why I'm in that dressing-room, and that's why I'll write to your husband, so sure as you give me the slightest uneasiness; and you had better think well what you do.'

The old lady, in a towering passion, with a fierce lustre in her cheeks, and eyes flashing lightning over the face of her opponent, vanished from the room.

Lady Alice had crossed the disputed territory of the Window dressing-room, and found herself in her elected bed-room before she had come to herself. She saw Lady Jane's face still before her, with the lurid astonishment and fear, white and sharp, on it, as when she had threatened a letter to General Lennox.

She sat down a little stunned and confused about the whole thing, incensed and disgusted with Lady Jane, and confirmed in her suspicion by a look she did not like in that young lady's face, and which her peroration had called up. She did not hear the shrilly rejoinder that pursued her through the shut door. She had given way to a burst of passion, and felt a little hot and deaf and giddy.

When the party assembled at dinner Lady Jane exerted herself more than usual. She was agreeable, and even talkative, and her colour had not been so brilliant since her arrival. She sat next to Guy Strangways, and old Lady Alice at the other side of the table did not look triumphant, but sick and sad; and to look at the two ladies you would have set HER down as the defeated and broken-spirited, and Lady Jane as the victrix in the late encounter.

The conversation at this end of the table resembled a dance, in which sometimes each man sets to his partner and turns her round, so that the whole company is frisking and spinning together; sometimes two perform; sometimes a *cavalier seul.* Thus was it with the talk of this section of the dinner-table, above the salt, at which the chief people were seated.

'I've just been asked by Lady Blunket how many miles it is to Wardlock, and I'm ashamed to say I can't answer her,' cried Sir Jekyl diagonally to Lady Alice, so as to cut off four people at his left hand, whose conversation being at the moment in a precarious way, forthwith expired, and the Baronet and his mother-in-law were left in possession of this part of the stage.

The old lady, as I have said, looked ill and very tired, and as if she had grown all at once very old; and instead of answering, she only nodded once or twice, and signed across the table to Lady Jane.

'Oh! I forgot,' said Sir Jekyl; 'you know Wardlock and all our distances, don't you, Lady Jane—can you tell me?'

'I don't remember,' said Lady Jane, hardly turning toward him; 'ten or twelve miles—is not it? it may be a good deal more. I don't really recollect;' and this was uttered with an air which plainly said, 'I don't really care.'

'I generally ride my visits, and a mile or two more or less does not signify; but one ought to know all the distances for thirty miles round; you don't know otherwise who's your neighbour.'

'Do you think it an advantage to know that any particular person *is* your neighbour?' inquired impertinent Drayton, with his light moustache, leaning back and looking drowsily into his glasses after his wont.

'Oh! Mr. Drayton, the country without neighbours — how dreadful!' exclaimed Miss Blunket. 'Existence without friends.'

'Friends—bosh!' said Drayton, confidentially, to his wine.

'There's Drayton scouting friendship, the young cynic!' cried Sir Jekyl. 'Do call him to order, Lady Jane.'

'I rather incline to agree with Mr. Drayton,' said Lady Jane, coldly.

'Do you mean to say you have no friends?' said Sir Jekyl, in well-bred amazement.

'Quite the contrary—I have too many.'

'Come—that's a new complaint. Perhaps they are very new friends?' inquired the Baronet.

'Some of them very old, indeed; but I've found that an old friend means only an old person privileged to be impertinent.'

Lady Jane uttered a musical little laugh that was very icy as she spoke, and her eye flashed a single insolent glance at old Lady Alice.

At another time perhaps a retort would not have been wanting, but now the old woman's eye returned but a wandering look, and her face expressed nothing but apathy and sadness.

'Grandmamma, dear, I'm afraid you are very much tired,' whispered Beatrix when they reached the drawing-room, sitting beside her after she had made her comfortable on the sofa, with cushions to her back; 'you would be better lying down, I think.'

'No, dear—no, darling. I think in a few minutes I'll go to my room. I'm not very well. I'm tired—*very* tired.'

And poor old granny, who was speaking very gently, and looking very pale and sunken, sighed deeply—it was almost a moan.

Beatrix was growing very much alarmed, and accompanied, or rather assisted, the old lady up to the room, where, aided by her and her maid, she got to her bed in silence, sighing deeply now and then.

She had not been long there when she burst into tears; and after a violent paroxysm she beckoned to Beatrix, and threw her lean old arms about her neck, saying—

'I'm sorry I came, child; I don't know what to think. I'm too old to bear this agitation—it will kill me.'

Then she wept more quietly, and kissed Beatrix, and whispered—'Send her out of the room—let her wait in the dressing-room.'

The maid was sitting at the further end of the apartment, and the old lady was too feeble to raise her voice so as to be heard there. So soon as her maid had withdrawn, Lady Alice said—

'Sit by me, Beatrix, darling. I am very nervous, and tell me who is that young man who sat beside Jane Lennox at dinner.'

As she ended her little speech Lady Alice, who, though I dare say actually ill enough, yet did not want to lose credit for all the exhaustion she fancied beside, closed her eyelids, and leaned a little back on her pillow motionless. This prevented her seeing

that if she were nervous Beatrix was so also, though in another
way, for her colour was heightened very prettily as she answered.

'You mean the tall, slight young man at Lady Jane's right?'
inquired Beatrix.

'That beautiful but melancholy-looking young man whom we
saw at Wardlock Church,' said Lady Alice, forgetting for the
moment that she had never divulged the result of her observations
from the gallery to any mortal but Sir Jekyl. Beatrix, who forgot nothing, and knew that her brief walk at Wardlock with
that young gentleman had not been confessed to anyone, was confounded on hearing herself thus, as she imagined, taxed with
her secret.

She was not more secret than young ladies generally are; but
whom could she have told at Wardlock? which of the old women
of that time-honoured sisterhood was she to have invited to talk
romance with her? and now she felt very guilty, and was blush-
ing in silent confusion at the pearl ring on her pretty, slender
finger, not knowing what to answer, or how to begin the confession which she fancied her grandmamma was about to extort.

Her grandmamma, however, relieved her on a sudden by
saying—

'I forgot, dear, I told you nothing of that dreadful day at
Wardlock Church, the day I was so ill. I told your papa *only;*
but the young man is here, and I may as well tell you now that
he bears a supernatural likeness to my poor lost darling. Jekyl
knew how it affected me, and he never told me. It was so like
Jekyl. I think, dear, I should not have come here at all had I
known that dreadful young man was here.'

'Dreadful! How is he dreadful?' exclaimed Beatrix.

'From his likeness to my lost darling—my dear boy—my poor,
precious, murdered Guy,' answered the old lady, lying back, and
looking straight toward the ceiling with upturned eyes and clasped
hands. She repeated—'Oh! Guy—Guy—Guy—my poor child!'

She looked like a dying nun praying to her patron saint.

'His name is Strangways—Mr. Guy Strangways,' said Beatrix.

'Ah, yes, darling! Guy was the name of my dear boy, and

Strangways was the name of his companion—an evil companion, I dare say.'

Beatrix knew that the young man whom her grandmamma mourned had fallen in a duel, and that, reasonably or unreasonably, her father was blamed in the matter. More than this she had never heard. Lady Alice had made her acquainted with thus much; but with preambles so awful that she had never dared to open the subject herself, or to question her 'Granny' beyond the point at which her disclosure had stopped.

That somehow it reflected on Sir Jekyl prevented her from inquiring of any servant, except old Donica, who met her curiosity with a sound jobation, and told her if ever she plagued her with questions about family misfortunes like that, she would speak to Sir Jekyl about it. Thus Beatrix only knew how Guy Deverell had died—that her grandmamma chose to believe he had been murdered, and insisted beside in blaming her father, Sir Jekyl, somehow for the catastrophe.

CHAPTER XXII.

HOW EVERYTHING WENT ON.

' Go down, dear, to your company,' resumed Lady Alice, sadly; ' they will miss you. And tell your father, when he comes to the drawing-room, I wish to see him, and won't detain him long.'

So they parted, and a little later Sir Jekyl arrived with a knock at the old lady's bed-room door.

' Come in—oh! yes—Jekyl—well, I've only a word to say. Sit down a moment at the bedside.'

' And how do you feel now, you dear old soul ?' inquired the Baronet, cheerfully. He looked strong and florid, as gentlemen do after dinner, with a genial air of contentment, and a fragrance of his wonderful sherry about him : all which seemed somehow brutal to the nervous old lady.

' Wonderfully, considering the surprise you had prepared for me, and which might as well have killed me as not,' she made answer.

'I know, to be sure—Strangways, you mean. Egad! I forgot. Trixie ought to have told you.'

'*You* ought to have told me. I don't think I should have come here, Jekyl, had I known it.'

'If I had known *that*,' thought Sir Jekyl, with a regretful pang, 'I'd have made a point of telling you.' But he said aloud—

'Yes. It was a *sottise*; but *I*'ve got over the likeness so completely that I forgot how it agitated you. But I ought to tell you they have no connexion with the family—none in the world. Pelter and Crowe, you know—devilish sharp dogs—my lawyers in town—they are regular detectives, by Jove! and know everything —and particularly have had for years a steady eye upon them and their movements; and I have had a most decided letter from them, assuring me that there has not been the slightest movement in that quarter, and therefore there is, absolulely, as I told you from the first, nothing in it.'

'And what Deverells are now living?' inquired the old lady, very pale.

'Two first cousins, they tell me—old fellows now; and one of them has a son or two; but not one called Guy, and none answering this description, you see; and neither have a shadow of a claim, or ever pretended; and as for that unfortunate accident——'

'Pray *spare* me,' said the old lady, grimly.

'Well, they did not care a brass farthing about the poor fellow, so they would never move to give me trouble in that matter; and, in fact, people never do stir in law, and put themselves to serious expense, purely for a sentiment—even a bad one.'

'I remember some years ago you *were* very *much* alarmed, Jekyl.'

'No, I was not. Who the plague says that? There's nothing, thank Heaven, I need fear. One does not like to be worried with lawsuits—that's all—though there is and can be no real danger in them.'

'And was it from these cousins you apprehended lawsuits?' inquired Lady Alice.

'No, not exactly—no, not at all. I believe that fellow Strangways—that fellow that used to live on poor Guy—I fancy he was the mover of it—indeed I know he was.'

'What did they proceed for?' asked the old lady. 'You never told me—you are so secret, Jekyl.'

'They did not proceed at all—how could I? Their attorneys had cases before counsel affecting me—that's all I ever heard; and they say now it was all Strangways' doing—that is, Pelter and Crowe say so. I wish I *were* secret.'

Old Lady Alice here heaved a deep groan, and said, not with asperity, but with a fatigued abhorrence—

'Go away; I wonder I can bear you near me.'

'Thank you very much,' said the Baronet, rising, with one of his pleasant chuckles. 'I can't tell you how glad I am to see you here, and I know you'll be very glad to see me in the morning, when you are a little rested.'

So he kissed the tips of his fingers and touched them playfully to the back of her thin hand, which she withdrew with a little frown, as if they chilled her. And by her direction he called in her maid, whom he asked very smilingly how she did, and welcomed to Marlowe; and she, though a little *passé*, having heard of the fame of Sir Jekyl, and many stories of his brilliant adventures, was very modest and fluttered on the occasion. And with another little petting speech to Lady Alice, the radiant Baronet withdrew.

It is not to be supposed that Lady Alice's tremors communicated themselves to Beatrix. Was it possible to regard that handsome, refined young man, who spoke in that low, sweet voice, and smiled so intelligently, and talked so pleasantly, and with that delicate flavour of romance at times, in the light of a goblin?

The gentlemen had made their whist-party. The Rev. Dives Marlowe was chatting to, not with, Lady Jane, who sat listlessly on an ottoman. That elderly girl, Miss Blunket, with the *naïve* ways, the animated, smiling, and rather malevolent countenance,

had secured little Linnett, who bore his imprisonment impatiently
and wearily it must be owned. When Miss Blunket was enthusiastic it was all very well; but her playfulness was wicked, and her
satire gaily vitriolic.

'Mr. Marlowe is fascinated, don't you think?' she inquired of
harmless little Linnett, glancing with an arch flash of her fierce
eyes at the Rev. Dives.

'She's awfully handsome,' said Linnett, honestly.

'Oh, dear, you wicked creature, you can't think I meant that.
She is some kind of cousin, I think—is not she? And her husband
has that great living—what's its name?—and no relation in the
Church; and Lady Jane, they say, rules him—and Sir Jekyl, some
people say, rules her.'

Linnett returned her arch glance with an honest stare of surprise.

'I had no idea of that, egad,' said he.

'She thinks him so wise in all worldly matters, you know; and
people in London fancied she would have been the second Lady
Marlowe, if she had not met General Lennox just at a critical
time, and fallen in love with him;' and as she said this she
laughed.

'Really!' exclaimed Linnett; and he surveyed Lady Jane in
this new light wonderingly.

'I really don't know; I heard it said merely; but very likely,
you know, it is not true,' she answered with an artless giggle.

'I knew you were quizzing—though, by Jove, you did sell me at
first; but I really think Sir Jekyl's a little spooney on that pretty
little Mrs. Maberly. Is she a widow?'

'Oh, dear, no—at least, not quite; she has a husband in India,
but then, poor man, he's so little in the way she need hardly wish
him dead.'

'I *see*,' said Linnett, looking at Mrs. Maberly, with a grave
interest.

While Miss Blunket was entertaining and instructing little
Linnett with this sort of girlish chatter, and from the whist-table,
between the deals, arose those critical discussions and reviews,

relieved now and then by a joke from the Baronet, or from his partner, Colonel Doocey, at the piano, countenanced by old Lady Blunket, who had come to listen and remained to doze, Beatrix, her fingers still on the keys, was listening to young Strangways.

There are times, lights, accidents, under which your handsome young people become incredibly more handsome, and this Guy Strangways now shared in that translated glory, as he leaned on the back of a tall carved chair, sometimes speaking, sometimes listening.

' It is quite indescribable, Miss Marlowe, how your music interests me—I should say, haunts me. I thought at first it was because you loved ballad music, which I also love ; but it is not that—it is something higher and more peculiar.'

' I am sure you were right at first, for I *know* I am a very in-different musician,' said Beatrix, looking down under her long lashes on the keys over which the jewelled fingers of her right hand wandered with hardly a tinkle, just tracing dreamily one of those sweet melancholy airs which made in fancy an accompaniment to the music of that young fellow's words.

How beautiful she looked, too, with eyes lowered and parted lips, and that listening smile—not quite a smile—drinking in with a strange rapture of pride and softness the flatteries which she refused and yet invited.

' It *is* something higher and mysterious, which, perhaps, I shall never attempt to explain, unless, indeed, I should risk talking very wildly—too wildly for you to understand, or, if you did, perhaps—to forgive.'

' You mentioned a Breton ballad you once heard,' said Beatrix, frightened, as girls will sometimes become whenever the hero of their happy hours begins on a sudden to define.

' Yes,' he said, and the danger of the crisis was over. ' I wish so much I could remember the air, you would so enter into its character, and make its wild unfathomable melancholy so beauti-fully touching in your clear contralto.'

' You must not flatter me ; I want to hear more of that ballad.'

'If flattery be to speak more highly than one thinks, who can flatter Miss Marlowe?' Again the crisis was menacing. 'Besides, I did not tell you we are leaving, I believe, in a day or two, and on the eve of so near a departure, may I not improve the few happy moments that are left me, and be permitted the privilege of a leave-taking, to speak more frankly, and perhaps less wisely than one who is destined to be all his life a neighbour?'

'Papa, I am sure, will be very sorry to hear that you and Monsieur Varbarriere are thinking of going so soon; I must try, however, to improve the time, and hear all you can tell me of those interesting people of Brittany.'

'Yes, they are. I will make them another visit — a sadder visit, Mademoiselle — for me a far more interesting one. You have taught me how to hear and see them. I never felt the spirit of Villemarque, or the romance and melancholy of that antique region, till I had the honour of knowing you.'

My friends always laughed at me about Brittany. I suppose different people are interested by different subjects; but I do not think anyone could read at all about that part of the world and not be fascinated. You promised to tell all you remember of that Breton ballad.'

'Oh, yes; the haunted lady, the beautiful lady, the heiress of Carlowel, now such a grand ruin, became enamoured of a myste-rious cavalier who wooed her; but he was something not of flesh and blood, but of the spirit world.'

'There is exactly such a legend, so far, at least, of a castle on the Rhine. I must show it to you. Do you read German?'

'Yes, Mademoiselle.'

'And does the ballad end tragically?'

'Most tragically. You shall hear.'

'Where are you, Guy?' in French, inquired a deep ringing voice.

And on the summons, Guy glanced over his shoulder, and replied.

'Oh,' exclaimed the same voice, 'I demand pardon. I am dis-turbing conversation, I fear; but an old man in want of assistance will be excused. I want my road book, Guy, and you have got it. Pray, run up stairs and fetch it.'

With great pleasure, of course, Guy Strangways ran up-stairs to tumble over block-books, letters, diaries, and the general residuum of a half-emptied valise.

Miss Beatrix played a spirited march, which awoke Lady Blunket, whom she had forgotten; and that interesting woman, to make up for lost time, entertained her with a history of the unreasonableness of Smidge, her maid, and a variety of other minute afflictions, which, she assured Beatrix seriously, disturbed her sleep.

CHAPTER XXIII.

THE DIVAN.

THAT night Sir Jekyl led the gentlemen in a body to his outpost quarters, in the rear of civilization, where they enjoyed their cigars, brandy and water, and even 'swipes,' prodigiously.. It is a noble privilege to be so rich as Sir Jekyl Marlowe. The Jewish price for frankincense was thrice its own weight in gold. How much did that aromatic blue canopy that rolled dimly over this Turkish divan cost that off-handed Sybarite? How many scruples of fine gold were floating in that cloud?

Varbarriere was in his way charmed with his excursion. He enjoyed the jokes and stories of the younkers, and the satiric slang and imperturbable good-humour of their host. The twinkle of his eye, from its deep cavern, and the suavity of his solemn features, testified to his profound enjoyment of a meeting to which he contributed, it must be owned, for his own share, little but smoke.

In fact, he was very silent, very observant—observant of more things than the talk perhaps.

All sorts of things were talked about. Of course, no end of horse and dog anecdote—something of wine, something of tobacco, something of the beauties of the opera and the stage, and those sad visions, the fallen angelic of the demimonde—something, but

only the froth and sparkle of politics — light conjecture, and
pungent scandal, in the spirit of gay satire and profligate comedy.

'He's a bad dog, St. Evermore. Did not you hear that about
the duel?' said Drayton.

'What?' asked the Baronet, with an unconscious glance at
Guy Strangways.

'He killed that French fool—what's his name?—unfairly, they
say. There has been a letter or something in one of the Paris
papers about it. Fired before his time, I think, and very ill feeling against the English in consequence.'

'Oh!' said the Baronet.

'But you know,' interposed Doocey, who was an older clubman
than Drayton, and remembering further back, thought that sort
of anecdote of the duel a little maladroit just then and there, 'St.
Evermore has been talked about a good deal; there were other
things—that horse, you know; and they say, by Jove! he was
licked by Tromboni, at the wings of the opera, for what he called
insulting his wife; and Tromboni says he's a marquess, and devil
knows what beside, at home, and wanted to fight, but St. Evermore wouldn't, and took his licking.'

'He's not a nice fellow by any means; but he's devilish good
company—lots of good stories and capital cigars,' said Drayton.

At this point M. Varbarriere was seized with a fit of coughing;
and Sir Jekyl glanced sharply at him; but no, he was not
laughing.

The conversation proceeded agreeably, and some charming
stories were told of Sir Paul Blunket, who was not present; and
in less than an hour the party broke up and left Sir Jekyl to his
solitary quarters.

The Baronet bid his last guest good-night at the threshold, and
then shut his door and locked himself in. It was his custom,
here, to sleep with his door locked.

'What was that fellow laughing at—Varbarriere? I'm certain he was laughing. I never saw a fellow so completely the cut
of a charlatan. I'll write to Charteris to-night. I *must* learn all
about him.'

Then Sir Jekyl yawned, and reflected what a fool Drayton was, what a fellow to talk, and what asses all fellows were at that age; and, being sleepy, he postponed his letter to Charteris to the next morning, and proceeded to undress.

Next morning was bright and pleasant, and he really did not see much good in writing the letter; and so he put it off to a more convenient time.

Shortly after the ladies had left the drawing-room for their bedrooms, Beatrix, having looked in for a moment to her grandmamma's room, and with a kiss and a good-night, taken wing again, there entered to Lady Alice, as the old plays express it, then composing herself for the night, Lady Jane's maid, with—

'Please, my lady, my lady wants to know if your ladyship knows where her ladyship's key may be?'

' *What* key?'

'The key of her bedchamber, please, my lady.'

'Oh! the key of my dressing-room. Tell Lady Jane that I have got the key of the Window dressing-room, and mean to keep it,' replied the old lady, firmly.

The maid executed a courtesy, and departed; and Lady Alice sank back again upon her pillow, with her eyes and mouth firmly closed, and the countenance of an old lady who is conscious of having done her duty upon one of her sex.

About two minutes later there came a rustle of a dressing-gown and the patter of a swift-slippered tread through the short passage from the dressing-room, and, without a knock, Lady Jane, with a brilliant flush on her face, ruffled into the room, and, with her head very high, and flashing eyes, demanded—

'Will you be so good, Lady Alice Redcliffe, as to give me the key of my bedroom?'

To which Lady Alice, without opening her eyes, and with her hands mildly clasped, in the fashion of a mediæval monument, over her breast, meekly and firmly made answer—

'If you mean the key of the Window dressing-room, Jane, I have already told your maid that I mean to *keep* it!'

'And I'll not leave the room till I get it,' cried Lady Jane, standing fiercely beside the monument.

'Then you'll not leave the room to-night, Jane,' replied the statuesque sufferer on the bed.

'We shall *see* that. Once more, will you give me my key or not?'

'The key of my dressing-room door is in my possession, and I mean to keep it,' repeated the old lady, with a provoking mildness.

'You shan't, madam—you'll do no such thing. You shall give up the key you have stolen. I'll lose my life but I'll make you.'

'Jane, Jane,' said the old lady, 'you are sadly changed for the worse since last I saw you.'

'And if *you're* not, it's only because there was no room for it. Sadly changed indeed—very true. I don't suffer you to bully me as you used at Wardlock.'

'May heaven forgive and pardon you!' ejaculated the old lady, with great severity, rising perpendicularly and raising both her eyes and hands.

'Keep your prayers for yourself, madam, and give me my key,' demanded the incensed young lady.

'I'll do no such thing; I'll do as I said; and I'll pray how I please, ma'am,' retorted the suppliant fiercely.

'Your prayers don't signify twopence. You've the temper of a fiend, as all the world knows; and no one can live in the same house with you,' rejoined Lady Jane.

'That's a wicked lie: my servants live all their days with me.'

'Because they know no one else would take them. But you've the temper of a fury. You haven't a friend left, and everyone hates you.'

'Oh! oh! oh!' moaned Lady Alice, sinking back, with her hand pressed to her heart piteously, and closing her eyes, as she recollected how ill she was.

'Ho! dear me!' exclaimed Lady Jane, in high disdain. 'Had not you better restore my key before you die, old lady?'

'Jane!' exclaimed Lady Alice, recovering in an instant, 'have you no feeling—you know the state I'm in; and you're bent on killing me with your unfeeling brutality?'

'You're perfectly well, ma'am, and you look it. I wish I was half as strong; you oblige me to come all this way, this bitter night, you odious old woman.'

'I see how it is, and why you want the key. A very little more, and I'll write to General Lennox.'

'Do; and he'll horsewhip you.'

Lady Jane herself was a little stunned at this speech, when she heard it from her own lips; and I think would have recalled it.

'Thank you, Jane; I hope you'll *remember* that. Horsewhip me! No doubt you wish it; but General Lennox is a gentleman, I hope, *although* he has married you; and I don't suppose he would murder a miserable old woman to gratify you.'

'You know perfectly what I mean—if you were a *man* he would horsewhip you; you have done nothing but insult me ever since you entered this house.'

'Thank you; it's quite plain. I shan't forget it. I'll ask him, when he comes, whether he's in the habit of beating women. It is not usual, I believe, among British officers. It *usen't* at least; but everything's getting on—young ladies, and, I suppose, old men—all getting on famously.'

'Give me my key, if you please; and cease talking like a fool,' cried Lady Jane.

'And what *do* you want of that key? Come, now, young lady, what is it?'

'I don't choose to have my door lie open, and I won't. I've no bolt to the inside, and I *will* have my key, madam.'

'If that's your object, set your mind at ease. I'll lock your door myself when you have got to your bed.'

'So that if the house takes fire I shall be burnt to death!'

'Pooh! nonsense!'

'And if I am they'll hang *you*, I hope.'

'Thank you. Flogged and hanged!' And Lady Alice laughed an exceeding bitter laugh. 'But the wicked violence of your language and *menaces* shan't deter me from the duty I've prescribed to myself. I'll define my reasons if you like, and I'll write as soon as you please to General Lennox.'

'I think you're *mad*—I do, I assure you. I'll endure it for once, but depend on it I'll complain to Sir Jekyl Marlowe, in my husband's absence, in the morning; and if this sort of thing is to go on, I had better leave the house forthwith—that's all.'

And having uttered these dignified sentences with becoming emphasis, she sailed luridly away.

'Good night, Jane,' said Lady Alice, with a dry serenity.

'Don't dare, you insupportable old woman, to wish me good-night,' burst out Lady Jane, whisking round at the threshold.

With which speech, having paused for a moment in defiance, she disappeared, leaving the door wide open, which is, perhaps, as annoying as clapping it, and less vulgar.

CHAPTER XXIV.

GUY STRANGWAYS AND M. VARBARRIERE CONVERSE.

WHEN M. Varbarriere and his nephew this night sat down in their dressing-room, the elder man said—

'How do you like Sir Jekyl Marlowe ?'

'A most agreeable host—very lively—very hospitable,' answered Guy Strangways.

'Does it strike you that he is *anxious* about anything ?'

The young man looked surprised.

'No; that is, I mean, he appears to me in excellent spirits. Perhaps, sir, I do not quite apprehend you ?'

'Not unlikely,' said the old gentleman. 'He does not question you ?'

'No, sir.'

'Yet he suspects me, and I think suspects you,' observed M. Varbarriere.

The young man looked pained, but said nothing.

'That room where poor Lady Marlowe was—was so shocked—

the green chamber—it is connected with the misfortunes of your family.'

'How, sir?'

'Those papers you have heard my lawyer mention as having been lost at Dubois' Hotel in London, by your grandfather, it is my belief were lost in this house and in that room.'

A gentleman smoking a cigar must be very much interested indeed when he removes his weed from his lips and rests the hand whose fingers hold it upon his knee, to the imminent risk of its going out while he pauses and listens.

'And how, sir, do you suppose this occurred—by what agency?' inquired the handsome young gentleman.

'The ghost,' answered M. Varbarriere, with a solemn sneer.

Guy Strangways knew he could not be serious, although, looking on his countenance, he could discern there no certain trace of irony as he proceeded.

'Many years later, poor Lady Marlowe, entering that room late at night—her maid slept there, and she being ill, for a change, in the smaller room adjoining (you don't know those rooms, but I have looked in at the door)—beheld what we call the ghost, and never smiled or held up her head after,' said the portly old gentleman between the puffs of his cigar.

'Beheld the ghost!'

'So they say, and I believe it—what they *call* the ghost.'

'Did she make an alarm or call her husband?'

'Her husband slept in that remote room at the very back of the house, which, as you see, he still occupies, quite out of hearing. You go down-stairs first, then up-stairs; and as he slept the greater part of two hundred feet away from the front of the house, of course he was out of the question;' and M. Varbarriere sneered again solemnly.

'A housekeeper named Gwynn, I am told, knows all about it, but I believe she is gone.'

'And do you really think, sir, that my grandfather lost those deeds *here?*'

'I always thought so, and so I told your father, and my information got him into a bad scrape.'

'You don't, I know, think it occurred supernaturally?' said
Guy, more and more bewildered.

'Supernaturally; of course it was—how else could it be?' answered the old gentleman, with a drowsy irony. 'That room has
been haunted, as I have heard, by a devil from the time it was
built, in the reign of George II. Can you imagine why General
Lennox was put to sleep there?'

The young man shook his head. The old one resumed his
smoking, leaving his problem unsolved.

'It shall be my business to evoke and to lay that devil,' said
the elderly gentleman, abruptly.

'Ought not Lady Jane Lennox to be warned if you really think
there is any—any *danger?*'

'The danger is to *General* Lennox, as I suppose.'

'I don't understand, sir.'

'No, you don't—better not. I told your poor father my belief
once, and it proved fatal knowledge to him. In the day that he
ate thereof he died. Bah! it is better to keep your mind to yourself until you have quite made it up—you understand?—and even
then till the time for action has come, and not even then, unless
you want help. Who will sum up the mischief one of those
prating fellows does in a life-time?'

The gentlemen were silent hereupon for a period which I may
measure by half a cigar.

'That green chamber—it is a hypocrite,' said the solemn old man,
looking drowsily on the smoke that was ascending the chimney,
into which he threw the butt-end of his cigar—'mind you, a
hypocrite. I have my theory. But we will not talk; no—*you*
will be less embarrassed, and *I* more useful, with this reserve.
For the purpose I have in view I will do fifty things in which you
could and would have no partnership. Will you peep into that
letter, Monsieur?' The ponderous gentleman grew dramatic here.
'Will you place your ear to that door, *si'l vous plait*—your eye to
that keyhole? Will you oblige me by bribing that domestic

with five pounds sterling ? Bah! I will be all ear, all eye—om-
nipresent, omniscient, omnipotent !—by *all* means for this END—
ay, all means—what *you* call secret, shabby, blackguard ;' and
the sonorous voice of the old man, for the first time since his arrival, broke into clangorous burst of laughter, which, subsiding
into a sort of a growl, died, at last, quite away. The old gentleman's countenance looked more thoughtful and a shade darker
than he had seen it. Then rising, he stood with his back to the
fire, and fumbled slowly at the heavy links of his watch-chain,
like a ghostly monk telling his beads, while he gazed, in the abstraction of deep thought, on the face of the young man.

Suddenly his face grew vigilant, his eyes lighted up, and
some stern lines gathered about them, as he looked down full upon
his nephew.

'Guy,' said he, ' you'll keep your promise—your word—your
oath—that not one syllable of what passes between us is divulged
to mortal, and that all those points on which I have enjoined reserve shall be held by you scrupulously secret.'

Guy bowed his acquiescence.

'What nonsense was that going on at the piano to-night?
Well, you need not answer, but there must be no more of it. I
won't burden you with painful secrets. You will understand me
hereafter ; but no more of *that*—observe me.'

The old gentleman spoke this injunction with a lowering nod,
and that deliberate and peremptory emphasis to which his metallic
tones gave effect.

Guy heard this, leaning in an unchanged attitude on his elbow
over the chimney-piece, in silence and with downcast eyes.

'Yes, Guy,' said the old man, walking suddenly up to him, and
clapping his broad hand upon his shoulder, 'I will complete the
work I have begun for you. Have confidence in me, don't mar it,
and you shall know all, and after I am gone, perhaps admire the
zealous affection with which I laboured in your interest. Good-
night, and Heaven bless you dear Guy ;' and so they parted for
the night.

Guy Strangways had all his life stood in awe of this reserved

despotic uncle—kind, indulgent in matters of pleasure and of
money, but habitually secret, and whenever he imposed a command, tyrannical. Yet Guy felt that even here there was kindness ; and though he could not understand his plans, of his motives
he could have no doubt.

For M. Varbarriere, indeed, his nephew had a singular sort
of respect. More than one-half of his character was enveloped in
total darkness to his eyes. Of the traits that were revealed some
were positively evil. He knew, by just one or two proofs, that
he was proud and vindictive, and could carry his revenge for a
long time, like a cold stone, in his sleeve. He could break out
into a devil of a passion, too, on occasion ; he could be as un-
scrupulous, in certain ways, as Machiavel ; and, it was fixed in
Guy's mind, had absolutely no religion whatsoever. What were
the evidences ?   M. Varbarriere led a respectable life, and showed
his solemn face and person in church with regularity, and was on
very courteous relations with the clergy, and had built the greater
part of a church in Pontaubrique, where prayers are, I believe,
still offered up for him. Ought not all this to have satisfied Guy ?
And yet he knew quite well that solemn M. Varbarriere did not
believe one fact, record, tradition, or article of the religion he
professed, or of any other. Had he denounced, ridiculed, or con-
troverted them ?—Never. On the contrary, he kept a civil tongue
in his head, or was silent. What, then, were the proofs which had
long quite settled the questi n in Guy's mind ? They consisted of
some half-dozen smiles and shrugs, scattered over some fifteen
years, and delivered impressively at significant moments.

But with all this he was kindly. The happiness of a great
number of persons depended upon M. Varbarriere, and they were
happy. His wine-estates were well governed. His great silk-
factory in the south was wisely and benevolently administered.
He gave handsomely to every deserving charity. He smiled on
children and gave them small coins. He loved flowers, and no
man was more idolised by his dogs.

Guy was attached by his kindness, and he felt that be his moral
system exactly what it might, he had framed one, and acted under

it, and he instinctively imbibed for him that respect which we always cherish for the man who has submitted his conduct consistently to a code or principle self-imposed by intellect—even erring.

CHAPTER XXV.

LADY ALICE TALKS WITH GUY STRANGWAYS.

WHEN Guy had bid this man good-night and entered his chamber, he threw himself into his easy-chair beside the fire, which had grown low and grey in the grate. He felt both sad and alarmed. He now felt assured that M. Varbarriere was fashioning and getting together the parts of a machine which was to work evil against their host and his family. His family? His *daughter* Beatrix. He had no other.

Already implicated in deception, the reasons for which he knew not, the direction of which he only suspected—bound as he was to secrecy by promises the most sacred, to his stern old kinsman and benefactor, he dared not divulge the truth. Somehow the blow meditated, he was confident, against this Baronet, was to redound to *his* advantage. What a villain should he appear when all was over! Sir Jekyl his host, too, frank and hospitable—how could he have earned the misfortune, be it great or small, that threatened? And the image of Beatrix—like an angel—stood between her father and the unmasked villain, Guy, who had entered the house in a borrowed shape, ate and drank and slept, talked and smiled, and, he now feared, *loved*, and in the end--struck!

When Mr. Guy Strangways came down next morning he looked very pale. His breakfast was a sham. He talked hardly at all, and smiled but briefly and seldom.'

M. Varbarriere, on the contrary, was more than usually animated, and talked in his peculiar vein rather more than was his wont; and after breakfast, Sir Jekyl placed his hand kindly on

Guy Strangways' arm as he looked dismally from the window. The young man almost started at the kindly pressure.

'Very glad to hear that Monsieur Varbarriere has changed his mind,' said Sir Jekyl, with a smile.

What change was this? thought Guy, whose thoughts were about other plans of his uncle's, and he looked with a strange surprise in Sir Jekyl's face.

'I mean his ill-natured idea of going so soon. I'm so glad. You know you have seen nothing yet, and we are going to kill a buck to-day, so you had better postpone the moor to-morrow, and if you like to take your rod in the afternoon, you will find—Barron tells me—some very fine trout, about half a mile lower down the stream than you fished yesterday—a little below the bridge.'

Guy thanked him, I fancy, rather oddly. He heard him in fact as if it was an effort to follow his meaning, and he really did feel relieved when his good-natured host was called away, the next moment, to settle a disputed question between the two sportsmen, Linnett and Doocey.

'How is grandmamma this morning?' inquired Sir Jekyl of Beatrix, before she left the room.

'Better, I think. She says she will take a little turn up and down the broad walk, by-and-bye, and I am to go with her.'

'Very pleasant for you, Trixie,' said her papa, with one of his chuckles. 'So you can't go with your ladies to Lonsted to-day?'

'No—it can't be helped; but I'm glad poor granny can take her little walk.'

'Not a bit of you, Trixie.'

'Yes, *indeed*, I am. Poor old granny!'

The incredulous Baronet tapped her cheek with his finger, as he chuckled again roguishly, and with a smile and a shake of his head, their little talk ended.

In the hall he found Guy Strangways in his angling garb, about to start on a solitary excursion. He preferred it. He was very much obliged. He did not so much care for the chase, and liked walking even better than riding.

The Baronet, like a well-bred host, allowed his guests to choose

absolutely their own method of being happy, but he could not but
perceive something in the young gentleman's manner that was
new and uncomfortable. Had he offended him—had anything
occurred during the sitting after dinner last night? Well, he
could not make it out, but his manner was a little odd and constrained, and in that slanting light from above, as he had stood
before him in the hall, he certainly did look confoundedly like
that other Guy whose memory was his chief spoil-sport. But it
crossed him only like a neuralgic pang, to be forgotten a minute
later. And so the party dispersed—some mounted, to the park;
others away with the keeper and dogs for the moor; and Strangways, dejected, on his solitary river-side ramble.

His rod and fly-book were but pretexts—his object was solitude.
It was a beautiful autumnal day, a low sun gilding the red and
yellow foliage of wood and hedgerow, and the mellow songs of
birds were quivering in the air. The cheer and the melancholy of
autumn were there—the sadness of a pleasant farewell.

'It is well,' thought Strangways, 'that I have been so startled
into consciousness, while I yet have power to escape my fate—that
beautiful girl! I did not know till last night how terrible I shall
find it to say farewell. But, cost what it may, the word must be
spoken. She will never know what it costs me. I may call it a
dream, but even dreams of paradise are forgotten; my dream—
never! All after-days dark without her. All my future life a
sad reverie—a celestial remembrance—a vain yearning. These
proud English people—and those dark designs, what are they?
No, they shan't hurt her—never. I'll denounce him first. What
is it to me what becomes of me if I have saved her—in so few days
grown to be so much to me—my idol, my darling, though she may
never know it?'

Guy Strangways, just five-and-twenty, had formed, on the
situation, many such tremendous resolutions as young gentlemen
at that period of life are capable of. He would speak to her no
more; he would think of her no more; he would brave his uncle's
wrath—shield her from all possibility of evil—throw up his own

stakes, be they what they might—and depart in silence, and never see Beatrix again.

The early autumn evening had begun to redden the western clouds, as Guy Strangways, returning, approached the fine old house, and passing a thick group of trees and underwoods, he suddenly found himself before Beatrix and Lady Alice. I dare say they had been talking about him, for Beatrix blushed, and the old lady stared at him from under her grey brows, with lurid half-frightened eyes, as she leaned forward, her thin fingers grasping the arms of the rustic chair, enveloped in her ermine-lined mantle.

Lady Alice looked on him as an old lady might upon a caged monster—with curiosity and fear. She was beginning to endure his presence, though still with an awe nearly akin to horror—though that horror was fast disappearing—and there was a strange yearning, too, that drew her towards him.

He had seen Beatrix that morning. The apparition had now again risen in the midst of his wise resolutions, and embarrassed him strangely. The old lady's stare, too, was, you may suppose, to a man predisposed to be put out, very disconcerting. The result was that he bowed very low indeed before the ladies, and remained silent, expecting, like a ghost, to be spoken to.

' Come here, sir, if you please,' said the old lady, with an odd mixture of apprehension and command. 'How d'ye do, Mr. Strangways? I saw you yesterday, you know, at dinner; and I saw you some weeks since at Wardlock Church. I have been affected by a resemblance. Merciful Heaven, it *is* miraculous! And things of that sort affect me now more than they once might have done. I'm a sickly old woman, and have lost most of my dearest ties on earth, and cannot expect to remain much longer behind them.'

It was odd, but the repulsion was still active, while at the same time she was already, after a fashion, opening her heart to him.

It was not easy to frame an answer, on the moment, to this strange address. He could only say, as again he bowed low—

'I do recollect, Lady Alice, having seen you in Wardlock Church. My uncle, Monsieur Varbarriere——'

At this point the handsome young gentleman broke down. His uncle had whispered him, as they sat side by side—

' Look at that old lady costumed in mourning, in the seat in the gallery with the marble tablet and two angels—do you see ?— on the wall behind. That is Lady Alice Redcliffe. I'll tell you more about her by-and-by.'

' By-and-by,' as Guy Strangways had come to know, indicated in M. Varbarriere's vocabulary that period which was the luminous point in his perspective, at which his unexplained hints and pro- ceedings would all be cleared up. The sudden rush of these recollections and surmises in such a presence overcame Guy Strang- ways, and he changed colour and became silent.

The old lady, however, understood nothing of the causes of his sudden embarrassment, and spoke again.

' Will you forgive an old woman for speaking with so little reserve ?—your voice, too, sir, so wonderfully resembles it— wonderfully.'

Old Lady Alice dried her eyes a little here, and Guy, who felt that his situation might soon become very nearly comical, said very gently—

' There are, I believe, such likenesses. I have seen one or two such myself.' And then to Beatrix, aside, ' My presence and these recollections, I fear, agitate Lady Alice.'

But the old lady interposed in a softened tone—' No, sir; pray don't go ; pray remain. You've been walking, fishing. What a sweet day, and charming scenery near here. I know it all very well. In my poor girl's lifetime I was a great deal here. She was very accomplished—she drew beautifully—poor thing ; my pretty Beatrix here is very like her. You can't remember your poor mamma ? No, hardly.'

All this time Lady Alice was, with aristocratic ill-breeding, contemplating the features of Guy Strangways, as she might a picture, with saddened eyes. She was becoming accustomed to the apparition. It had almost ceased to frighten her; and she liked it even, as a help to memory.

Five minutes later she was walking feebly up and down the plateau, in the last level beams of the genial sunset, leaning on the arm of the young man, who could not refuse this courtesy to the garrulous old lady, although contrary to his prudent resolutions— it retained him so near to Beatrix.

' And, Mr. Strangways, it is not every day, you know, I can walk out; and Trixie here will sometimes bring her work into the boudoir—and if you would pay me a visit there, and read or talk a little, you can't think what a kindness you would do me.'

What could he do but hear and smile, and declare how happy it would make him? Although here, too, he saw danger to his wise resolutions. But have not the charities of society their claims?

These were their parting words as they stood on the stone plat-form under the carved armorial bearings of the Marlowes, at the hall-door; and old Lady Alice, when she reached her room, wept softer and happier tears than had wet her cheeks for many a year.

<hr>

CHAPTER XXVI.

SOME TALK OF A SURVEY OF THE GREEN CHAMBER.

THE red sunset beam that had lighted the group we have just been following, glanced through the windows of M. Varbarriere's dressing-room, and lighted up a letter he was at that moment reading. It said—

' The woman to whom you refer is still living. We heard fully about her last year, and, we are informed, is now in the service of Lady Alice Redcliffe, of Wardlock, within easy reach of Marlowe. We found her, as we thought, reliable in her statements, though impracticable and reserved; but that is eight years since. She was, I think, some way past fifty then.'

M. Varbarriere looked up here, and placed the letter in his pocket, beholding his valet entering.

'Come in, Jacques,' exclaimed the ponderous old gentleman, in the vernacular of the valet.

He entered gaily bowing and smiling.

'Well, my friend,' he exclaimed good-humouredly, 'you look very happy, and no wonder—you, a lover of beauty, are fortunate in a house where so much is treasured.'

'Ah! Monsieur mocks himself of me. But there are many beautiful ladies assembled here, my faith!'

'What do you think of Lady Jane Lennox?'

'Oh, heavens! it is an angel!'

'And only think! she inhabits, all alone, that terrible green chamber!' exclaimed the old gentleman, with an unwonted smile, 'I have just been wondering about that green chamber, regarding which so many tales of terror are related, and trying from its outward aspect to form some conjecture as to its interior, you understand, its construction and arrangements. It interests me so strangely. Now, I dare say, by this time so curious a sprite as you—so clever—so potent with that fair sex who hold the keys of all that is worth visiting, there is hardly a nook in this house, from the cellar to the garret, worth looking at, into which you have not contrived a peep during this time?'

'Ah, my faith! Monsieur does me too much honour. I may have been possibly, but I do not know to which of the rooms they accord that name.'

Now upon this M. Varbarriere described to him the exact situation of the apartment.

'And who occupies the room at present, Monsieur?'

'Lady Jane Lennox, I told you.'

'Oh! then I am sure I have not been there. That would be impossible.'

'But there must be no impossibility here,' said the old gentleman with a grim 'half joke and whole earnest' emphasis. 'If you satisfy me during our stay in this house I will make you a present of five thousand francs—you comprehend?—this day three weeks. I am

curious in my way as you are in yours.   Let us see whether your
curiosity cannot subserve mine.   In the first place, on the honour
of a gentleman—your father was a Captain of Chasseurs, and his
son will not dishonour him—you promise to observe the strictest
silence and secrecy.'

Jacques bowed and smiled deferentially; their eyes met for a
moment, and Monsieur Varbarriere said—

'You need not suppose anything so serious—*mon ami*—there is
no tragedy or even *fourberie* intended.   I have heard spiritual
marvels about that apartment; I am inquisitive.   Say, I am
composing a philosophy and writing a book on the subject, and
I want some few facts about the proportions of it.   See, here
is a sketch—oblong square—that is the room.   You will visit
it—you take some pieces of cord—you measure accurately the
distance from this wall to that—you see?—the length; then
from this to this—the breadth.   If any projection or recess, you
measure its depth or prominence most exactly.   If there be any
door or buffet in the room, beside the entrance, you mark where.
You also measure carefully the thickness of the wall at the
windows and the door.   I am very curious, and all this you shall
do.'

The courier shrugged, and smiled, and pondered.

'Come, there may be difficulties, but such as melt before the
light of your genius and the glow of this,' and he lifted a little
column of a dozen golden coins between his finger and thumb.

'Do you think that when we, the visitors, are all out walking
or driving, a chambermaid would hesitate for a couple of these
counters to facilitate your enterprise and enable you to do all this?
Bah! I know them too well.'

'I am flattered of the confidence of Monsieur.   I am *ravi* of the
opportunity to serve him.'

There was something perhaps cynical in the imposing solemnity
of gratitude with which M. Varbarriere accepted these evidences of
devotion.

'You must so manage that she will suppose nothing of the fact
that it is *I* who want all these foolish little pieces of twine,' said

the grave gentleman; ' she would tell everybody. What will you say to her ?'

' Ah, Monsieur, please, it will be Margery. She is a charming rogue, and as discreet as myself. She will assist, and I will tell her nothing but fibs; and we shall make some money. She and I together in the servants' hall—she shall talk of the ghosts and the green chamber, and I will tell how we used to make wagers who would guess, without having seen it, the length of such a room in the Château Mauville, when we were visiting there—how many windows—how high the chimneypiece; and then the nearest guesser won the pool. You see, Monsieur—you understand ? Margery and I, we will play this little trick. And so she will help me to all the measurements before, without sharing of my real design, quite simply.'

' Sir, I admire your care of the young lady's simplicity,' said M. Varbarriere, sardonically. ' You will procure all this for me as quickly as you can, and I shan't forget my promise.'

Jacques was again radiantly grateful.

' Jacques, you have the character of being always true to your chief. I never doubted your honour, and I show the esteem I hold you in by undertaking to give you five thousand francs in three weeks' time, provided you satisfy me while here. It would not cost me much, Jacques, to make of you as good a gentleman as your father.'

Jacques here threw an awful and indescribable devotion into his countenance.

' I don't say, mind you, I'll do it—only that if I pleased I very easily might. You shall bring me a little plan of that room, including all the measurements I have mentioned, if possible to-morrow—the sooner the better; that to begin with. Enough for the present. Stay; have you had any talk with Sir Jekyl Marlowe—you must be quite frank with me—has he noticed you ?'

' He has done me that honour.'

' Frequently ?'

' Once only, Monsieur.'

' Come, let us hear what passed.'

M. Varbarriere had traced a slight embarrassment in Jacques' countenance.

So with a little effort and as much gaiety as he could command, Jacques related tolerably truly what had passed in the stable-yard.

A lurid flash appeared on the old man's forehead for a moment, and he rang out fiercely—

'And why the devil, sir, did you not mention that before ?'

'I was not aware, Monsieur, it was of any importance,' he answered deferentially.

' Jacques, you must tell me the whole truth—did he make you a present ?'

'No, Monsieur.'

' He gave you nothing then or since ?'

' *Pas un sous, Monsieur*—nothing.'

' Has he *promised* you anything ?'

'Nothing, Monsieur.'

' But you understand what he means ?'

' Monsieur will explain himself.'

' You understand he has made you an offer in case you consent to transfer your service.'

' Monsieur commands my allegiance.'

' You have only to say so if you wish it.'

' Monsieur is my generous chief. I will not abandon him for a stranger—never, while he continues his goodness and his preference for me.'

' Well, you belong to *me* for a month, you know, by our agreement. After that you may consider what you please. In the meantime be true to me ; and not one word, if you please, of me or my concerns to anybody.'

' Certainly Monsieur. I shall be found a man of honour now as always.'

' I have no doubt, Jacques ; as I told you, I know you to be a gentleman—I rely upon you.'

M. Varbarriere looked rather grimly into his eye as he uttered this compliment ; and when the polite little gentleman had left the room, M. Varbarriere bethought him how very little he had to betray—how little he knew about him, his nephew, and his plans; and although he would not have liked his inquiries to be either baulked or disclosed, he could yet mentally snap his fingers at Monsieur.

CHAPTER XXVII.

M. VARBARRIERE TALKS A LITTLE MORE FREELY.

AFTER his valet left him, M. Varbarriere did not descend, but remained in his dressing-room, thinking profoundly; and, after a while, he opened his pocket-book, and began to con over a number of figures, and a diagram to which these numbers seemed to refer.

Sometimes standing at the window, at others pacing the floor, and all the time engrossed by a calculation, like a man over a problem in mathematics.

For two or three minutes he had been thus engaged when Guy Strangways entered the room.

'Ho! young gentleman, why don't you read your prayer-book?' said the old man, with solemn waggery.

'I don't understand,' said the young gentleman.

'No, you don't. I am the old sphynx, you see, and some of my riddles I can't make out, even myself. My faith! I have been puzzling my head till it aches over my note-book; and I saw you walking with that old lady, Lady Alice Redcliffe, up and down so affectionately. *There* is another riddle! My faith! the house itself is an enigma. And Sir Jekyl—what do you think of *him*; is he going to marry?'

'To marry!' echoed Guy Strangways.

'Ay, to marry. I do not know, but he is so sly. We must not let him marry, you know; it would be so cruel to poor little Mademoiselle Beatrix—eh?

Guy Strangways looked at him doubtingly.

'He is pretty old, you know, but so am I, and *older*, my faith! But I think he is making eyes at the *married* ladies—eh ?'

'I have not observed—perhaps so,' answered Guy, carelessly. 'He does walk and talk a great deal with that pretty Madame Maberly.'

'Madam Maberly? Bah!' And M. Varbarriere's 'bah' sounded like one of those long sneering slides played sometimes on a deep chord of a double bass. 'No, no, it is that fine woman, Miladi Jane Lennox.'

'Lady Jane! I fancied she did not like him. I mean that she positively *dis*liked him; and to say truth, I never saw, on his part, the slightest disposition to make himself agreeable.'

'I do not judge by words or conduct—in presence of others those are easily controlled; it is when the eyes meet—you can't mistake. Bah! I knew the first evening we arrived. Now, see, you must have your eyes about you, Guy. It is *your* business, not mine. Very important to you, mon petit garçon; of no·sort of imaginable consequence to me, except as your friend; therefore you shall watch and report to me. You understand?'

Guy flushed with a glow of shame and anger, and looked up with gleaming eyes, expecting to meet the deep-set observation of the old man. Had their eyes encountered, perhaps a quarrel would have resulted, and the fates and furies would have had the consequences in their hands; but M. Varbarriere was at the moment reading his attorney's letter again. Guy looked out of the window, and thought resolutely.

'One duplicity I have committed. It is base enough to walk among these people masked; but to be a spy—*never*.'

And he clenched his hand and pressed his foot upon the floor.

It was dreadful to know that these moral impossibilities were expected of him. It was terrible to feel that a rupture with his best, perhaps his only friend, was drawing slowly but surely on; but he was quite resolved. Nothing on earth could tempt him to the degradation of which his kinsman seemed to think so lightly.

Happily, perhaps, for the immediate continuance of their amicable relations, the thoughts of M. Varbarriere had taken a new turn, or rather reverted to the channel from which they had only for a few minutes diverged.

'You were walking with that old woman, Lady Alice Redcliffe. She seemed to talk a great deal. How did she interest you all that time?'

'To say truth, she did *not* interest me all that time. She talked vaguely about family afflictions, and the death of her son; and she looked at me at first as if I were a brigand, and said I was very like some one whom she had lost.'

'Then she's a friendly sort of old woman, at least on certain topics, and garrulous? Who's there? Oh! Jacques; very good, you need not stay.'

The old gentleman was by this time making his toilet.

'Did she happen to mention a person named Gwynn, a house-keeper in her service?'

'No.'

'I'm glad she is an affable old lady; we shall be sure to hear something useful,' said the old gentleman, with an odd smile. 'That housekeeper I must see and sift. They tell me she's im-practicable; *they* found her so. I shall see. While you live, Guy, do your own business; no one else will do it, be sure. I did mine, and I've got on.'

The old gentleman, who was declaiming before the looking-glass in his shirt-sleeves and crimson silk suspenders, brushing up that pyramid of grizzled hair which added to the solemnity of his effect, now got into his black silk waistcoat. The dressing-bell had rung, and the candles had superseded daylight.

'You'll observe all I told you, Guy. Sir Jekyl shan't marry—he would grow what they call impracticable, like Madame Gwynn; Miss Beatrix, *she* shan't marry either—it would make, perhaps, new difficulties; and you, I may as well tell you, *can't* marry her. When you know the reasons you will see that such an event *could not be contemplated*. You understand?'

And he dropped his haircomb, with which he had been bestow-ing a last finish on his spire of hair, upon his dressing-table, with a slight emphasis.

' Therefore, Guy, you will understand you must not be a fool about that young lady ; there are many others to speak to ; and if you allow yourself to like her, you will be a miserable stripling till you forget her.'

' There is no need, sir, to warn me ; I have resolved to avoid any such feeling. I have sense enough to see that there are obstacles insurmountable to my ever cherishing that ambition, and that I never could be regarded as worthy.'

' Bravo ! young man, that is what I like ; you are as modest as the devil ; and *here*, I can tell you, modesty, which is so often silly, is as wise as the serpent. You understand ?'

The large-chested gentleman was now getting into his capacious coat, having buttoned his jewelled wrist-studs in ; so he contemplated himself in the glass, with a touch and a pluck here and there.

' One word more, about that old woman. Talk to her all you please, and let *her* talk—and talk *more* than you, so much the better ; but observe, she will question you about yourself, and your connections, and one word you shall not answer ; observe she learns nothing from you, that is, in the spirit of your solemn promise to me.'

M. Varbarriere had addressed this peremptory reminder over his shoulder, and now retouched his perpendicular cone of hair, which waved upwards like a grey flame.

' Guy, you will be late,' he called over his shoulder. ' Come, my boy ; we must not be walking in with the entremets.'

And he plucked out that huge chased repeater, a Genevan masterpiece, which somehow harmonised with his air of wealth and massiveness, and told him he had but eight minutes left ; and with an injunction to haste, which Guy, with a start, obeyed, this sable and somewhat mountainous figure swayed solemnly from the room.

' Who *is* that Monsieur Varbarriere ?' inquired Lady Alice of her host, as the company began to assemble in the drawing-room, before that gentleman had made his appearance.

' I have not a notion.'

'Are you serious ? No, you're *not* serious,' observed Lady Alice.

'I'm *always* serious when I talk to you.'

'Thank you. I'm sure that is meant for a compliment,' said the old lady, curtly.

'And I assure you I mean what I say,' continued Sir Jekyl, not minding the parenthesis. 'I really don't know, except that he comes from France—rather a large place, you know—*where* he comes from. I have not a notion what his business, calling or trade may be.'

'*Trade!*' replied Lady Alice, with dry dignity.

'Trade, to be sure. *You're* a tradesman yourself, you know— a miner—*I* bought twenty-two shares in that for you in June last; you're an iron ship-builder—you have fifteen in that; you're a 'bus-man—you have ten there; and you were devilish near being a brewer, only it stopped.'

'Don't talk like a fool—a joint-stock company I hope is one thing, and a—a—the other sort of thing quite another, I fancy.'

'You fancy, yes; but it is not. It's a firm—Smith, Brown, Jones, Redcliffe, and Co., omnibus drivers, brewers, and so forth. So if he's not a rival, and doesn't interfere with *your* little trade, I really don't care, my dear little mamma, what sort of shop my friend Varbarriere may keep; but as I said, I don't know; maybe he's too fine a fellow to meddle, like us, with vats and busses.'

'It appears odd that you should know absolutely nothing about your own guests,' remarked Lady Alice.

'Well, it would be odd, only I do,' answered Sir Jekyl—'all one needs to know or ask. He presented his papers, and comes duly accredited—a letter from old Philander the Peer. Do you remember Peery still? I don't mind him; he was always a noodle, though in a question of respectability he's not quite nothing; and another from Bob Charteris—you don't know him— Attaché at Paris; a better or more reliable quarter one could not hear from. I'll let you read them to-morrow; they speak un-

equivocally for his respectability; and I think the inference is
even that he has a soul above 'busses. Here he is.'

M. Varbarriere advanced with the air of a magician about to
conduct a client to his magic mirror, toward Lady Alice, before
whom he made a low bow, having been presented the day before,
and he inquired with a grave concern how she now felt herself,
and expressed with a sonorous suavity his regrets and his hopes.

Lady Alice, having had a good account of him, received him on
the whole very graciously; and being herself a good Frenchwoman,
the conversation flowed on agreeably.

CHAPTER XXVIII.

SOME PRIVATE TALK OF VARBARRIERE AND LADY ALICE AT THE DINNER-TABLE.

AT dinner he was placed beside the old lady. He understood
good cookery, and with him to dine was to analyse and contemplate. He was usually taciturn and absorbed during the process;
but on this occasion he made an effort, and talked a good deal
in a grave, but, as the old lady thought, an agreeable and kindly
vein.

Oddly enough, he led the conversation to his nephew, and found
his companion very ready indeed to listen, as perhaps he had anti-
cipated, and even to question him on this theme with close but
unavowed interest.

'He bears two names which, united, remind me of some of my
bitterest sorrows—Guy was my dear son's Christian name, and
Mr. Strangways was his most particular friend; and there is a
likeness too,' she continued, looking with her dim and clouded
eyes upon Guy at the other side, whom fate had placed beside
Miss Blunket—'a likeness so wonderful as to make me, at times,
quite indescribably nervous; at times it is—how handsome! don't
you consider him wonderfully handsome?—at times the likeness
is so exact as to become all but insupportable.'

She glanced suddenly as she spoke, and saw an expression on the countenance of M. Varbarriere, who looked for no such inspection at that moment, which she neither liked nor understood.

No, it was *not* pleasant, connected with the tone in which she spoke, the grief and the agitation she recounted, and above all with the sad and horrible associations connected indissolubly in her mind with those names and features. It was a face both insincere and mocking — such a countenance as has perhaps shocked us in childhood, when in some grief or lamentation, looking up for sympathy, we behold a face in which lurks a cruel enjoyment, or a sense of an undivulged joke.

Perhaps he read in the old lady's face something of the shock she experienced ; for he said, to cover his indiscretion, 'I was, at the moment, reminded of a strange mistake which once took place in consequence of a likeness. Some of the consequences were tragic, but the rest so ridiculous that I can never call the adventure to mind without feeling the comedy prevail. I was thinking of relating it, but, on recollection, it is too vulgar.'

M. Varbarriere, I am certain, was telling fibs ; but he did it well. He did not hasten to change his countenance, but allowed that expression to possess his features serenely after she had looked, and only shifted it for a grave and honest one when he added—

' You think then, perhaps, that my nephew had formerly the honour of being a companion of Mr. Redcliffe, your son ?'

' Oh, dear, no. He was about Jekyl's age. I dare say I had lost him before that young man was born.'

' Oh! that surprises me very much. Monsieur Redcliffe—your son—is it possible he should have been so much older ?'

' My son's name was Deverell,' said the old lady, sadly.

'Ah! that's very odd. He, Guy, then, had an uncle who had a friend of that name—Guy Deverell—long ago in this country. That is very interesting.'

' *Is* not it ?' repeated Lady Alice, with a gasp. ' I feel, somehow, it must be he—a tall, slight young man.'

'Alas! madam, he is much changed if it be he. He must have been older than your son, madam. He must be, I think, near

sixty now, and grown rather stout.   I've heard him talk at times
of his friend Guy Deverell.'

' And with affection, doubtless.'

' Well, yes, with affection, certainly, and with great indignation of his death—the mode of it.'

'Ah! yes,' said Lady Alice, flushing to the roots of her grey
hair, and looking down on her plate.

Here there was silence for the space of a minute or more.

' Yes, Monsieur Varbarriere; but you know, even though we
cannot always forget, we must forgive.'

' Champagne, my lady ?' inquired the servant over her shoulder.

' *No*, thank you,' murmured Lady Alice.

M. Varbarriere took some and sipped it, wondering how Sir
Jekyl contrived to get such wines, and mentally admitting that
even in the champagne countries it would task him—M. Varbarriere—to find its equal.   And he said—

' Yes, Lady Alice, divine philosophy, but not easy to practise.
I fear it is as hard to do one as the other.'

' And how *is* Mr. Strangways ?' inquired Lady Alice.

They were talking very confidentially and in a low tone, as if
old Strangway's health was the subject of conspiracy.

' Growing old, Lady Alice; he has not spared himself; otherwise well.'

'And this, you say, is his nephew ?' continued the old lady.
' And you ?'

' I am Guy's uncle— his *mother's* brother.'

' And his mother, is *she* living ?'

' No, poor thing! gone long ago.'

Lady Alice looked again unexpectedly into M. Varbarriere's
face, and there detected the same unreliable expression.

' Monsieur Varbarriere,' said old Lady Alice a little sternly in
his ear, 'you will pardon me, but it seems to me that you are
trifling, and not quite sincere in all you tell me.'

In a moment the gravity of all the Chief Justices that ever sat in
England was gathered in his massive face.

' I am shocked, madam, at your thinking me capable of trifling.

How have I showed, I entreat, any evidences of a disposition so contrary to my feelings?'

'I tell you frankly—in your countenance, Monsieur Varbarriere; and I observed it before, Monsieur.'

'Believe me, I entreat, madam, when I assure you, upon the honour of a gentleman, every word I have said is altogether true. Nor would it be easy for me to describe how profound is my sympathy with you.'

From this time forth Lady Alice saw no return of that faint but odious look of banter that had at first shocked and then irritated her; and fortified by the solemn assurance he had given, she fell into a habit of referring it to some association unconnected with herself, and tried to make up for her attack upon him by an increased measure of courtesy.

Dwelling on those subjects that most interested Lady Alice, he and she grew more and more confidential, and she came, before they left the parlour, to entertain a high opinion of both the wisdom and the philanthropy of M. Varbarriere.

CHAPTER XXIX.

THE LADIES AND GENTLEMEN RESUME CONVERSATION IN THE DRAWING-ROOM.

'DIVES, my boy,' said the Baronet, taking his stand beside his brother on the hearth-rug, when the gentlemen had followed the ladies into the drawing-room, and addressing him comfortably over his shoulder, 'the Bishop's coming to-morrow.'

'Ho!' exclaimed Dives, bringing his right shoulder forward, so as nearly to confront his brother. They had both been standing side by side, with their backs, according to the good old graceful English fashion, to the fire.

'Here's his note—came to-night. He'll be here to dinner, I suppose, by the six o'clock fast train to Slowton.'

'Thanks,' said Dives, taking the note and devouring it energetically.

'Just half a dozen lines of three words each—always so, you know. Poor old Sammy! I always liked old Sammy—a good old cock at school he was—great fun, you know, but always a gentleman.'

Sir Jekyl delivered these recollections standing with his hands behind his back, and looking upwards with a smile to the ceiling, as the Rev. Dives Marlowe read carefully every word of the letter.

'Sorry to see his hand begins to shake a little,' said Dives, returning the interesting manuscript.

'Time for it, egad! He's pretty well on, you know. We'll all be shaky a bit before long, Dives.'

'How long does he stay?'

'I think only a day or two. I have his first note up-stairs, if I did not burn it,' answered the Baronet.

'I'm glad I'm to meet him—*very* glad indeed. I think it's five years since I met his lordship at the consecration of the new church of Clopton Friars. I always found him very kind—very. He likes the school-house fellows.'

'You'd better get up your parochial experiences a little, and your theology, eh? They say he expects his people to be alive. You used to be rather good at theology—usen't you?'

Dives smiled.

'Pretty well, Jekyl.'

'And what do you want of him, Dives?'

'Oh! he could be useful to me in fifty ways. I was thinking—you know there's that archdeaconry of Priors,' Dives replied pretty nearly in a whisper.

'By Jove! yes—a capital thing—I forgot it;' and Sir Jekyl laughed heartily.

'Why do you laugh, Jekyl?' he asked a little drily.

'I—I really don't know,' said the Baronet, laughing on.

'I don't see anything absurd or unreasonable in it. That archdeaconry has always been held by some one connected with the county families. Whoever holds it must be fit to associate with the people of that neighbourhood, who won't be intimate, you know, with everybody; and the thing really is little more than a feather, the house and place are expensive, and no one that has not something more than the archdeaconry itself can afford it.'

The conversation was here arrested by a voice which inquired—

'Pray, can you tell me what day General Lennox returns?'

The question was Lady Alice's. She had seemed to be asleep—probably was—and opening her eyes suddenly, had asked it in a hard, dry tone.

'*I?*' said Sir Jekyl. 'I don't know, I protest—may be to-night—may be to-morrow. Come when he may, he's very welcome.'

'You have not heard?' she persisted.

'No, I have not,' he answered, rather tartly, with a smile.

Lady Alice nodded, and raised her voice—

'Lady Jane Lennox, you've heard, no doubt—pray, when does the General return?'

If the scene had not been quite so public, I dare say this innocent little inquiry would have been the signal for one of those keen encounters to which these two fiery spirits were prone.

'He has been detained unexpectedly,' drawled Lady Jane.

'You hear from him constantly?' pursued the old lady.

'Every day.'

'It's odd he does not say when you may look for him,' said Lady Alice.

'Egad, you want to make her jealous, I think,' interposed Sir Jekyl.

'Jealous? Well, I think a young wife may very reasonably be jealous, though not exactly in the vulgar sense, when she is left without a clue to her husband's movements.'

'You said you were going to write to him. I wish you would, Lady Alice,' said the young lady, with an air of some contempt.

'I can't believe he has not said how soon his return may be looked for,' observed the old lady.

'I suppose he'll say whenever he can, and in the meantime I don't intend plaguing him with inquiries he can't answer.' And with these words she leaned back fatigued, and with a fierce glance at Sir Jekyl, who was close by, she added, so loud that I wonder Lady Alice did not hear her—'Why don't you stop that odious old woman?'

'Stop an odious old woman!—why, who ever did? Upon my honour, I know no way but to kill her,' chuckled the Baronet.

Lady Jane deigned no reply.

'Come here, Dives, and sit by me,' croaked the old lady, beckoning him with her thin, long finger. 'I've hardly seen you since I came.'

'Very happy, indeed—very much obliged to you, Lady Alice, for wishing it.'

And the natty but somewhat forbidding-looking Churchman sat himself down in a prie-dieu chair vis-à-vis to the old gentlewoman, and folded his hands, expecting her exordium.

'Do you remember, Sir Harry, your father?'

'Oh, dear, yes. I recollect my poor father very well. We were at Oxford then, or just going. How old was I?—pretty well out of my teens.'

It must be observed that they sat in a confidential proximity—nobody listened—nobody cared to approach.

'You remember when he died, poor man?'

'Yes—poor father!—we were at home—Jekyl and I—for the holidays—I believe it *was*—a month or so. The Bishop, you know, was with him.'

'I know. He's coming to-morrow.'

'Yes; so my brother here just told me—an excellent, exemplary, pious prelate, and a true friend to my poor father. He posted fifty miles—from Doncaster—in four hours and a half, to be with him. And a great comfort he was. I shall never forget it to him.'

'I don't think you cared for your father, Dives; and Jekyl positively disliked him,' interposed Lady Alice agreeably.

'I trust there was no feeling so unchristian and monstrous ever harboured in my brother's breast,' replied Dives, loftily, and with a little flush in his cheeks.

'You can't believe any such thing, my dear Dives; and you

know you did not care if he was at the bottom of the Red Sea, and I don't wonder.'

' Pray don't, Lady Alice. If you think such things, I should prefer not hearing them,' murmured Dives, with clerical dignity.

' And what I want to ask you now is this,' continued Lady Alice; ' you are of course aware that he told the Bishop that he wanted that green chamber, for some reason or another, pulled down ?'

Dives coughed, and said—

' Well, yes, I *have* heard.'

' What was his reason, have you any notion ?'

' He expressed none. My father gave, I believe, no reason. I never heard any,' replied the Reverend Dives Marlowe.

' You may be very sure he had a reason,' continued Lady Alice.

' Yes, very likely.'

' And why is it not done ?' persisted Lady Alice.

' I can no more say why, than you can,' replied Dives.

' But why don't you see to it ?' demanded she.

' See to it! Why, my dear Lady Alice, you must know I have no more power in the matter than Doocey there, or the man in the moon. The house belongs to Jekyl. Suppose you speak to him.'

' You've a tongue in your head, Dives, when you've an object of your own.'

Dives flushed again, and looked, for an apostle, rather forbidding.

' I have not the faintest notion, Lady Alice, to what you allude.'

' Whatever else he may have been, Dives, he was your father,' continued Lady Alice, not diverted by this collateral issue ; ' and as his son, it was and is your business to give Jekyl no rest till he complies with that dying injunction.'

' Jekyl's his own master ; what can I do ?'

' Do as you do where your profit's concerned ; tease him as you would for a good living, if he had it to give.'

' I don't press my interests much upon Jekyl. I've never teased him or anybody else, for anything,' answered Dives, grandly.

'Come, come, Dives Marlowe; you have duties on earth, and something to think of besides yourself.'

'I trust I don't need to be reminded of that, Lady Alice,' said the cleric, with a bow and a repulsive meekness.

'Well, speak to your brother.'

'I *have* alluded to the subject, and an opportunity *may* occur again.'

'*Make* one—make an opportunity, Dives.'

'There are rules, Lady Alice, which we must all observe.'

'Come, come, Dives Marlowe,' said the lady, very tartly, 'remember you're a clergyman.'

'I hope I *do*, madame; and I trust *you* will too.'

And the Rector rose, and with an offended bow, and before she could reply, made a second as stiff, and turned away to the table, where he took up a volume and pretended to read the title.

'Dives,' said the old lady, making no account of his huff, 'please to tell Monsieur Varbarriere that I should be very much obliged if he would afford me a few minutes here, if he is not better engaged; that is, it seems to me he has nothing to do there.'

M. Varbarriere was leaning back in his chair, his hands folded, and the points of his thumbs together; his eyes closed, and his bronzed and heavy features composed, as it seemed, to deep thought; and one of his large shining shoes beating time slowly to the cadences of his ruminations.

The Reverend Dives Marlowe was in no mood just at that moment to be trotted about on that offensive old lady's messages. But it is not permitted to gentlemen, even of his sacred calling, to refuse, in this wise, to make themselves the obedient humble servants of the fair sex, and to tell them to go on their own errands.

Silently he made her a slight bow, secretly resolving to avail himself sparingly of his opportunities of cultivating her society for the future.

Perhaps it was owing to some mesmeric reciprocity; but exactly at this moment M. Varbarriere opened his eyes, arose, and walked towards the fireplace, as if his object had been to contemplate the ornaments over the chimneypiece; and arriving at the hearthrug,, and beholding Lady Alice, he courteously drew near, and accosted her with a deferential gallantry, saving the Reverend Dives Marlowe, who was skirting the other side of the round table, the remainder of his tour.

~~~~~~~~~~

CHAPTER XXX.

VARBARRIERE PICKS UP SOMETHING ABOUT DONICA GWYNN.

DRAWING-ROOM conversation seldom opens like an epic in the thick of the plot, and the introductory portions, however graceful, are seldom worth much. M. Varbarriere and Lady Alice had been talking some two or three minutes, when she made this inquiry.

'When did you last see the elder Mr. Strangways, whom you mentioned at dinner ?'

'Lately, very lately—within this year.'

'Did he seem pretty well ?'

'Perfectly well.'

'What does he think about it all ?'

'I find a difficulty. If Lady Alice Redcliffe will define her question——'

'I mean—well, I should have asked you first, whether he ever talked to you about the affairs of that family—the Deverell family —I mean as they were affected by the loss of a deed. I don't understand these things well; but it involved the loss, they say, of an estate; and then there was the great misfortune of my life.'

M. Varbarriere here made a low and reverential bow of sympathy; he knew she meant the death of her son.

'Upon this latter melancholy subject he entirely sympathises with you. His grief of course has long abated, but his indignation survives.'

'And well it may, sir. And what does he say of the paper that disappeared ?'

'He thinks, madam, that it was stolen.'

'Ha ! So do I.'

The confidential and secret nature of their talk had drawn their heads together, and lowered their voices.

'He thinks it was abstracted by one of the Marlowe family.'

'Which of them?　Go on, sir.'

'Well, by old Sir Harry Marlowe, the father of Sir Jekyl.'

'It certainly *was* he; it could have been no other; it was stolen, that is, I don't suppose by his hand; I don't know, perhaps it was; he was capable of a great deal; *I* say nothing, Monsieur Varbarriere.'

Perhaps that gentleman thought she had said a good deal; but he was as grave on this matter as she.

'You seem, madam, very positive.　May I be permitted to inquire whether you think there exists proof of the fact?'

'I don't speak from proof, sir.'

Lady Alice sat straighter, and looked full in his face for a moment, and said—

'I am talking to you, Monsieur Varbarriere, in a very confidential way.　I have not for ever so many years met a human being who cared, or indeed knew anything of my poor boy as his friend.　I have at length met you, and I open my mind, my conjectures, my suspicions; but, you will understand, in the strictest confidence.'

'I have so understood all you have said, and in the same spirit I have spoken and mean to speak, madam, if you permit me, to you.　I [do feel an interest in that Deverell family, of whom I have heard so much.　There was a servant, a rather superior order of person, who lived as housekeeper—a Mrs. Gwynn—to whom I would gladly have spoken, had chance thrown her in my way, and from whom it was hoped something important might be elicited.'

'She is my housekeeper now,' said Lady Alice.

'Oh! and——'

'I think she's a sensible person; a respectable person, I believe, in her rank of life, although they chose to talk scandal about her; as what young woman who lived in the same house with that vile old man, Sir Harry Marlowe, could escape scandal?　But, poor thing! there was no evidence that ever I could learn; nothing but lies and envy: and she has been a very faithful servant to the family.'

'And is now in your employment, madam ?'

'My housekeeper at Wardlock,' responded Lady Alice.

'Residing there now ?' inquired M. Varbarriere.

Lady Alice nodded assent.

I know not by what subtle evidences, hard to define, seldom if ever remembered, we sometimes come to a knowledge, by what seems an intuition, of other people's intentions. M. Varbarriere was as silent as Lady Alice was; his heavy bronzed features were still, and he looking down on one of those exquisite wreaths of flowers that made the pattern of the carpet; his brown, fattish hands were folded in his lap. He was an image of an indolent reverie.

Perhaps there was something special and sinister in the composure of those large features. Lady Alice's eye rested on his face, and instantly a fear smote her. She would have liked to shake him by the arm, and cry, 'In God's name, do you mean us any harm ?' But it is not permitted even to old ladies such as she to explode in adjuration, and shake up old gentlemen whose countenances may happen to strike them unpleasantly.

As people like to dispel an omen, old Lady Alice wished to disturb the unpleasant pose and shadows of those features. So she spoke to him, and he looked up like his accustomed self.

'You mentioned Mr. Herbert Strangways just now, Monsieur. I forget what relation you said he is to the young gentleman who accompanies you, Mr. Guy Strangways.'

'Uncle, madam.'

'And, pray, does he perceive—did he ever mention a most astonishing likeness in that young person to my poor son ?'

'He has observed a likeness, madam, but never seemed to think it by any means so striking as you describe it. Your being so much moved by it has surprised me.'

Here Lady Alice's old eyes wandered toward the spot where Guy Strangways stood, resting them but a moment; every time she looked so at him, this melancholy likeness struck her with a new force. She sighed and shuddered, and removed her eyes. On looking again at M. Varbarriere, she saw the same slightly truculent shadow over his features, as again he looked drowsily upon the carpet.

She had spent nearly a quarter of a century in impressing her limited audience with the idea that if there were thunderbolts in heaven they ought to fall upon Sir Jekyl Marlow. Yet, now that she saw in that face something like an evil dream, a promise of judgment coming, a feeling of compunction and fear agitated her.

She looked over his stooping shoulders and saw pretty Beatrix leaning on the back of her father's chair, the young lady pleading gaily for some concession, Sir Jekyl laughing her off.

'How pretty she looks to-night—poor Trixie!' said Lady Alice, unconsciously.

M. Varbarriere raised his head, and looked, directed by her gaze, toward father and daughter. But his countenance did not brighten. On the contrary, it grew rather darker, and he looked another way, as if the sight offended him.

'Pretty creature she is—pretty Beatrix!' exclaimed the old lady, looking sadly and fondly across at her.

No response was vouchsafed by M. Varbarriere.

'Don't you think so? Don't you think my granddaughter very lovely?'

Thus directly appealed to, M. Varbarriere conceded the point, but not with effusion.

'Yes, Mademoiselle is charming—she is very charming—but I am not a critic. I have come to that time of life, Lady Alice, at which our admiration of mere youth, with its smooth soft skin and fresh tints, supersedes our appreciation of beauty.'

In making this unsatisfactory compliment, he threw but one careless glance at Beatrix.

'That girl, you know, is heiress of all this—nothing but the title goes to Dives, and the small estate of Grimalston,' said Lady Alice. 'Of course I love my grandchild, but it always seems to me wrong to strip a title of its support, and send down the estates by a different line.

'Miss Beatrix Marlowe has a great deal too much for her own happiness. It is a disproportioned fortune, and in a young lady so sensible will awake suspicions of all her suitors. "You are at my feet, sir," she will think, "but is your worship inspired by love or by avarice ?" She is in the situation of that prince who turned all he touched into gold ; while it feeds the love of money, it starves nature.'

'I don't think it has troubled her head much as yet. If she had no dot whatever, she could not be less conscious,' said the old lady.

'Some people might go through life and never feel it ; and even of those who do, I doubt if there is one who would voluntarily surrender the consequence or the power of exorbitant wealth for the speculative blessing of friends and lovers more sincere. I could quite fancy, notwithstanding, a lady, either wise or sensitive, choosing a life of celibacy in preference to marriage under conditions so suspicious. Miss Marlowe would be a happier woman with only four or five hundred pounds a-year.'

'Well, maybe so,' said the old lady, dubiously, for she knew something of the world as well as of the affections.

'She will not, most likely, give it away; but if it were taken, she would be happier. Few people have nerve for an operation, and yet many are the more comfortable when it is performed.'

'Beatrix has only been out one season, and that but interruptedly. She has been very much admired, though, and I have no doubt will be very suitably married.

'There are disadvantages, however.'

'I don't understand,' said Lady Alice, a little stiffly.

'I mean the tragedy in which Sir Jekyl is implicated,' said M. Varbarriere, rising, and looking, without intending it, so sternly at Lady Alice, that she winced under it.

'Yes, to be sure, but you know the world does not mind that —the world does not choose to believe ill of fortune's minions— at least, to remember it. A few old-fashioned people view it as you and I do; but Jekyl stands very well. It is a wicked world Monsieur Varbarriere.'

'It is not for me to say. Every man has profited, more or less, at one time or another, by its leniency. Perhaps I feel in this particular case more strongly than others; but, notwithstanding the superior rank, wealth, and family of Sir Jekyl Marlowe, I should not, were I his equal, like to be tied to him by a close family connexion.'

Lady Alice did not feel anger, nor was she pleased. She did not look down abashed at discovering that this stranger seemed to resent on so much higher ground than she the death of her son. She compressed her thin lips, looking a little beside the stern gentleman in black, at a distant point on the wall, and appeared to reflect.

CHAPTER XXXI.

LADY JANE PUTS ON HER BRILLIANTS.

THAT evening, by the late post, had arrived a letter, in old General Lennox's hand, to his wife. It had come at dinner time, and it was with a feeling of *ennui* she read the address. It was one of those billets which, in Swift's phrase, would 'have kept cool;' but, subsiding on the ottoman, she opened it—conjugal relations demanded this attention; and Lady Jane, thinking 'what a hand he writes!' ran her eye lazily down those crabbed pages in search of a date to light her to the passage where he announced his return but there was none, so far as she saw.

'What's all this about? "Masterson, the silkmercer at Marlowe—a very"—something—"fellow—*honest*." Yes, that's the word. So he may be, but I shan't buy his horrid trash, if that's what you mean,' said she, crumpling up the stupid old letter, and leaning back, not in the sweetest temper, and with a sidelong glance of lazy defiance through her half-closed lashes, at the unconscious Lady Alice.

And now arrived a sleek-voiced servant, who, bowing beside
Lady Jane, informed her gently that Mr. Masterson had arrived
with the parcel for her ladyship.

'The parcel! what parcel?'

'I'm not aware, my lady.'

'Tell him to give it to my maid. Ridiculous rubbish!' murmured Lady Jane, serenely.

But the man returned.

'Mr. Masterson's direction from the General, please, my lady,
was to give the parcel into your own hands.'

'Where is he?' inquired Lady Jane, with a lofty fierceness.

'In the small breakfast-parlour, my lady.'

'Show me the way, please.'

When Lady Jane Lennox arrived she found Mr. Masterson cloaked
and muffled, as though off a journey, and he explained, that having
met General Lennox yesterday accidentally in Oxford Street, in
London, from whence he had only just returned, he had asked him
to take charge of a parcel, to be delivered into her ladyship's own
hands, where, accordingly, he now placed it.

Lady Jane did not thank him; she was rather conscious of
herself conferring a favour by accepting anything at his hands;
and when he was gone she called her maid, and having reached
her room and lighted her candles, she found a very beautiful set of
diamonds.

'Why, these are really superb, beautiful brilliants!' exclaimed
the handsome young lady. The cloud had quite passed away, and
a beautiful light glowed on her features.

Forthwith to the glass she went, in a charming excitement.

'Light all the candles you can find!' she exclaimed.

'Well, my eyes, but them is beautiful, my lady!' ejaculated the
maid, staring with a smirk, and feeling that at such a moment she
might talk a little, without risk, which, indeed, was true.

So with bed-room and dressing-room candles, and a pair pur-
loined even from old Lady Alice's room, a tolerably satisfactory
illumination was got up, and the jewels did certainly look dazzling.

The pendants flashed in her ears—the exquisite collar round her

beautiful throat—the tiara streamed livid fire over her low Venus-
like forehead, and her eager eyes and parted lips expressed her
almost childlike delight.

There are silver bullets against charmed lives. There are women
from whose snowy breasts the fire-tipped shafts of Cupid fall
quenched and broken; and yet a handful of these brilliant pellets
will find their way through that wintry whiteness, and lie lodged
in her bleeding heart.

After I know not how long a time spent before the glass, it
suddenly struck Lady Jane to inquire of the crumpled letter,
in which the name of Masterson figured, and of whose contents she
knew, in fact, nothing, but that they named no day for the
General's return. She had grown curious as to who the donor
might be. Were those jewels a gift from the General's rich old
sister, who had a splendid suit, she had heard, which she would
never put on again? Had they come as a bequest? How was it,
and whose were they?

And now with these flashing gems still dangling so prettily in
her ears, and spanning her white throat, as she still stood before
the glass, she applied herself to spell out her General's meaning in
better temper than for a long time she had read one of that gallant
foozle's kindly and honest rigmaroles. At first the process was
often interrupted by those glances at the mirror which it is impossible under ordinary circumstances to withhold; but as her
interest deepened she drew the candle nearer, and read very
diligently the stiffly written lines before her.

They showed her that the magnificent present was from himself
alone. I should be afraid to guess how many thousand pounds had
been lavished upon those jewels. An uxurious fogey—a wicked
old fool—perhaps we, outside the domestic circle, may pronounce
him. Lady Jane within that magic ring saw differently.

The brief, blunt, soldier-like affection that accompanied this
magnificent present, and the mention of a little settlement of the
jewels, which made them absolutely hers in case her 'old man'
should die, and the little conjecture 'I wonder whether you would
sometimes miss him?' smote her heart strangely.

'What a gentleman—what an old darling!'—and she—how heinously had she requited his manly but foolish adoration!

'I'll write to him this moment,' she said, quite pale.

And she took the casket in her hands and laid it on her bed, and sat down on the side of it, and trembled very much, and suddenly burst into tears, insomuch that her maid was startled, and yielding forthwith to her sympathy, largely leavened with curiosity, she came and stood by her and administered such consolation as people will who know nothing of your particular grief, and like, perhaps, to discover its causes.

But after a while her mistress asked her impatiently what she meant, and, to her indignation and surprise, ordered her out of the room.

'I wish he had not been so good to me. I wish he had ever been unkind to me. I wish he would beat me. Good heaven! is it all a dream?'

So, quite alone, with one flashing pendant in her ear, with the necklace still on—incoherently, wildly, and affrighted—raved Lady Jane, with a face hectic and wet with tears.

Things appeared to her all on a sudden, quite in a new character, as persons suddenly called on to leave life, see their own doings as they never beheld them before; so with a shock, and an awakening, tumbled about her the whole structure of her illusions, and a dreadful void with a black perspective for the first time opened round her.

She did not return to the drawing-room. When Beatrix, fearing she might be ill, knocked at the door of the green chamber, and heard from the far extremity Lady Jane's clear voice call 'Come in,' she entered. She found her lying in her clothes, with the counterpane thrown partially over her, upon the funereal-looking old bed, whose dark green curtains depended nearly from the ceiling.

'Well?' exclaimed Lady Jane, almost fiercely, rising to her elbow, and staring at Beatrix.

'I—you told me to come in. I'm afraid I mistook.'

'Did I? I dare say. I thought it was my maid. I've got such a bad headache.'

'I'm very sorry. Can I do anything?'

'No, Beatrix—no, thank you; it will go away of itself.'

'I wish so much, Lady Jane, you would allow me to do anything for you. I—I sometimes fear I have offended you. You seemed to like me, I thought, when I saw you this spring in London, and I've been trying to think how I have displeased you.'

'*Displeased* me! *you* displease *me!* Oh! Beatrix, Beatrix, dear, you don't know, you can never know. I—it is a feeling of disgust and despair. I hate myself, and I'm frightened and miserable, and I wish I dare cling to you.'

She looked for a moment as if she would have liked to embrace her, but she turned away and buried her face in her pillow.

'Dear Lady Jane, you must not be so agitated. You certainly are not well,' said Beatrix, close to the bedside, and really a good deal frightened. 'Have you heard—I hope you have not—any ill news?'

If Lady Jane had been dead she could not have seemed to hear her less.

'I hope General Lennox is not ill?' inquired she timidly.

'Ill? No—I don't know; he's very well. I hope he's very well. I hope he is; and—and I know what I wish for myself.'

Beatrix knew what her grandmamma thought of Lady Jane's violence and temper, and she began to think that something must have happened to ruffle it that evening.

'I wish you'd go dear, you *can* do nothing for me,' said Lady Jane, ungraciously, with a sudden and sombre change of manner.

'Well, dear Lady Jane, if you think of anything I can do for you, pray send for me; by-and by you might like me to come and read to you; and would you like me to send your maid?'

'Oh! no—no, no, *no*—nothing—good-night,' repeated Lady Jane, impatiently.

So Beatrix departed, and Lady Jane remained alone in the vast chamber, much more alone than one would be in a smaller one.

CHAPTER XXXII.

CONCILIATION.

THAT night again, old Lady Alice, just settling, and having actually swallowed her drops, was disturbed by a visit from Lady Jane, who stood by her dishevelled, flushed, and with that storm-beaten look which weeping leaves behind it. She looked eager, even imploring, so that Lady Alice challenged her with—

'What on earth, Jane, brings you to my bedside at this hour of the night.'

'I've come to tell you, Lady Alice, that I believe I was wrong the other night to speak to you as I did.'

'I thought, Jane,' replied the old lady with dignity, 'you would come to view your conduct in that light.'

'I thought you were right all the time; that is, I thought you meant kindly. I wished to tell you so,' said Lady Jane.

'I am glad, Jane, you can now speak with temper.'

'And I think you are the only person alive, except poor Lennox, who really cares for me.'

'I knew, Jane, that reflection and conscience would bring you to this form of mind,' said Lady Alice.

'And I think, when I come to say all this to you, you ought not to receive me so.'

'I meant to receive you kindly, Jane; one can't always in a moment forget the pain and humiliation which such scenes produce. It will help me, however, your expressing your regret as you do.'

'Well, I believe I am a fool—I believe I deserve this kind of treatment for lowering myself as I have done. The idea of my coming in here, half dressed, to say all this, and being received in this—in this indescribable way!'

'If you don't feel it, Jane, I'm sorry you should have expressed any sorrow for your misconduct,' replied Lady Alice, loftily.

'Sorrow, madam! I never said a word about sorrow. I said

I thought you cared for me, and I don't think so now. I am sure
you don't, and I care just as little for you, not a pin, madam,
with your ridiculous airs.'

'Very good, dear—then I suppose you are quite satisfied with
your former conduct?'

'Perfectly—of *course* I am, and if I had had a notion what
kind of person you are I should not have come near you, I promise
you.'

Lady Alice smiled a patient smile, which somehow rather provoked the indignant penitent.

'I'd as soon have put my hand in the fire, madam. I've borne
too much from you—a great deal too much; it is you who should
have come to me, madam, and I don't care a farthing about you.'

'And I'm still under sentence, I presume, when General Lennox returns with his horsewhip,' suggested Lady Alice, meekly.

'It would do you nothing but good.'

'You are excessively *impertinent*,' said Lady Alice, a little
losing her self-command.

'So are you, madam.'

'And I desire you'll leave my room,' pursued Lady Alice.

'And don't you address me while we remain in this house,' exclaimed Lady Jane, with flaming cheeks.

'Quit the room!' cried Lady Alice, sitting up with preter-
natural rigidity.

'Open the door!' exclaimed Lady Jane, fiercely, to the scared
maid, 'and carry this candle.'

And the maid heard her mutter forcibly as she marched before
her through the passage—'wicked old frump.'

I am afraid it was one of those cases of incompatibility of temper, or faults on both sides, in which it is, on the whole, more for
the interests of peace and goodwill that people should live apart,
than attempt that process under the same roof.

There was a smoking party that night in Sir Jekyl's room. A
line had reached him from General Lennox, regretting his long
stay in town, and fearing that he could hardly hope to rejoin his
agreeable party at Marlowe before a week or possibly ten days.

But he hoped that they had not yet shot all the birds—and so, with that mild joke and its variations, the letter humorously concluded.

He had also had a letter from the London legal firm—this time the corresponding limb of the body was Crowe—who, in reply to some fresh interrogatories of the Baronet's, wrote to say that his partner, Mr. Pelter, being called to France by legal business connected with Craddock and Maddox, it devolved on him to 'assure Sir Jekyl that, so far as they could ascertain, everything in the matter to which he referred was perfectly quiet, and that no ground existed for apprehending any stir whatsoever.'

These letters from Pelter and Crowe, who were shrewd and by no means sanguine men of business, had always a charming effect on his spirits—not that he quite required them, or that they gave him any new ideas or information, but they were pleasant little fillips, as compliments are to a beauty. He was, therefore, this evening, more than usually lively, and kept the conversation in a very merry amble.

Guy Strangways was absent; but his uncle, M. Varbarriere, was present, and in his solemn, sly, porcine way, enjoyed himself with small exertion and much unction, laughing sometimes sardonically and without noise, at things which did not seem to amuse the others so much; but, in all he said, very courteous, and in his demeanour sauve and bowing. He was the last man to take leave of his host, on the threshold, that night.

'I always lock myself in,' said Sir Jekyl, observing his guest's eye rest for a moment on the key, on which his own finger rested, 'and I can't think why the plague I do,' he added, laughing, 'except that my father did so before me.'

'It makes your pleasant room more a hermitage, and you more of a recluse,' said Monsieur Varbarriere.

'It is very well to be a recluse at pleasure, and take monastic vows of five hours' duration, and shut yourself up from the world, with the key of the world, nevertheless, in your pocket,' said Sir Jekyl.

Monsieur Varbarriere laughed, and somehow lingered, as if he expected more.

'You don't mean that you assert your liberty at capricious hours, and affright your guests in the character of a ghost?' said Monsieur Varbarriere, jocosely.

Sir Jekyl laughed.

'No,' said he, 'on the contrary, I make myself more of a prisoner than you imagine. My man sleeps in the little room in which you now stand, and draws his little camp-bed across the door. I can't tell you the least why I do this, only it was my father's custom also, and I fancy my throat would be cut if my guard did not lie across the threshold. The world is a mad tree, and we are branches, says the Italian proverb. Good-night, Monsieur Varbarriere.'

'Good-night,' said the guest, with a bow and a smile; and both, with a little laugh, shook hands and parted.

Monsieur Varbarriere was a tolerably early riser, and next morning was walking in the cheering morning sun, under the leaves of the evergreens, glittering with dew. A broad walk, wide enough for a pony-carriage, sweeps along a gentle wooded elevation, commanding a wide prospect of that rich country.

He leaned on the low parapet, and with his pocket field-glass lazily swept the broad landscape beneath. Lowering his telescope, he stood erect, and looked about him, when, to his surprise, for he did not think that either was an early riser, he saw Sir Jekyl Marlowe and Lady Jane Lennox walking side by side, and approaching.

Monsieur Varbarriere was blessed with very long and clear sight, for his time of life. There was something in the gait of these two persons, and in the slight gesture that accompanied their conversation, as they approached, which struck M. Varbarriere as indicating excitement though of different kinds.

In the pace of the lady, who carried her head high, with a slight wave sometimes to this side, sometimes to that, was as much of what we term swagger as is compatible with feminine grace. Sometimes a sudden halt, for a moment, and a 'left-face' movement on her companion. Sir Jekyl, on the other hand, bore himself, he thought, like a gentleman, a good deal annoyed and irritated.

All this struck M. Varbarriere in a very few seconds, during which, uncertain whether he ought to come forward or not, he hesitated where he stood.

It was plain, however, that he was quite unobserved standing in the recess of the evergreens; so he leaned once more upon the parapet, and applied his glass to his eye.

Now he was right in his conjecture. This had been a very stormy walk, though the cool grey light of morning is not the season for exciting demonstrations. We will take them up in the midst of their conversation, a little before Monsieur Varbarriere saw them—just as Sir Jekyl said with a slight sneer—

'Oh, of course, it was very kind.'

'More, it's *princely*, sir,' cried Lady Jane.

'Well, princely—very princely—only, pray, dear Jane, do not talk so very loud; you can't possibly wish the keepers and milk-maids to hear every word you say.'

'I don't care, Jekyl. I think you have made me mad.'

'You *are* a bit mad, Jane, but it is not I who made you so.'

'Yes, Jekyl, you've made me mad—you have made me a fiend; but, bad as I am, I can never face that good man more.'

'Now don't—now don't. What *can* be the matter with you?' urged Sir Jekyl in a low tone.

'This, sir—I'll see him no more—you must. You *shall* take me away.'

'Now, now, now—*come!* Are you talking like a sane person, Janet? What the devil can have come over you about these trumpery diamonds?'

'You shan't talk that way.'

'Come! I venture to say they are nothing like as valuable as you fancy, and whatever they are, Lennox got them a devilish good bargain, rely on it. He knows perfectly well what he's about. Everyone knows how rich he is, and the wife of a fellow like that ought to have jewels; people would talk—I give you my honour they would, if you had not; and then he is in town, with nothing to keep him there—no business, I mean—an old military man, and he wants to keep you in good humour.'

'It's a lie. I know what you mean.'

'Upon my soul, it's a fact,' he laughed, looking very pale. 'Surely you don't mistake an old East Indian general for a Joseph!'

'Talk any way but that, you wretch! I know him. It's no use—he's the soul of honour. Oh Jekyl, Jekyl! why did not you marry me when you might, and save me from all this?'

'Now, Janet, *is* this reasonable—you know you never thought of it—you know it would not have done—would you have liked Beatrix? Besides, you have really done better—a great *deal* better—he's not so old as he looks—I dare say not much older than I—and a devilish deal richer, and—a—what the devil you want, for the life of me, I can't see.'

It was about at this point in their conversation that, on a sudden, they came upon Monsieur Varbarriere, looking through his field-glass. Lady Jane moved to turn short about, but Sir Jekyl pressed his arm on hers impatiently, and keep her straight.

<hr />

CHAPTER XXXIII.

LADY JANE AND BEATRIX PLAY AT CROQUET.

'GOOD MORNING, Monsieur Varbarriere,' cried the Baronet, who divined truly that the fattish elderly gentleman with the bronzed features, and in the furred surtout, had observed them.

'Ah!' cried Monsieur Varbarriere, turning toward them genially, his oddly shaped felt hat in one hand, and his field-glass still extended in the other. 'What a charming morning! I have been availing myself of the clear sunlight to study this splendid prospect, partly as a picture, partly as a map.'

Lady Jane with her right hand plucked some wild flowers from the bank, which at that side rises steeply from the walk, while the gentlemen exchanged salutations.

'I've just been pointing out some of our famous places to Lady Jane Lennox. A little higher up the walk the view is much more commanding. What do you say to a walk here after breakfast? There's a capital glass in the hall, much more powerful than that can be. Suppose we come by-and-by?'

'You are very good—I am so obliged—my curiosity has been so very much piqued by all I have seen.'

Monsieur Varbarriere was speaking, as usual, his familiar French, and pointed with his telescope toward a peculiarly shaped remote hillock.

'I have just been conjecturing could that be that Gryston which we passed by on our way to Marlowe.'

'Perfectly right, by Jove! what an eye for locality you must have!'

'Have I? Well, sometimes, perhaps,' said the foreign gentleman, laughing.

'The eye of a general. Yes, you are quite right—it is Gryston.'

Now Sir Jekyl was frank and hearty in his talk; but there was an air—a something which would have excited the observation of Monsieur Varbarriere, even had he remarked nothing peculiar in the bearing of his host and his companion as they approached. There was a semi-abstraction, a covert scrutiny of that gentleman's countenance, and a certain sense of uneasiness.

Some more passed—enough to show that there was nothing in the slightest degree awkward to the two pedestrians in having so unexpectedly fallen into an ambuscade while on their route—and then Sir Jekyl, with a word of apology to Lady Jane, resumed his walk with her towards the pleasure-grounds near the house.

That day Lady Jane played croquet with Beatrix, while Sir Jekyl demonstrated half the country, from the high grounds, to Monsieur Varbarriere.

The croquet-ground is pretty—flower-beds lie round it, and a 'rockery,' as they called it, covered with clambering flowers and plants, and backed by a thick grove of shrubs and evergreens, fenced it in to the north.

Lady Jane was kind, ill-tempered, capricious; played wildly, lazily, badly.

‘ Do you like people in spite of great faults ever, Beatrix ?’ she asked, suddenly.

‘ Every one has great faults,’ said Trixie, sporting a little bit of philosophy.

‘ No, they have not ; there are very good people, and I hate them,’ said Lady Jane, swinging her mallet slowly like a pendulum, and gazing with her dark deep eyes full into her companion’s face.

‘ Hate the good people !’ exclaimed Beatrix ; ‘ then how do you feel towards the bad ?’

‘ There are some whose badness suits me, and I like them; there are others whose badness does not, and them I hate as much as the good almost.’

Trixie was puzzled ; but she concluded that Lady Jane was in one of her odd moods, and venting her ill-temper in those shocking eruptions of levity.

‘ How old are you, Beatrix ?’

‘ Nineteen.’

‘ Ha! and I am five-and-twenty—six years. There is a great deal learned in those six years. I don’t recollect what I was like when I was nineteen.’

She did not sigh; Lady Jane was not given to sighing, but her face looked sad and sullen.

‘ It all came of my having no friend,’ she said, abruptly. ‘ Not one. That stupid old woman might have been one, but she would not. I had no one—it was fate ; and here I am, such as I am, and I don’t blame myself or anything. But I wish I had one true friend.’

‘ I am sure, Lady Jane, you must have many friends,’ said Beatrix.

‘ Don’t be a little hypocrite, Beatrix ; why should I more than another ? Friends are not picked up like daisies as we walk along.

If you have neither mother nor sisters, nor kith nor kin to care about you, you will find it hard to make strangers do so. As for old Lady Alice, I think she always hated me ; she did nothing but pick holes in everything I said or did ; I never heard anything from her but the old story of my faults. And then I was thrown among women of the world—heartless, headless creatures. I don't blame them, they knew no better—perhaps there *is* no better ; but I do blame that egotistical old woman, who, if she had but controlled her temper, might have been of so much use to me, and *would* not. Religion, and good principles, and all that, whether it is true or false, is the safest plan ; and I think if she had been moderately kind and patient, she might have made me as good as others. Don't look at me as if I had two heads, dear. I'm not charging myself with any enormity. I only say it is the happiest way, even if it be the way of fools.'

'Shall we play any more ?' inquired Beatrix, after a sufficient pause had intervened to soften the transition.

'Yes, certainly. Which is my ball ?'

'The red. You are behind your hoop.'

'Yes ; and—and it seems to me, Beatrix, you are a cold little stick, like your grandmamma, as you call her, though she's no grandmamma of yours.'

'Think me as stupid as you please, but you must not think me cold ; and, indeed, you wrong poor old granny.'

'We'll talk no more of her. I think her a fool and a savage. Come, it's your turn, is not it to play ?'

So the play went on for a while in silence, except for those questions and comments without which it can hardly proceed.

'And now you have won, have not you ?' said Lady Jane.

'Should you like another game ?' asked Beatrix.

'Maybe by-and-by ; and — I sometimes wish you liked me, Beatrix ; but I don't know you, and you are little better than a child still ; and—no—it could not be—it never could—you'd be sure to hate me in a little while.'

'But I do like you, Lady Jane. I liked you very much in London, you were so kind ; and I don't know why you were so changed to me when you came here; you seem to have taken a positive dislike to me.'

' So I had, child—I detested you,' said Lady Jane, but in a tone that had something mocking in it. ' Everything has grown —how shall I express it ?—disgusting to me—yes, *disgusting*. You had done nothing to cause it; you need not look so contrite. I could not help it either. I am odious—and I can't love or like anybody.'

' I am sure, Lady Jane, you are not at all like what you describe.'

' You think me faultless, do you ?'

Beatrix smiled.

' Well, I see you don't. What *is* my fault ?' demanded Lady Jane, looking on her not with a playful, but with a lowering countenance.

' It is a very conceited office—pointing out other people's faults, even if one understood them, which I do not.'

' Well, I give you leave; tell me one, to begin with,' persisted Lady Jane Lennox.

Beatrix laughed.

' I wish, Lady Jane, if you insist on my telling your faults, that you would not look so stern.'

' Stern—do I ?' said Lady Jane; ' I did not intend; it was not with you, but myself, that I was angry; not angry either, for my faults have been caused by other people, and to say truth, I don't very much wish to mend them.'

' No, Lady Jane,' said Beatrix, merrily. I won't say in cold blood anything 'disagreeable. I don't say, mind, that I really could tell you any one fault you may fancy you have—but I won't try.'

' Well, let us walk round this oval; I'll tell you what you think. You think I am capricious—and so I may appear—but I am not; on the contrary, my likings or aversions are always on good grounds, and last very long. I don't say people always know the grounds. but they know it is not whim; they know—those that have experienced either—that my love and aversion are both very steady. You think I am ill-tempered, too, but I am not—I am isolated and unhappy ; but my temper is easy to get on with—and I don't know why I am talking to you,' she exclaimed, with a sudden change in her look and tone, ' as if you and I could ever by any possibility become friends. Good-bye, Beatrix ; I see your grandmamma beckoning.'

So she was—leaning upon the arm of her maid, a wan lank figure—motioning her toward her.

' Coming, grandmamma,' cried Beatrix, and smiled, and turning to say a parting word to Lady Jane, she perceived that she was already moving some way off toward the house.

CHAPTER XXXIV.

GENERAL LENNOX RECEIVES A LETTER.

MONSIEUR VARBARRIERE was charmed with his host this morning. Sir Jekyl spent more than an hour in pointing out and illustrating the principal objects in the panorama that spread before and beneath them as they stood with field-glasses scanning the distance, and a very agreeable showman he made.

Very cheery and healthful among the breezy copse to make this sort of rural survey. As they parted in the hall, Monsieur Varbarriere spoke his eloquent appreciation of the beauties of the surrounding country ; and then, having letters to dispatch by the post, he took his leave, and strode up with pounding steps to his dressing-room.

Long before he reached it, his smile had quite subsided, and it was with a solemn and stern countenance that he entered and nodded to his valet, whom he found awaiting him there.

' Well, Jacques, any more offers ? Does Sir Jekyl still wish to engage you ?'

' I can assure Monsieur there has not been a word since upon that affair.'

'*Good!*' said Monsieur Varbarriere, after a second's scrutiny of the valet's dark, smirking visage.

The elderly gentleman unlocked his desk, and taking forth a large envelope, he unfolded the papers enclosed in it.

'Have we anything to note to-day about that apartment verd? Did you manage the measurement of the two recesses?'

'They are three feet and a half wide, two feet and a half deep, and the pier between them is, counting in the carved case, ten feet and six inches; and there is from the angle of the room at each side, that next the window and that opposite, to the angle of the same recesses, counting in, in like manner, the carved case, two feet and six inches exactly. Here monsieur has the threads of measurement,' added Jacques, with a charming bow, handing a little paper, containing certain pieces of tape cut at proper lengths and noted in pen and ink, to his master.

'Were you in the room yourself since?'

'This afternoon I am promised to be again introduced.'

'Try both—particularly that to your right as you stand near the door—and rap them with your knuckles, and search as narrowly as you can.'

Monsieur Jacques bowed low and smiled.

'And now about the other room,' said Monsieur Varbarriere; 'have you had an opportunity?'

'I have enjoyed the permission of visiting it, by the kindness of Sir Jekyl's man.'

'He does not suppose any object?' inquired Monsieur Varbarriere.

'None in the world—nothing—merely the curiosity of seeing everything which is common in persons of my rank.'

Monsieur Varbarriere smiled dimly.

'Well, there is a room opening at the back of Sir Jekyl's room—what is it?'

'His study.'

Varbarriere nodded—'Go on.'

'A room about the same size, surrounded on all sides except the window with books packed on shelves.'

' Where is the door ? '

' There is no door, visible at least, except that by which one enters from Sir Jekyl Marlowe's room,' answered Monsieur Jacques.

' Any sign of a door ? '

Monsieur Jacques smiled a little mysteriously.

' When my friend, Monsieur Tomlinson, Sir Jekyl's gentleman, had left me alone for a few minutes, to look at some old books of travels with engravings, for which I had always a liking, I did use my eyes a little, Monsieur, upon other objects, but could see nothing. Then, with the head of my stick I took the liberty to knock a little upon the shelves, and one place I did find where the books are not real, but made of wood.'

' Made of wood ? ' repeated Monsieur Varbarriere.

' Yes—bound over to imitate the tomes ; and all as old and dingy as the books themselves.'

' You knew by the sound ? '

' Yes, Monsieur, by the sound. I removed, moreover, a real book at the side, and I saw there wood.'

' Whereabout is that in the wall ? '

' Next to the corner, Monsieur, which is formed by the wall in which the windows are set—it is a dark corner, nearly opposite the door by which you enter.'

' That's a door,' said Monsieur Varbarriere, rising deliberately as if he were about to walk through it.

' I think Monsieur conjectures sagely.'

' What more did you see, Jacques ? ' demanded Monsieur Varbarriere, resuming his seat quietly.

' Nothing, Monsieur ; for my good friend returned just then, and occupied my attention otherwise.'

' You did not give him a hint of your discovery ? '

' Not a word, sir.'

' Jacques, you must see that room again, quietly. You are very much interested, you know, in those books of travel. When you have a minute there to yourself again, you will take down in turn every volume at each side of that false bookcase, and search

closely for hinge or bolt—there must be something of the kind—
or keyhole—do you see? Rely upon me, I will not fail to consider the service handsomely. Manage that if possible, to-day.'

'I will do all my possible, Monsieur.'

'I depend upon you, Jacques. Adieu.'

With a low bow and a smirk, Jacques departed.

Monsieur Varbarriere bolted his dressing-room door, and sat
down musing mysteriously before his paper. His large, fattish,
freckled hand hung down over the arm of the low chair, nearly to
the carpet, with his heavy gold pencil-case in its fingers. He
heaved one deep, unconscious sigh, as he leaned back. It was not
that he quailed before any coming crisis. He was not a soft-
hearted or nervous general, and had quite made up his mind.
But he was not without good nature in ordinary cases, and the
page he was about to open was full of terror and bordered all
round with black.

Lady Jane Lennox was at that moment seated also before her
desk, very pale, and writing a few very grateful and humble lines
of thanks to her General—vehement thanks—vehement self-
abasement—such as surprised him quite delightfully. He read
them over and over, smiling with all his might, under his stiff
white moustache, and with a happy moisture in his twinkling grey
eyes, and many a murmured apostrophe, 'Poor little thing—how
pleased she is—poor little Janet!' and resolving how happy they
two should be, and how much sunshine was breaking into their
world.

Monsieur Varbarriere was sitting in deep thought before his
desk.

'Yes, I think I *may*,' was the result of his ruminations.

And in his bold clear hand he indited the following letter, which
we translate :—

Private and Confidential.

Marlowe Manor,—th October, 1849.

General Lennox.

SIR,—I, in the first place, beg you to excuse the apparent presumption of my soliciting a private audience of a gentleman to whom I have the honour to be but so slightly known, and of claiming the protection of an honourable secrecy. The reason of my so doing will be obvious when I say that I have certain circumstances to lay before you which nearly affect your honour. I decline making any detailed statement by letter, nor will I explain my meaning at Marlowe Manor ; but if, without *fracas*, you will give me a private meeting, at any place between this and London, I will make it my business to see you, when I shall satisfy you that I have not made this request without the gravest reasons. May I entreat that your reply may be addressed to me, *poste restante*, Slowton.

> Accept the assurance, &c., &c., &c.,
>   H. VARBARRIERE.

Thus was the angelic messenger, musical with silvery wings, who visited honest General Lennox in his lodgings off Piccadilly, accompanied all the way, in the long flight from Slowton to the London terminus, by a dark spirit of compensation, to appal him with a doubt.

Varbarriere's letter had been posted at Wardlock by his own servant Jacques—a precaution he chose to adopt, as he did not care that anyone at the little town of Marlowe, far less at the Manor, should guess that he had anything on earth to say to General Lennox.

When the two letters reached that old gentleman, he opened Lady Jane's first ; for, as we know, he had arrived at the amorous age, and was impatient to read what his little Jennie had to say; and when he had read it once, he had of course to read it all over again ; then he kissed it and laughed tremulously over it, and was nearer to crying than he would have confessed to anyone— even to her ; and he read it again at the window, where he was seen by seedy Captain Fezzy, who was reading *Bell's Life*, across the street, in the three-pair-of-stairs window, and by Miss Dignum, the proprietress, from the drawing-room, with a countenance so radiant and moved as to interest both spectators from their different points of view.

Thus, with many re-perusals and pleasant castle-buildings, and some airs gently whistled in his reveries, he had nearly forgotten M. Varbarriere's letter.

He was so gratified—he always knew she cared for her old man, little Jennie—she was not demonstrative, all the better perhaps for that; and here, in this delightful letter, so grateful, so sad, so humble, it was all confessed—demonstrated, at last; and old General Lennox thought infinitely better of himself, and far more adoringly of his wife than ever, and was indescribably proud and happy. Hitherto his good angel had had it all his own way; the other spirit was now about to take his turn—touched him on the elbow and presented Monsieur Varbarriere's letter, with a dark smile.

'Near forgetting this, by Jove!' said the old gentleman with the white moustache and eyebrows, taking the letter in his gnarled pink fingers.

'What the devil can the fellow mean? I think he's a fool,' said the General, very pale and stern, when he had read the letter twice through.

If the people at the other side had been studying the transition of human countenance, they would have had a treat in the General's, now again presented at his drawing-room window, where he stood leaning grimly on his knuckles.

Still oftener, and more microscopically, was this letter spelled over than the other.

'It can't possibly refer to Jane. It *can't*. I put that out of my head—*quite*,' said the poor General energetically to himself, with a short wave of his hand like a little sabre-cut in the air.

But what could it be? He had no kinsman near enough in blood to 'affect his honour.' But these French fellows had such queer phrases. The only transaction he could think of was the sale of his black charger in Calcutta for two hundred guineas, to that ill-conditioned fellow, Colonel Bardell, who, he heard, had been grumbling about that bargain, as he did about every other.

'I should not be surprised if he said I cheated him about that horse!'

And he felt quite obliged to Colonel Bardell for affording this hypothesis.

'Yes, Bardell was coming to England—possibly at Marlowe now. He knows Sir Jekyl. Egad, that's the very thing. He's been talking; and this officious old French bourgeois thinks he's doing a devilish polite thing in telling me what a suspected dog I am.'

The General laughed, and breathed a great sigh of relief, and recalled all the cases he could bring up in which fellows had got into scrapes unwittingly about horse-flesh, and how savagely fellows sometimes spoke when they did not like their bargains.

CHAPTER XXXV.

THE BISHOP AT MARLOWE.

So he laboured in favour of his hypothesis with an uneasy sort of success; but, for a few seconds, on one sore point of his heart had there been a pressure, new, utterly agonising, and there remained the sense of contusion.

The General took his hat, and came and walked off briskly into the city a long way, thinking he had business; but when he reached the office, preferring another day—wishing to be back at Marlowe—wishing to see Varbarriere—longing to know the worst.

At last he turned into a city coffee-house, and wrote a reply on a quarto sheet of letter-paper to Monsieur Varbarriere. He was minded first to treat the whole thing with a well-bred contempt, and simply to mention that as he expected soon to be at Marlowe, he would not give Monsieur Varbarriere the trouble of making an appointment elsewhere.

But, seated in his box, he read Monsieur Varbarriere's short letter over again before committing himself, and it struck him that it was *not* an intimation to be trifled with—it had a certain gravity which did not lose its force by frequent reading. The gentleman himself, too—reserved, shrewd, with an odd mixture of the unctuous and the sardonic—his recollection of this person, the writer, came unpleasantly in aid of the serious impression which his letter was calculated to make; and he read again—

'I have certain circumstances to lay before you which nearly affect your honour.'

The words smote his heart again with a tremendous augury; somehow they would not quite fit his hypothesis about the horse, but it might be something else. Was there any lady who might conceive herself jilted? Who could guess what it might be?

Jennie's letter he read then again in his box, with the smell of beef-steaks, the glitter of pewter pots, and the tread of waiters about him.

Yes, it was—he defied the devil himself to question it—an affectionate, loving, grateful letter. And Lady Alice had gone to Marlowe, and was staying there—Lady Alice Redcliffe, that stiff, austere duenna—Jane's kinswoman. He was glad of it, and often thinking of it. But, no—oh!—no—it could not possibly refer to Jane: upon that point he had perfectly made up his mind.

Well, with his pen between his fingers, he considered when he could go, and where he should meet this vulgar Frenchman. He could not leave London to-morrow, nor next day, and the day following he had to give evidence on the question of compensation to that native prince, and so on; so at last he wrote, naming the nearest day he could command, and requesting, in a postscript which he opened the letter to add, that Monsieur Varbarriere would be so very good as to let him know a little more distinctly to what specific subject his letter referred, as he had in vain taxed his recollection for the slightest clue to his meaning; and although he was perfectly satisfied that he could not have the smallest difficulty in clearing up anything that could possibly be alleged against him as a soldier or a gentleman—having, he thanked

Heaven, accomplished his career with honour—he yet could not feel quite comfortable until he heard something more explicit.

As the General, with this letter in his pocket, was hurrying to the post-office, the party at Marlowe were admiring a glorious sunset, and Monsieur Varbarriere was describing to Lady Jane Lennox some gorgeous effects of sunlight which he had witnessed from Lisbon on the horizon of the Atlantic.

The bishop had already arrived, and was in his dressing-room, and Dives was more silent and thoughtful than usual.

Yes, the Bishop had arrived. He was venerable, dignified, dapper, with, for his time of life, a wonderfully shapely leg in his black silk stocking. There was in his manner and tones that suavity which reminds one at the same time of heaven and the House of Lords. He did not laugh. He smiled and bowed sometimes. There was a classical flavour in his conversation with gentlemen, and he sometimes conversed with ladies, his leg crossed horizontally, the ankle resting on his knee, while he mildly stroked the shapely limb I have mentioned, and murmured well-bred Christianity, to which, as well as to his secular narratives, the ladies listened respectfully.

Don't suppose he was a hypocrite or a Pharisee. He was as honest as most men, and better than many Christians. He was a bachelor, and wealthy; but if he had amassed a good deal of public money, he had also displayed a good deal of public spirit, and had done many princely and even some kind actions. His family were not presentable, making a livelihood by unmentionable practices, such as shopkeeping and the like. Still he cut them with moderation, having maintained affable though clandestine relations with his two maiden aunts, who lived and died in Thames Street, and having twice assisted a nephew, though he declined seeing him, who was a skipper of a Russian brig.

He was a little High-Church. But though a disciplinarian in ecclesiastical matters, and with notions about self-mortification, his rule as master of the great school he had once governed had been kindly and popular as well as firm. I do not know exactly what interest got him his bishopric. Perhaps it was his reputation only;

and that he was thinking of duty, and his fasts, and waked in his cell one morning with a mitre on instead of his night-cap. The Trappist, mayhap, in digging his grave had lighted on a pot of gold.

'I had no idea,' exclaimed Miss Blunket, when the Bishop's apron and silk stockings had moved with the Rev. Dives Marlowe to the opposite extremity of the drawing-room, where the attentive Rector was soon deep in demonstrations, which evidently interested the right reverend prelate much, drawn from some manuscript notes of an ancestor of Dives's who had filled that see, which had long known him no more, and where he had been sharp in his day in looking up obscure rights and neglected revenues.

'I had no idea the Bishop was so young; he's by *no means* an old-looking man ; and so very admirable a prelate—is not he ?'

'He has neglected one of St. Paul's conditions though,' said Sir Jekyl; 'but you will not think the worse of him for that. It may be mended, you know.'

'What's that ?' inquired Miss Blunket.

'Why, he's not the husband of one wife.'

'Nonsense, you wretch!' cried Miss Blunket, with a giggle, jerking a violet which she was twiddling between her fingers at the Baronet.

'He has written a great deal, has not he ?' continued Miss Blunket. 'His tract on mortification has gone to fifteen thousand copies, I see by the newspaper.'

'I wonder he has never married,' interposed Lady Blunket, drowsily, with her usual attention to the context.

'I wonder he never tried it as a species of mortification,' suggested Sir Jekyl.

'You horrid Vandal! Do you hear him, mamma ?' exclaimed Miss Blunket.

Lady Blunket rather testily—for she neither heard nor understood very well, and her daughter's voice was shrill—asked—

'*What* is it ? You are always making mountains of molehills, my dear, and *startling* one.'

Old Lady Alice Redcliffe's entrance at this moment made a

diversion. She entered, tall, grey, and shaky, leaning on the arm of pretty Beatrix, and was encountered near the door by the right reverend prelate, who greeted her with a dignified and apostolic gallantry, which contrasted finely with Sir Jekyl's jaunty and hilarious salutation.

The Bishop was very much changed since she had seen him last. He, no doubt, thought the same of her. Neither intimated this little reflection to the other. Each estimated, with something of wonder and pity, the other's decay, and neither appropriated the lesson.

'I dare say you think me very much altered,' said Lady Alice, so soon as she had made herself comfortable on the ottoman.

' I was about putting the same inquiry of myself, Lady Alice; but, alas! why should we? "Never continueth in one stay," you know; change is the universal law, and the greatest, last.'

The excellent prelate delivered this *ex cathedrâ*, as an immortal to a mortal. It was his duty to impress old Lady Alice, and he courteously included himself, being a modest priest, who talked of sin and death as if bishops were equally subject to them with other men.

<hr>

CHAPTER XXXVI.

OLD SCENES RECALLED.

AT dinner the prelate, who sat beside Lady Alice, conversed in the same condescending spirit, and with the same dignified humility, upon all sorts of subjects—upon the new sect, the Huggletonians, whom, with doubtful originality, but considerable emphasis, he likened to 'lost sheep.'

' Who's lost his sheep, my lord?' inquired Sir Paul Blunket across the table.

'I spoke metaphorically, Sir Paul. The Huggletonians, the sheep who should have been led by the waters of comfort, have been suffered to stray into the wilderness.'

' Quite so—I see. Shocking name that—the Huggletonians. I should not like to be a Huggletonian, egad!' said Sir Paul Blunket, and drank some wine. ' Lost sheep, to be sure—yes; but that thing of bringing sheep to water—you see—it's a mistake. When a wether takes to drinking water, it's a sign he's got the rot.'

The Bishop gently declined his head, and patiently allowed this little observation to blow over.

Sir Paul Blunket, having delivered it, merely added, after a decent pause, as he ate his dinner—

' Dartbroke mutton this—five years old—eh ?'

' Yes. I hope you like it,' answered his host.

Sir Paul Blunket, having a bit in his mouth, grunted politely—

' Only for your own table, though ?' he added, when he'd swallowed it.

' That's all,' answered Sir Jekyl.

' Never pay at market, you know,' said Sir Paul Blunket.　' I consider any sheep kept beyond two years as lost.'

' A lost sheep, and sell him as a Huggletonian,' rejoined Sir Jekyl.

' It is twenty years,' murmured the Bishop in Lady Alice's ear, for he preferred not hearing that kind of joke, ' since I sate in this parlour.'

' Ha !' sighed Lady Alice.

' Long *before* that I used, in poor Sir Harry's time, to be here a good deal—a hospitable, kind man, in the main.'

' I never liked him,' croaked Lady Alice, and wiped her mouth.

They sat so very close to Sir Jekyl that the Bishop merely uttered a mild ejaculation, and bowed toward his plate.

' The arrangements of this room—the portraits—are just what I remember them.'

' Yes, and you were here—let me see—just thirty years since, when Sir Harry died—weren't you ?'

' So I was, my dear Lady Alice—very true,' replied the Bishop in his most subdued tones, and he threw his head back a little, and nearly closed his eyes; and she fancied he meant, in a dignified way, to say, 'I should prefer not speaking of those particular recollections while we sit so near our host.' The old lady was much of the same mind, and said to him quietly—

'I'll ask you a few questions by-and-bye. You remember Donica Gwynn. She's living with me now—the housekeeper, you know.'

'Yes, perfectly, a very nice-looking quiet young woman—how is she?'

'A dried-up old woman now, but very well,' said Lady Alice.

'Yes, to be sure; she must be elderly now,' said he, hastily; and the Bishop mentally made up one of those little sums in addition, the result of which surprises us sometimes in our elderly days so oddly.

When the party transferred themselves to the drawing-room, Lady Alice failed to secure the Bishop, who was seized by the Rev. Dives Marlowe and carried into a recess—Sir Jekyl having given his clerical brother the key of a cabinet in which were deposited more of the memoranda, and a handsome collection of the official and legal correspondence of that episcopal ancestor whose agreeable MSS. had interested the Bishop so much before dinner.

Jekyl, indeed, was a good-natured brother. As a match-making mother will get the proper persons under the same roof, he had managed this little meeting at Marlowe. When the ladies went away to the drawing-room, he had cried—

'Dives, I want you here for a moment,' and so he placed him on the chair which Lady Jane Lennox had occupied beside him, and what was more to the purpose, beside the Bishop; and, as Dives was a good scholar, well made up on controversies, with a very pretty notion of ecclesiastical law and a turn for Latin verse, he and the prelate were soon in a state of very happy and intimate confidence. This cabinet, too, was what the game of chess is to the lovers—a great opportunity—a seclusion; and Dives, knowing all about the papers, was enabled really to interest the Bishop very keenly.

So Lady Alice, who wanted to talk with him, was doomed to a jealous isolation, until that friend, of whom she was gradually coming to think very highly indeed, Monsieur Varbarriere, drew near, and they fell into conversation, first on the recent railway collision, and then on the fruit and flower show, and next upon the Bishop.

They both agreed what a charming and venerable person he was, and then Lady Alice said—

'Sir Harry Marlowe, I told you—the father, you know, of Jekyl there,' and she dropped her voice as she named him, 'was in possession at the time when the deed affecting my beloved son's rights was lost.'

'Yes, madame.'

'And it was the Bishop there who attended him on his death-bed.'

'Ho!' exclaimed M. Varbarriere, looking more curiously for a moment at that dapper little gentleman in the silk apron.

'They said he heard a great deal from poor wretched Sir Harry. I have never had an opportunity of asking him in private about it, but I mean to-morrow, please Heaven.'

'It may be, madame, in the highest degree important,' said Monsieur Varbarriere, emphatically.

'How can it be? My son is dead.'

'Your son is'——and M. Varbarriere, who was speaking sternly and with a pallid face, like a man deeply excited, suddenly checked himself, and said—

'Yes, very true, your son is dead. Yes, madame, he is dead.'

Old Lady Alice looked at him with a bewildered and frightened gaze.

'In Heaven's name, sir, what do you mean?'

'Mean—mean—why, what have I said?' exclaimed Monsieur Varbarriere, very tartly, and looking still more uncomfortable.

'I did not say you had said anything, but you do mean something.'

'No, madame, I *forgot* something; the tragedy to which you referred is not to be supposed to be always as present to the mind of another as it naturally is to your own. We forget in a moment

of surprise many things of which at another time we need not to
be reminded, and so it happened with me.'

Monsieur Varbarriere stood up and fiddled with his gold double
eye-glasses, and seemed for a while disposed to add more on that
theme, but, after a pause, said—

' And so it was to the *Bishop* that Sir Harry Marlowe communicated his dying wish that the green chamber should be shut
up ?'

' Yes, to him ; and I have heard that more passed than is suspected, but of that I know nothing; only I mean to put the
question to him directly, when next I can see him alone.'

Monsieur Varbarriere again looked with a curious scrutiny at
the Bishop, and then he inquired—

' He is a prelate, no doubt, who enjoys a high reputation for
integrity ?'

' This I know, that he would not for worlds utter an untruth,'
replied Lady Alice.

' What a charming person is Lady Jane Lennox !' exclaimed
Monsieur Varbarriere, suddenly diverging.

' H'm ! do you think so ? Well, yes, she *is* very much admired.'

' It is not often you see a pair so unequal in years so affectionately attached,' said Monsieur Varbarriere.

' I have never seen her husband, and I can't, therefore, say how
they get on together ; but I'm glad to hear you say so. Jane has
a temper, you know, which *every* one might not get on with ; that
is,' she added, fearing lest she had gone a little too far, ' sometimes it is not quite pleasant.'

' No doubt she was much admired and much pursued,' observed
Varbarriere.

' Yes, I said she was admired,' answered Lady Alice, drily.

' How charming she looks, reading her book at this moment !'
exclaimed Varbarriere.

She was leaning back on an ottoman, with a book in her hand ;
her rich wavy hair, her jewels and splendid dress, her beautiful
braceleted arms, and exquisitely haughty features, and a certain

negligence in her *pose*, recalled some of those voluptuous portraits of the beauties of the Court of Charles II.

Sir Jekyl was seated on the other side of the cushioned circle, leaning a little across, and talking volubly, and, as it seemed, earnestly. It is one of those groups in which, marking the silence of the lady and the serious earnestness of her companion, and the flush of both countenances, one concludes, if there be nothing to forbid, that the talk is at least romantic.

Lady Alice was reserved, however; she merely said—

'Yes, Jane looks very well; she's always well got up.'

Monsieur Varbarriere saw her glance with a shrewd little frown of scrutiny at the Baronet and Lady Jane, and he knew what was passing in her mind; she, too, suspected what was in his, for she glanced at him, and their eyes met for a moment and were averted. Each knew what the other was thinking; so Lady Alice said—

'For an old gentleman, Sir Jekyl is the most romantic I know; when he has had his wine, I think he'd flirt with any woman alive. I dare say he's boring poor Jane to death, if we knew but all. She can't read her book. I assure you I've seen him, when nobody better was to be had, making love to old Susan Blunket— Miss Blunket there—after dinner, of course: and by the time he has played his rubber of whist he's quite a sane man, and continues so until he comes in after dinner next evening. We all know Jekyl, and never mind him.'

Having thus spoken, she asked Monsieur Varbarriere whether he intended a long stay in England, and a variety of similar questions.

CHAPTER XXXVII.

IN WHICH LADY ALICE PUMPS THE BISHOP.

LADY JANE LENNOX, who complained of a headache, departed early for her room. The Baronet's passion for whist returned, and he played with more than his usual spirit and hilarity; Monsieur

Varbarriere, his partner, was also in great force, and made some
very creditable sallies between the deals.   All went, in fact, merry
as a marriage-bell.   But in that marriage-bell booms unmarked
the selfsame tone which thrills in the funeral-knell.   There was
its somewhat of bitter rising probably in each merry soul in that
gay room.   Black care walked silently among those smiling
guests, and on an unseen salver presented to each his sprig of rue
or rosemary.   Another figure also, lank, obsequious, smirking
dolorously, arrayed in the Marlowe livery, came in with a bow,
and stood with an hour-glass in his long yellow claw at the back
of Sir Jekyl's chair; you might see the faint lights of his hollow
eyes reflected on the Baronet's cards.

'A little chilly to-night, is not it?' said Sir Jekyl, and shook
his shoulders.   'Have we quite light enough, do you think?'

In that serene company there were two hearts specially sore,
each with a totally different anguish.

In Lady Alice's old ears continually beat these words, 'Your
son is——' ending, like an interrupted dream, in nothing.   Before
her eyes was Varbarriere's disturbed countenance as he dropped
the curtain over his meaning, and affected to have forgotten the
death of Guy Deverell.

'Your son is——' Merciful Heaven! could he have meant
living?

Could that shape she had seen in its coffin, with the small blue
mark in its serene forehead, where the bullet had entered, been a
simulacrum—not her son—a cast—a fraud?

Her reason told her loudly such a thought was mere insanity;
and yet what could that sudden break in Varbarriere's sentence
have been meant to conceal, and what did that recoiling look
imply?

'Your son is——' It was for ever going on.   She knew there
was something to tell, something of which M. Varbarriere was
thoroughly cognisant, and about which nothing could ever induce
him to open his lips.

If it was not 'your son is living,' she cared not what else it
might be, and *that*—could it?—no, it could not be.   A slight

hectic touched each thin cheek, otherwise she looked as usual. But as she gazed dreamily over the fender, with clouded eyes, her temples were throbbing, and she felt sometimes quite wild, and ready to start to her feet and adjure that awful whist-player to disclose all he knew about her dead boy.

Beatrix was that evening seated near the fireplace, and Drayton making himself agreeable, with as small trouble as possible to himself. Drayton! Well, he was rather amusing—cleverish— well enough up upon those subjects which are generally supposed to interest young ladies; and, with an affectation of not caring really exerting himself to be entertaining. Did he succeed? If you were to judge by her animated looks and tones, you would have said very decidedly. Drayton's self-love was in a state of comfort, even of luxury, that evening. But was there anything in the triumph?

A pale face, at the farther end of the room, with a pair of large, dark, romantic eyes, a face that had grown melancholy of late, she saw every moment, though she had not once looked in that direction all the evening.

As Drayton saw her smile at his sallies, with bright eyes and heightened colour, leaning back in her cushioned chair, and looking under her long lashes into the empty palm of her pretty hand, he could not see that little portrait—painted on air with the colours of memory—that lay there like a locket;—neither his nor any other eyes, but hers alone.

Guy Strangways was at the farther end of the room, where were congregated Lady Blunket and her charming daughter, and that pretty Mrs. Maberly of whom we have spoken; and little Linnett, mounted straddlewise on his chair, leaning with his elbows on the back, and his chin on his knuckles, helped to entertain them with his inexhaustible agreeabilities. Guy Strangways had indeed very little cast upon him, for Linnett was garrulous and cheerful, and reinforced beside by help from other cheery spirits.

Here was Guy Strangways undergoing the isolation to which he had condemned himself; and over there, engrossed by Drayton, the lady whose peer he had never seen. Had she missed him? He saw no sign. Not once even casually had she looked in his direction; and how often, though she could not know it, had his eyes wandered toward her! Dull to him was the hour without her, and she was engrossed by another, who, selfish and shallow, was merely amusing himself and pleasing his vanity.

How is it that people in love see so well without eyes? Beatrix saw without a glance, exactly where Guy Strangways was. She was piqued and proud, and chose perhaps to show him how little he was missed. It was his presence, though he suspected it so little, that sustained that animation which he resented; and had *he* left the room, Drayton would have found, all at once, that she was tired.

Next day was genial and warm, one of those days that bygone summer sometimes gives us back from the past to the wintry close of autumn, as in an old face that we love we sometimes see a look transitory and how pathetic, of the youth we remember. Such days, howsoever pleasant, come touched with the melancholy of a souvenir. And perhaps the slanting amber light nowhere touched two figures more in harmony with its tone than those who now sat side by side on the rustic seat, under the two beech trees at the farther end of the pleasure-ground of Marlowe.

Old Lady Alice, with her cushions disposed about her, and her cloaks and shawls, had one arm of the seat; and the Bishop, gaitered and prudently buttoned up in a surtout of the finest black cloth, and with that grotesque (bequeathed of course by the Apostles) shovel-hat upon his silvery head, leaned back upon the other, and, with his dapper leg crossed, and showing the neat sole of his shoe to Lady Alice, stroked and patted, after his wont, the side of his calf.

'Upwards of three-and-thirty years,' said the Bishop.

'Yes, about that—about three-and-thirty years; and what did you think of him? A very bad man, I'm sure.'

'Madam, *de mortuis*. We have a saying, " concerning the dead, nothing but good." '

'Nothing but *truth*, say I,' answered Lady Alice. 'Praise can do them no good, and falsehood will do us a great deal of harm.'

'You put the point strongly, Lady Alice ; but when it is said, "nothing but good," we mean, of course, nothing but the good we may *truly* speak of them.'

'And that, as you know, my lord, in his case was not much. You were with him to the moment of his death—nearly a week, was it not ?'

'Three days precisely.'

'Did he know from the first he was dying ?' inquired Lady Alice.

'He was not aware that his situation was desperate until the end of the second day. Nor was it ; but he knew he was in danger, and was very much agitated, poor man ; very anxious to live and lead a better life.'

'And you prayed with him ?'

'Yes, yes; he was very much agitated, though ; and it was not easy to fix his thoughts, poor Sir Harry! It was very sad. He held my hand in his—my hand—all the time I sat by the bed, saying, "Don't you think I'll get over it ?—I feel that I shall—I feel quite safe while I hold your hand." I never felt a hand tremble as his did.

'You prayed for him, and read with him ?' said Lady Alice. 'And you acted, beside, as his confessor, did not you, and heard some revelation he had to make ?'

'You forget, my dear Lady Alice, that the office of confessor is unknown to the Church. It is not according to our theory to extract a specific declaration of particular sins.'

'H'm! I remember they told me that you refused at school to read the Absolution to the boys of your house until they had made confession and pointed out an offender they were concealing.'

The Bishop hemmed and slightly coloured. It might have amused an indifferent auditor to see that eminent and ancient divine taken to task, and made even to look a little foolish, by this old woman, and pushed into a corner, as a wild young curate might be by him on a question of Church doctrine.

'Why, as to that, the fact may be so; but it was under very special circumstances, Lady Alice. The Church refuses even the Sacrament of the Lord's Supper to an intending communicant who is known to be living in wilful sin; and here was a wilful concealment of a grave offence, to which all had thus made themselves, and were continuing to make themselves, accessory. It is, I allow, a doubtful question, and I do not say I should be prepared to adopt that measure now. The great Martin Luther has spoken well and luminously on the fallacy of taking his convictions at any one period of his life as the measure of his doctrine at a later one. The grain of mustard-seed, the law of perpetual expansion and development, applies to faith as well as to motive and action, to the Christian as a spiritual individual as well as to the Church as an aggregate.'

This apology for his faith did the Right Reverend the Lord Bishop of Queen's Copely urge in his citation before old Lady Alice Redcliffe, whom one would have thought he might have afforded to despise in a Christian way; but for wise purposes the instincts of self-defence and self-esteem, and a jealousy of even our smallest neighbour's opinion, is so deeply implanted, that we are ready to say a good word for ourselves to anyone who misconceives the perfect wisdom of our words, or the equally perfect purity of our motives.

CHAPTER XXXVIII.

LADY ALICE AND VARBARRIERE TÈTE-À-TÊTE IN THE LIBRARY.

'WELL, he told you something, did not he?' persisted Lady Alice.

'In the sense of a distinct disclosure, nothing,' said the Bishop, looking demurely over his horizontal leg on the neatly-shorn grass. 'He did speak to me upon subjects—his wishes, and I have no doubt he intended to have been much more explicit. In fact, he intimated as much; but he was overtaken by death—unable to speak when I saw him next morning.'

'He spoke to you, I know, about pulling down or blowing up that green chamber,' said Lady Alice, whose recollections grew a little violent in proportion to the Bishop's reserve and her own impatience.

'He did not suggest quite such strong measures, but he did regret that it had ever been built, and made me promise to urge upon his son, as you once before mentioned you were aware, so soon as he should come of age, to shut it up.

'And you did urge him?'

'Certainly, Lady Alice,' said the Bishop, with dignity. 'I viewed it in the light of a duty, and a very sacred one, to do so.'

'He told you the reason, then?' inquired Lady Alice.

'He gave me no reason on earth for his wish; perhaps, had he been spared for another day, he would have done so; but he expressed himself strongly indeed, with a kind of horror, and spoke of the Italian who built, and his father who ordered it, in terms of strong disapprobation, and wished frequently it had never been erected. Perhaps you would like to take a little turn. How very pretty the flowers still are!'

'Very. No, thank you, I'll sit a little. And there was something more. I know perfectly there was, my lord; what was it, pray?' answered the old lady.

'It was merely something that I took charge of,' said the Bishop, cautiously.

'You need not be so reserved with me, my lord; I'm not, as you very well know, a talking old woman, by any means. I know something of the matter already, and have never talked about it; and as the late Lady Marlowe was my poor daughter by marriage, you may talk to me, I should hope, a little more freely than to a total stranger.'

The Bishop, I fancy, thought there was something in this appeal, and was, perhaps, amused at the persistency of women, for he smiled sadly for a second or two on his gaiter, and he said, looking before him with his head a little on one side—

' You give me credit, my dear Lady Alice, for a great deal more reserve than I have, at least on this occasion, exercised. I have very little to disclose, and I am not forbidden by any promise, implied or direct, to tell you the very little I know.'

He paused.

' Well, my lord, *pray* go on,' insisted Lady Alice.

' Yes, on the whole,' said the Bishop, thoughtfully, ' I prefer telling you. In the room in which he died, in this house, there is, or was, a sort of lock-up place.'

' That was the room in which Jekyl now sleeps,' interrupted Lady Alice.

' I am not aware.'

' The room at the extreme back of the house. You go through a long passage on the same level as the hall, and then, at the head of the far back-stair, into a small room on your left, and through that into the bedroom, I mean. It was there, I know, his coffin lay, for I saw him in it.'

' As well as I recollect, that must have been the room. I know it lay as you describe. He gave me some keys that were placed with his purse under his pillow, and directed me to open the press, and take out a box, resembling a small oak plate-chest, which I did, and, by his direction, having unlocked it, I took out a very little trunk-shaped box, covered with stamped red leather, and he took it from me, and the keys, and that time said no more.'

' Well ?'

' In the evening, when I returned, he said he had been thinking about it, and wished to place it and the key in my care, as his boy was not of age, and it contained something, the value of which, as I understood, might be overlooked, and the box mislaid. His direction to me was to give it to his son, the present Sir Jekyl, on his coming of age, and to tell him from him that he was to do what was right with it. I know those were his words, for he was exhausted, and not speaking very distinctly; and I repeated them carefully after him, and as he said, " correctly;" after a short time he added, " I think I shall tell you more about it to-morrow;" but, as I told you, he was unable to speak next morning.'

' And what did that red box contain ?' asked Lady Alice.

' I can't tell. I never unlocked it. I tied it round with a tape and sealed it, and so it remained.'

' Then, Jekyl got it when he came of age ?'

' I had him, about that time, at my house. He examined the box, and, when he had satisfied himself as to its contents, he secured it again with his own seal, and requested me to keep it for him for some short time longer.'

' Have you got it still in your possession ?'

' No. I thought it best to insist at last on his taking it into his own keeping. I've brought it with me here—and I gave it to him on the day of my arrival.'

' Very heavy, was it ?'

' On the contrary, very light.'

' H'm ! Thank you, my lord; it is very good of you to converse so long with an old woman such as I.'

' On the contrary, Lady Alice, I am much obliged to you. The fact is, I believe it is better to have mentioned these circumstances. It may, perhaps, prove important that some member of the family should know exactly what took place between me and the late Sir Harry Marlowe during his last illness. You now know everything. I have reminded him, as I thought it right, of the earnest injunction of his father, first with respect to that room, the green chamber; and he tells me that he means to comply with it when his party shall have broken up. And about the other matter, the small box, I mentioned that he should do what is right with it. He asked me if I had seen what the box contained; and on my saying no, he added that he could not tell what his father meant by telling him to do what was right with it—in fact, that he could do nothing with it.'

' Quite an Italian evening !' exclaimed the Bishop, after a pause, rising, and offering his arm to Lady Alice.

And so their conference ended.

Next day, contrary to her secluded custom, and for the first time, Lady Alice glided feebly into the new library of Marlowe, of which all the guests were free.

Quite empty, except of that silent company in Russia leather and gold, in vellum, and other fine suits; all so unobtrusive and quiet; all so obsequiously at her service; all ready to speak their best, their brightest, and wisest thoughts, or to be silent and neglected, and yet never affronted; always alert to serve and speak, or lie quiet.

Quite deserted! No, not quite. There, more than half hidden by that projection and carved oak pilaster, sate Monsieur Varbarriere, in an easy-chair and a pair of gold spectacles, reading easily his vellum quarto.

'Pretty room!' exclaimed Lady Alice in soliloquy, so soon as she had detected the corpulent and grave student.

Monsieur Varbarriere laid down his book with a look of weariness, and seeing Lady Alice, smiled benignly, and rose and bowed, and his sonorous bass tones greeted her courteously from the nook in which he stood framed in oak, like a portrait of a rich and mysterious burgomaster.

'What a pretty room!' repeated the old lady; 'I believe we are *tête-à-tête*.'

'Quite so; I have been totally alone; a most agreeable surprise, Lady Alice. Books are very good company; but even the best won't do always; and I was beginning to weary of mine.'

M. Varbarriere spoke French, so did Lady Alice; in fact, for that gentleman's convenience, all conversations with him in that house were conducted in the same courtly language.

Lady Alice looked round the room to satisfy herself that they were really alone; and having made her commendatory criticisms on the apartment once more,

'Very pretty,' echoed Monsieur Varbarriere; 'I admire the oak, especially in a library, it is so solemn and contemplative. The Bishop was here to-day, and admired the room very much. An agreeable and good man the Bishop appears to be.'

'Yes; a good man; an excellent man. I had a very interesting conversation with him yesterday. I may as well tell you,

Monsieur Varbarriere—I know I may rely upon you—I have not
come to my time of life without knowing pretty well, by a kind of
instinct, whom I may trust; and I well know how you sympathise
with me about my lost son.'

'Profoundly, madame;' and Monsieur Varbarriere, with his
broad and brown hand on his breast, bowed slowly and very deep.

CHAPTER XXXIX.

M. VARBARRIERE ORDERS HIS WINGS.

In her own way, with interjections, and commentary and occasional
pauses for the sake of respiration, old Lady Alice related the substance of what the Bishop had communicated to her.

'And what do you suppose, Monsieur Varbarriere, to have been
the contents of that red leather box?' asked Lady Alice.

Monsieur Varbarriere smiled mysteriously and nodded.

'I fancy, Lady Alice, I have the honour to have arrived at
precisely the same conclusion with yourself,' said he.

'Well, I dare say. You see now what is involved. You
understand now why I should be, for his own sake, more than
ever grieved that my boy is gone,' she said, trembling very much.

Monsieur Varbarriere bowed profoundly.

'And why it is, sir, that I do insist on your explaining your
broken phrase of the other evening.'

Monsieur Varbarriere in his deep oak frame stood up tall, portly,
and erect. A narrow window, with stained heraldic emblazonry,
was partly behind him, and the light from above fell askance on
one side of his massive countenance, throwing such dark down-
ward bars of shadow on his face, that Lady Alice could not tell
whether he was scowling or smiling, or whether the effect was an
illusion.

'What phrase, pray, does you ladyship allude to?' he inquired.

'You spoke of my boy—my poor Guy—as if you knew more of
him than you cared to speak—as if you were on the point of

disclosing, and suddenly recollected yourself,' replied Lady Alice.

' You mean when I had the honour to converse with you the night before last in the drawing-room,' said he, a little brusquely, observing that the old lady was becoming vehemently excited.

' Yes ; when you left me under the impression that you thought my son still living,' half screamed Lady Alice, like a woman in a fury.

' Bah !' thundered the sneering diapason of Monsieur Varbarriere, whose good manners totally forsook him in his angry impatience, and his broad foot on the floor enforced his emphasis with a stamp.

' What do you mean, you foreign masquerader, whom nobody knows ? What *can* it be ? Sir, you have half distracted me. I've heard of people getting into houses—I've heard of magicians —I've heard of the devil—I have heard of charlatans, sir. I'd like to know what right, if you know nothing of my dear son, you have to torture me with doubts——'

' Doubts !' repeated Varbarriere, if less angrily, more contemptuously. ' Pish !'

' You may say *pish*, sir, or any rudeness you please ; but depend upon this, if you do know *anything*, of any kind, about my darling son, I'll have it from you if there be either laws or men in England,' shrieked Lady Alice.

Varbarriere all at once subsided, and looked hesitatingly. In tones comparatively quiet, but still a little ruffled, he said—

' I've been, I fear, very rude ; everyone that's angry is. I think you are right. I ought never to have approached the subject of your domestic sorrow. It was not my doing, Madame; it was *you* who insisted on drawing me to it.'

' You told me that you had seen my son, and knew Mr. Strangways intimately.'

' I did *not!*' cried Varbarriere sternly, with his head thrown back ; and he and Lady Alice for a second or two were silent. ' That is, I beg pardon, you *misapprehended* me. I'm sure I never could have said I had seen your son, Mr. Guy Deverell, or that I had a particularly intimate acquaintance with Mr. Strangways.'

'It won't do,' burst forth Lady Alice again; 'I'll not be fooled—I won't be fooled, sir.'

'Pray, then, pause for one moment before you have excited an alarm in the house, and possibly decide me on taking my leave for ever,' said Varbarriere, in a low but very stern tone. 'Whatever I may be—charlatan, conjurer, devil—if you but knew the truth, you would acknowledge yourself profoundly and everlastingly indebted to me. It *is* quite true that I am in possession of facts of which you had not even a suspicion; it is true that the affairs of those nearest to you in blood have occupied my profoundest thoughts and most affectionate care. I believe, if you will but exercise the self-command of which I have no doubt you are perfectly capable, for a very few days, I shall have so matured my plans as to render their defeat impracticable. On the other hand, if you give me any trouble, or induce the slightest suspicion anywhere that I have taken an interest of the kind I describe, I shall quit England, and you shall go down to your grave in *darkness*, and with the conviction, moreover, that you have blasted the hopes for which you ought to have sacrificed not your momentary curiosity only, but your unhappy life.'

Lady Alice was awed by the countenance and tones of this strange man, who assumed an authority over her, on this occasion, which neither of her deceased lords had ever ventured to assert in their lifetimes.

Her fearless spirit would not, however, succumb, but looked out through the cold windows of her deep-set eyes into the fiery gaze of her *master*, as she felt him, daringly as before.

After a short pause, she said—

'You would have acted more wisely, Monsieur Varbarriere, had you spoken to me on other occasions as frankly as you have just now done.'

'Possibly, madame.'

'Certainly, monsieur.'

M. Varbarriere bowed.

'Certainly, sir. But having at length heard so much, I am willing to concede what you say. I trust the delay may not be

long. I think you ought to tell me soon. I suppose we had better
talk no more in the interim,' she added, suddenly turning as she
approached the threshold of the room, and recovering something of
her lofty tone—'upon that, to me, terrible subject.'

'*Much* better, madame,' acquiesced M. Varbarriere.

'And we meet otherwise as before,' said the old lady, with a
disdainful condescension and a slight bow.

'I thank you, madame, for that favour,' replied M. Varbarriere,
reverentially, approaching the door, which, as she drew near to
withdraw, he opened for her with a bow, and they parted.

'I hope she'll be quiet, that old grey wild-cat. I must get a
note from her to Madame Gwynn. The case grows stronger ; a
little more and it will be irresistible, if only that stupid and ill-
tempered old woman can be got to govern herself for a few days.'

That evening, in the drawing-room, Monsieur Varbarriere was
many degrees more respectful than ever to that old grey wild-cat,
at whom that morning he had roared in a way so utterly ungen-
tlemanlike and ferocious.

People at a distance might have almost fancied a sexagenarian
caricature of a love-scene. There had plainly been the lovers'
quarrel. The lady carried her head a little high, threw sidelong
glances on the carpet, had a little pink flush in her cheeks, and
spoke little ; listened, but smiled not ; while the gentleman sat as
close as he dare, and spoke earnestly and low.

Monsieur Varbarriere was, in fact, making the most of his time,
and recovering all he could of his milder influence over Lady
Alice, and did persuade and soften ; and at length he secured a
promise of the note he wanted to Mrs. Gwynn, pledging his honour
that she would thoroughly approve the object of it, so soon as he
was at liberty to disclose it.

That night, taking leave of Sir Jekyl, Monsieur Varbarriere
said—

'You've been so good as to wish me to prolong my visit, which
has been to me so charming and so interesting. I have ventured,
therefore, to enable myself to do so, by arranging an absence of

two days, which I mean to devote to business which will not bear postponement.'

'Very sorry to lose you, even for the time you say; but you must leave your nephew, Mr. Strangways, as a hostage in our hands to secure your return.'

'He shall remain, as you are so good as to desire it, to enjoy himself. As for me, I need no tie to hold me to my engagement, and only regret every minute stolen for other objects from my visit.'

There was some truth in these complimentary speeches. Sir Jekyl was now quite at ease as to the character of his guests, whom he had at first connected with an often threatened attack, which he profoundly dreaded, however lightly he might talk of its chances of success. The host, on the whole, liked his guests, and really wished their stay prolonged; and Monsieur Varbarriere, who silently observed many things of which he did not speak, was, perhaps, just now particularly interested in his private perusal of that little romance which was to be read only at Marlowe Manor.

'I see, Guy, you have turned over a new leaf—no fooling now— you must not relapse, mind. I shall be away for two days. If longer, address me at Slowton. May I rely on your good sense and resolution—knowing what are our probable relations with this family—to continue to exercise the same caution as I have observed in your conduct, with much satisfaction, for the last two evenings? Well, I suppose I may. If you cannot trust yourself—fly. Get away—pack. You may follow me to Slowton, make what excuse you please; but don't loiter here. Good night.'

Such was the farewell spoken by Varbarriere to his nephew, as he nodded his good-night on the threshold of their dressing-room.

In the morning Monsieur Varbarriere's place knew him no more at the breakfast-table. With his valise, despatch-box, and desk, he had glided away, in the frosty sunlight, in a Marlowe post-chaise, to the 'Plough Inn,' on the Old London Road, where, as. we know, he had once sojourned before. It made a slight round-about to the point to which his business really invited his route;

ınd as he dismissed his vehicle here, I presume it was done with a
view to mystify possible inquirers.

At the 'Plough Inn' he was received with an awful bustle and
reverence. The fame of the consideration with which he was
entertained at Marlowe had reached that modest hostelry, and
Monsieur Varbarriere looked larger, grander, more solemn in its
modest hall, than ever ; his valise was handled with respect, and
lifted in like an invalid, not hauled and trundled like a prisoner ;
and the desk and despatch-box, as the more immediate attendants
on his person, were eyed with the respect which such a confidenc o
could not fail to inspire.

So Monsieur Varbarriere, having had his appetising drive through
a bright country and keen air, ate his breakfast very comfortably ;
and when that meal was over, ordered a 'fly,' in which he proceeded to Wardlock, and pulled up at the hall-door of Lady
Alice's reserved-looking, but comfortable old red-brick mansion.

CHAPTER XL.

MONSIEUR VARBARRIERE TALKS WITH DONICA GWYNN.

THE footman opened the door in deshabille and unshorn, with a
countenance that implied his sense of the impertinence of this
disturbance of his gentlemanlike retirement. There was, however,
that in the countenance of Monsieur Varbarriere, as well as the
intangible but potent 'aura' emitted by wealth, which surrounded
him—an influence which everybody feels and no one can well
define, which circumambiates a rich person and makes it felt,
nobody knows how, that he *is* wealthy—that brought the flunkey to
himself ; and adjusting his soiled necktie hastily with one hand, he
ran down to the heavy but commanding countenance that loomed
on his from the window of the vehicle.

' This is Wardlock ?' demanded the visitor.

' Wardlock Manor ?—yes, sir,' answered the servant.

'I've a note from Lady Alice Redcliffe, and a few words to Mrs. Gwynn the housekeeper. She's at home?'

'Mrs. Gwynn?—yes, sir.'

'Open the door, please,' said Monsieur Varbarriere, who was now speaking good frank English with wonderful fluency, considering his marked preference for the French tongue elsewhere.

The door flew open at the touch of the footman; and Monsieur Varbarriere entered the staid mansion, and was shown by the servant into the wainscoted parlour in which Lady Alice had taken leave of the ancient retainer whom he was about to confer with.

When Mrs. Gwynn, with that mixture of curiosity and apprehension which an unexpected visit is calculated to inspire, entered the room, very erect and natty, she saw a large round-shouldered stranger, standing with his back toward her, arrayed in black, at the window, with his grotesque high-crowned hat on.

Turning about he removed this with a slight bow and a grave smile, and with his sonorous foreign accent inquired—

'Mrs. Gwynn, I suppose?'

'Yes, sir, that is my name, if you please.'

'A note, Mrs. Gwynn, from Lady Alice Redcliffe.'

And as he placed it in the thin and rather lady-like fingers of the housekeeper, his eyes rested steadily on her features, as might those of a process-server, whose business it might be hereafter to identify her.

Mrs. Gwynn read the note, which was simply an expression of her mistress's wish that she should answer explicity whatever questions the gentleman, M. Varbarriere, who would hand it to her, and who was, moreover, a warm friend of the family, might put to her.

When Mrs. Gwynn, with the help of her spectacles, had spelled through this letter, she in turn looked searchingly at Monsieur Varbarriere, and began to wonder unpleasantly what line his examination might take.

'Will you, Mrs. Gwynn, allow me the right to sit down, by yourself taking a chair?' said Monsieur Varbarriere, very politely, smiling darkly, and waving his hand toward a seat.

'I'm very well as I am, I thank you, sir,' replied Gwynn, who did not very much like the gentleman's looks, and thought him rather like a great roguish Jew pedlar whom she had seen long ago at the fair of Marlowe.

'Nay, but pray sit down—I can't while you stand—and our conversation may last some time—pray do.'

'I can talk as well, sir, one way as t'other,' replied she, while at the same time, with a sort of fidgeted impatience, she did sit down and fold her hands in her lap.

'We have all, Mrs. Gwynn, a very high opinion of you; I mean Lady Alice and the friends of her family, among whom I reckon myself.'

'It's only of late as I came to my present misses, you're aware, sir, 'aving been, from, I may say, my childhood in the Marlowe family.'

'I know—the Marlowe family—it's all one, in fact; but I may say, Mrs. Gwynn, that short, comparatively, as has been your time with Lady Alice, you are spoken of with more respect and liking by that branch of the family than by Sir Jekyl.'

'I've done nothing to disoblege Sir Jekyl, as Lady Alice knows. Will you be so kind, sir, as to say what you want of me, having business to attend to up stairs?'

'Certainly, it is only a trifle or two.'

Monsieur Varbarriere cleared his voice.

'Having ascertained all about that *secret door* that opens into the green chamber at Marlowe, we would be obliged to you to let us know at what time, to your knowledge, it was first used.'

His large full eyes, from under his projecting brows, stared full upon her shrinking gaze as he asked this question in tones deep and firm, but otherwise as civil as he could employ.

It was vain for Mrs. Gwynn to attempt to conceal her extreme agitation. Her countenance showed it—she tried to speak, and failed; and cleared her throat, and broke down again.

'Perhaps you'd like some water,' said Varbarriere, rising and approaching the bell.

'No,' said Donica Gwynn, rising suddenly and getting before him. 'Let be.'

He saw that she wished to escape observation.

'As you please, Mrs. Gwynn—sit down again—I shan't without your leave—and recover a little.'

'There's nothing wrong with me, sir,' replied Donica, now in possession of her voice, very angrily, 'there's nothing to cause it.'

'Well, Mrs. Gwynn, it's quite excusable; I know all about it.'

'What *are* you, a builder or a hartist?'

'Nothing of the kind; I'm a gentleman without a profession, Mrs. Gwynn, and one who will not permit you to be compromised; one who will protect you from the slightest suspicion of anything unpleasant.'

'I don't know what you're a-driving at,' said Mrs. Gwynn, still as white as death, and glancing furiously.

'Come, Mrs. Gwynn, you're a sensible woman. You *do* know *perfectly*. You have maintained a respectable character.'

'Yes, sir!' said Donica Gwynn, and suddenly burst into a paroxysm of hysterical tears.

'Listen to me: you have maintained a respectable character, I know it; nothing whatever to injure that character shall ever fall from my lips; no human being—but two or three just as much interested in concealing all about it as you or I—shall ever know anything about it; and Sir Jekyl Marlowe has consented to take it down, so soon as the party at present at Marlowe shall have dispersed.'

'Lady Alice—I'll never like to see her again,' sobbed Donica.

'Lady Alice has no more suspicion of the existence of that door than the Pope of Rome has; and what is more, never shall. You may rely upon me to observe the most absolute silence and secrecy—nay, more, if necessary for the object of concealment—so to mislead and mystify people, that they can never so much as surmise the truth, *provided*—pray observe me—*provided* you treat me with the most *absolute candour*. You must not practise the least reserve or concealment. On tracing the slightest shadow of either in your communication with me, I hold myself free to deal with the facts in my possession, precisely as may seem best to myself. You understand?'

'Not Lady Alice, nor none of the servants, nor—nor a creature living, please.'

'*Depend* on me,' said Varbarriere.

'Well, sure I may; a gentleman would not break his word with such as me,' said Donica, imploringly.

'We can't spend the whole day repeating the same thing over and over,' said Varbarriere, rather grimly; 'I've said my say— I know everything that concerns *you* about it, without your opening your lips upon the subject. You occupied that room for two years and a half during Sir Harry's lifetime—you see I know it all. *There!* you are perfectly safe. I need not have made you any promise, but I do—perfectly safe with me—and the room shall vanish this winter, and no one but ourselves know anything of that door—do you understand?—*provided*——'

'Yes, sir, please—and what do you wish to know more from me? I don't know, I'm sure, why I should be such a fool as to take on so about it, as if *I* could help it, or was ever a bit the worse of it myself. There's been many a one has slep' in that room and never so much as knowed there was a door but that they came in by.'

'To be sure; so tell me, do you recollect Mr. Deverell's losing a paper in that room?'

'Well, I do mind the time he said he lost it there, but I know no more than the child unborn.'

'Did Sir Harry never tell you?'

'They said a deal o' bad o' Sir Harry, and them that should a' stood up for him never said a good word for him. Poor old creature!—I doubt if he had pluck to do it. I don't think he had, poor fellow!'

'Did he ever *tell* you he had done it! Come, remember your promise.'

'No, upon my soul—never.'

'Do you *think* he took it?'

Their eyes met steadily.

' Yes, I do,' said she, with a slight defiant frown.

' And *why* do you think so ?'

' Because, shortly after the row began about that paper, he talked with me, and said there was something a-troubling of him, and he wished me to go and live in a farm-house at Applehythe, and keep summat he wanted kep safe, as there was no one in all England so true as me—poor old fellow ! He never told me, and I never asked. But I laid it down in my own mind it was the paper Mr. Deverell lost, that's all.'

' Did he ever show you that paper ?'

' No.'

' Did he tell you where it was ?'

' He never said he had it.'

' Did he show you where that thing was which he wanted you to take charge of ?'

' Yes, in the press nigh his bed's head.'

' Did he open the press ?'

' Ay.'

' Well ?'

' He showed me a sort of a box, and he said that was all.'

' A little trunk of stamped red leather—was that like it ?'

' That was just it.'

' Did he afterwards give it into anybody's charge ?'

' I know no more about it. I saw it there, that's all. I saw it once, and never before nor since.'

' Is there more than one secret door into that room ?' pursued Varbarriere.

' More than one ; no, never as I heard or thought.'

' Where is the door placed with which *you* are acquainted ?'

' Why ? Don't you know ?'

' Suppose I know of two. We have discovered a second. Which is the one you saw used ? *Come !*'

Parenthetically it is to be observed that no such discovery had been made, and Varbarriere was merely fishing for information without disclosing his ignorance.

'In the recess at the right of the bed's head.'

'Yes; and how do you open it? I mean from the green chamber?'

'I never knowd any way how to open it—it's from t'other side. There's a way to bolt it, though.'

'Ay? How's that?

'There's an ornament of scrowl-work, they calls it, bronze-like, as runs down the casing of the recess, shaped like letter esses. Well, the fourteenth of them, reckoning up from the bottom, next the wall, turns round with your finger and thumb'; so if anyone be in the green chamber, and knows the secret, they can stop the door being opened.'

'I see—thank you. You've been through the passage leading from Sir Harry's room that was—Sir Jekyl Marlowe's room, at the back of the house, to the secret door of the green chamber?'

'No, never. I know nothink o' that, no more nor a child.'

'No?'

'No, nothink at all.'

Varbarriere had here been trying to establish another conjecture.

There was a pause. Varbarriere, ruminating darkly, looked on Donica Gwynn. He then closed his pocket-book, in which he had inscribed a few notes, and said—

'Thank you, Mrs. Gwynn. Should I want anything more I'll call again; and you had better not mention the subject of my visit. Let me see the pictures—that will be the excuse—and do *you* keep *your* secret, and I'll keep mine.'

'No, I thank you, sir,' said Donica, drily, almost fiercely, drawing back from his proffered douceur.

'Tut, tut,—pray do.'

'No, I thank you.'

So he looked at the pictures in the different rooms, and at some old china and snuff-boxes, to give a colour to his visit; and with polite speeches and dark smiles, and a general courtesy that was unctuous, he took his leave of Donica Gwynn, whom he left standing in the hall with a flushed face and a sore heart.

CHAPTER XLI.

A STORY OF A MAGICIAN AND A VAMPIRE.

THE pleasant autumn sun touched the steep roofs and mullioned windows of Marlowe Manor pleasantly that morning, turning the thinning foliage of its noble timber into gold, and bringing all the slopes and undulations of its grounds into relief in its subdued glory. The influence of the weather was felt by the guests assembled in the spacious breakfast-parlour, and gay and animated was the conversation.

Lady Jane Lennox, that ' superbly handsome creature,' as old Doocey used to term her, had relapsed very much into her old ways. Beatrix had been pleased when, even in her impetuous and uncertain way, that proud spirit had seemed to be drawn toward her again. But that was past, and that unruly nature had broken away once more upon her own solitary and wayward courses. She cared no more for Beatrix, or, if at all, it was plainly not kindly.

In Lady Jane's bold and mournful isolation there was something that interested Beatrix, ungracious as her ways often were, and she felt sore at the unjust repulse she had experienced. But Beatrix was proud, and so, though wounded, she did not show her pain—not that pain, nor another far deeper.

Between her and Guy Strangways had come a coldness unintelligible to her, an estrangement which she would have felt like an insult, had it not been for his melancholy looks and evident loss of spirits.

There is a very pretty room at Marlowe; it is called (*why*, I forget) Lady Mary's boudoir; its door opens from the first landing on the great stair. An oak floor, partly covered with a Turkey carpet, one tall window with stone shafts, a high old-fashioned stone chimneypiece, and furniture perhaps a little incongruous, but pleasant in its incongruity. Tapestry in the Teniers style— Dutch village festivals, with no end of figures, about half life-size,.

dancing, drinking, making music ; old boors, and young and fair-haired maidens, and wrinkled vraus, and here and there gentlemen in doublets and plumed hats, and ladies, smiling and bare-headed, and fair and plump, in great stomachers. These pleasant subjects, so life-like, with children, cocks and hens, and dogs interspersed, helped, with a Louis Quatorze suit of pale green, and gold chairs cushioned with Utrecht velvet, to give to this room its character so mixed, of gaiety and solemnity, something very quaint and cheery.

This room had old Lady Alice Redcliffe selected for her sitting-room, when she found herself unequal to the exertion of meeting the other ladies in the drawing-room, and hither she had been wont to invite Guy Strangways, who would occasionally pass an hour here wonderfully pleasantly and happily—in fact, as many hours as the old lady would have permitted, so long as Beatrix had been her companion.

But with those self-denying resolutions we have mentioned came a change. When Beatrix was there the young gentleman was grave and rather silent, and generally had other engagements which at least shortened his visit. This was retorted by Beatrix, who, a few minutes after the arrival of the visitor whom old Lady Alice had begun to call her secretary, would, on one pretence or another, disappear, and leave the old princess and her secretary to the uninterrupted enjoyment of each other's society.

Now since the night on which Varbarriere in talking with Lady Alice had, as we have heard, suddenly arrested his speech respecting her son—leaving her in uncertainty how it was to have been finished—an uncertainty on which her morbid brain reflected a thousand horrid and impossible shapes, the old lady had once more conceived something of her early dread of Guy Strangways. It was now again subsiding, although last night, under the influence of laudanum, in her medicated sleep her son had been sitting at her bedside, talking incessantly, she could not remember what.

Guy Strangways had just returned from the Park for his fishing-rod and angler's gear, when he was met in the hall by the

grave and courteous butler, who presented a tiny pencilled note
from Lady Alice, begging him to spare her half an hour in Lady
Mary's boudoir.

Perhaps it was a bore. But habitual courtesy is something
more than 'mouth honour, breath.' Language and thought
react upon one another marvellously. To restrain its expression is
in part to restrain the feeling; and thus a well-bred man is not
only in words and demeanour, but inwardly and sincerely, more
gracious and noble than others.

How oddly things happen sometimes!

Exactly as Guy Strangways arrived on the lobby, a little gloved
hand—it was Beatrix's—was on the door-handle of Lady Mary's
boudoir. It was withdrawn, and she stood looking for a second
or two at the young gentleman, who had evidently been going in
the same direction. He, too, paused; then, with a very low bow,
advanced to open the door for Miss Marlowe.

'No, thank you—I—I think I had better postpone my visit to
grandmamma till I return. I'm going to the garden, and should
like to bring her some flowers.'

'I'm afraid I have arrived unluckily—she would, I know, have
been so glad to see you,' said Guy Strangways.

'Oh, I've seen her twice before to-day. You were going to
make her a little visit now.'

'I—if you wish it, Miss Marlowe, I'll defer it.'

'She would be very little obliged to me, I'm sure; but I must
really go,' said Beatrix, recollecting on a sudden that there was
no need of so long a parley.

'It would very much relieve the poor secretary's labours, and
make his little period of duty so much happier,' said Guy, forgetting his wise resolutions strangely.

'I am sure grandmamma would prefer seeing her visitors singly
—it makes a great deal more of them, you know.'

And with a little smile and such a pretty glow in her cheeks,
she passed him by. He bowed and smiled faintly too, and for a
moment stood gazing after her into the now vacant shadow of the
old oak wainscoting, as young Numa might after his vanished

Egeria, with an unspoken, burning grief and a longing at his heart.

' I'm sure she can't like me—I'm sure she *dis*likes me. So much the better—Heaven knows I'm glad of it.'

And with an aching heart he knocked, turned the handle, and entered the pretty apartment in which Lady Alice, her thin shoulders curved, as she held her hands over the fire, was sitting alone.

She looked at him over her shoulder strangely from her hollow eyes, without moving or speaking for a time. He bowed gravely, and said—

' I have this moment received your little note, Lady Alice, and have hastened to obey.'

She sat up straight and sighed.

' Thanks—I have not been very well—so nervous—so very nervous,' she repeated, without removing her sad and clouded gaze from his face.

' We all heard with regret that you had not been so well,' said he.

' Well, we'll not talk of it—you're very good—I'm glad you've come—very nervous, and almost wishing myself back at Wardlock —where indeed I should have returned, only that I should have been wishing myself back again before an hour — miserably nervous.'

And Lady Alice sniffed at her smelling-salts, and added—

' And Monsieur Varbarriere gone away on business for some days—is not he?'

' Yes—quite uncertain—possibly for two, or perhaps three, he said,' answered Guy.

' And he's very—he knows—he knows a great deal—I forget what I was going to say—I'm half asleep to-day—no sleep—a very bad night.'

And old Lady Alice yawned drearily into the fire.

' Beatrix said she'd look in ; but everyone forgets—you young people are so selfish.'

' Mademoiselle Marlowe was at the door as I came in, and said she would go on instead to the garden first, and gather some flowers for you.'

' Oh! h'm!—very good—well, I can't talk to-day ; suppose you choose a book, Mr. Strangways, and read a few pages—that is, if you are quite at leisure ?'

' Perfectly—that is, for an hour—unfortunately I have then an appointment.   What kind of book shall I take ?' he asked, approaching one of the two tall bookstands that flanked an oval mirror opposite the fireplace.

' Anything, provided it is old.'

Nearly half an hour passed in discussing what to read—the old lady not being in the mood that day to pursue the verse readings which had employed Guy Strangways hitherto.

' This seems a curious old book,' he said, after a few moments. ' Very old French—I think upon witchcraft, and full of odd narratives.'

' That will do very well.'

' I had better try to translate it—the language is so antiquated.'

He leaned the folio on the edge of the chimneypiece, and his elbow beside it, supporting his head on his hand, and so read aloud to the *exigeante* old lady, who liked to see people employed about her, even though little of comfort, amusement, or edification resulted from it.

The narrative which Lady Alice had selected was entitled thus :—

' CONCERNING A REMARKABLE REVENGE AFTER SEPULTURE.'

' In the Province of Normandy, in the year of grace 1405, there lived a young gentleman of Styrian descent, possessing estates in Hungary, but a still more opulent fortune in France.   His park abutted on that of the Chevalier de St. Aubrache, who was a man also young, of ancient lineage, proud to excess, and though wealthy, by no means so wealthy as his Styrian neighbour.

' This disparity in riches excited the wrath of the jealous nobleman, who having once admitted the passions of envy and hatred to his heart, omitted no opportunity to injure him.

'The Chevalier de St. Aubrache, in fact, succeeded so well——'

Just at this point in the tale, Beatrix, with her flowers, not expecting to find Guy Strangways still in attendance, entered the room.

'You need not go; come in, dear—you've brought me some flowers—come in, I say; thank you, Beatrix, dear—they are very pretty, and very sweet too. Here is Mr. Strangways—sit by me, dear—reading a curious old tale of witchcraft. Tell her the beginning, pray.'

So Strangways told the story over again in his best way, and then proceeded to read as follows:—

'The Chevalier de St. Aubrache, in fact, succeeded so well, that on a point of law, aided by a corrupt judge in the Parliament of Rouen, he took from him a considerable portion of his estate, and subsequently so managed matters without committing himself, that he lost his life unfairly in a duel, which the Chevalier secretly contrived.

'Now there was in the household of the gentleman so made away with, a certain Hungarian, older than he, a grave and politic man, and reputed to have studied the art of magic deeply. By this man was the corpse of the deceased gentleman duly coffined, had away to Styria, and, it is said, there buried according to certain conditions, with which the Hungarian magician, who had vowed a terrible revenge, was well acquainted.

'In the meantime the Chevalier de St. Aubrache had espoused a very beautiful demoiselle of the noble family of D'Ayenterre, by whom he had one daughter, so beautiful that she was the subject of universal admiration, which increased in the heart of her proud father that affection which it was only natural that he should cherish for her.

'It was about the time of Candlemas, a full score of years after the death of his master, that the Hungarian magician returned to Normandy, accompanied by a young gentleman, very pale indeed, but otherwise so exactly like the gentleman now so long dead, that no one who had been familiar with his features could avoid being struck, and indeed, affrighted with the likeness.

'The Chevalier de St. Aubrache was at first filled with horror, like the rest; but well knowing that the young man whom he, the stranger, so resembled, had been actually killed as aforesaid, in combat, and having never heard of vampires, which are among the most malignant and awful of the manifestations of the Evil One, and not recognising at all the Hungarian magician, who had been careful to disguise himself effectually; and, above all, relying on letters from the King of Hungary, with which, under a feigned name, as well as with others from the Archbishop of Toledo in Spain, he had come provided, he received him into his house; when the grave magician, who resembled a doctor of a university, and the fair-seeming vampire, being established in the house of their enemy, began to practise, by stealth, their infernal arts.'

The old lady saw that in the reader's countenance, as he read this odd story, which riveted her gaze. Perhaps conscious of her steady and uncomfortable stare, as well as of a real parallel, he grew obviously disconcerted, and at last, as it seemed, even agitated as he proceeded.

'Young man, for Heaven's sake, will you tell me who you are?' said Lady Alice, her dark old eyes fixed fearfully on his face, as she rose unconsciously from her chair.

The young man, very pale, turned a despairing and almost savage look from her to Beatrix, and back to her again.

'You are not a Strangways,' she continued.

He looked steadily at her, as if he were going to speak, then dropped his glance suddenly and remained silent.

'I say, I know your name is not Strangways,' said the old lady, in increasing agitation.

'I can tell you nothing about myself,' said he again, fixing his great dark eyes, that looked almost wild in his pallid face, full upon her, with a strange expression of anguish.

'In the Almighty's name, are you Guy Deverell?' she screamed, lifting up her thin hands between him and her in her terror.

The young man returned her gaze, oddly with, she fancied, a

look of baffled horror in his face. It seemed to her like an evil spirit detected.

He recovered, however, for a few seconds, something of his usual manner. Instead of speaking, he bowed twice very low, and, on the point of leaving the room, he suddenly arrested his departure, turning about with a stamp on the floor; and walking back to her, he said, very gently—

'Yes, yes, why should I deny it? My name *is* Guy Deverell.'

And was gone.

CHAPTER XLII.

FAREWELL.

'Oh! grandmamma, *what* is it?' said Beatrix, clasping her thin wrist.

The old lady, stooping over the chair on which she leaned, stared darkly after the vanished image, trembling very much.

'*What* is Deverell—why should the name be so dreadful— is there anything—oh! grandmamma, *is* there anything very bad?'

'I don't know—I am confused—did you ever see such a face? My gracious Heaven!' muttered Lady Alice.

'Oh! grandmamma, darling, tell me what it is, I implore of you.'

'Yes, dear, everything; another time. I can't now. I might do a mischief. I might prevent—you must promise me, darling, to tell no one. You must not say his name is Deverell. *You* say nothing about it. That dreadful, dreadful story!'

The folio was lying with crumpled leaves, back upward, on the floor, where it had fallen.

'There is something plainly fearful in it. *You* think so, grandmamma; something discovered; something going to happen. Send after him, grandmamma; call him back. If it is anything you can prevent, I'll ring.'

'Don't *touch* the bell,' cried granny, sharply, clutching at her hand, 'don't *do* it. See, Beatrix, you promise me you say nothing to anyone of what you've witnessed—*promise*. I'll tell you all I know when I'm better. He'll come again. I *wish* he'd come again. I'm sure he will, though I hardly think I could bear to see him. I don't know what to think.'

The old lady threw herself back in her chair, not affectedly at all, but looking so awfully haggard and agitated that Beatrix was frightened.

'Call nobody, there's a darling; just open the window; I shall be better.'

And she heaved some of those long and heavy sighs which relieve hysterical oppression; and, after a long silence she said—

'It is a long time since I have felt so ill, Beatrix. Remember this, darling, my papers are in the black cabinet in my bed-room at home—I mean Wardlock. There is not a great deal. My jointure stops, you know; but whatever little there is, is for you, darling.'

'You're not to talk of it, granny, darling, you'll be quite well in a minute; the air is doing you good. May I give you a little wine?—Well, a little water?'

'Thanks, dear; I *am* better. Remember what I told you, and particularly your promise to mention what you heard to no one. I mean the—the—strange scene with that young man. I think I will take a glass of wine. I'll tell you all when I'm better —when Monsieur Varbarriere comes back. It is important for a time, especially having heard what I have, that I should wait a little.'

Granny sipped a little sherry slowly, and the tint of life, such as visits the cheek of the aged, returned to hers, and she was better.

'I'd rather not see him any more. It's all like a dream. I don't know what to make of it,' muttered granny! and she began audibly to repeat passages, tremblingly and with upturned eyes, from her prayer-book.

Perplexed, anxious, excited, Beatrix looked down on the

collapsed and haggard face of the old lady, and listened to the moaned petition, 'Lord, have mercy upon us!' which trembled from her lips as it might from those of a fainting sinner on a death-bed.

Guy Deverell, as I shall henceforward call him, thinking of nothing but escape into solitude, was soon a good way from the house. He was too much agitated, and his thoughts too confused at first, to estimate all the possible consequences of the sudden disclosure he had just made.

What would Varbarriere, who could be stern and violent, say or do, when he learned it? Here was the one injunction on which he had been ever harping violated. He felt how much he owed to the unceasing care of that able and disinterested friend through all his life, and how had he repaid it all!

'Anything but deception—anything but that. I could not endure the agony of my position longer—yes, agony.'

He was now wandering by the bank of the solitary river, and looked back at the picturesque gables of Marlowe Manor through the trees; and he felt that he was leaving all that could possibly interest him in existence in leaving Marlowe. Always was rising in his mind the one thought, 'What does she think of my deception and my agitation—what can she think of *me*?'

It is not easy, even in silence and alone, when the feelings are at all ruffled, to follow out a train of thought. Guy thought of his approaching farewell to his uncle: he sometime heard his great voice thundering in despair and fury over his ruined schemes —schemes, be they what they might, at least unselfish. Then he thought of the effect of the discovery on Sir Jekyl, who, no doubt, had special reasons for alarm connected with this name —a secret so jealousy guarded by Varbarriere. Then he thought of his future. His commission in the French army awaited him. A life of drudgery or listlessness? No such thing! a career of adventure and glory—ending in a baton or death! Death is so romantic in the field! There are always some beautiful eyes to drop in secret those tears which are worth dying for

It is not a crowded trench, where fifty corpses pig together in the last noisome sleep—but an apotheosis !

He was sure he had done well in yielding to the impulse that put an end to the tedious treachery he had been doomed to practise; and if well, then *wisely*—so, no more retrospection.

All this rose and appeared in fragments like a wreck in the eddies of his mind.

One thing was clear—he must leave Marlowe forthwith. He could not meet his host again. He stood up. It is well to have hit upon anything to be done—anything quite certain.

With rapid steps he now returned to Marlowe, wondering how far he had walked, as it seemed to him, in so mere a moment of time.

The house was deserted; so fine a day had tempted all its inmates but old Lady Alice abroad. He sent to the village of Marlowe for a chaise, while Jacques, who was to await where he was the return of his master, Monsieur Varbarriere, got his luggage into readiness, and he himself wrote, having tried and torn up half a dozen, a note to Sir Jekyl, thanking him for his hospitality, and regretting that an unexpected occurrence made his departure on so short notice unavoidable. He did not sign it. He would not write his assumed name. Sir Jekyl could have no difficulty in knowing from which of his guests it came, perhaps would not even miss the signature.

The chaise stood at the door-steps, his luggage stowed away, his dark short travelling cloak about his shoulders, and his note to Sir Jekyl in his fingers.

He entered the great hall, meaning to place it on the marble table where Sir Jekyl's notes and newspapers usually awaited him, and there he encountered Beatrix.

There was no one else. She was crossing to the outer door, and they almost met before they came to a stop.

'Oh! Mr. Strangways.'

'Pray call me by my real name, Deverell. Strangways was my mother's; and in obedience to those who are wiser than I, during my journey I adopted it, although the reasons were not told me.'

There was a little pause here.

'I am very glad I was so fortunate as to meet you, Miss Marlowe, before I left. I'm just going, and it would be such a privilege to know that you had not judged me very hardly.'

'I'm sure papa will be very sorry you are going—a break-up is always a sad event—we miss our guests so much,' she said, smiling, but a little pale.

'If you knew my story, Miss Marlowe, you would acquit me,' he said, bursting forth all at once. 'Misfortune overtook me in my early childhood, before I can remember. I have no right to trouble you with the recital; and in my folly I superadded this— the worst—that madly I gave my love to one who could not return it—who, perhaps, ought not to have returned it. Pardon me, Miss Marlowe, for talking of these things ; but as I am going away, and wished you to understand me, I thought, perhaps, you would hear me. Seeing how hopeless was my love, I never told it, but resolved to see her no more, and so to the end of my days will keep my vow ; but this is added, that for her sake my life becomes a sacrifice—a real one—to guard her from sorrows and dangers, which I believe *did* threaten her, and to save her from which I devote myself, as perhaps she will one day understand. I thought I would just tell you so much before I went, and—and—that *you* are that lady. Farewell, dear Miss Marlowe, most beautiful—beloved.'

He pressed her hand, he kissed it passionately, and was gone.

It was not until she had heard the vehicle drive rapidly away, that she quite recovered herself. She went into the front hall, and through the window, standing far back, watched the receding chaise. When it was out of sight, humming a gay air, she ran up-stairs, and into her bed-room, when, locking the door, she wept the bitterest tears, perhaps, she had ever shed, since the days of her childhood.

CHAPTER XLIII.

AT THE BELL AND HORNS.

WITH the reader's permission, I must tell here how Monsieur Varbarriere proceeded on his route to Slowton.

As he mounted his vehicle from the steps of Wardlock, the flunkey, who was tantalised by the very unsatisfactory result of his listening at the parlour-door, considered him curiously.

'Go on towards the village,' said M. Varbarriere to the driver, in his deep foreign accents.

And so soon as they were quite out of sight of the Wardlock flunkey, he opened the front window of his nondescript vehicle, and called—

'Drive to Slowton.'

Which, accordingly, was done. M. Varbarriere, in profound good-humour, a flood of light and certainty having come upon him, sat back luxuriously in a halo of sardonic glory, and was smiling to himself, as men sometimes will over the chess-board when the rest of their game is secure.

At the Bell and Horns he was received with a reverential welcome.

'A gentleman been inquiring for Monsieur Varbarriere?' asked the foreign gentleman in black, descending.

'A gentleman, sir, as has took number seven, and expects a gentleman to call, but did not say who, which his name is Mr. Rumsey?'

'Very good,' said Monsieur Varbarriere.

Suddenly he recollected that General Lennox's letter might have reached the post-office, and, plucking a card from his case, wrote an order on it for his letters, which he handed to Boots, who trudged away to the post-office close by.

Varbarriere was half sorry now that he had opened his correspondence with old General Lennox so soon. He had no hope that Donica Gwynn's reserves would have melted and given way so rapidly in the interview which had taken place. He was a man who cared nothing about penal justice, who had embraced the world's ethics early, and looked indulgently on escapades of human nature, and had no natural turn for cruelty, although he could be cruel enough when an object was to be accomplished.

' I don't think I'd have done it, though he deserves it richly, and has little right to look for quarter at my hands.'

And whichever of the gentlemen interested he may have alluded to, he cursed him under his breath ardently.

In number seven there awaited him a tall and thin man of business, of a sad countenance and bilious, with a pale drab-coloured and barred muslin cravat, tied with as much precision as a curate's; a little bald at the very top of his head; a little stooped at his shoulders. He did not smile as Monsieur Varbarriere entered the room. He bowed in a meek and suffering way, and looked as if he had spent the morning in reading Doctor Blewish's pamphlet ' On the Ubiquity of Disguised Cholera Morbus,' or our good Bishop's well-known tract on ' Self-Mortificatiou.' There was a smell of cigars in the room, which should not have been had he known that Monsieur Varbarriere was to be here so early. His chest was weak, and the doctors ordered that sort of fumigation.

Monsieur Varbarriere set his mind at ease by preparing himself to smoke one of the notable large cigars, of which he carried always a dozen rounds or so in his case.

' You have brought the cases and opinions with you ?' inquired Varbarriere.

The melancholy solicitor replied by opening a tin box, from which he drew several sheafs of neatly labelled papers tied up in red tape; the most methodical and quiet of attorneys, and ̄one of the most efficient to be found.

' Smoke away; you like it, so do I ; we can talk too, and look at these,' said Varbarriere, lighting his cigar.

Mr. Rumsey bowed, and meekly lighted his also.

Then began the conference on business.

' Where are Gamford's letters ?—these ?—ho !'

And as Monsieur Varbarriere read them, puffing away as fast as a furnace, and threw each down as he would play a card, in turn, he would cry ' Bah !'—' Booh !'—or, ' Did you ever read such Gelamathias ?'—and, at last—

' Who was right about that *benet*—you or I ? I told you what he was.'

' You will perceive just now, I think, sir, that there are some things of value there notwithstanding. You can't see their importance until you shall have looked into the enlarged statement we have been enabled by the result of some fresh discoveries to submit to counsel.'

' Give me that case. Fresh discoveries, have you ? I venture to say, when you've heard my notes, you'll open your eyes. No, I mean the cigar-case ; well, you may give me that too.'

So he took the paper, with its bluish briefing post pages, and broad margin, and the opinions of Mr. Serjeant Edgeways and Mr. Whaulbane, Q.C., copied in the same large, round hand at the conclusion.

' Well, these opinions are stronger than I expected. There is a bit here in Whaulbane's I don't like so well—what you call fishy, you know. But you shall hear just now what I can add to our proofs, and you will see what becomes of good Mr. Whaulbane's doubts and queries. You said always you did not think they had destroyed the deed ?'

' If well advised, they did not. I go that length. Because the deed, although it told against them while a claimant in the Deverell line appeared, would yet be an essential part of their case in the event of their title being attacked from the Bracton quarter ; and therefore the fact is, they could not destroy it.'

' They are both quite clear upon the question of secondary evidence of the contents of a lost deed, I see,' said Varbarriere, musingly, ' and think our proof satisfactory. Those advocates, however—*why* do they ?—always say their say with so many reserves and misgivings, that you begin to think they know very little more of the likelihoods of the matter, with all their pedantry than you do yourself.'

' The glorious uncertainty of the law !' ejaculated Mr. Rumsey, employing a phrase which I have heard before, and with the nearest approach to a macerated smile which his face had yet worn.

'Ay,' said Varbarriere, in his metallic tones of banter, 'the glorious uncertainty of the law. That must be true, for you're always saying it; and it must be pleasant too, if one could only see it; for, my faith! you look almost cheerful while you say it.'

'It makes counsel cautious, though it does not cool clients when they're once fairly blooded,' said Mr. Rumsey. 'A client is a wonderful thing sometimes. There would not be half the money made of our profession if men kept their senses when they go into law; but they seldom do. Lots of cool gamblers at every other game, but no one ever keeps his head at law.'

'That's encouraging; thank you. Suppose I take your advice, and draw stakes?' said Varbarriere.

'You have no notion,' said Mr. Rumsey, resignedly.

'Well, I believe you're right, monsieur; and I believe *I* am right too; and if you have any faith in your favourite oracles, so must you; but, have you done your cigar? Well, take your pen for a moment and listen to me, and note what I say. When Deverell came down with his title-deeds to Marlowe, they gave him the Window dressing-room for his bed-room, and the green-chamber, with the bed taken down, for his dressing-room; and there he placed his papers, with the key turned in the door. In the morning his attorney came. It was a meeting about a settlement of the mortgage; and when the papers were overhauled it was found that that deed had been abstracted. Very good. Now listen to what I have to relate concerning the peculiar construction of that room.

So Monsieur Varbarriere proceeded to relate minutely all he had ascertained that day, much to the quiet edification of Mr. Rumsey, whose eyes brightened, and whose frontal wrinkles deepened as he listened.

'I told you I suspected some legerdemain about that room long ago; the idea came to me oddly. When on a visit to the Marquis de Mirault he told me that in making alterations in the château they had discovered a false door into one of the bed-rooms. The tradition of this contrivance, which was singularly artful, was lost. It is possible that the secret of it perished with its first possessor. By means of this door the apartment in question was placed in almost immediate conjunction with another, which, except through this admirably concealed door, could not be reached from it without a long circuit. The proximity of the rooms, in fact, had been, by reason of the craft with which they were apparently separated, entirely overlooked.'

The attorney observed, sadly—

'The French are an ingenious people.'

'The curiosity of my friend was excited,' continued Varbarriere, 'and with some little search among family records he found that this room, which was constructed in the way of an addition to the château, had been built about the beginning of the eighteenth century, during the marquisate of one of the line, who was celebrated as *un homme a bonnes fortunes*, you understand, and its object was now quite palpable.'

'A man, no doubt, of ability—a long-headed gentleman,' mused the melancholy attorney.

'Well, at Marlowe I saw a collection of elevations of the green chamber, as it is called, built only two or three years later—and, mind this, by the same architect, an Italian, called Paulo Abruzzi, a remarkable name, which I perfectly remembered as having been mentioned by my friend the Marquis as the architect of his ancestral relic of Cupid's legerdemain. But here is the most remarkable circumstance, and to which my friend Sir Jekyl quite innocently gave its proper point. The room under this chamber, and, of course, in the same building, was decorated with portraits painted in the panel, and one of them was this identical Marquis de Mirault, with the date 1711, and the Baronet was good enough to tell me that he had been a very intimate friend, and had visited his grandfather, at Marlowe.'

CHAPTER XLIV.

M. VARBARRIERE'S PLANS.

VARBARRIERE solemnly lighted a cigar, and squinted at its glowing point with his great dark eyes, in which the mild attorney saw the lurid reflection. When it was well lighted he went on—

'You may suppose how this confirmed my theory. I set about my enquiries quietly, and was convinced that Sir Jekyl knew all about it, by his disquietude whenever I evinced an interest in that portion of the building. But I managed matters very slyly, and collected proof very nearly demonstrative; and at this moment he has not a notion who I am.'

'No. It will be a surprise when he does learn,' answered the attorney, sadly.

'A fine natural hair-dye is the air of the East Indies: first it turns light to black, and then black to grey. Then, my faith!—a bronzed face with plenty of furrows, a double chin, and a great beard to cover it, and eleven stone weight expanded to seventeen stone—*Corpo di Bacco!*—and six pounds!'

And Monsieur Varbarriere laughed like the clang and roar of a chime of cathedral bells.

'It will be a smart blow,' said the attorney, almost dreamily.

'Smash him,' said Varbarriere. 'The Deverell estate is something over five thousand a-year; and the mesne rates, with four per cent. interest, amount to 213,000*l.*

'He'll defend it,' said the knight of the sorrowful countenance, who was now gathering in his papers.

'I hope he will,' growled Varbarriere, with a chuckle. 'He has not a leg to stand on—all the better for *you*, at all events; and then I'll bring down that other hammer on his head.'

'The criminal proceedings?' murmured the sad attorney.

'Ay. I can prove that case myself—he fired before his time, and killed him, I'm certain simply to get the estate. I was the only person present—poor Guy! Jekyl had me in his pocket then.

The rascal wanted to thrust me down and destroy me afterwards. He employed that Jew house, Robenzahl and Isaacs—the villain! Luck turned, and I am a rich fellow now, and his turn is coming. Vive la justice eternelle! Vive la bagatelle! Bravo! Bah!'

Monsieur Varbarriere had another pleasant roar of laughter here, and threw his hat at the solemn attorney's head.

'You'll lunch with me,' said Varbarriere.

'Thanks,' murmured the attorney.

'And now the war,—the campaign—what next?'

'You'll make an exact note,' the attorney musingly replied, ' of what that woman Wynn or Gwynn can prove ; also what the Lord Bishop of what's-his-name can prove ; and it strikes me we shall have to serve some notice to intimidate Sir Jekyl about that red-leather box, to prevent his making away with the deed, and show him we know it is there ; or perhaps apply for an order to make him lodge the deed in court ; but Tom Weavel—he's always in town—will advise us. You don't think that women will leave us in the lurch ?'

'No,' said Varbarriere, as if he was thinking of something else. 'That Donica Gwynn, you mean. She had that green chamber to herself, you see, for a matter of three years.'

'Yes.'

'And she's one of those old domestic Dianas who are sensitive about scandal—you understand—and she knows what ill-natured people would say ; so I quieted her all I could, and I don't think she'll venture to recede. No ; she certainly won't.'

'How soon can you let me have the notes, sir ?'

'To-morrow, when I return. I've an appointment to keep by rail to-night, and I'll make a full memorandum from my notes as I go along.'

'Thanks—and what are your instructions ?'

'Send back the cases with copies of the new evidence.'

'And assuming a favourable opinion, sir, are my instructions to proceed ?'

'Certainly, my son, forthwith—the grass it must not grow under our feet.'

'Of course subject to counsel's opinion?' said the attorney, sadly.

'To be sure.'

'And which first—the action or the indictment? or both together?' asked Mr. Rumsey.

'*That* for counsel too. Only my general direction is, let the onset be as sudden, violent, and determined as possible. You see?'

The attorney nodded gently, tying up his last bundle of papers as softly as a lady might knot her ribbon round the neck of her lap-dog.

'You see?'

'Yes, sir; your object is destruction. Delenda est Carthago—that's the word,' murmured Mr. Rumsey, plaintively.

'Yes—ha, ha!—what you call double him up!' clanged out Varbarriere, with an exulting oath and a chuckle.

The attorney had locked up his despatch-box now, and putting the little bunch of keys deep into his trousers pocket, he said, 'Yes, that's the word; but I suppose you have considered'——

'*What?* I'm tired considering.'

'I was going to say whether some more certain result might not be obtainable by negotiation; that is, if you thought it a case for negotiation.'

'*What* negotiation? What do you mean?'

'Well, you see there are materials—there's something to yield at both sides,' said the attorney, very slowly, in a diplomatic reverie.

'But why should you think of a compromise, the worst thing I fancy could happen *you?*'

There was a general truth in this. It is not the ferryman's interest to build a bridge, nor was it Mr. Rumsey's that his client should walk high and dry over those troubled waters through which it was his privilege and profit to pilot him. But he had not quite so much faith in this case as Monsieur Varbarriere had, and he knew that his wealthy and resolute client could grow savage enough in defeat, and had once or twice had stormy interviews with him after failures.

'If the young gentleman and young lady liked one another, for instance, the conflicting claims might be reconciled, and a marriage would in that case arrange the difference.'

'There's nothing very deep in that,' snarled Varbarriere, but there is everything impracticable. 'Do you think Guy Deverell, whose father that *lache* murdered before my eyes, could ever endure to call *him* father? Bah! If I thought so I would drive him from my presence and never behold him more. No, no, no! There is more than an estate in all this—there is justice, there is *punishment.*'

Monsieur Varbarriere, with his hands in his pockets, took a turn up and down the room, and his solemn steps shook the floor, and his countenance was agitated by violence and hatred.

The pale, thin attorney eyed him with a gentle and careworn observation. His respected client was heaving with a great toppling swagger as he to-ed and fro-ed in his thunderstorm, looking as black as the Spirit of Evil.

This old-maidish attorney was meek and wise, but by no means timid. He was accustomed to hear strong language, and sometimes even oaths, without any strange emotion. He looked on this sort of volcanic demonstration scientifically, as a policeman does on drunkenness—knew its stages, and when it was best left to itself.

Mr. Rumsey, therefore, poked the fire a little, and then looked out of the window.

'You don't go to town to-night?'

'Not if you require me here, sir.'

'Yes, I shall have those memoranda to give you—and tell me now, I think you know your business. Do you think, as we now stand, success is *certain?*'

'Well, sir, it certainly is very strong—very; but I need not tell you a case will sometimes take a queer turn, and I never like to tell a client that anything is absolutely certain—a case is sometimes carried out of its legitimate course, you see; the judges may go wrong, or the jury bolt, or a witness may break down, or else a bit of evidence may start up—it's a responsibility we never take on ourselves to say that of any case; and you know there has been a good deal of time—and that sometimes raises a feeling with a jury.'

'Ay, a quarter of a century, but it can't be helped. For ten years of that time I could not show, I owed money to everybody. Then, when *I* was for striking on the criminal charge for *murder*, or *manslaughter*, or whatever you agreed it was to be, you all said I must begin with the civil action, and first oust him from Guy Deverell's estate. Well, *there* you told me I could not move till he was twenty-five, and now you talk of the good deal of time— *ma foi!*—as if it was I who delayed, and not *you*, messieurs. But enough, past is past. We have the present, and I'll use it.'

'We are to go on, then?'

'Yes, we've had to wait too long, Stop for nothing, drive right on, you see, at the fastest pace counsel can manage If I saw the Deverell estate where it should be, and a judgment for the mesne rates, and Sir Jekyl Marlowe in the dock for his crime, I don't say I should sing *nunc dimittis*; but, *parbleu*, sir, it would be very agreeable—ha! ha! ha!'

~~~~~~~~~~

CHAPTER XLV.

TEMPEST.

'Does Mr. Guy Deverell know anything of the measures you contemplate in his behalf?' inquired the attorney.

'Nothing. Do you think me a fool? Young men *are* such asses!'

'You know, however, of course, that he will act. The proceedings, you know, must be in his name.'

'Leave that to me.'

Varbarriere rang the bell and ordered luncheon. There were grouse and trout—he was in luck—and some cream cheese, for

which rural delicacy he had a fancy. They brew very great ale at
Slowton, like the Welsh, and it was a novelty to the gentleman
of foreign habits, who eat as fastidiously as a Frenchman, and as
largely as a German. On the whole it was satisfactory, and the
high-shouldered, Jewish-looking sybarite shook hands in a very
friendly way with his attorney in the afternoon, on the platform at
Slowton, and glided off toward Chester, into which ancient town he
thundered, screaming like a monster rushing on its prey; and a
victim awaited him in the old commercial hotel; a tall, white-
headed, military-looking man, with a white moustache twirled up
fiercely at the corners; whose short pinkish face and grey eyes, as
evening deepened, were pretty constantly presented at the window
of the coffee-room next the street door of the inn. From that post
he saw all the shops and gas-lamps, up and down the street,
gradually lighted. The gaselier in the centre of the coffee-room,
with its six muffed glass globes, flared up over the rumpled and
coffee-stained morning newspapers and the almanac, and the
battered and dissipated-looking railway guide, with corners curled
and back coming to pieces, which he consulted every ten minutes
through his glasses.

How many consultations he had had with the waiter upon the
arrival of trains due at various hours, and how often the injunction
had been repeated to see that no mistake occurred about the
private room he had ordered; and how reiterated the order that
any gentleman inquiring for General Lennox should be shown at
once into his presence, the patient waiter with the bilious com-
plexion could tell.

As the time drew near, the General having again conferred with
the waiter, conversed with the porter, and even talked a little with
Boots—withdrew to his small square sitting-room and pair of
candles upstairs, and awaited the arrival of Monsieur Varbarriere,
with his back to the fire, in a state of extreme fidget.

That gentleman's voice he soon heard upon the passage, and the
creaking of his heavy tread! and he felt as he used, when a young
soldier, on going into action.

The General stepped forward. The waiter announced a gentle-

man who wished to see him; and Varbarriere's dark visage and
mufflers, and sable mantle loomed behind; his felt hat in his hand,
and his wavy cone of grizzled hair was bowing solemnly.

'Glad you're come—how d'ye do?' and Varbarriere's fat brown
hand was seized by the General's pink and knotted fingers in a
very cold and damp grasp. 'Come in and sit down, sir. What
will you take?—tea, or dinner, or what?'

'Very much obliged. I have ordered something, by-and-by, to
my room—thank you very much. I thought, however, that you
might possibly wish to see me immediately, and so I am here, at
all events, as you soldiers say, to report myself,' said Varbarriere,
with his unctuous politeness.

'Yes, it *is* better, I'd rather have it now,' answered the General,
in a less polite and more literal way. 'A chair, sir;' and he
placed one before the fire, which he poked into a blaze. 'I—I
hope you are not fatigued,'—here the door shut, and the waiter
was gone; 'and I want to hear, sir, if you please, the—the meaning of the letter you favoured me with.'

The General by this time had it in his hand open, and tendered
it, I suppose for identification, to M. Varbarriere, who, however,
politely waved it back.

'I quite felt the responsibility I took upon myself when I wrote
as I did. That responsibility of course I accept; and I have come
all this way, sir, for no other purpose than to justify my expressions, and to invite you to bring them to the test.'

'Of *course*, sir. Thank you,' said the General.

Varbarriere had felt a momentary qualm about this particular
branch of the business which he had cut out for himself. When
he wrote to General Lennox he was morally *certain* of the existence
of a secret passage into that green room, and also of the relations
which he had for some time suspected between Sir Jekyl and his
fair guest. On the whole it was not a bad *coup* to provide, by
means of the old General's jealousy, such literal proof as he
still required of the concealed entrance, through which so much
villany had been accomplished—and so his letter—and now its
consequences—about which it was too late to think.

General Lennox, standing by the table, with one candle on the
chimneypiece and his glasses to his eyes, read aloud, with some
little stumbling, these words from the letter of Monsieur Varbarriere :—

'The reason of my so doing will be obvious when I say that I
have certain circumstances to lay before you which nearly affect
your honour. I decline making any detailed statement by letter ;
nor will I explain my meaning at Marlowe Manor. But if, without *fracas*, you will give me a private meeting, at any place
between this and London, I will make it my business to see you,
when I shall satisfy you that I have not made this request without
the gravest reasons.'

'Those are the passages, sir, on which you are so good as to
offer me an explanation ; and first, there's the phrase, you know,
" certain circumstances to lay before you which nearly affect your
honour ;" that's a word, you know, sir, that a fellow *feels* in a
way—in a way that can't be trifled with.'

'Certainly. Put your question, General Lennox, how you
please,' answered Varbarriere, with a grave bow.

'Well, how—how—exactly—I'll—I will put my question. I'd
like to know, sir, in what relation—in—yes—in what relation, as
a soldier, sir, or as a gentleman, sir, or as—*what ?*'

'I am very much concerned to say, sir, that it is in the very
nearest and most sacred interest, sir—as a *husband*.'

General Lennox had sat down by this time, and was gazing
with a frank stern stare full into the dark countenance of his
visitor ; and in reply he made two short little nods, clearing his
voice, and lowering his eyes to the table.

It was a very trifling way of taking it. But Varbarriere saw
his face flush fiercely up to the very roots of his silver hair, and he
fancied he could see the vessels throbbing in his temples.

'I—very good, sir—thank you,' said the General, looking up
fiercely and shaking his ears, but speaking in a calm tone.

'Go on, pray—let me know—I say—in God's name, don't keep
me.'

'Now, sir, I'll tell it to you briefly—I'll afterwards go into whatever proof you desire. I have reason, I deeply regret it, to believe—in fact to know—that an immoral intimacy exists between Sir Jekyl Marlowe and Lady Jane Lennox.'

' It's a lie, sir !' screamed the General—' a damned lie, sir—a damned lie, sir—a *damned* lie, sir.'

His gouty claw was advanced trembling as if to clutch the muffler that was folded about Monsieur Varbarriere's throat, but he dropped back in his seat again shaking, and ran his fingers through his white hair several times. There was a silence which even M. Varbarriere did not like.

Varbarriere was not the least offended at his violence. He knew quite well that the General did not understand what he said, or mean, or remember it—that it was only the wild protest of agony. For the first time he felt a compunction about that old foozle, who had hitherto somehow counted for nothing in the game he was playing, and he saw him, years after, as he had shrieked at him that night, with his claw stretched towards his throat, ludicrous, and also terrible.

' My God! sir,' cried the old man, with a quaver that sounded like a laugh, ' do you tell me so ?'

' It's true, sir.' said Varbarriere.

' Now, sir, I'll not interrupt you—tell all, pray—hide nothing,' said the General.

' I was, sir, accidentally witness to a conversation which is capable of no other interpretation; and I have legal proof of the existence of a secret door, connecting the apartment which has been assigned to you, at Marlowe, with Sir Jekyl's room.'

' The damned villain ! What a fool,' and then very fiercely he suddenly added, ' You can prove all this, sir ? I hope you can.'

' All this, and more, sir. I suspect, sir, there will hardly be an attempt to deny it.'

' Oh, sir, it's terrible ; but I was such a fool. I had no business—I deserve it all. Who'd have imagined such villains ? But, d—— me, sir, I can't believe it.'

There was a tone of anguish in the old man's voice which made even his grotesque and feeble talk terrible.

' I say there can't be such devils on earth;' and then he broke
into an incoherent story of all his trust and love, and all that Jane
owed him, and of her nature which was frank and generous, and
how she never hid a thought from him—open as heaven, sir.
What business was it of his, d—— him! What did he mean by
trying to set a man against his wife? No one but a scoundrel
ever did it.

Varbarriere stood erect.

' You may submit how you like, sir, to your fate; but you
shan't insult me, sir, without answering it. My note left it
optional to you to exact my information or to remain in the darkness, which it seems you prefer. If you wish it, I'll make my
bow—it's nothing to me, but two can play at that game. I've
fought perhaps oftener than you, and you shan't bully *me*.'

' I suppose you're right, sir—don't go, pray—I think I'm half
mad, sir,' said General Lennox, despairingly.

' Sir, I make allowance—I forgive your language, but if you
want to talk to me, it must be with proper respect. I'm as good
a gentleman as you; my statement is, of course, strictly true, and
if you please you can test it.'

CHAPTER XLVI.

GUY DEVERELL AT SLOWTON.

' COME, sir, I have a right to know it—have you not an object in
fooling me?' said General Lennox, relapsing all on a sudden into
his ferocious vein.

' In telling you the truth, sir, I *have* an object, perhaps—but
seeing that it *is* the truth, and concerns you so nearly, you need
not trouble yourself about *my* object,' answered Varbarriere, with
more self-command than was to have been expected.

' I *will* test it, sir. I will try you,' said the General, sternly.
By —— I'll sift it to the bottom.'

'So you ought, sir; that's what I mean to help you to,' said Varbarriere.

'How, sir?—say *how*, and by Heaven, sir, I'll shoot him like a dog.'

'The way to do it I've considered. I shall place you *probably* in possession of such proof as will thoroughly convince you.'

'Thank you, sir, go on.'

'I shall be at Marlowe to-morrow—you must arrive late—on no account earlier than half-past twelve. I will arrange to have you admitted by the glass door—through the conservatory. Don't bring your vehicle beyond the bridge, and leave your luggage at the Marlowe Arms. The object, sir, is this,' said Varbarriere, with deliberate emphasis, observing that the General's grim countenance did not look as apprehensive as he wished, 'that your arrival shall be unsuspected. No one must know anything of it except myself and another, until you shall have reached your room. Do you see?'

'Thanks, sir—yes,' answered the General, looking as unsatisfactorily as before.

'There are two recesses with shelves—one to the right, the other to the left of the bed's head as you look from the door. The secret entrance I have mentioned lies through that at the right. You must not permit any alarm which may be intended to reach Sir Jekyl. Secure the door, and do you sit up and watch. There's a way of securing the secret door from the inside—which I'll explain—that would *prevent* his entrance—don't allow it. The whole—pardon me, sir—*intrigue* will in that case be disclosed without the possibility of a prevarication. You have followed me, I hope, distinctly.'

'I—I'm a little flurried, I believe, sir; I have to apologise. I'll ask you, by-and-by, to repeat it. I think I should like to be alone, sir. She wrote me a letter, sir—I wish I had died when I got it.'

When Varbarriere looked at him, he saw that the old East Indian was crying.

'Sir, I grieve with you,' said Varbarriere, funereally, 'You can command my presence whenever you please to send for me. I shall remain in this house. It will be absolutely necessary, of course, that you should see me again.'

'Thank you, sir. I know—I'm sure you mean kindly—but God only knows all it is.'

He had shaken his hand very affectionately, without any meaning—without knowing that he had done so.

Varbarriere said—

'Don't give way, sir, too much. If there is this sort of misfortune, it is much better discovered—*much* better. You'll think so just now. You'll view it quite differently in the morning. Call for me the moment you want me—farewell, sir.'

So Varbarriere was conducted to his bed-room, and made, beside his toilet, conscientious inquiries about his late dinner, which was in an advanced state of preparation; and when he went down to partake of it, he had wonderfully recovered the interview with General Lennox. Notwithstanding, however, he drank two glasses of sherry, contrary to gastronomic laws, before beginning. Then, however, he made, even for him, a very good dinner.

He could not help wondering what a prodigious fuss the poor old fogey made about this little affair. He could not enter the least into his state of mind. She was a fine woman, no doubt; but there were others—no stint—and he had been married quite long enough to sober and acquire an appetite for liberty.

What was the matter with the old fellow? But that it was insufferably comical, he could almost find it in his heart to pity him.

Once or twice as he smoked his cigar he could not forbear shaking with laughter, the old Philander's pathetics struck him so sardonically.

I really think the state of that old gentleman, who certainly had attained to years of philosophy, was rather serious. That is, I dare say that a competent medical man with his case under observation at that moment would have pronounced him on the verge either of a fit or of insanity.

When Varbarriere had left the room, General Lennox threw

himself on the red damask sofa, which smelled powerfully of
yesterday's swell bagman's tobacco, never perceiving that stale
fragrance, nor the thinness of the cushion which made the ribs and
vertebræ of the couch unpleasantly perceptible beneath. Then,
with his knees doubled up, and the 'Times' newspaper over his
face, he wept, and moaned, and uttered such plaintive and hideous
maunderings as would do nobody good to hear of.

A variety of wise impulses visited him. One was to start
instantaneously for Marlowe and fight Sir Jekyl that night by
candle-light; another, to write to his wife for the last time as his
wife—an eternal farewell—which perhaps would have been highly
absurd, and affecting at the same time.

About two hours after Varbarriere's departure for dinner, he
sent for that gentleman, and they had another, a longer, and a
more collected interview—if not a happier one.

The result was, that Varbarriere's advice prevailed, as one
might easily foresee, having a patient so utterly incompetent to
advise himself.

The attorney having shaken hands with Monsieur Varbarriere,
and watched from the platform the gradual disappearance of the
train that carried him from the purlieus of Slowton, with an
expression of face plaintive as that with which Dido on the wild
sea banks beheld the receding galleys of Æneas, loitered back
again dolorously to the hostelry.

He arrived at the door exactly in time to witness the descent of
Guy Deverell from his chaise. I think he would have preferred
not meeting him, it would have saved him a few boring questions;
but it was by no means a case for concealing himself. He therefore met him with a melancholy frankness on the steps.

The young man recognised him.

'Mr. Rumsey?—How do you do? Is my uncle here?'

'He left by the last train. I hope I see you well, sir.'

'Gone? and where to?'

'He did not tell me.' That was true, but the attorney had
seen his valise labelled 'Chester' by his direction. 'He went by

the London train, but he said he would be back to-morrow. Can *I* do anything ? Your arrival was not expected.'

'Thank you. I think not. It was just a word with my uncle I wished. You say he will be here again in the morning ?'

'Yes, so he said. I'm waiting to see him.'

'Then I can't fail to meet him if I remain.' The attorney perceived, with his weatherwise experience, the traces of recent storm, both in the countenance and the manner of this young man, whose restiveness just now might be troublesome.

'Unless your business is urgent, I think—if you'll excuse me—you had better return to Marlowe,' remarked the attorney. 'You'll find it more comfortable quarters, a good deal, and your uncle will be very much hurried while here, and means to return to Marlowe to-morrow evening.'

'But I shan't. I don't mean to return ; in fact, I wish to speak to him here. I've delayed you on the steps, sir, very rudely ; the wind is cold.'

So he bowed, and they entered together, and the attorney, whose curiosity was now a little piqued, found he could make nothing of him, and rather disliked him ; his reserve was hardly fair in so very young a person, and practised by one who had not yet won his spurs against so redoubted a champion as the knight of the rueful countenance.

Next morning, as M. Varbarriere had predicted, General Lennox, although sleep had certainly had little to do with the change, was quite a different man in some respects—in no wise happier, but much more collected ; and now he promptly apprehended and retained Monsieur Varbarriere's plan, which it was agreed was to be executed that night.

More than once Varbarriere's compunctions revisited him as he sped onwards that morning from Chester to Slowton. But as men will, he bullied these misgivings and upbraidings into submission. He had been once or twice on the point of disclosing this portion of the complication to his attorney, but an odd sort of shyness prevented. He fancied that possibly the picture and his part in it were not altogether pretty, and somehow he did not care to expose himself to the secret action of the attorney's thoughts.

Even in his own mind it needed the strong motive which had first prompted it. Now it was no longer necessary to explore the mystery of that secret door through which the missing deed, and indeed the Deverell estate, had been carried into old Sir Harry's cupboard. But what was to be done? He had committed himself to the statement. General Lennox had a right to demand— in fact, *he* had promised—a distinct explanation.

Yes, a distinct explanation, and, further, a due corroboration by proof of that explanation. It was all due to Monsieur Varbarriere, who had paid that debt to his credit and conscience, and behold what a picture! Three familiar figures, irrevocably transformed, and placed in what a halo of infernal light.

'The thing could not be helped, and, whether or no, it was only right. Why the devil should I help Jekyl Marlowe to deceive and disgrace that withered old gentleman? I don't think it would have been a pleasant position for me.'

And all the respectabilities hovering near cried 'hear, hear, hear!' and Varbarriere shook up his head, and looked magisterial over the havoc of the last livid scene of the tragedy he had prepared; and the porter crying 'Slowton!' opened the door, and released him.

CHAPTER XLVII.

UNCLE AND NEPHEW.

WHEN he reached his room, having breakfasted handsomely in the coffee-room, and learned that early Mr. Rumsey had accomplished a similar meal in his own sitting-room, he repaired thither, and entered forthwith upon their talk.

It was a bright and pleasant morning; the poplar trees in front of the hotel were all glittering in the mellow early sunlight, and the birds twittering as pleasantly as if there was not a sorrow or danger on earth.

' Well, sir, true to my hour,' said Monsieur Varbarriere, in his deep brazen tones, as smiling and wondrously he entered the attorney's apartment.

' Good morning, sir—how d'ye do ? Have you got those notes prepared you mentioned ?'

' That I have, sir, as you shall see, pencil though ; but that doesn't matter—no ?'

The vowel sounded grandly in the upward slide of Varbarriere's titantic double bass.

The attorney took possession of the pocket-book containing these memoranda, and answered—

' No, I can read it very nicely. Your nephew is here, by-the-bye ; he came last night.'

' Guy ? What's brought him here ?'

M. Varbarriere's countenance was overcast. What had gone wrong ? Some chamber in his mine had exploded, he feared, prematurely.

Varbarriere opened the door, intending to roar for Guy, but remembering where he was, and the dimensions of the place, he tugged instead at the bell-rope, and made his summons jangle wildly through the lower regions.

' Hollo !' cried Varbarriere from his threshold, anticipating the approaching waiter ; ' a young gentleman—a Mr. Guy Strang-ways, arrived last evening ?'

' Strangways, please, sir ? Strangways ? No, sir, I don't think we 'av got no gentleman of that name in the 'ouse, sir.'

' But I know you *have*. Go, make out where he is, and let him know that his uncle, Monsieur Varbarriere, has just arrived, and wants to see him—*here*, may I ?' with a glance at the attorney.

' Certainly.'

' There's some mischief,' said Varbarriere, with a lowering glance at the attorney.

' It looks uncommon like it,' mused that gentleman, sadly.

' Why doesn't he come ?' growled Varbarriere, with a motion of his heel like a stamp. 'What do you think he has done? Some cursed sottise.'

'Possibly he has proposed marriage to the young lady, and been refused.'

'Refused! I hope he has.'

At this juncture the waiter returned.

'Well?'

'No, sir, please. No one hin the 'ouse, sir. No such name.'

'Are you sure?' asked Varbarriere of the attorney, in an under diapason.

'Perfectly—said he'd wait here for you. I told him you'd be here this morning,' answered he, dolorously.

'Go down, sir, and get me a list of the gentlemen in the house. I'll pay for it,' said Varbarriere, with an imperious jerk of his hand.

The ponderous gentleman in black was very uneasy, and well he might. So he looked silently out of the window which commands a view of the inn yard, and his eyes wandered over a handsome manure-heap to the chicken-coop and paddling ducks, and he saw three horses' tails in perspective in the chiaro-oscuro of the stable, in the open door of which a groom was rubbing a curb chain. He thought how wisely he had done in letting Guy know so little of his designs. And as he gloomily congratulated himself on his wise reserve, the waiter returned with a slate, and a double column of names scratched on it.

Varbarriere having cast his eye over it, suddenly uttered an oath.

'Number 10—that's the gentleman. Go to number 10, and tell him his uncle wants him here,' roared Varbarriere, as if on the point of knocking the harmless waiter down. 'Read there!' he thundered, placing the slate, with a clang, before the meek attorney, who read opposite to number 10, 'Mr. G. Deverell.'

He pursed his mouth and looked up lackadaisically at his glowering client, saying only 'Ha!'

A minute after and Guy Deverell in person entered the room. He extended his hand deferentially to M. Varbarriere, who on his

part drew himself up black as night, and thrust his hands half
way to the elbows in his trowsers pockets, glaring thunderbolts in
the face of the contumacious young man.

' You see *that ?*' jerking the slate with another clang before
Guy.   ' Did *you* give that name?   Look at number *ten*, sir.'
Varbarriere was now again speaking French.

' Yes, sir, Guy Deverell—my own name.   I shall never again
consent to go by any other.   I had no idea what it might involve
—never.'

The young man was pale, but quite firm.

' You've broken your word, sir; you have ended your relations
with me,' said Varbarriere, with a horrible coldness.

' I am sorry, sir—I *have* broken my promise, but when I could
not keep it without a worse deception.   To the consequences, be
they what they may, I submit, and I feel, sir, more deeply than
you will ever know all the kindness you have shown me from my
earliest childhood until now.'

' Infinitely flattered,' sneered Varbarriere, with a mock bow.
' You have, I presume, disclosed your name to the people at Marlowe as frankly as to those at Slowton?'

' Lady Alice Redcliffe called me by my true name, and insisted
it was mine.   I could not deny it—I admitted the truth.   Mademoiselle Marlowe was present also, and heard what passed.   In
little more than an hour after this scene I left Marlowe Manor.   I
did not see Sir Jekyl, and simply addressed a note to him saying
that I was called away unexpectedly.   I did not repeat to him the
disclosure made to Lady Alice.   I left that to the discretion of
those who had heard it.'

' Their *discretion*—very good—and now, Monsieur Guy Deverell,
I have *done* with you.   I shan't leave you as I took you up, absolutely penniless.   I shall so place you as to enable you with dili-
gence to earn your bread without degradation—that is all.   You
will be so good as to repair forthwith to London and await me at
our quarters in St. James's Street.   I shall send you, by next post,
a cheque to meet expenses in town—no, pray don't thank me; you
might have thanked me by your obedience.   I shan't do much

more to merit thanks. Your train starts from hence, I think, in half an hour.'

Varbarriere nodded angrily, and moved his hand towards the door.

'Farewell, sir,' said Guy, bowing low, but proudly.

'One word more,' said Varbarriere, recollecting suddenly; 'you have not arranged a correspondence with any person? answer me on your honour.'

'No, sir, on my honour.'

'Go, then. Adieu!' and Varbarriere turned from him brusquely, and so they parted.

'Am I to understand, sir,' inquired the attorney, 'that what has just occurred modifies our instructions to proceed in those cases?'

'Not at all, sir,' answered Varbarriere, firmly.

'You see the civil proceedings must all be in the name of the young gentleman—a party who is of age—and you see what I mean.'

'I undertake personally the entire responsibility; you are to proceed in the name of Guy Deverell, and what is more, use the utmost despatch, and spare no cost. When shall we open the battle?'

'Why, I dare say next term.'

'That is less than a month hence?'

'Yes, sir.'

'By my faith, his hands will be pretty full by that time,' said Varbarriere, exultingly. 'We must have the papers out again. I can give you all this day, up to half-past five o'clock. We must get the new case into shape for counsel. You run up to town this evening. I suspect I shall follow you to-morrow; but I must run over first to Marlowe. I have left my things there, and my servant; and I suppose I must take a civil leave of my enemy— there are courtesies, you know—as your prize-fighters shake hands in the ring.'

The sun was pretty far down in the west by the time their sede-runt ended. M. Varbarriere got into his short mantle and mufflers, and donned his ugly felt hat, talking all the while in his deep metallic tones, with his sliding cadences and resounding emphases. The polite and melancholy attorney accompanied his nutritious client to the door, and after he had taken his seat in his vehicle, they chatted a little earnestly through the window, agreeing that they had grown very 'strong' indeed—anticipating nothing but victory, and in confidential whispers breathing slaughter.

As Varbarriere, with his thick arm stuffed through one of the upholstered leathern loops with which it is the custom to flank the windows of all sorts of carriages, and his large varnished boot on the vacant cushion at the other side, leaned back and stared darkly and dreamily through the plate glass on the amber-tinted landscape, he felt rather oddly approaching such persons and such scenes—a crisis with a remoter and more tremendous crisis behind —the thing long predicted in the whisperings of hope—the real thing long dreamed of, and now greeted strangely with a mixture of exultation and disgust.

There are few men, I fancy, who so thoroughly enjoy their revenge as they expected. It is one of those lusts which has its *gout de revers*—' sweet in the mouth, bitter in the belly ;' one of those appetites which will allow its victim no rest *till* it is gratified, and no peace *afterward*. Now, M. Varbarriere was in for it, he was already coming under the solemn shadow of its responsibilities, and was chilled. It involved other people, too, besides its proper object—people who, whatever else some of them might be, were certainly, as respected him and his, innocent. Did he quail, and seriously think of retiring *re infectâ ?* No such thing! It is wonderful how steadfast of purpose are the disciples of darkness, and how seldom, having put their hands to the plough, they look back.

All this while Guy Deverell, in exile, was approaching London with brain, like every other, teeming with its own phantasmagoria. He knew not what particular danger threatened Marlowe Manor, which to him was a temple tenanted by Beatrix alone, the living idol whom he worshipped. He was assured that somehow his consent, perhaps co-operation, was needed to render the attack effectual, and here would arise his opportunity, the self-sacrifice which he contemplated with positive pleasure, though, of course, with a certain awe, for futurity was a murky vista enough beyond it.

Varbarriere's low estimate of young men led *him* at once to conclude that this was an amorous escapade, a bit of romance about that pretty wench, Mademoiselle Beatrix. Why not ? The fool, fooling according to his folly, should not arrest wisdom in her march. Varbarriere was resolved to take all necessary steps in his nephew's name, without troubling the young man with a word upon the subject. He would have judgment and execution, and he scoffed at the idea that his nephew, Guy, would take measures to have him—his kinsman, guardian, and benefactor—punished for having acted for his advantage without his consent.

CHAPTER XLVIII.

IN LADY MARY'S BOUDOIR.

THE red sunset had faded into darkness as M. Varbarriere descended from his carriage at the door-steps of Marlowe. The dressing-bell had not yet rung. Everyone was quite well, the solemn butler informed him graciously, as if *he* had kept them in health to oblige M. Varbarriere. That gentleman's dark countenance, however, was not specially illuminated on the occasion. The intelligence he really wanted referred to old Lady Alice, to whom the inexcusable folly and perfidy of Guy had betrayed his name.

Upon this point he had grown indescribably uncomfortable as he drew near to the house. Had the old woman been conjecturing and tattling ? Had she called in Sir Jekyl himself to counsel ? How was he, Varbarriere, to meet Sir Jekyl ? He must learn from Lady Alice's lips how the land lay.

'And Lady Alice,' he murmured with a lowering countenance, 'pretty well, I hope? Down-stairs to-day, eh?'

The butler had not during his entire visit heard the 'foreign chap' talk so much English before.

'Lady Halice was well in 'ealth.'

'In the drawing-room?'

'No, sir, in Lady Mary's boudoir.'

'And Sir Jekyl?'

'In 'is hown room, sir.'

'Show me to the boudoir, please; I have a word for Lady Alice.'

A few moments more and he knocked at the door of that apartment, and was invited to enter with a querulous drawl that recalled the association of the wild cat with which in an irreverent moment he had once connected that august old lady.

So Varbarriere entered and bowed and stood darkly in the doorframe, reminding her again of the portrait of a fat and cruel burgomaster. 'O! it's you? come back again, Monsieur Varbarriere? Oh!—I'm very glad to see you.'

'Very grateful—very much flattered; and your ladyship, how are *you?*'

'Pretty well — ailing — always ailing — delicate health and *cruelly* tortured in mind. What else can I expect, sir, but sickness?'

'I hope your mind has not been troubled, Lady Alice, since I had the honour of last seeing you.'

'Now, *do* you really hope that? Is it *possible* you *can* hope that my mind, in the state in which you left it, has been one minute at ease since I saw you? Beside, sir, I have heard something that for reasons quite inexplicable *you* have chosen to conceal from me.'

'May I ask what it is? I shall be happy to explain.'

'Yes, the name of that young man—it is *not* Strangways, that was a falsehood; his name, sir, is Guy Deverell!'

And saying this, Lady Alice, after her wont, wept passionately.

'That is perfectly true, Lady Alice; but I don't see what value that information can have, apart from the explanatory particulars I promised to tell you; but not for a few days. If, however, you desire it, I shall postpone the disclosure no longer. You will, I am sure, first be so good as to tell me, though, whether anyone but you knows that the foolish young man's name is Deverell?'

'No; no one, except Beatrix, not a creature. She was present, but has been, at my request, perfectly silent,' answered Lady Alice, eagerly, and gaped darkly at Varbarriere, expecting his revelation.

M. Varbarriere thought, under the untoward circumstances, that a disclosure so imperfect as had been made to Lady Alice was a good deal more dangerous than one a little fuller. He therefore took that lady's hand very reverentially, and looking with his full solemn eyes in her face, said—

'It is not only true, madam, that his name is Guy Deverell, but equally true that he is the lawful son, as well as the namesake, of that Guy Deverell, your *son*, who perished by the hand of Sir Jekyl Marlowe in a duel. Shot down foully, as that Mr. Strangways avers who was his companion, and who was present when the fatal event took place.'

'Gracious Heaven, sir! My son married?'

'Yes, madam, *married* more than a year before his death. All the proofs are extant, and at this moment in England.'

'Married! my boy married, and never told his mother! Oh, Guy, Guy, *Guy*! is it credible?'

'It is not a question, madam, but an absolute certainty, as I will show you whenever I get the papers to Wardlock.'

'And to whom, sir, pray, was my son married?' demanded Lady Alice, after a long pause.

'To my sister, madam.'

Lady Alice gaped at him in astonishment.

'Was she a person at all his equal in life?—a person of—of any education, I mean?' inquired Lady Alice, with a gasp, sublimely unconscious of her impertinence.

'As good a lady as you are,' replied Varbarriere, with a swarthy flush upon his forehead.

'I should like to *know* she was a *lady*, at all events.'

'She was a lady, madam, of pure blood, incapable of a mean thought, incapable, too, of anything low-bred or impertinent.'

His sarcasm sped through and through Lady Alice without producing any effect, as a bullet passes through a ghost.

'It is a great surprise, sir, but *that* will be satisfactory. I suppose you can show it?'

Varbarriere smiled sardonically and answered nothing.

'My son married to a Frenchwoman! Dear, dear, *dear!* Married! You can feel for me, monsieur, knowing as I do nothing of the person or family with whom he connected himself.'

Lady Alice pressed her lean fingers over her heart, and swept the wall opposite, with dismal eyes, sighing at intervals, and gasping dolorously.

The old woman's egotism and impertinence did not vex him long or much. But the pretence of being absolutely above irritation from the feminine gender, in any extant sage, philosopher, or saint, is a despicable affectation. Man and woman were created with inflexible relations; each with the power in large measure or in infinitesimal doses, according to opportunity, to infuse the cup of the other's life with sweet or bitter—with nectar or with poison. Therefore great men and wise men have winced and will wince under the insults of small and even of old women.

'A year, you say, before my poor boy's death?'

'Yes, about that; a little more.'

'Mademoiselle Varbarriere! H'm,' mused Lady Alice.

'I did not say Varbarriere was the name,' sneered he, with a deep-toned drawl.

'Why, you said, sir, did not you, that the Frenchwoman he married was your sister?'

'I said the lady who accepted him was my sister. I never said her name was Varbarriere, or that she was a Frenchwoman.'

'Is not your name Varbarriere, sir?' exclaimed Lady Alice, opening her eyes very wide.

'Certainly, madam. A *nom de guerre*, as we say in France, a name which I assumed with the purchase of an estate, about six years ago, when I became what you call a naturalized French subject.'

'And pray, sir, what *is* your name ?'

'*Varbarriere*, madam. I did bear an English name, being of English birth and family. May I presume to enquire particularly whether you have divulged the name of my nephew to anyone ?'

' No, to no one; neither has Beatrix, I am certain.'

' You now know, madam, that the young man is your own grandson, and therefore entitled to at least as much consideration from you as from me ; and I again venture to impress upon you this fact, that if prematurely his name be disclosed, it may, and indeed *must* embarrass my endeavours to reinstate him in his rights.'

As he said this Varbarriere made a profound and solemn bow ; and before Lady Alice could resume her catechism, that dark gentleman had left the room.

As he emerged from the door he glanced down the broad oak stair, at the foot of which he heard voices. They were those of Sir Jekyl and his daughter. The Baronet's eye detected the dark form on the first platform above him.

' Ha ! Monsieur Varbarriere—very welcome, monsieur—when did you arrive ?' cried his host in his accustomed French.

' Ten minutes ago.'

' Quite well, I hope.'

' Perfectly ; many thanks—and Mademoiselle Beatrix ?'

The large and sombre figure was descending the stairs all this time, and an awful shadow, as he did so, seemed to overcast the face and form of the young lady, to whom, with a dark smile, he extended his hand.

' Quite well, Beatrix, too—*all* quite well—even Lady Alice in her usual health,' said Sir Jekyl.

' *Better*—I'm glad to hear,' said Varbarriere.

' Better ! Oh dear, no—that would never do. But her temper

is just as lively, and all her ailments flourishing. By-the-bye, your nephew had to leave us suddenly.'

'Yes—business,' said Varbarriere, interrupting.

Beatrix, he was glad to observe, had gone away to the drawing-room.

'He'll be back, I hope, immediately?' continued the Baronet. 'He's a fine young fellow. Egad, he's about as good-looking a young fellow as I know. I should be devilish proud of him if I were you. When does he come back to us?'

'Immediately, I hope; business, you know; but nothing very long. We are both, I fear, a very tedious pair of guests; but you have been so pressing, so hospitable,——'

'Say rather, so selfish, monsieur,' answered Sir Jekyl, laughing. 'Our whist and cigars have languished ever since you left.'

M. Varbarriere laughed a double-bass accompaniment to the Baronet's chuckle, and the dressing-bell ringing at that moment, Sir Jekyl and he parted agreeably.

CHAPTER XLIX.

THE GUESTS TOGETHER.

VARBARRIERE marched slowly up, and entered his dressing-room with a 'glooming' countenance and a heavy heart. Everything looked as if he had left it but half an hour ago. He poked the fire and sat down.

He felt like a surgeon with an operation before him. There was a loathing of it, but he did not flinch.

Reader, you think you understand other men. Do you understand yourself? Did you ever quite succeed in defining your own motives, and arriving at the moral base of any action you ever did? Here was Varbarriere sailing with wind and tide full in his favour, right into the haven where he would be—yet to look in his face you would have said '*there* is a sorrowful man,' and had you been able to see within, you would have said, '*there* is a man divided against himself.' Yes, as every man *is*. Several spirits, quite distinct, not blending, but pleading and battling very earnestly on opposite sides, all in possession of the 'house' —but one dominant, always with a disputed sway, but always carrying his point—always the prosperous bully.

Yes, every man is a twist of many strands. Varbarriere was compacted of several Varbarrieres—one of whom was the stronger and the most infernal. His feebler associates commented upon him—despised him—feared him—sought to restrain him, but knew they could not. He tyrannised, and was to the outer world the one and indivisible Varbarriere.

Monsieur Varbarriere the tyrant was about to bring about a *fracas* that night, against which the feebler and better Varbarrieres protested. Varbarriere the tyrant held the knife over the throat of a faithless woman—the better Varbarrieres murmured words of pity and of faint remonstrance. Varbarriere the tyrant scrupled not to play the part of spy and traitor for his ends; the nobler Varbarrieres upbraided him sadly, and even despised him. But what were these feeble angelic Varbarrieres? The ruler is the state, *l'etat c'est moi*! and Varbarriere the tyrant carried all before him.

As the dark and somewhat corpulent gentleman before the glass adjusted his necktie and viewed his shirt-studs, he saw in his countenance, along with the terrible resolution of that tyrant, the sorrows and fears of the less potent spirits; and he felt, though he would not accept, their upbraidings and their truth; so with a stern and heavy heart he descended to the drawing-room.

He found the party pretty nearly assembled, and the usual buzz and animation prevailing, and he smiled and swayed from group to group, and from one chair to another.

Doocey was glad, monstrous glad to see him.

'I had no idea how hard it was to find a good player, until you left us—our whist has been totally ruined. The first night we tried Linnett; he thinks he plays, you know; well, I do assure you, you never *witnessed* such a thing—such a *caricature*, by

Jupiter—forgetting your lead—revoking—*every*thing, by Jove. You may guess what a chance we had—*my* partner, I give you my honour, against old Sir Paul Blunket, as dogged a player as there is in England, egad, and Sir Jekyl there. We tried Drayton next night—the most conceited fellow on earth, and *no head*— Sir Paul had him. I never saw an old fellow so savage. Egad, they were calling one another names across the table—you'd have *died* laughing; but we'll have some play now you've come back, and I'm very glad of it.'

Varbarriere, while he listened to all this, smiling his fat dark smile, and shrugging and bowing slightly as the tale required these evidences, was quietly making his observations on two or three of the persons who most interested him. Beatrix, he thought, was looking ill—certainly much paler, and though very pretty, rather sad—that is, she was ever and anon falling into little abstractions, and when spoken to, waking up with a sudden little smile.

Lady Jane Lennox—she did not seem to observe him—was seated like a sultana on a low cushioned seat, with her rich silks circling grandly round her. He looked at her a little stealthily and curiously, as men eye a prisoner who is about to suffer execution. His countenance during that brief glance was unobserved, but you might have read there something sinister and cruel.

'I forget—*had* the Bishop come when you left us?' said Sir Jekyl, laying his hand lightly from behind on the arm of Varbarriere. The dark-featured man winced—Sir Jekyl's voice sounded unpleasantly in his reverie.

'Ah! Oh! The Bishop? Yes—the Bishop was here when I left; he had been here a day or two,' answered Varbarriere, with a kind of effort.

'Then I need not introduce you—you're friends already,' said Sir Jekyl.

At which moment the assembled party learned that dinner awaited them, and the murmured arrangements for the procession commenced, and the drawing-room was left to the click of the Louis Quatorze clock and the sadness of solitude.

'We had such a dispute, Monsieur Varbarriere, while you were away,' said Miss Blunket.

'About me, I hope,' answered the gentleman addressed, in tolerable English, and with a gallant jocularity.

'Well, no—not about you,' said old Miss Blunket, timidly. 'But I so wished for you to take part in the argument.'

'And why wish for me?' answered the sardonic old fellow, amused, maybe the least bit in the world flattered.

'Well, I think you have the power, Monsieur Varbarriere, of putting a great deal in very few words—I mean, of making an argument so clear and short.'

Varbarriere laughed indulgently, and began to think Miss Blunket a rather intelligent person.

'And what was the subject, pray?'

'Whether life was happier in town or country.'

'Oh! the old debate—country mouse against town mouse,' replied Varbarriere.

'Ah, just so—so true—I don't think *any*-one said that, and—and—I do wish to know which side you would have taken.'

'The condition being that it should be all country or all town, of course, and that we were to retain our incomes?'

'Yes, certainly,' said Miss Blunket, awaiting his verdict with a little bit of bread suspended between her forefinger and thumb.

'Well, then, I should pronounce at once for the country,' said Varbarriere.

'I'm so glad—that's just what I said. I'm sure, said I, I should have Monsieur Varbarriere on my side if he were here. I'm so glad I was right. Did not you hear me say that?' said she, addressing Lady Jane Lennox, whose steady look, obliquely from across the table a little higher up, disconcerted her.

Lady Jane was not thinking of the debate, and asked in her quiet haughty way—

'What is it?'

'Did I not say, yesterday, that Monsieur Varbarriere would vote for the country, in our town or country argument, if he were here?'

'Oh! did you? Yes, I believe you did. I was not listening.'

'And which side, pray, Lady Jane, would you have taken in that ancient debate?' inquired Varbarriere, who somehow felt constrained to address her.

'Neither side,' answered she.

'What! neither town nor country—and how then?' inquired Varbarriere, with a shrug and a smile.

'I think there is as much hypocrisy and slander in one as the other, and I should have a new way—people living like the Chinese, in boats, and never going on shore.'

Varbarriere laughed—twiddled a bit of bread between his finger and thumb, and leaned back, and looked down, still smiling, by the edge of his plate; and was there not a little flush under the dark brown tint of his face?

'That would be simply prison,' ejaculated Miss Blunket.

'Yes, prison; and is not anything better than liberty with its liabilities? Why did Lady Hester Stanhope go into exile in the East, and why do sane men and women go into monasteries?'

Varbarriere looked at her with an odd kind of interest, and sighed without knowing it; and he helped himself curiously to sweetbread, a minute later, and for a time his share in the conversation flagged.

Lady Jane, he thought, was looking decidedly better than when he left—very well, in fact—very well indeed—not at all like a person with anything pressing heavily on her mind.

He glanced at her again. She was talking to old Sir Paul Blunket in a bold careless way, which showed no sign of hidden care or fear.

'Have you been to town since!' inquired Sir Jekyl, who happened to catch Varbarriere's eye at that moment, and availed himself of a momentary lull in what we term the conversation, to put his question.

'No; you think I have been pleasuring, but it was good honest business, I assure you.'

'Lady Alice here fancied you might have seen the General, and learned something about his plans,' continued Sir Jekyl.

'What General?—Lennox—eh?' inquired Varbarriere.

'Yes. What's your question, Lady Alice?' said the Baronet, turning to that lady, and happily not observing an odd expression in Varbarriere's countenance.

'No question; he has not been to London,' answered the old lady, drawing her shawl which she chose to dine in about her, chillily.

'Is it anything *I* can answer?' threw in Lady Jane, who, superbly tranquil as she looked, would have liked to pull and box Lady Alice's ears at that moment.

'Oh no, I fancy not; it's only the old question, when are we to see the General; is he coming back at all?'

'I wish anyone could help me to an answer,' laughed Lady Jane, with a slight uneasiness, which might have been referred to the pique which would not have been unnatural in a handsome wife neglected.

'I begin to fear I shall leave Marlowe without having seen him,' said Lady Alice, peevishly.

'Yes, and it is not complimentary, you know; he disappeared just the day before you came, and he won't come back till you leave; men are such mysterious fellows, don't you think?' said Sir Jekyl.

'It doesn't look as if he liked her company. Did he ever meet you, Lady Alice?' inquired Sir Paul Blunket in his bluff way, without at all intending to be uncivil.

'*That*, you think, would account for it; much obliged to you, Sir Paul,' said Lady Alice, sharply.

Sir Paul did not see it, or what she was driving at, and looked at her therefore with a grave curiosity, for he did not perceive that she was offended.

'Sir Paul has a way of hitting people very hard, has not he, Lady Alice? and then leaving them to recover of themselves,' said Sir Jekyl.

'There's not a great deal of civility wasted among you,' observed Lady Alice.

'I only meant,' said Sir Paul, who felt that he should place himself right, 'that I could not see why General Lennox should avoid Lady Alice, unless he was acquainted with her. There's nothing in that.'

'By-the-bye, Lady Alice,' said Sir Jekyl, who apprehended a possible scene from that lady's temper, and like a good shepherd wished to see his flock pasture peaceably together—'I find I can let you have any quantity you like of that plant you admired yesterday. I forget its name, and the Bishop says he has got one at the Palace with a scarlet blossom : so, perhaps, if you make interest with him—what do you say, my lord ?'

So having engaged the good Bishop in floral conversation with that fiery spirit, the Baronet asked Sir Paul whether he believed all that was said about the great American cow; and what he thought of the monster parsnip; and thus he set him and Lady Alice ambling on different tracts, so that there was no risk of their breaking lances again.

CHAPTER L.

A VISITOR IN THE LIBRARY.

THE company were now pecking at those fruits over which Sir Jekyl was wont to chuckle grimly, making pleasant satire on his gardener, vowing he kept an Aladdin's garden, and that his green-gages were emeralds, and his gooseberries rubies.

In the midst of the talk, the grave and somewhat corpulent butler stood behind his master's chair, and murmured something mildly in his ear.

'What's his name ?' inquired Sir Jekyl.

'Pullet, please, sir.'

'Pullet! I never heard of him. If he had come a little earlier with a knife and fork in his back, we'd have given a good account of him.'

His jokes were chuckled to Lady Alice, who received them drowsily.

' Where have you put him ?'

' In the library, please, sir.'

' What kind of looking person ?'

' A middlish sort of a person, rayther respectable, I should say, sir ; but dusty from his journey.'

' Well, give him some wine, and let him have dinner, if he has not had it before, and bring in his card just now.'

All this occurred without exciting attention or withdrawing Sir Jekyl from any sustained conversation, for he and Lady Alice had been left high and dry on the bank together by the flow and ebb of talk, which at this moment kept the room in a rattle ; and Sir Jekyl only now and then troubled her with a word.

' Pullet !' thought Sir Jekyl, he knew not why, uneasily. ' Who the devil's Pullet, and what the plague can Pullet want ? It can't be Paulett—can it ? There's nothing on earth Paulett can want of me, and he would not come at this hour. Pullet—Pullet —let us see.' But he *could* not see, there was not a soul he knew who bore that name.

' He's eating his dinner, sir, the gentleman, sir, in the small parlour, and says you'll know him quite well, sir, when you see him,' murmured the butler, ' and more '——

' Have you got his card ?'

' He said, sir, please, it would be time enough when he had heat his dinner.'

' Well, so it will.'

And Sir Jekyl drank a glass of claret, and returned to his ruminations.

' So, I shall know Pullet quite well when I see him,' mused the Baronet, ' and he'll let me have his card when he has had his dinner—a cool gentleman, whatever else he may be.' About this Pullet, however, Sir Jekyl experienced a most uncomfortable suspense and curiosity. A bird of ill omen he seemed to him—an angel of sorrow, he knew not why, in a mask.

While the Baronet sipped his claret, and walked quite alone in the midst of his company, picking his anxious steps, and hearing strange sounds through his valley of the shadow of death, the promiscuous assemblage of ladies and gentlemen dissolved itself. The fair sex rose, after their wont, smiled their last on the sable file of gentlemen, who stood politely, napkin in hand, simpering over the backs of their chairs, and, some of them majestically alone, others sliding their fair hands affectionately within the the others' arms, glided through the door in celestial procession.

'I shall leave you to-morrow, Sir Jekyl,' began the Bishop, gravely changing his seat to one just vacated beside his host, and bringing with him his principal chattels, his wine-glasses and napkin.

'I do hope, my lord, you'll reconsider that,' interrupted Sir Jekyl, laying his fingers kindly on the prelate's purple sleeve. A dismal cloud in Sir Jekyl's atmosphere was just then drifting over him, and he clung, as men do under such shadows, to the contact of good and early friendship.

'I am, I assure you, very sorry, and have enjoyed your hospitality much— *very* much; but we can't rest long, you know: we hold a good many strings, and matters won't wait our convenience.'

'I'm only afraid you are overworked; but, of course, I understand how you feel, and shan't press,' said Sir Jekyl.

'And I was looking for you to-day in the library,' resumed the Bishop, 'anxious for a few minutes, on a subject I glanced at when I arrived.'

'I—I *know*,' said Sir Jekyl, a little hesitatingly.

'Yes, the dying wish of poor Sir Harry Marlowe, your father,' murmured the Bishop, looking into his claret-glass, which he slowly turned about by the stem; and, to do him justice, there was not a quarter of a glassful remaining in the bottom.

'I know—to be sure. I quite agree with your lordship's view. I wish to tell you that—quite, I assure you. I don't—I *really* don't at all understand his reasons; but, as you say, it is a case for implicit submission. I intend, I assure you, actually to take down that room during the spring. It is of no real use, and rather spoils the house.'

'I am happy, my dear Sir Jekyl, to hear you speak with so much decision on the subject—truly happy;' and the venerable prelate laid his hand with a gentle dignity on the cuff of Sir Jekyl's dress-coat, after the manner of a miniature benediction. 'I *may* then discharge *that* quite from my mind?'

'Certainly—quite, my lord. I accept your views implicitly.'

'And the *box* — the other wish — you know,' murmured the Bishop.

'I must honestly say, I can't the least understand what can have been in my poor father's mind when he told me to—to do what was right with it—was not that it? For I do assure you, for the life of me, I can't think of anything to *be* done with it but let it *alone*. I pledge you my honour, however, if I ever do get the least inkling of his meaning, I will respect it as implicitly as the other.'

'Now, now, that's exactly what I wish. I'm perfectly satisfied you'll do what's right.'

And as he spoke, the Bishop's countenance brightened, and he drank slowly, looking up toward the ceiling, that quarter of a glass of claret on which he had gazed for so long in the bottom of the crystal chalice.

Just then the butler once more inclined his head from the back of Sir Jekyl's chair, and presented a card to his master on the little salver at his left side. It bore the inscription, 'Mr. Pelter, Camelia Villa,' and across this, perpendicularly, after the manner of a joint 'acceptance' of the firm, was written—'Pelter and Crowe, Chambers, Lincoln's Inn Fields,' in bold black pencilled lines.

'Why did not you tell me that before?' whispered the Baronet, tartly, half rising, with the card in his hand.

'I was not haware, Sir Jekyl. The gentleman said his name exactly like Pullet.'

'In the library? Well—tell him I'm coming,' said Sir Jekyl; and his heart sank, he knew not why.

'Beg your pardon, my lord, for a moment—my man of business, all the way from London, and I fancy in a hurry. I shall get rid of him with a word or two—you'll excuse me ? Dives, will you oblige me—take my place for a moment, and see that the bottle does not stop ; or, Doocey, will you ?—Dives is doing duty at the foot.'

Doocey had hopes that the consultation with the butler portended a bottle of that wonderful Constantia which he had so approved two days before, and took his temporary seat hopefully.

Sir Jekyl, with a general apology and a smile, glided away without fuss, and the talk went on much as before.

When the parlour-door shut behind Sir Jekyl, his face darkened. ' I know it's some *stupid* thing,' he thought, as he walked down the gallery with rapid steps, toward the study, the sharp air agitating, as he did so, his snowy necktie and glossy curls.

' How d'ye do, Mr. Pelter ?—very happy to see you. I had not a notion it was you—the stupid fellow gave me quite another name. Quite well, I hope ?'

' Quite well, Sir Jekyl, I thank you—a—quite well,' said the attorney, a stoutish, short, wealthy-looking man, with a massive gold chain, a resolute countenance, and a bullet head, with close-cut greyish hair.

Pelter was, indeed, an able, pushing fellow, without Latin or even English grammar, having risen in the office from a small clerkship, and, perhaps, was more useful than his gentlemanlike partner.

' Well—a—well, and what has brought you down here ? Very glad to see you, you know ; but you would not run down for fun, I'm afraid,' said Sir Jekyl.

' Au—no—au, well, Sir Jekyl, it has turned out, sir—by gad, sir, I believe them fellows *are* in England, after all !'

' What do you mean by them fellows ?' said Sir Jekyl, with a very dark look, unconsciously repeating the attorney's faulty grammar.

' Strangways and Deverell, you know—I mean them—Herbert Strangeways, and a young man named Deverell—they're in England, I've been informed, very private—and Strangways has been with Smith, Rumsey, and Snagg—the office—you know; and there is something on the stocks there.'

As the attorney delivered this piece of intelligence he kept his eye shrewdly on Sir Jekyl, rather screwed and wrinkled, as a man looks against a storm.

'Oh!—is that all? There's nothing very alarming, is there, in that?—though, d—— me, I don't see, Mr. Pelter, how you reconcile your present statement with what you and your partner wrote to me twice within the last few weeks.'

'Very true, Sir Jekyl; perfectly true, sir. Our information misled us totally; they have been devilish sharp, sir—devilish sly. We never were misled before about that fellow's movements—not that they were ever of any real importance.'

'And why do you think them—but maybe you don't—of more consequence now?'

Pelter looked unpleasantly important, and shook his head.

'What is it—I suppose I may know?' said Sir Jekyl.

'It looks queerish, Sir Jekyl, there's no denying that—in fact, very queerish indeed—both me and my partner think so. You recollect the deed?'

'No—devil a deed—d—— them all!—I don't remember one of them. Why, you seem to forget it's nearly ten years ago,' interrupted the Baronet.

'Ah!—no—not ten—the copy of the deed that we got hold of, pretending to be a marriage settlement. It was brought us, you know, in a very odd way, but quite fair.'

'Yes, I do remember—yes, to be sure—that thing you thought was a forgery, and put in our way to frighten us. Well, and do you fancy that's a genuine thing now?'

'I always thought it might—I think it may—in fact, I think it is. We have got a hint they rely on it. And here's a point to be noted: the deed fixes five-and-twenty as the period of his majority; and just as he attains that age, his father being nearly that time dead, they put their shoulders to the wheel.'

'Put their d—d numbskulls under it, you mean. How can they move—how can they stir? I'd like to know how they can touch my title? I don't care a curse about them. What the plague's frightening you and Crowe *now?* I'm blest if I don't think you're growing old. Why can't you stick to your own view?—you say one thing one day and another the next. Egad, there's no knowing where to have you.'

The Baronet was talking bitterly, scornfully, and with all proper contempt of his adversaries, but there's no denying he looked very pale.

'And there certainly is activity there; cases have been with counsel on behalf of Guy Deverell, the son and heir of the deceased,' pursued Mr. Pelter, with his hands in his pockets, looking grimly up into the Baronet's face.

'Won't you sit down?—do sit down, Pelter; and you haven't had wine?' said Sir Jekyl.

'Thanks—I've had some sherry.'

'Well, you must have some claret. I'd like a glass myself.'

He had rung the bell, and a servant appeared.

'Get claret and glasses for two.'

The servant vanished deferentially.

'I'm not blaming you, mind; but is it not odd we should have known nothing of this son, and this pretended marriage till now?'

'Odd!—oh dear, no!—you don't often know half so much of the case at the other side—nothing at all often till it's on the file.'

'Precious satisfactory!' sneered Sir Jekyl.

'When we beat old Lord Levesham, in Blount and Levesham, they had not a notion, no more than the man in the moon, what we were going on, till we produced the release, and got a direction, egad.' And the attorney laughed over that favourite recollection.

CHAPTER LI.

PELTER OPENS HIS MIND.

'TAKE a glass of claret. This is '34. Maybe you'd like some port better.'

' No, thanks, this will do very nicely,' said the accommodating attorney. 'Thirty-four? So it is, egad: and uncommon fine too.'

' I hope you can give me a day or two—not business, of course —I mean by way of holiday,' said Sir Jekyl. 'A little country air will do you a world of good—set you up for the term.'

Mr. Pelter smiled, and shook his head shrewdly.

' Quite out of the question, Sir Jekyl, I thank you all the same —business tumbling in too fast just now—I daren't stay away another day—no, no—ha, ha, ha! no rest for us, sir—no rest for the wicked. But this thing, you know, looks rather queerish, we thought—a little bit urgent: the other party has been so sly; and no want of money, sir—the sinews of war—lots of tin there.'

' Yes, of course; and lots of tin here, too. I fancy fellows don't like to waste money only to hold their own; but, egad, if it comes to be a pull at the long purse, all the worse for them,' threw in the Baronet.

' And their intending, you know, to set up this marriage,' continued the attorney without minding; 'and that Herbert Strangways being over here with the young pretender, as we call him, under his wing; and Strangways is a deuced clever fellow, and takes devilish sound view of a case when he lays his mind to it. It was he that reopened that great bankruptcy case of Onslow and Grawley, you remember.'

Sir Jekyl assented, but did not remember.

' And a devilish able bit of chess-play that was on both sides— no end of concealed property—brought nearly sixty thousand pounds into the fund, egad! The creditors passed a vote, you

remember—spoke very handsomely of him.   Monstrous able fellow,
egad !'

'A monstrous able fellow he'll be if he gets my property, egad !
It seems to me you Pelter and Crowe are half in love with him,'
said Sir Jekyl, flushed and peevish.

'We'll hit him a hard knock or two yet, for all that—ha, ha !—
or I'm mistaken,' rejoined old Mr. Pelter.

'Do you know him ?' inquired Sir Jekyl ; and the servant at
the same time appearing in answer to his previous summons, he
said—

'Go to the parlour and tell Mr. Doocey—you know *quietly*—
that I am detained by business, but that we'll join them in a little
time in the drawing-room.'

So the servant, with a reverence, departed.

'I say, *do* you ?'

'Just a little.   Seven years ago, when I was in Havre, he was
stopping there too.   A very gentlemanlike man—sat beside him
twice at the table d'hôte.   I could see he knew d—d well who I
was—wide awake, very agreeable man, very—wonderfully well-
informed.   Wonderful ups and downs that fellow's had—clever
fellow—ha, ha, ha !—I mentioned you, Sir Jekyl ; I wanted to
hear if he'd say anything—fishing, hey ?   Old file, you know '—
and the attorney winked and grinned agreeably at Sir Jekyl.
'Capital claret this—cap-i-tal, by Jupiter !   It came in natural
enough.   We were talking of England, you see.   He was asking
questions ; and so, talking of country gentlemen, and county
influence, and parliamentary life, you know, I brought in *you*,
and asked him if he knew Sir Jekyl Marlowe.'   Another wink and
a grin here.   'I asked, a bit suddenly, you know, to see how he'd
take it.   Did not show, egad !   more than that decanter—ha, ha,
ha !—devilish cool dog—monstrous clever fellow—not a bit ; and
he said he did not know you—had not that honour ; but he knew
a great deal of you, and he spoke very handsomely—upon my
honour quite au—au—handsomely of you, he did.'

'Vastly obliged to him,' said Sir Jekyl ; but though he sneered I
think he was pleased.   'You don't recollect what he said, I dare say ?'

' Well, I can*not* exactly.'

' Did he mention any unpleasantness ever between us ?' continued Sir Jekyl.

' Yes, he said there had, and that he was afraid Sir Jekyl might not remember his name with satisfaction; but he, for his part, liked to forget and forgive—that kind of thing, you know, and young fellows being too hot-headed, you know. I really—I don't think he bears you personally any ill-will.'

' There has certainly been time enough for anger to cool a little, and I really, for my part, never felt anything of the kind towards him; I can honestly say *that*, and I dare say he knows it. I merely want to protect myself against—against madmen, egad !' said Sir Jekyl.

' I think that copy of a marriage settlement you showed me had no names in it,' he resumed.

' No, the case is all put like a moot point, not a name in it. It's all nonsense, too, because every man in my profession knows a copying clerk never has a notion of the meaning of anything— letter, deed, pleading—nothing he copies—not an iota, by Jove !'

' 'Finish the bottle; you must not send it away,' said Sir Jekyl.

' Thanks, I'm doing very nicely; and now as they may open fire suddenly, I want to know'—here the attorney's eyes glanced at the door, and his voice dropped a little—' any information of a confidential sort that may guide us in—in——'

' Why, I fancy it's *all* confidential, isn't it ?' answered Sir Jekyl.

' Certainly—but aw—but—I meant—you know—there was aw— a—there was a talk, you know, about a deed. Eh ?'

' I—I—*yes*, I've heard—I know what you mean,' answered Sir Jekyl, pouring a little claret into his glass. ' They—those fellows —they lost a deed, and they were d—d impertinent about it; they wanted—you know it's a long time ago—to try and slur my poor father about it—I don't know exactly how, only, I think, there would have been an action for slander very likely about it, if it had not stopped of itself.'

Sir Jekyl sipped his claret.

'I shan't start till three o'clock train to-morrow, if you have anything to say to me,' said the attorney, looking darkly and expectingly in Sir Jekyl's face.

'Yes, I'll think over everything. I'd like to have a good talk with you in the morning. You sleep here, you know, of course.'

'Very kind. I hope I shan't be in your way, Sir Jekyl. Very happy.'

Sir Jekyl rang the bell.

'I shan't let you off to-morrow, unless you really can't help it,' he said; and, the servant entering, 'Tell Mrs. Sinnot that Mr. Pelter remains here to-night, and would wish—*do* you?—to run up to your room. Where's your luggage?'

'Precious light luggage it is. I left it at the hotel in the town —a small valise, and a——'

'Get it up here, do you mind, and let us know when Mr. Pelter's room is ready.'

'Don't be long about dressing; we must join the ladies, you know, in the drawing-room. I wish, Pelter, there was no such thing as business; and that all attorneys, except you and Crowe, of course, were treated in this and the next world according to their deserts,' an ambiguous compliment at which Pelter nodded slyly, with his hands in his pockets.

'You'll have to get us all the information you can scrape together, Sir Jekyl. You see they may have evidence of that deed —I mean the lost one, you know—and proving a marriage and the young gentleman legitimate. It may be a serious case—upon my word a *very* serious case—do you see? And term begins, you know, immediately, so there really is no time to lose, and there's no harm in being ready.'

'I'll have a long talk with you about it in the morning, and I am devilish glad you came—curse the whole thing!'

The servant here came to say that Mr. Pelter's room was ready, and his luggage sent for to the town.

'Come up, then—we'll look at your room.'

So up they went, and Pelter declared himself charmed.

'Come to my room, Mr. Pelter—it's a long way off, and a confoundedly shabby crib; but I've got some very good cigars there,' said Sir Jekyl, who was restless, and wished to hear the attorney more fully on this hated business.

CHAPTER LXII.

THE PIPE OF PEACE.

SIR JEKYL marched Mr. Pelter down the great stair again, intending to make the long journey rearward. As they reached the foot of the stairs, Monsieur Varbarriere, candle in hand, was approaching it on the way to his room. He was walking leisurely, as large men do after dinner, and was still some way off.

'By Jove! Why did not you tell me?' exclaimed the attorney, stopping short. 'By the law! you've *got* him here.'

'Monsieur Varbarriere?' said the Baronet.

'Mr. Strangways, sir—*that's* he.'

'*That* Strangways!' echoed the Baronet.

'Herbert Strangways,' whispered Mr. Pelter, and by this time M. Varbarriere was under the rich oak archway, and stopped, smiling darkly, and bowing a little to the Baronet, who was for a moment surprised into silence.

'How do you do, Mr. Strangways, sir?' said the attorney, advancing with a shrewd resolute smile, and extending his hand.

M. Varbarriere, without the slightest embarrassment, took it, bowing with a courtly gravity.

'Ah, Monsieur Pelter?—yes, indeed—very happy to meet you again.'

'Yes, sir—very happy, Mr. Strangways; so am I. Did not know you were in this part of the world, Mr. Strangways, sir. You remember Havre, sir?'

'Perfectly—yes. You did not know me by the name of Var-

barriere, which name I adopted on purchasing the Varbarriere
estates shortly after I met you at Havre, on becoming a naturalized subject of France.'

'Wonderful little changed, Monsieur Barvarrian—fat, sir—a
'little stouter—in good case, Mr. Strangways; but six years, you
know sir, does not *count* for *nothing*—ha, ha, ha!'

'You have the goodness to flatter me, I fear,' answered Varbarriere, with a smile somewhat contemptuous, and in his deep tones
of banter.

'This is my friend, Mr. Strangways, if he'll allow me to call
him so—Mr. Herbert Strangways, Sir Jekyl,' said the polite attorney, presenting his own guest to the Baronet.

'And so, Monsieur Varbarriere, I find I have an additional
reason to rejoice in having made your acquaintance, inasmuch
as it revives a very old one, so old that I almost fear you may
have forgotten it. You remember our poor friend, Guy Deverell,
and '——

'Perfectly, Sir Jekyl, and I was often tempted to ask you the
same question; but—but you know there's a *melancholy*—and we
were so happy here, I had not courage to invite the sadness of the
retrospect, though a very remote one. I believe I was right, Sir
Jekyl. Life's true philosophy is to extract from the present all
it can yield of happiness, and to bury our dead out of our sight.'

'I dare say—I'm much of that way of thinking myself. And
—dear me!—I—I suppose I'm very much altered.' He was looking at Varbarriere, and trying to recover in the heavy frame and
ponderous features before him the image of that Herbert Strangways, whom, in the days of his early coxcombry, he had treated
with a becoming impertinence.

'No—you're wonderfully little changed—I say honestly—quite
wonderfully like what I remember you. And I—I know what a
transformation I am—perfectly,' said Varbarriere.

And he stood before Sir Jekyl, as he would display a portrait,
full front—Sir Jekyl held a silver candlestick in his hand, Monsieur Varbarriere his in his—and they stood face to face—in a
dream of the past.

Varbarriere's mystic smile expanded to a grin, and the grin broke into a laugh—deep and loud—not insulting—not sneering.

In that explosion of sonorous and enigmatic merriment Sir Jekyl joined—perhaps a little hesitatingly and coldly, for he was trying, I think, to read the riddle—wishing to be quite sure that he might be pleased, and accept these vibrations as sounds of reconciliation.

There was nothing quite to forbid it.

'I see,' said Monsieur Varbarriere, in tones still disturbed by laughter, 'in spite of your politeness, Sir Jekyl, what sort of impression my metamorphosis produces. Where is the raw-boned youth—so tall and gawky, that, egad! London bucks were ashamed to acknowledge him in the street, and when they did speak could not forbear breaking his gawky bones with their jokes?—ha, ha, ha! Now, lo! here he stands—the grand old black swine, on hind legs—hog-backed—and with mighty paunch and face all draped in fat. Bah! ha, ha, ha! What a magician is Father Time! Look and laugh, sir—you cannot laugh more than I.'

'I laugh at your fantastic caricature, so utterly unlike what I see. There's a change, it's true, but no more than years usually bring; and, by Jove! I'd much rather any day grow a little full, for my part, than turn, like some fellows, into a scarecrow.'

'No, no—no scarecrow, certainly,' still laughed Varbarriere.

'Egad, no,' laughed the attorney in chorus. 'No corners there, sir—ribs well covered—hey? nothing like it coming on winter;' and grinning pleasantly, he winked at Sir Jekyl, who somehow neither heard nor saw him, but said—

'Mr. Pelter, my law adviser here, was good enough to say he'd come to my room, which you know so well, Monsieur Varbarriere, and smoke a cigar. You can't do better—pray let me persuade you.'

He was in fact tolerably easily persuaded, and the three gentlemen together—Sir Jekyl feeling as if he was walking in a

dream, and leading the way affably—reached that snuggery which
Varbarriere had visited so often before.

'Just *one*—they *are* so good,' said he.   'We are to go to the
drawing-room—arn't we?'

'Oh, certainly.   I think you'll like these—they're rather good,
Mr. Pelter.   You know them, Monsieur Varbarriere.'

'I've hardly ever smoked such tobacco.   Once, by a chance, at
Lyons, I lighted on a box very like these—that is, about a third
of them—but hardly so good.'

'We've smoked some of these very pleasantly together,' said Sir
Jekyl, cultivating genial relations.

Varbarriere, who had already one between his lips, grunted a
polite assent with a nod.   You would have thought that his whole
soul was in his tobacco, as his dark eyes dreamily followed the
smoke that thinly streamed from his lips.   His mind, however,
was busy in conjecturing what the attorney had come about, and
how much he knew of his case and his plans.   So the three gentlemen puffed away in silence for a time.

'Your nephew, Mr. Guy Strangways, I hope we are soon to
see him again?' asked Sir Jekyl, removing his cigar for a
moment.

'You are very good.   Yes, I hope.   In fact, though I call it
business, it is only a folly which displeases me, which he has
promised shall end ; and whenever I choose to shake hands, he
will come to my side.   There is no real quarrel, mind,' and Varbarriere laughed, 'only I must cure him of his nonsense.'

'Well, then we may hope very soon to see Mr. Strangways.   I
call him Strangways, you know, because he has assumed that name,
I suppose, permanently.'

'Well, I think so.   His real name is Deverell—a very near relation, and, in fact, representative of our 'poor friend Guy.   His
friends all thought it best he should drop it, with its sad associations, and assume a name that may be of some little use to him
among more affluent relatives,' said M. Varbarriere, who had resolved to be frank as day and harmless as doves, and to disarm
suspicion adroitly.

'A particularly handsome fellow—a distinguished-looking young man. How many things, Monsieur Varbarriere, we wish undone as we get on in life!'

The attorney lay back in his chair, his hands in his pockets, his heels on the carpet, his cigar pointing up to the ceiling, and his eyes closed luxuriously. He intended making a note of everything.

'I hope to get him on rapidly in the French service,' resumed Varbarriere, 'and I can make him pretty comfortable myself while I live, and more so after I'm gone; and in the meantime I am glad to put him in a field where he must exert himself, and see something of labour as well as of life.'

There was a knock at the door, and the intelligence that Mr. Pelter's luggage was in his room. He would have stayed, perhaps, but Sir Jekyl, smiling, urged haste, and as his cigar was out, he departed. When he was quite gone, Sir Jekyl rose smiling, and extended his hand to Varbarriere, who took it smiling in his own way; also, Sir Jekyl was looking in the face of the large man who stood before him, and returning his gaze a little cloudily; and laughing, both shook hands for a good while, and there was nothing but this lowtoned laughter between them.

'At all events, Herbert, I'm glad we have met, very glad— very, very. I did not think I'd have felt it quite this way. I've your forgiveness to ask for a great deal. I never mistook a man so much in my life. I believe you are a devilish good fellow; but—but I fancied, you know, for a long time, that you had taken a hatred to me, and—and I have done you great injustice; and I wish very much I could be of any use to—to that fine young fellow, and show any kindness worth the name towards you.'

Sir Jekyl's eyes were moist, he was smiling, and he was shaking Varbarriere's powerful hand very kindly. I cannot analyse his thoughts and feelings in that moment of confusion. It had overcome him suddenly—it had in some strange way even touched Varbarriere. Was there dimly seen by each a kindly solution of a life-long hatred—a possibility of something wise, perhaps self-sacrificing, that led to reconciliation and serenity in old days?

Varbarriere leaned his great shoulders to the wall, his hand still in Sir Jekyl's, still smiling, and looked almost sorrowfully, while he uttered something between a long pant and a sigh.

'Wonderful thing life is—terrible battle, life!' murmured Varbarriere, leaning against the wall, with his dark eyes raised to the far cornice, and looking away and through and beyond it into some far star.

There are times when your wide-awake gentlemen dream a little, and Sir Jekyl laughed a pensive and gentle little laugh, shaking his head and smiling sadly in reply.

'Did you ever read Vathek?' asked the Baronet, 'rather a good horror—the fire, you know—ah, ha!—that's a fire every fellow has a spark of in him; I know I have. I've had everything almost a fellow wants; but this I know, If I were sure that death was only rest and darkness, there's hardly a day I live I would not choose it.' And with this sentiment came a sincere and odd little laugh.

'My faith! I believe it's true,' said Varbarriere with a shrug, and a faint smile of satiety on his heavy features.

'We must talk lots together, Herbert—talk a great deal. You'll find I'm not such a bad fellow after all. Egad, I'm *very* glad you're here!'

CHAPTER LIII.

A RENCONTRE IN THE GALLERY.

IT was time now, however, that they should make their appearance in the drawing-room; so, for the present, Varbarriere departed. He reached his dressing-room in an undefined state—a sort of light, not of battle fires, but of the dawn in his perspective; when, all on a sudden, came the image of a white-moustached, white-browed, grim old military man, glancing with a clear, cold eye, that could be cruel, from the first-class carriage window, up and down the platform of a gas-lit station, some hour and a half away from Slowton, and then sternly at his watch.

'The stupid old fogey !' thought Varbarriere, with a pang, as he revised his toilet hurriedly for the drawing-room. 'Could that episode be evaded ?'

There was no time to arrive at a clear opinion on this point, nor, indeed, to ascertain very clearly what his own wishes pointed at. So, in a state rather anarchic, he entered the gallery, *en route* for the drawing-room.

Monsieur Varbarriere slid forth, fat and black, from his doorway, with wondrous little noise, his bulk considered, and instantly on his retina, lighted by the lamp at the cross galleries, appeared the figure of a tall thin female, attired in a dark cloak and bonnet, seated against the opposite wall, not many steps away. Its head turned, and he saw Donica Gwynn. It was an odd sort of surprise; he had just been thinking of her.

'Oh! I did not think as you were here, sir; I thought you was in Lunnon.'

'Yet here I am, and you too, both unexpectedly.' A suspicion had crossed his mind. 'How d'ye do, Mrs. Gwynn ?'

'Well, I thank you, sir.'

'Want *me* here ?'

'No, sir; I was wrote for by missus, please.'

'Yes,' he said very slowly, looking hard at her. 'Very good, Mrs. Gwynn ; have you anything to say to me ?'

It would not do, of course, to protract this accidental talk ; he did not care to be seen *tête-à-tête* with Donica Gwynn in the gallery.

'No sir, please, I han't nothing to say, sir,' and she courtesied.

'Very well, Mrs. Gwynn; we're quite secret, hey ?' and with another hard look, but only momentary, in her face, he proceeded toward the head of the staircase.

'Beg parding, sir, but I think you dropt something.' She was pointing to a letter, doubled up, and a triangular corner of which stuck up from the floor, a few yards away.

'Oh! thank you,' said Varbarriere, quickly retracing his steps, and picking it up.

A terrible fact for the world to digest is this, that some of our gentlemen attorneys are about the most slobbering men of business to be found within its four corners. They will mislay papers, and even lose them; they are dilatory and indolent—quite the reverse of our sharp, lynx-eyed, energetic notions of that priesthood of Themis, and prone to every sort and description of lay irregularity in matters of order and pink tape.

Our friend Pelter had a first-rate staff, and a clockwork partner beside in Crowe, so that the house was a very regular one, and was himself, in good measure, the fire, bustle, and impetus of the firm. But every virtue has its peccant correspondent. If Pelter was rapid, decided, daring, he was also a little hand-over-hand. He has been seen in a hurry to sweep together and crunch like a snowball a drift of banknotes, and stuff them so impressed into the bottom of his great-coat pocket! What more can one say?

This night, fussing out at his bed-room door, he plucked his scented handkerchief from his pocket, and, as he crossed his threshold, with it flirted forth a letter, which had undergone considerable attrition in that receptacle, and was nothing the whiter, I am bound to admit, especially about the edges, for its long sojourn there.

Varbarriere knew the handwriting and I. M. M. initials in the left-hand lower angle. So, with a nod and a smile, he popped it into his trousers pocket, being that degree more cautious than Pelter.

Sir Jekyl was once more in high spirits. To do him justice, he had not affected anything. There had been an effervescence—he hardly knew how it came about. But his dangers seemed to be dispersing; and, at the worst, were not negotiation and compromise within his reach?

Samuel Pelter, Esq., gentleman attorney and a solicitor of the High Court of Chancery, like most prosperous men, had a comfortable confidence in himself; and having heard that Lady Alice

Redcliffe was quarrelling with her lawyer, thought there could be no harm in his cultivating her acquaintance.

The old lady was sitting in a high-backed chair, very perpendicularly, with several shawls about and around her, stiff and pale; but her dusky eyes peered from their sunken sockets, in grim and isolated observation.

Pelter strutted up. He was not perhaps, a distinguished-looking man—rather, I fear, the contrary. His face was broad and smirking, with a short, broad, blue chin, and a close crop of iron-grey on his round head, and plenty of crafty crow's-feet and other lines well placed about.

He stood on the hearthrug, within easy earshot of Lady Alice, whom he eyed with a shrewd glance, 'taking her measure,' as his phrase was, and preparing to fascinate his prey.

'Awful smash that, ma'am, on the Smather and Slam Junction', said Pelter, having fished up a suitable topic. 'Frightful thing—fourteen killed—and they say upwards of seventy badly hurt. I'm no chicken, Lady Alice, but by Jove, ma'am, I can't remember any such casualty—a regular ca-tas-trophe, ma'am!'

And Pelter, with much feeling, gently lashed his paunch with his watch-chain and bunch of seals, an obsolete decoration, which he wore—I believe still wears.

Lady Alice, who glowered sternly on him during this speech, nodded abruptly with an inarticulate sound, and then looked to his left, at a distant picture.

'I trust I see you a great deal better, Lady Alice. I have the pleasure, I believe, to address Lady Alice Redcliffe—aw, haw, h'm,' and the attorney executed his best bow, a ceremony rather of agility than grace. 'I had the honour of seeing you, Lady Alice Redcliffe, at a shower-flow—flower-show, I mean—in the year—let me see—egad, ma'am, twelve—no—no—*thirteen* years ago. How time does fly! Of course all them years—*thirteen*, egad!—has not gone for nothing. I dare say you don't perceive the alterations in yourself—no one does—I wish no one else did—that was always my wish to Mrs. P. of a morning—*my* good lady, Mrs. Pelter—ha, ha, ha! Man can't tether time or tide, as the Psalm

says, and every year scribbles a wrinkle or two.   You were suffer--
ing, I heard then, ma'am, chronic cough, ma'am—and all that.   I
hope it's abated—I know it will, ma'am—my poor lady is a martyr
to it—troublesome thing—very—awful troublesome !   Lady Alice.'

There was no reply, Lady Alice was still looking sternly at the
picture.

' I remember so well, ma'am, you were walking a little lame
then, linked with Lord Lumdlebury—(we have had the honour to
do business occasionally for his lordship)—and I was informed by a
party with me that you had been with Pincendorf.   I don't think
much of them jockeys, ma'am, for my part; but if it was anything of a callosity'—

Without waiting for any more, Lady Alice Redcliffe rose in
solemn silence to her full height, beckoned to Beatrix, and said.
grimly—

' I'll change my seat, dear, to the sofa—will you help me with
these things ?'

Lady Alice glided awfully to the sofa, and the gallant Mr.
Pelter instituted a playful struggle with Beatrix for possession of
the shawls.

' I remember the time, miss, I would not have let you carry your
share ; but, as I was saying to Lady Alice Redcliffe'—

He was by this time tucking a shawl about her knees, which, so
soon as she perceived, she gasped to Beatrix—

' Where's Jekyl ?—I can't have *this* any longer—call him here.'

' As I was saying to you, Lady Alice, ma'am, our joints grow a
bit rusty after sixty ; and talking of feet, I passed the Smather
and Slam Junction, ma'am, only two hours after the collision ;
and, egad ! there were three feet all in a row cut off by the instep,.
quite smooth, ma'am, lying in the blood there, a pool as long as
the passage up stairs—awful sight !'

Lady Alice rose up again, with her eyes very wide, and her
mouth very close, apparently engaged in mental prayer, and her
face angry and pink, and she beckoned with tremulous fingers to
Sir Jekyl, who was approaching with one of his provoking smiles.

'I say, Mr. Pelter, my friend Doocey wants you over there; they're at loggerheads about a law point, and I can't help them.'

'Hey! if it's *practice* I can give them a wrinkle maybe;' and away stumped the attorney, his fists in his pockets, smirking, to the group indicated by his host.

'Hope I haven't interrupted a conversation? What can I do for you?' said Sir Jekyl, gaily.

'What do you *mean*, Jekyl Marlowe—what *can* you mean by bringing such persons here? What pleasure can you *possibly* find in low and *dreadful* society?—none of your family liked it. Where did you find that man? How on earth did you procure such a person? If I *could*—if I had been well enough, I'd have rung the bell and ordered your servant to remove him. I'd have gone to my bed-room, sir, only that even there I could not have felt safe from his intrusions. It's utterly intolerable and prepos·terous!'

'I had no idea my venerable friend, Pelter, could have pursued a lady so cruelly; but rely upon me, I'll protect you.'

'I think you had better cleanse your house of such persons; at all events, I insist they shan't be allowed to make their horrible sport of me!' said Lady Alice, darting a fiery glance after the agreeable attorney.

CHAPTER LIV.

OLD DONNIE AND LADY JANE.

'Can you tell me, child, anything about that horrible fat old Frenchman, who has begun to speak English since his return?' asked Lady Jane Lennox of Beatrix, whom she stopped, just touching her arm with the tip of her finger, as she was passing. Lady Jane was leaning back indolently, and watching the movements of M. Varbarriere with a disagreeable interest.

'That's Monsieur Varbarriere,' answered Beatrix.

'Yes, I know that; but who is he—what is he? I wish he were gone,' replied she.

'I really know nothing of him,' replied Beatrix, with a smile.

'Yes, you do know something about him; for instance, you know he's the uncle of that handsome young man who accompanied him.' This Lady Jane spoke with a point which caused on a sudden a beautiful scarlet to tinge the young girl's cheeks.

Lady Jane looked at her, without a smile, without archness, with a lowering curiosity and something of pain, one might fancy, even of malignity.

Lady Jane hooked her finger in Beatrix's bracelet, and lowering her eyes to the carpet, remained silent, it seemed to the girl undecided whether to speak or not on some doubtful subject. With a vague interest Beatrix watched her handsome but sombre countenance, till Lady Jane appearing to escape from her thoughts, with a little toss of her beautiful head and a frown, said, looking up—

'Beatrix, I have such frightful dreams sometimes, I am ill, I think; I am horribly nervous to-night.'

'Would you like to go to your room? Maybe if you were to lie down, Lady Jane'——

'By-and-by, perhaps—yes.' She was still stealthily watching Varbarriere.

'I'll go with you—shall I?' said Beatrix.

'No, you shan't,' answered Lady Jane, rudely.

'And why, Lady Jane?' asked Beatrix, hurt and surprised.

'You shall never visit my room; you are a good little creature. I could have loved you, Beatrix, but now I can't.'

'Yet I like you, and you meet me so! why is this?' pleaded Beatrix.

'I can't say, little fool; who ever knows why they like or dislike? I don't. The fault, I suppose, is mine, not yours. I never said it was yours. If you were ever so little wicked,' she added, with a strange little laugh, 'perhaps I could; but it is not worth talking about,' and with a sudden change from this sinister levity to a seriousness which oscillated strangely between crnelty and sadness, she said—

'Beatrix, you like that young man, Mr. Strangways?' Again poor Beatrix blushed, and was about to falter an exculpation and a protest; but Lady Jane silenced it with a grave and resolute '*Yes—you like him*;' and after a little pause, she added—'Well, if you don't marry *him*, marry no one else;' and shortly after this, Lady Jane sighed heavily.

This speech of hers was delivered in a way that prevented evasion or girlish hypocrisy, and Beatrix had no answer but that blush which became her so; and dropping her eyes to the ground, she fell into a reverie, from which she was called up by Lady Jane, who said suddenly—

'What can that fat Monsieur Varbarriere be?' He looks like Torquemada, the Inquisitor—mysterious, plausible, truculent—what do you think?' Don't you fancy he could poison you in an ice or a cup of coffee; or put you into Cardinal Ballue's cage, and smile on you once a year through the bars?'

Beatrix smiled, and looked on the unctuous old gentleman with an indulgent eye, comparatively.

'I can't see him so melodramatically, Lady Jane,' she laughed. 'To me he seems a much more commonplace individual, a great deal less interesting and atrocious, and less like the abbot.'

'What abbot?' said Lady Jane, sharply. 'Now really that's very odd.'

'I meant,' said Beatrix, laughing, 'the Abbot of Quidlinberg, in Canning's play, who is described, you know, as very corpulent and cruel.'

'Oh, I forgot: I don't think I ever read it; but it chimed in so oddly with my dreams.'

'How, what do you mean?' cried Beatrix, amused.

'I dreamed some one knocked at night at my door, and when I said "come in," that Monsieur Varbarriere put in his great face, with a hood on like a friar's, smiling like—like an assassin; and somehow I have felt a disgust of him ever since.'

'Well, I really think he would look rather well in a friar's frock and hood,' said Beatrix, glancing at the solemn old man again with a little laugh. 'He would do very well for Mrs. Radcliff's one-handed monk, or Schedone, or some of those awful ecclesiastics that scare us in books.'

' I think him positively odious, and I hate him,' said Lady Jane, quietly rising. ' I mean to steal away—will you come with me to the foot of the stair ?'

' Come,' whispered Beatrix ; and as Lady Jane lighted her candle, in that arched recess near the foot of the stair, where, in burnished silver, stand the files of candles, awaiting the fingers which are to bear them off to witness the confidences of toilet or of dejection, she said—

' Well, as you won't take me with you, we must part here. Good-night, Lady Jane.'

Lady Jane turned as if to kiss her, but only patted her on the cheek, and said coldly—

' Good-bye, little fool—now run back again.'

When Lady Jane reached the gallery at the top of the staircase, she, too, saw Donica Gwynn seated where Varbarriere had spoken to her.

' Ha ! Donica,' cried she suddenly, in the accents of early girlhood, ' I'm so glad to see you, Donica. You hardly know me now ?'

And Lady Jane, in the light of one transient, happy smile, threw her jewelled arms round the neck of the old housekeeper, whose visits of weeks at a time to Wardlock were nearly her happiest remembrances of that staid old mansion.

' You dear old thing ! you were always good to me ; and I such a madcap and such a fury ! Dull enough now, Donnie, but not a bit better.'

' My poor Miss Jennie !' said old Donica Gwynn, with a tender little laugh, her head just a little on one side, looking on her old pet and charge with such a beautiful, soft lighting up of love in her hard old face as you would not have fancied could have beamed there. Oh ! most pathetic mystery, how in our poor nature, layer over layer, the angelic and the evil, the mean and the noble, lie alternated. How sometimes, at long intervals, in the wintriest life and darkest face, the love of angels will suddenly beam out, and show you, still unwrecked, the eternal capacity for heaven.

'And grown such a fine 'oman—bless ye—I allays said she would—didn't I ?'

'You always stood up for me, old Donnie Don. Come into my room with me now, and talk. Yes—come, and talk, and talk, and talk—I have no one, Donnie, to talk with now. If I had I might be different—I mean better. You remember poor mamma, Donnie—don't you ?'

'*Dear!* to be sure—yes, and a nice creature, and a pretty—there's a look in your face sometimes reminds me on her, Miss Jennie. And I allays said you'd do well—didn't I ?—and see what a great match, they tell me, you a' made! Well well! and how you *have* grown!—a fine lady, bless you,' and she laughed so softly over those thin, girlish images of memory, you'd have said the laugh was as far away and as sad as the remembrance.

'Sit down, Donnie Don,' she said, when they had entered the room. 'Sit down, and tell me everything—how all the old people are, and how the old place looks—you live there now ? *I* have nothing to tell, only I'm married, as you know—and—and I think a most good-for-nothing creature.'

'Ah, no, pretty Miss Jane, there was good in you always, only a little bit hasty, and *that* anyone as had the patience could see ; and I knowed well you'd be better o' that little folly in time.'

'I'm not better, Donnie—I'm worse—I *am* worse, Donnie. I know I am—not better.'

'Well, dear! and jewels, and riches, and coaches, and a fine gentleman adoring you—not very young, though. Well, maybe all the better. Did you never hear say, it's better to be an old man's darling than a young man's slave ?'

'Yes, Donnie, it's very well; but let us talk of Wardlock—and he's *not* a fine man, Donnie, who put that in your head—he's old, and ugly, and'—she was going to say stupid, but the momentary bitterness was rebuked by an accidental glimpse of the casket in which his splendid present was secured—' and tell me about Wardlock, and the people—is old Thomas Jones there still ?'

'No, he's living at Glastonhowe now, with his grandson that's married—very happy ; but you would not believe how old he looks, and they say can't remember nothink as he used to, but very comfortable.'

'And Turpin, the gardener?'

'Old Turpin be dead, miss, two years agone; had a fit a few months before, poor old fellow, and never was strong after. Very deaf he was of late years, and a bit cross sometimes about the vegetables, they do say; but he was a good-natured fellow, and decent allays; and though he liked a mug of ale, poor fellow now and then, he was very regular at church.'

'Poor old Turpin dead! I never heard it—and *old?* he used to wear a kind of flaxen wig.'

'Old! dearie me, that he was, miss, you would not guess how old—there's eighty-five years on the grave-stone that Lady Alice put over him, from the parish register, in Wardlock churchyard, bless ye!'

'And—and as I said just now about my husband, General Lennox, that he was old—well, he *is* old, but he's a good man, and kind, and such a gentleman.'

'And you love him—and what more is needed to make you both happy?' added Donica; 'and glad I am, miss, to see you so comfortably married—and such a nice, good, grand gentleman; and don't let them young chaps be coming about you with their compliments, and fine talk, and love-making.'

'What do you mean, woman? I should hope I know how to behave myself as well as ever Lady Alice Redcliffe did. It is *she* who has been talking to you, and, I suppose, to every one, the stupid, wicked hag.'

'Oh, Miss Jennie, dear!'

CHAPTER LV.

ALONE—YET NOT ALONE.

'Well, Donnie, don't talk about *her;* talk about Wardlock, and the people, and the garden, and the trees, and old Wardlock church,' said Lady Jane, subsiding almost as suddenly as she flamed up. 'Do you remember the brass tablet about Eleanor Faukes, well-beloved and godly, who died in her twenty-second year, in the year of grace sixteen hundred and thirty-four? See how I remember it! Poor Eleanor Faukes! I often think of her—and do you remember how you used to make me read the two lines at the end of the epitaph? "What you are I was; what I am you shall be." Do you remember?'

'Ay, miss, that I do. I wish I could think o' them sorts o' things allays—it's very good, miss.'

'Perhaps it is, Donnie. It's very sad and very horrible, at all events, death and judgment,' answered Lady Jane.

'Have you your old Bible yet, miss?'

'Not here,' answered Lady Jane, colouring a little; but recollecting, she said, 'I *have* got a very pretty one, though, and she produced a beautiful volume bound in velvet and gold.

'A deal handsomer, Miss Jennie, but not so well read, I'm afeared,' said Donica Gwynn, looking at the fresh binding and shining gilt leaves.

'There it is, Donnie Don; but I feel like you, and I *do* like the old one best, blurred and battered; poor old thing, it looked friendly, and this like a fashionable chaplain. I have not seen it for a long time, Donnie; perhaps it's lost, and this is only a show one, as you see.'

And after a few seconds she added, a little bitterly, almost angrily, 'I never read my Bible now. I never open it,' and then came an unnatural little laugh.

'Oh! Miss Jennie, dear—I mean my Lady Jane—don't say

that, darling—*that* way, anyhow, don't say it. Why should not you read your Bible, and love it, better now nor ever, miss—the longer you live the more you'll want it, and when sorrow comes, what have you but that?'

'It's all denunciation, all hard names, and threats, Donnie. If people believed themselves what they *say* every Sunday in church, miserable sinners, and I dare say they are, they'd sicken and quake at sight of it. I hope I may come to like it some day, Donnie,' she added, with a short sigh.

'I mind, Miss Jennie—I mean my Lady Jane.'

'No, you're to call me Jennie still, or I'll drop Donnie Don, and call you Mrs. Gwynn,' said Lady Jane, with her hands on Donica's thin shoulders, playfully, but with a very pensive face and tone.

Donica smiled for a moment, and then her face saddened too, and she said—

'And I mind, Miss Jennie, when it was the same way with me, only with better reason, for I was older than you, and had lived longer than ever you did without a thought of God ; but I tell you, miss, you'll find your only comfort there at last; it is not much, maybe, to the like o' me, that can't lay her mind down to it, but it's *some-think* ; ay, I mind the time I durst not open it, thinking I'd only meet summat there to vex me. But 'tisn't so : there's a deal o' good nature in the Bible, and ye'll be sure to stumble on some-think kind whenever you open it.'

Lady Jane made no answer. She looked down with a careworn gaze on her white hand, the fleeting tenement of clay ; jewelled rings glimmered on its fingers—the vanities of the world, and under it lay the Bible, the eternal word. She was patting the volume with a little movement that made the brilliants flash. You would have thought she was admiring her rings, but that her eyes were so sad and her gaze so dreamy.

'And I hear the mistress, Lady Alice, a-coming up—yes, 'tis her voice. Good-night, Miss Jennie, dear.'

'Good-night, dear old Donnie.'

'And you'll promise me you'll read a bit in it every night.'

'Where's the use in promising, Donnie ? Don't we promise

everything—the whole Christian religion, at our baptism—and how do we keep it ?'

'You must promise you'll read, if 'twas only a verse every night, Miss Jennie, dear—it may be the makin' o' ye. I hear Lady Alice a-calling.'

'You're a good old thing—I like you, Donnie—you'd like to make me better—happier, that is—and I love you—and I promise for this night, at all events, I will read a verse, and maybe more, if it turns out good-natured, as you say. Good-night.'

And she shook old Gwynn by both hands, and kissed her; and as she parted with her, said—

'And, Donnie, you must tell my maid I shan't want her to-night—and I *will* read, Donnie—and now, good-night again.'

So handsome Lady Jane was alone.

'It seems to me as if I had not time to think—God help me, God help me,' said Lady Jane. 'Shall I read it? That odious book, that puts impossibilities before us, and calls eternal damnation eternal justice!'

'Good-night, Jane,' croaked Lady Alice's voice, and the key turned in the door.

With a pallid glance from the corners of her eyes, of intense contempt—*hatred*, even, at the moment, she gazed on the door, as she sate with her fingers under her chin; and if a look could have pierced the panels, hers would have shot old Lady Alice dead at the other side. For about a minute she sat so, and then a chilly little laugh rang from her lips; and she thought no more for a while of Lady Alice, and her eyes wandered again to her Bible.

'Yes, that odious book! with just power enough to distract us, without convincing—to embitter our short existence, without directing it; I *hate* it.'

So she said, and looked as if she would have flung it into the farthest corner of the room. She was spited with it, as so many others are, because it won't do for us what we must do for ourselves.

'When sorrow comes, poor Donnie says—*when* it comes—little she knows how long it has been here! Life—such a dream—such an agony often. Surely it pays the penalty of all its follies. Judgment indeed! The all-wise Creator sitting in judgment upon creatures like us, living but an hour, and walking in a dream!'

This kind of talk with her, as with many others, was only the expression of a form of pain. She was perhaps in the very mood to read, that is, with the keen and anxious interest that accompanies and indicates a deep-seated grief and fear.

It was quite true what she said to old Donica. These pages had long been sealed for her. And now, with a mixture of sad antipathy and interest, as one looks into a coffin, she did open the book, and read here and there in a desultory way, and then, leaning on her hand, she mused dismally ; then made search for a place she wanted, and read and wept, wept aloud and long and bitterly.

The woman taken, and ' set in the midst,' the dreadful Pharisees standing round. The Lord of life, who will judge us on the last day, hearing and *saving !* Oh, blessed Prince, whose service is perfect freedom, how wise are thy statutes ! 'More to be desired are they than gold—*sweeter* also than honey.' Standing between thy poor tempted creatures and the worst sorrow that can befall them—a sorrow that softens, not like others, as death approaches, but is transformed, and stands like a giant at the bedside. May they see thy interposing image—may they see thy face now and for ever.

Rest for the heavy-laden ! The broken and the contrite he will not despise. Read and take comfort, how he dealt with that poor sinner. Perfect purity, perfect mercy. Oh, noblest vision that ever rose before contrite frailty ! Lift up the downcast head—let the poor heart break no more—you shall rise from the dust an angel.

Suddenly she lifted up her pale face, with an agony and a light on her countenance, with hands clasped, and such a look from the abyss, in her upturned eyes.

Oh! was it possible—could it be true ? A *friend*—such a *friend !*

Then came a burst of prayer—wild resolutions—agonised tears. She knew that in all space, for her, was but one place of safety— to lie at the wounded feet of her Saviour, to clasp them, to bathe them with her tears. An hour—more—passed in this agony of stormy hope breaking in gleams through despair. Prayer—cries for help, as from the drowning, and vows frantic—holy, for the future.

'Yes, once more, thank God, I can dare with safety—here and now—to see him for the last time. In the morning I will conjure old Lady Alice to take me to Wardlock. I will write to London. Arthur will join me there. I'd like to go abroad never into the world again—never—never—never. He will be pleased. I'll try to make amends. He'll never know what a wretch I've been. But he shall see the change, and be happier. Yes, yes, yes.' Her beautiful long hair was loose, its rich folds clasped in her strained fingers—her pale upturned face bathed in tears and quivering—'The Saviour's feet!—No happiness but there—wash them with my tears—dry them with this hair.' And she lifted up her eyes and hands to heaven.

Poor thing! In the storm, as cloud and rack fly by, the momentary gleam that comes—what is it? Do not often these agitations subside in darkness? Was this to be a lasting sunshine, though saddened for her? Was she indeed safe now and for ever?

But is there any promise that repentance shall arrest the course of the avenger that follows sin on earth? Are broken health or blighted fame restored when the wicked man 'turneth away from the wickedness that he hath committed;' and do those consequences that dog iniquity with 'feet of wool and hands of iron,' stay their sightless and soundless march so soon as he begins to do 'that which is lawful and right?' It is enough for him to know that he that does so 'shall save his soul alive.'

CHAPTER LVI.

'MAY I see you, Monsieur Varbarriere, to-morrow, in the room in which I saw you to-day, at any hour you please after half-past eleven?' inquired Lady Alice, a few minutes after that gentleman had approached her.

'Certainly, madam; perhaps I can at this moment answer you upon points which cause you anxiety; pray command me.'

And he sate like a corpulent penitent on a low prie-dieu chair beside her knee, and inclined his ear to listen.

'It is only to learn whether my—my poor boy's son, my grand-son, the young man in whom I must feel so deep an interest, is about to return here?'

'I can't be quite certain, madam, of that; but I can promise that he will do himself the honour to present himself before you, whenever you may please to appoint, at your house of Wardlock.'

'Yes, that would be better still. He could come there and see his old grandmother. I would like to see him soon. I have a great deal to say to him, a great deal to tell him that would in-terest him; and the pictures; I know you will let him come. Do you really mean it, Monsieur Varbarriere?'

M. Varbarriere smiled a little contemptuously, and bowed most deferentially.

'Certainly madam, I mean what I say; and if I did *not* mean it, still I would say I do.'

There was something mazy in this sentence which a little be-wildered old Lady Alice's head, and she gazed on Varbarriere with a lack-lustre frown.

'Well, then, sir, the upshot of the matter in that *I may* rely on what you say. and expect my grandson's visit at Ward-lock?'

'Certainly, madam, you *may* expect it,' rejoined Varbarriere, oracularly.

'And pray, Monsieur Varbarriere, are you married?' inquired the old lady, with the air of a person who had a right to be informed.

'Alas, madam, may I say Latin?—Infandum, regina, jubes renovare dolorem; you stir up my deepest grief. I am, indeed, what you call an old bachelor.

'Well, so I should suppose; I don't see what business you would have had to marry.'

'Nor I either,' he replied.

'And you are very rich, I suppose.'

'The rich man never says he is rich, and the poor man never says he is poor. What shall I say? Pretty well? Will that do?'

'H'm, yes; you ought to make a settlement, Monsieur Varbarriere.'

'On your grandson, madam?'

'Yes, my grandson, he's nothing the worse of that, sir—and your nephew.'

'Madam, the idea is beneficent, and does honour to your heart. I have, to say truth, had an idea of doing something for him by my will, though not by settlement; you are quite in advance of me, madam—I shall reflect.'

Monsieur Varbarriere was, after his wont, gravely amusing himself, so gravely that old Lady Alice never suspected an irony. Old Lady Alice had in her turn taken up the idea of a solution of all family variance, by a union between Guy Deverell and Beatrix, and her old brain was already at the settlements.

'Lady Alice, you must positively give us up our partner, Monsieur Varbarriere, our game is arrested; and, egad, Pelter, poor fellow, is bursting with jealousy!'

Lady Alice turned disdainfully from Sir Jekyl.

'Monsieur Varbarriere, pray don't allow me to detain you now. I should be very glad to see you, if you had no particular objection, to-morrow.'

'Only too happy; you do me, madam, a great deal of honour;' and with a bow and a smile Monsieur Varbarriere withdrew to the whist-table.

He did not play that night by any means so well as usual. Doocey, who was his partner, was, to say the least, disappointed, and Sir Jekyl and Sir Paul made a very nice thing of it, in that small way which makes domestic whist-players happy and serene. When they wound up, Doocey was as much irritated as a perfectly well-bred gentleman could be.

'Well, Sir Paul, we earned our winnings, eh? Four times the trick against honours, not bad play, I think,' said Sir Jekyl, as they rose.

'Captain Doocey thinks our play had nothing to do with it,' observed Sir Paul, with a faint radiance of complacent banter over his bluff face, as he put his adversary's half-crowns into his trousers pocket.

'I never said *that*, Sir Paul, of course; you mistake me, but *we* might, don't you think, Monsieur Varbarriere, have played a little better? for instance, we should have played our queen to the lead of spades. I'm sure that would have given us the trick, don't you see, and you would have had the lead, and played diamonds, and forced Sir Jekyl to ruff with his ace, and made my knave good, and that would have given us the lead and trick.'

'Our play goes for nothing, you see, Sir Paul,' said Sir Jekyl.

'No; Captain Doocey thinks play had nothing to do with it,' said Sir Paul Blunket.

''Gad, I think play had *every*thing to do with it—not *yours*, though,' said Doocey, a little tartly.

'I must do you *all* justice,' interposed Varbarriere, 'you're all right—everyone played well except me. I do pretty well when I'm in the vein, but I'm not to-night; it was a very bad performance. I played execrably, Captain Doocey.'

'Oh! no, I won't allow that; but you know once or twice you certainly did not play according to your own principles, I mean, and I couldn't therefore see exactly what you meant, and I dare say it was as much my fault as yours.'

And Doocey, with his finger on Varbarriere's sleeve, fell into one of those *resumés* which mysteriously interest whist-players, and Varbarriere listened to his energetic periods with his hands in his pockets, benignant but bored, and assented with a good grace to his own condemnation. And smothering a yawn as he moved away, again pleaded guilty to all the counts, and threw himself on the mercy of the court.

'What shall we do to-morrow?' exclaimed Sir Jekyl, and he heard a voice repeat 'to-morrow,' and so did Varbarriere. 'I'll turn it over, and at breakfast I'll lay half a dozen plans before you, and you shall select. It's a clear frosty night; we shall have a fine day. You don't leave us, Mr. Pelter, till the afternoon, d'ye see? and mind, Lady Alice Redcliffe sits in the boudoir, at the first landing on the great stair; the servant will show you the way; don't fail to pay her a visit, d'ye mind, Pelter; she's huffed, you left her so suddenly; don't mind her at first; just amuse her a little, and I think she's going to change her lawyer.'

Pelter, with his hands in his pockets, smiled shrewdly and winked on Sir Jekyl.

'Thanks; I know it, I heard it; you can give us a lift in that quarter, Sir Jekyl, and I shan't forget to pay my respects.'

When the ladies had gone, and the gentlemen stood in groups by the fire, or sat listless before it, Sir Jekyl, smiling, laid his hand on Varbarriere's shoulder, and asked him in a low tone—

'Will you join Pelter in my room, and wind up with a cigar?'

'I was going, that is, tempted, only ten minutes ago, to ask leave to join your party,' began Varbarriere.

'It is not a party—we should be only three,' said Sir Jekyl, in an eager whisper.

'All the more inviting,' continued Varbarriere, smiling. 'But I suddenly recollected that I shall have rather a busy hour or two, three or four letters to write. My people of business in France never give me a moment; they won't pay my rent or cork a bottle, my faith! without a letter.'

'Well, I'm sorry you can't; but you must make it up to me,

and see, you must take two or three of these to your dressing-room,' and he presented his case to M. Varbarriere.

'Ha! you are very good ; but, *no ;* I like to connect them with your room, they must not grow too common, they shall remain a treat. No, no, I won't; ha, ha, ha! Thank you very much,' and he waved them off, laughing and shaking his head.

Somehow he could not brook accepting this trifling present. To be sure, here he was a guest at free quarters, but at this he stuck ; he drew back and waved away the cigar-case. It was not logical, but he could not help it.

When Pelter and Sir Jekyl sat in the Baronet's chamber, under their canopy of tobacco-smoke over their last cigar,

'See, Pelter,' said Sir Jekyl, ' it won't do to *seem* anxious ; the fact is [I'm *not* anxious ; I believe he has a lot of money to leave that young fellow. Suppose they marry ; the Deverells are a capital old family, don't you see, and it will make up everything, and stop people talking about—about old nonsense. I'll settle all, and I don't care a curse, and I'll not be very long in the way. I can't keep always young, I'm past fifty.'

'Judging by his manner, you know, I should say any proposition you may have to make he'd be happy to listen to,' said Mr. Pelter.

'You're sleepy, Pelter.'

'Well, a little bit,' said the attorney, blinking, yawning, and grinning all together.

'And, egad, I think you want to be shaved,' said Sir Jekyl, who did not stand on ceremony with his attorney.

'Should not wonder,' said Mr. Pelter, feeling his chin over sleepily with his finger and thumb. ' My shave was at half-past four, and what is it now ?—half-past eleven, egad ! I thought it was later. Good-night, Sir Jekyl—those *are* cigars, magnificent, by Jove!—and about the Strangways' business, I would not be in too great a hurry, do you see ? I would not open anything, till I saw whether they were going to move, or whether there was anything in it. I would not put it in his head, d'ye see, hey ?' and from habit Pelter winked.

And with that salutation, harmless as the kiss apostolic, Mr. Pelter, aided by a few directions from Sir Jekyl, toddled away to his bedchamber yawning, and the Baronet, after his wont, locked himself into his room in very tolerable spirits.

There was a sofa in Varbarriere's dressing-room, on which by this time, in a great shawl dressing-gown, supine lay our friend; like the painted stone monument of the Chief Justice of Chester in Wardlock church, you could see on the wall sharply defined in shadow the solemn outline of his paunch. He was thinking—not as we endeavour to trace thought in narrative, like a speech, but crossing zigzag from point to point, and back and forward. A man requires an audience, and pen and paper, to think in train at all. His ideas whisked and jolted on somewhat in this fashion :—

'It is to be *avoided*, if possible. My faith! it is now just twelve o'clock! A dangerous old blockhead. I must avoid it, if only for time to think in. There was nothing this evening to imply such relations—Parbleu! a pleasant situation if it prove all a mistake. These atrabilious countrymen and women of mine are so odd, they may mislead a fellow accustomed like me to a more intriguing race and a higher *finesse*. Ah! no; it is certainly true. The *fracas* will end everything. That old white monkey will be sure to blunder me into it. Better reconsider things, and wait. What shall I tell him? No excuse, I must go through with it, or I suppose he will call for pistols—curse him! I'll give Sir Jekyl a hint or two. He must see her, and make all ready. The old fool will blaze away at me, of course. Well! I shall fight him or not, as I may be moved. No one in this country need fight now who does not wish it. Rather a comfortable place to live in, if it were not for the climate. I forgot to ask Jacques whether Guy took all his luggage! What o'clock now? Come, by my faith! it is time to decide.'

CHAPTER LVII.

M. VARBARRIERE DECIDES.

VARBARRIERE sat up on the side of his sofa.

'Who brought that woman, Gwynn, here ?   What do they want of her ?' It was only the formula by which interrogatively to express the suspicion that pointed at Sir Jekyl and his attorney. 'Soft words for me while tampering with my witnesses, then laugh at me.   Why did not I ask Lady Alice whether she really wrote for her ?'

Thus were his thoughts various as the ingredients of that soup called harlequin, which figures at low French taverns, in which are floating bits of chicken, cheese, potato, fish, sausage, and so forth —the flavour of the soup itself is consistent, nevertheless.   The tone of Varbarriere's ruminations, on the whole, was decided.   He wished to avert the exposure which his interference alone had invited.

He looked at his watch—he had still a little more than half an hour for remedial thought and action—and now, what is to be done to prevent *cet vieux singe blanc* from walking into the green chamber, and keeping watch and ward at his wife's bedside until that spectre shall emerge through the wall, whom with a curse and a stab he was to lay ?

Well, what precise measures were to be taken ?   First he must knock up Sir Jekyl in his room, and tell him positively that General Lennox was to be at Marlowe by one o'clock, having heard stories in town, for the purpose of surprising and punishing the guilty.   Sir Jekyl would be sharp enough to warn Lady Jane ; or should he suggest that it would be right to let her know, in order to prevent her from being alarmed at the temper and melo-dramatics of her husband, and to secure the coolness and prepara-tion which were necessary ?   It required some delicacy and tact, but he was not afraid.   Next, he must meet General Lennox, and tell him in substance that he had begun to hope that he had been himself practised upon. Yes, that would do—and he might be as dark as he pleased on the subject of his information.

Varbarriere lighted his bed-room candle, intending to march forthwith to Sir Jekyl's remote chamber.

Great events, as we all know, turn sometimes upon small pivots. Before he set out, he stood for a moment with his candle in one hand, and in his reverie he thrust the other into the pocket of his voluminous black trousers, and there he encountered, unexpectedly, the letter he had that evening picked up on the floor of the gallery. It had quite dropped out of his mind. Monsieur Varbarriere was a Jupiter Scapin. He had not the smallest scruple about reading it, and afterwards throwing it into the fire, though it contained other men's secrets, and was another man's property.

This was a letter from Sir Jekyl Marlowe to Pelter and Crowe, and was in fact upon the special subject of Herbert Strangways. Unlucky subject! unlucky composition! Now there was, of course, here a great deal of that sort of communication which occurs between a clever attorney and his clever client, which is termed 'privileged,' and is not always quite fit to see the light. Did ever beauty read letter of compliment and adoration with keener absorption?

Varbarriere's face rather whitened as he read, and his fat sneer was not pleasant to see.

He got through it, and re-commenced. Sometimes he muttered and sometimes he thought; and the notes of this oration would have read nearly thus:—

'So the question is to be opened whether the *anonymous payment*—he lies, it was in *my name!*—through the bankers protects me technically from pursuit; and I'm to be "run by the old Hebrew pack from cover to cover," over the Continent—bravo!— till I vanish for seven years more.' Here Monsieur Varbarriere laughed in lurid contempt.

The letter went on in the same vein—contemptuous, cruel, he fancied. Everyone *is* cruel in self-defence; and in its allusions and spirit was something which bitterly recalled the sufferings which in younger and weaker days that same Baronet, pursuing the same policy, had inflicted upon him. Varbarriere remembered when he was driven to the most ignominious and risky shifts, to ridiculous disguises; he remembered his image in the cracked shaving-glass in the garret in his lair near Notre Dame—the red wig and moustache, and the goggles.

How easily an incautious poke will re-awake the dormant neuralgia of toothache; and tooth, cheek, ear, throat, brain, are all throbbing again in the re-induced anguish! With these sharp and vivid recollections of humiliation, fear, and suffering, all stirred into activity by this unlucky letter, that savage and vindictive feeling which had for so long ruled the life of Herbert Strangways, and had sunk into an uneasy dose under the narcotic of this evening's interview, rose up suddenly, wide awake and energetic.

He looked at his watch. The minute-hand showed him exactly how long he had been reading this confidence of client to attorney. 'You will, will you?' murmured Varbarriere, with his jaw a little fiercely set, and a smile. ' He will *checkmate* me, he thinks, in two or three moves. He does not see, clever fellow, that I will checkmate him in *one!*'

Now, this letter had *preceded* all that had occurred this evening to soften old animosities—though, strictly examined, that was not very much. It did not seem quite logical then, that it should work so sudden a revolution. I cannot, however, say positively; for in Varbarriere's mind may have long lain a suspicion that Sir Jekyl was not now altogether what he used to be, that he did not quite know all he had inflicted, and that time had made him wiser, and therefore gentler of heart. If so, the letter had knocked down this hypothesis, and its phrases, one or two of them, were of that unlucky sort which not only recalled the thrill of many an old wound, but freshly galled that vanity which never leaves us, till ear and eye grow cold, and light and sound are shut out by the coffin-lid.

So Varbarriere, being quite disenchanted, wondered at his own illusions, and sighed bitterly when he thought what a fool he had been so near making of himself. And thinking of these things, he stared grimly on his watch, and by one of those movements that betray one's abstraction, held it to his ear, as if he had fancied it might have gone down.

There it was, thundering on at a gallop. The tread of unseen fate approaching. Yes, it was time he should go. Jacques peeped in.

'You've done as I ordered?'

'Yes, Monsieur.'

'Here, lend me a hand with my cloak—very good. The servants, the butler, have they retired?'

'So I believe, Monsieur.'

'My hat — thanks. The lights all out on the stairs and lobbies?'

'Yes, Monsieur.'

'Go before—is that lighted?'

'Yes, sir.'

This referred to one of those little black lanterns which belong to Spanish melodrama, with a semi cylindrical horn and a black slide. We have most of us seen such, and handled if not possessed them.

'Leporello! hey, Jacques?' smiled Varbarriere sardonically, as he drew his short black cloak about him.

'Monsieur is always right,' acquiesced the man, who had never heard of Leporello before.

'Get on, then.'

And the valet before, the master following, treading cautiously, they reached the stair-head, where Varbarriere listened for a moment, then descended and listened again at the foot, and so through the hall into the long gallery, near the end of which is a room with a conservatory.

This they entered. The useful Jacques had secured the key of the glass door into the conservatory, which also opened the outer one; and Varbarriere, directing him to wait there quietly till his return, stepped out into the open air and faint moonlight. A moment's survey was enough to give him the lie of the ground, and recognizing the file of tufted lime-trees, rising dark in the

mist, he directed his steps thither, and speedily got up the
broad avenue, bordered with grass and guarded at either side by
these rows of giant limes.

On reaching the carriage-way, standing upon a slight eminence,
Varbarriere gazed down the misty slope toward the gate-house,
and then toward Marlowe Manor, in search of a carriage or a
human figure. Seeing none, he strolled onward toward the gate,
and soon *did* see, airy and faint in the haze and distance, a vehicle approaching. It stopped some two hundred yards nearer the
gate than he, a slight figure got out, and after a few words apparently, the driver turned about, and the slim, erect figure came
gliding stiffly along in his direction. As he approached Varbarriere stood directly before him.

'Ha! here I am waiting, General,' said Varbarriere, advancing.
'I—I suppose we had better get on at once to the house?'

General Lennox met him with a nod.

'Don't care, sir. Whatever you think best,' answered the
General, as sternly as if he were going into action.

'Thanks for your confidence, General. I think so;' and side by
side they walked in silence for a while toward the house.

'Lady Alice Redcliffe here?'

'Yes, sir.'

'That's well. And, sir,' he continued, suddenly stopping short,
and turning full on Varbarriere—'for God's sake, *do* you think it
is *certainly true?*'

'You had better come, sir, and judge for yourself,' pursued
Varbarriere.

'D—— you, sir—you think I'll wait over your cursed riddles.
I'd as soon wait in hell, sir. You don't know, sir—it's the tortures of the damned. Egad, no man has a right—no man could
stand it.'

'I think it *is*, sir. I think it's *true*, sir. I *think* it's true.
I'm nearly *sure* it's true,' answered Varbarriere, with a pallid
frown, not minding his anathema. 'How *can* I say more?'

General Lennox looked for a while on the ground, then up and about dismally, and gave his neck a little military shake, as if his collar sat uneasily.

'A lonely life for me, sir. I wish to God the villain had shot me first. I was very fond of her, sir—desperately fond—madness, sir. I was thinking I would go back to India. Maybe you'll advise with me, sir, to-morrow? I have no one.'

CHAPTER LVIII.

AT THE GREEN CHAMBER.

As they approached the house, Jacques, who sat awaiting M. Varbarriere's return, behind the door facing the conservatory, was disagreeably surprised by a visit from the butler.

'Here I am!' exclaimed Jacques very cheerfully, feeling that he could not escape.

'Ow! haw! Mr. Jack, by gad!' exclaimed the butler, actually jumping back in panic, and nearly extinguishing his candle on his breast.

It was his custom, on hearing a noise or seeing a light, to make a ceremonious reconnoissance in assertion of his character, not of course in expectation of finding anything; and here at length he thought he had lighted on a burglar, and from the crown of his head to his heels froze thrills of terror. 'And what the devil, Mr. Jack, are you doing here, please, sir?'

'Waiting, my friend, to admit Monsieur, my master,' answered Jacques, who was adroit enough to know that it is sometimes cunning to be frank.

In fact it was the apparition of M. Varbarriere, in his queer hat and cloak, crossing a window, which had inspired the butler with a resolution to make his search.

'Haw! dear me! yes, I saw him, Mr. Jack, I did; and what, Mr. Jack, is the doors opened for at these hours, unbeknown to me?'

' My most dear friend, I am taking every care, as you see; but my master, he choose to go out, and he choose to come in. Jacques is nothing but what you call the latch-key.'

' And what is he a-doing hout o' doors this time o'night, Mr. Jack? I never knowd afore sich a think to 'appen. Why it looks like a stragethim, that's what it does, Mr. Jack—a stragethim.'

And the butler nodded with the air of a moral constable.

' It's a folly, Monsieur. My faith! a little *ruse* of love I imagine.'

' You don't mean to say he's hout a-larkin?'

Jacques, who only conjectured the sense of the sentence, winked and smiled.

' Well, I don't think it's not the way he should be.'

' My master is most generous man. My friend, you shall see he shall know how kind you have been. Monsieur, my master, he is a *prince!*' murmured Jacques, eloquently, his fingers on the butler's cuff, and drew back to read in his countenance how it worked.

' It must not hoccur again, Mr. Jack, wile ere,' replied the butler, with another grave shake of his head.

' Depend yourself on me,' whispered Jacques again in his ear, while he squeezed the prudent hand of the butler affectionately. ' But you must go way.'

' I do depend on you, Mr. Jack, but I don't like it, mind— I don't like it, and I won't say nothink of it till I hear more from you.'

So the butler withdrew, and the danger disappeared.

' You will please to remember, sir,' said Varbarriere, as they approached the house, ' that this is of the nature of a military movement—a surprise; there must be no sound—no alarm.'

' Quite so,' whispered old Lennox, with white lips. He was clutching something nervously under the wide sleeve of his loose drab overcoat. He stopped under the shadow of a noble clump of trees about fifty steps away from the glass door they were approaching.

'I—I almost wish, sir—I'll go back—I don't think I can go on, sir.'

Varbarriere looked at his companion with an unconscious sneer, but said nothing.

'By ——, sir, if I find it true, I'll kill him, sir.'

The old man had in his gouty grip one of those foolish daggers once so much in vogue, but which have now gone out of use, and Varbarriere saw it glimmer in the faint light.

'Surely, Colonel Lennox, you don't mean—you can't mean—you're not going to resort to violence, sir?'

'By ——, sir, he had best look to it.'

Varbarriere placed his hand on the old man's sleeve, he could feel the tremor of his thin wrist through it.

'General Lennox, if I had fancied that you could have harboured such a thought, I never should have brought you here.'

The General, with his teeth clenched, made him no reply but a fierce nod.

'Remember, sir, you have the courts of law, and you have the code of honour—either or both. One step more I shall not take with you, if you mean that sort of violence.'

'What do you mean, sir?' asked the General, grimly.

'I mean this, sir, you shall learn nothing by this night's procedure, unless you promise me, upon your honour as a soldier, sir, and a gentleman, that you will not use that dagger or any other weapon.'

General Lennox looked at him with a rather glassy stare.

'You're right, sir, I dare say, said Lennox, suddenly and helplessly.

'You promise?'

'Ay, sir.'

'Upon your honour?'

'Upon my honour; ay, sir, my honour.'

'I'm satisfied, General. Now observe, you must be silent, and as noiseless as you can. If Sir Jekyl be apprised of your arrival, of course the—the experiment fails.'

General Lennox nodded. Emerging into the moonlight, Varbarriere saw how pale and lean his face looked.

Across the grass they pace side by side in silence. The glass door opened without a creak or a hitch. Jacques politely secured it, and, obeying his master's gesture, led the way through the gallery to the hall.

'You'll remember, General, that you arrived late; you understand? and having been observed by me, were admitted; and—and all the rest occurred naturally.'

'Yes, sir, any d—d lie you like. All the world's lying—why should not I?'

At the foot of the staircase, Jacques was dismissed, having lighted bed-room candles for the two gentlemen, so that they lost something of their air of Spanish conspirators, and they mounted the stairs together in a natural and domestic fashion.

When they had crossed the lobby, and stood at the door of the dressing-room, Varbarriere laid his hand on General Lennox's arm—

'Stop here a moment; you must knock at Lady Alice's door over there, and get the key of your room. She locks the door and keeps the key at night. Make no noise, you know.'

They had been fortunate hitherto in having escaped observation; and Varbarriere's strategy had, up to this point, quite succeeded.

'Very quietly, mind,' whispered he, and withdrew behind the angle of the wall, toward the staircase.

Old Lennox was by this time at the door which he had indicated, and knocked. There was a little fuss audible within, but no answer. He knocked again more sharply, and he heard the gabble of female voices; and at last a rather nervous inquiry, 'Who's there, please?'

'General Lennox, who wants the key of his room,' answered he, in no mood to be trifled with. The General was standing, grim as fate, and stark as Corporal Trim, bed-room candle in hand, outside her door.

'He's *not* General Lennox — send him about his business,' exclaimed an imperious female voice from the state bed, in which

Lady Alice was sitting, measuring some mysterious drops in a graduatéd glass.

'My lady says she's sorry she can't find it to-night, sir, being at present in bed, please, sir.'

'Come, child—no nonsense—I want my key, and I'll have it,' replied the General, so awfully that the maid recoiled.

'I think, my lady, he'll be rude if he doesn't get it.'

'What's the man like?'

'A nice-spoken gentleman, my lady, and dressed very respectable.'

'You never *saw* General Lennox?'

'No, my lady, please.'

Neither had Lady Alice; but she had heard him minutely described.

'A lean ugly old man is he, with white bristly whiskers, you know, and a white head, and little grey eyes, eh?'

They had no notion that their little confidence was so distinctly audible to the General without, who stood eyeing the panel fiercely as a sentry would a suspicious figure near his beat, and with fingers twitching with impatience to clutch his key.

'What sort of nose?' demanded the unseen speaker—'long or short?'

'Neither, please, my lady; bluish, rayther, I should say.'

'But it is either long or short, *decidedly*, and I forget which,' said Lady Alice—'*Tisn*'t he!'

The General ground his teeth with impatience, and knocked so sharp a signal at the door that Lady Alice bounced in her bed.

'Lord bless us! How dare he do that?—tell him how dare he.'

'Lady Alice, sir, would be much obliged if you'd be so good not knock so loud, sir, please,' said the maid at the door, translating the message.

'Tell your mistress I'm General Lennox, and must have my key,' glared the General, and the lady's-maid, who was growing nervous, returned.

'He looks, my lady, like he'd beat us, please, if he does not get the key, my lady.'

'Sha'n't have it, the brute! We don't know he is—a robber, maybe. Bolt the door, and tell him to bring Monsieur Varbarriere to the lobby, and if *he* says he's General Lennox he shall have the key.'

With trembling fingers the maid *did* bolt the door, and once more accost the soldier, who was chafing on the threshold.

'Please, sir, my lady is not well, having nervous pains, please sir, in her head to-night, and therefore would be 'appy if you would be so kind to bring Mister Barvarrian' (the name by which our corpulent friend was known in the servants' hall) 'to her door, please, when she'll try what she may do to oblige you, sir.'

'They don't know me,' said the General, accosting Varbarriere, who was only half a dozen steps removed, and whom he had rejoined. 'You must come to the door, they say, and tell them it's all right.'

Perhaps with some inward sense of the comic, Varbarriere presented himself at the door, when, his voice being recognised, and he himself reconnoitered through the keyhole and reported upon, the maid presented herself in an extemporised drapery of cloaks and shawls, like a traveller in winter, and holding these garments together with one hand, with the other presented the key, peering anxiously in the General's face.

'Key, sir, please.'

'I thank you,' said the General, with a nod, to which she responded with such a courtesy as her costume permitted. The door shut, and as the gentlemen withdrew they heard the voices of the inmates again busy with the subject.

'Good-night,' whispered Varbarriere, looking in the General's blue eye with his own full and steady gaze.

'I know you'll remember your promise,' said he.

'Yes—what ?'

'No *violence*,' replied Varbarriere.

'No, of course, I said so. Good-bye.'

'You must appear—your *manner*, mind—just as usual. Nothing to alarm—you may defeat all else.'

'I see.'

Varbarriere pressed his hand encouragingly. It felt like death.

'Don't fear me,' said General Lennox. 'We'll see—we'll see, sir; good-bye.'

He spoke in a low, short, resolute tone, almost defiant; but looked very ill. Varbarriere had never taken leave of a man on the drop, but thought that this must be like it.

He beckoned to him as the General moved toward the dressing-room door, and made an earnest signal of silence. Lennox nodded, applied the key, and Varbarriere was gone.

CHAPTER LIX.

IN THE GREEN CHAMBER.

GENERAL LENNOX opened the door suddenly, and stood in the green chamber, holding his candle above his temple, and staring with a rather wild countenance and a gathered brow to the further end of the room. A candle burned on the table, and the Bible lay beside it. No one was there but the inmate of the bed, who sat up with a scared face. He locked the door in silence, and put the key in his pocket.

'Who's there?—who is it? O my God! Arthur, is it you?' she cried. It was not a welcome. It was as if she had seen a ghost—but she smiled.

'You're well? quite well? and happy? no doubt happy?' said Lennox, setting down his candle on the table near the bed, 'and glad to see me?'

'Yes, Arthur; Arthur, what's the matter? You're ill—*are* you ill?'

'Ho! no, very well, quite well—very well indeed.'

There was that in his look and manner that told her she was ruined. She froze with a horror she had never dreamed of before.

'There's something, Arthur—there is—you won't tell me.'

'That's strange, and *you* tell *me* everything.'

'What do you *mean*, sir? Oh, Arthur, what *do* you mean?'

'Mean! Nothing!'

'I was afraid you were angry, and I've done nothing to vex you —nothing. You looked so angry—it's so unreasonable and odd of you. But I am glad to see you, though you don't seem glad to see me. You've been a long time away, Arthur, in London, very long. I hope all your business is settled—all well settled, I hope. And I'm very glad to hear you're not ill—indeed I am. Why are you vexed?'

'Vexed! ho! I'm vexed, am I? that's odd.'

She was making a desperate effort to seem as usual, and talked on.

'We have had old Lady Alice Redcliffe here, my chaperon, all this while, if you please, and takes such ridiculous care of me, and locks me into my room every night. She means kindly, but it is very foolish.'

'Yes, it is d—d foolish.'

'We have been employed very much as usual—walking, and driving, and croquet. Beatrix and I have been very much together, and Sir Paul and Lady Blunket still here. I don't think we have had any arrival since you left us. Mr. Guy Strangways has gone away, and Monsieur Varbarriere returned to-day.'

She was gabbling as merrily as she could, feeling all the time on the point of fainting.

'And the diamonds came?' the General said, suddenly, with a sort of laugh.

'Oh! yes, the diamonds, so beautiful. I did not thank you in my letter—not half enough. They are beautiful—so exquisitely beautiful—brilliants—and so becoming; you have no idea. I hope you got my letter. Indeed I felt it all, every word, Arthur, only I could not say half what I wished. Don't you believe me, Arthur.'

'Lie down, woman, and take your sleep; you sleep *well?* you *all* do—of course you sleep? Lie down.'

'You are angry, Arthur; you are excited; something has happened—something bad—what is it? For God's sake, Arthur, tell me what it is. Why won't you tell me?'

'Nothing—nothing strange—quite common.'

'Oh! Arthur, tell me at once, or kill me. You look as if you hated me.'

'*Hate* you!—There's a hereafter. God sees.'

'I can't understand you, Arthur; you wish to distract me. I'd rather know anything. For mercy's sake speak out.'

'Lie you down, and wait.'

She did lie down. The hour of judgment had come as a thief in the night. The blood in her temples seemed to drum on the pillow. There was not a clear thought in her brain, only the one stunning consciousness.

'He knows all! I am ruined.' Yet the feminine instinct of *finesse* was not quite overpowered.

Having placed the candle on the chimney-piece, so that the curtain at the foot of the bed threw its shadow over that recess in which the sorcerer Varbarriere had almost promised to show the apparition, old Lennox sat down at the bedside, next this mysterious point of observation. Suddenly it crossed him, as a break of moonlight will the blackest night of storm, that he must act more wisely. Had he not alarmed his wife, what signal might not be contrived to warn off her guilty accomplice?

'Jennie,' said he, with an effort, in a more natural tone, 'I'm tired, very tired. We'll sleep. I'll tell you all in the morning. Go to sleep.'

'Good-night,' she murmured.

'That will do; go to sleep,' he answered.

Gently, gently, she stole a peep at that pretty watch that stood in its little slanting stand at her bedside. There was still twenty minutes—Heaven be praised for its mercy!—and she heard old Lennox at the far side of this 'great bed of Ware,' making an ostentation of undressing. His boots tumbled on the floor. She heard his watch-guard jingle on the stand, and his keys and purse dropped in turn on the table. She heard him adjust the chair, as usual, on which he was wont to deposit his clothes as he removed them; she fancied she even heard him yawn. Her heart was throbbing as though it would choke her, and she was praying as she never prayed before—for a reprieve. And yet her respiration was long and deep, as if in the sleep she was counterfeiting.

Lennox, at the other side, put off his muffler, his outer coat, the frock-coat he wore, the waistcoat. She dared not look round to observe his progress. But at last he threw himself on the bed with a groan of fatigue, and pulled the coverlet over him, and lay without motion, like a man in need of rest.

Lady Jane listened. She could not hear him breathe. She waited some five minutes, and then she murmured, ' Arthur.' No answer. ' *Arthur.*' Again no answer ; and she raised herself on her elbow, cautiously, and listened ; and after a little pause, quick as light she got out of bed, glided to the chimneypiece, and lighted a taper at the candle there, listened again for a moment, and on tiptoe, in bare feet, glided round the foot of the bed, and approached the recess at the other side of the bed's head, and instantly her fingers were on one of those little flowers in the ormolu arabesque that runs along the edge of the wooden casing.

Before she could turn it, a gouty hand over her shoulder took hold of hers, and, with a low sudden cry, she saw her husband.

' Can't I do that for you ? What is it ?' said he.

Her lips were white, and she gazed in his face without saying a word.

He was standing there unbooted, in his trowsers, with those crimson silk suspenders on, with the embroidery of forget-me-nots, which she had described as ' her work '—I am afraid inaccurately —a love-token—hypocrisy on hypocrisy.

Asmodeus, seated on the bed's head, smirked down sardonically on the tableau, and clapped his apish hands.

' Get to your bed there. If you make a sign, by ——, I'll kill you.'

She made no answer. She gazed at him dumbly. He was not like himself. He looked like a villain.

He did not lie down again. He sat by the little table, on which his watch, his keys, and loose shillings lay. The night was chill, but he did not feel it then.

He sat in his shirt-sleeves, his chin on his breast, eyeing from under his stern white brows the shadowy arch through which the figure was to emerge.

Suddenly he heard the swift steps of little, naked feet on the carpet come round the foot of the bed, and his wife wildly threw herself at his feet, and clasped them in an agony. He could feel every sinew in her arms vibrate in the hysterical strain of her entreaty.

'Oh, Arthur! oh, darling, take me away from this, for God's sake. Come down with me; come to the drawing-room, or to the dressing-room; take me away; you'll be happier, indeed you will, than ever you were; you'll never repent it, darling; do what I say. I'll be the best wife, indeed I will. See, I've been reading my Bible; look at it. I'm quite changed—quite changed. God only knows how changed. Oh, Arthur, Arthur, if you ever loved me, take me away; come from this room—come, you'll never repent it. Oh, Arthur, be wise, be merciful! The more you forgive, the more you'll be loved. It is not I, but God says that. I'm praying to you as I would to Him, and He forgives us when we implore: take pity on me; you'll never be sorry. Have mercy, Arthur, have mercy—you are kind, I know you're kind, you would not ruin your wretched Jennie. Oh, take pity before it is too late, and take me from this dreadful room. You'll be glad, indeed you will; there never was such a wife as I'll be to you, the humblest, the most loving, and you'll be happier than ever you were. Oh, Arthur, Arthur, I'm praying to you as if you were God, for mercy; don't say no! Oh, can you; can you; can you?'

General Lennox was moved, but not from his course. He never saw before such a face of misery. It was like the despairing pleading of the last day. But alas! in this sort of quarrel there can be no compromise; reconciliation is dishonour.

'Go and lie down. It's all over between us,' said he in a tone that left her no room for hope. With a low, long cry, and her fingers clasped over her forehead, she retraced her steps, and lay down, and quietly drew her icy feet into the bed, awaiting the inevitable. Lennox resumed his watch.

CHAPTER LX.

THE MORNING.

MONSIEUR VARBARRIERE was standing all this while with his shadow to the door-post of the Window dressing-room, and his dark eyes fixed on the further door which admits to the green chamber. His bed-room candle, which was dwindling, stood on the table at his elbow.

' He heard a step crossing the lobby softly toward his own room, and whispered,

' Who's there ?'

' Jacques Duval, at Monsieur's service.'

Monsieur took his candle, and crossed the floor to meet Jacques, who was approaching, and he signed to him to stop. He looked at his watch. It was now twenty minutes past one.

' Jacques,' said he, in a whisper, ' there's no mistake about those sounds ?'

' No, Monsieur, not at all.'

' Three nights running, you say ?'

' Monsieur is perfectly right.'

' Steps, you say ?'

' Yes, sir, footsteps.'

' It could not have been the wind, the shaking or creaking of the floor or windows ?'

' Ah no, Monsieur, not at all as that.'

' The steps quick, not slow ; wasn't it ?'

' Quick, sir, as one in haste and treading lightly would walk.'

' And this as you sat in the butler's room ?'

' Monsieur recollects exactly.'

Varbarriere knew that the butler's room exactly underlay that dingy library that abutted on Sir Jekyl's bedchamber, and on that account had placed his sentinel to watch there.

' Always about the same time ?' he asked.

'Very nearly, Monsieur, a few minutes, sometimes before, some-times after; only trifle, in effect *nothing*,' answered Jacques.

'Jacques, you must leave my door open, so that, should I want you, you can hear me call from the door of that dressing-room; take care you keep awake, but don't move.'

So saying, Varbarriere returned to his place of observation. He set down his candle near the outer door, and listened, glower-ing as before at the far one. The crisis was near at hand, so near that, on looking at his watch again, he softly approached the door of the green chamber, and there, I am sorry to say, he listened diligently.

But all was disappointingly silent for a while longer. Suddenly he heard a noise. A piece of furniture shoved aside it seemed, a heavy step or two, and the old man's voice exclaim 'Ha!' with an interrogatory snarl in it. There was a little laugh, followed by a muffled blow or a fall, and a woman's cry, sharp and momen-tary—'Oh, God! oh, God!' and a gush of smothered sobs, and the General's grim voice calling 'silence!' and a few stern words from him, and fast talking between them, and Lady Jane calling for light, and then more wild sobbing. There had been no sound of a struggle.

Varbarriere stood, stooping, scowling, open-mouthed, at the door, with his fingers on the handle, hardly breathing. At last he gasped—

'That d—— old ape! has he hurt her?' He listened, but all was silent. Did he still hear smothered sobs? He could not be certain. His eyes were glaring on the panel of the door; but on his retina was a ghostly image of beautiful Lady Jane, blood-stained, with glazing eyes, like Cleopatra dying of her asps.

After a while he heard some words from the General in an odd ironical tone. Then came silence again—continued silence—half an hour's silence, and then a sound of some one stirring.

He knew the tread of the General about the room. Whatever was to occur *had* occurred. That was his conclusion. Perhaps the General was coming to *his* room to look for him. It was time he should withdraw, and so he did.

'You may get to your bed, Jacques, and come at the usual hour.'

So, with his accustomed civilities, Monsieur Jacques disappeared. But old Lennox did not visit Varbarriere, nor even emerge from his room.

After an hour Varbarriere revisited the dressing-room next the green chamber. He waited long without hearing anything, and at length he heard a step—was it the General's again, or Sir Jekyl's?—whoever it was, he seemed to be fidgeting about the room, collecting and packing his things, Varbarriere fancied, for a journey; and then he heard him draw the writing-table a little, and place a chair near it, and as the candle was shining through the keyhole, he supposed the General had placed himself to write at it.

Something had happened, he felt sure. Had Lennox despatched Sir Jekyl, or Sir Jekyl wounded the General? Or had Lady Jane been killed? Or was all right, and no one of the actors stretched on the green baize carpet before the floats? He would believe that, and got quickly to his bed, nursing that comfortable conclusion the while. But when he shut his eyes, a succession of pale faces smeared with blood came and looked at him, and would not be ordered away. So he lighted his candle again, and tried to exorcise these visitors with the pages of a French Review, until very late sleep overtook him.

Jacques was in his room at the usual hour, eight o'clock; and Varbarriere started up in his bed at sound of his voice, with a confused anticipation of a catastrophe. But the cheerful squire had nothing to relate except how charming was the morning, and to hand a letter to Monsieur.

Varbarriere's mind was not upon letters that morning, but on matters nearer home.

'General Lennox has not been down stairs yet?'

'No, Monsieur.'

'Nor Sir Jekyl?'

'No, Monsieur.'

'Where's my watch? there—yes—eight o'clock. H'm. When does Lady Jane's maid go to her?'

'Not until the General has advanced himself pretty well in his toilet, the entrance being through his dressing-room.'

'The General used to be down early?'

'Yes, Monsieur, half-past eight I remember.'

'And Sir Jekyl?'

'About the same hour.'

'And Lady Jane is called, I suppose, a little before that hour?'

'Yes, about a quarter past eight, Monsieur. Will Monsieur please to desire his cup of coffee?'

'Yes, everything—quickly—I wish to dress; and what's this? a letter.'

It was from Guy Deverell, as Varbarriere saw at a glance, and not through the post.

'My nephew hasn't come?' sternly demanded Varbarriere, with a kind of start, on reading the signature, which he did before reading the letter.

'No, Monsieur, a young man has conveyed it from Slowton.'

Whereupon Varbarriere, with a striped silk nightcap of many colours pending over his corrugated forehead, read the letter through the divided bed-curtains.

His nephew, it appeared, had arrested his course at Birmingham, and turned about, and reached Slowton again about the hour at which M. Varbarriere had met old Lennox in the grounds of Marlowe.

'What a fanfaronnade! These young fellows—what asses they are!' sneered Varbarriere.

It was not, in truth, very wise. This handsome youth announced his intention to visit Marlowe that day, to see Monsieur Varbarriere for, perhaps, the last time before setting forth for Algeria, where he knew a place would at once be found for him in the ranks of those brave soldiers whom France had sent there. His gratitude to his uncle years could never abate, but it was time he should cease to task his generosity, and he was quite resolved henceforward to fight his way single-handed in the world, as so many other young fellows did. Before taking his departure he thought he should present himself to say his adieux to M. Varbarriere—even to his host, Sir Jekyl Marlowe ; and there was a good deal more of such stuff.

'Sir Jekyl! stuff! His uncle! lanterns! He wants to see that pretty Miss Beatrix once more! *voila tout!* He has chosen his time well. Who knows what confusion may be here to-day ? No matter.'

By this time he had got his great quilted dressing-gown about him, in the folds of which Varbarriere looked more unwieldly still than in his drawing-room costume.

'I must read about that Algeria ; have they got any diseases there ? plague—yellow fever—ague ! By my faith ! if the place is tolerably healthy, it would be no such bad plan to let the young fool take a turn on that gridiron, and learn thoroughly the meaning of independence.'

So Monsieur Varbarriere, with a variety of subjects to think over, pursued his toilet.

CHAPTER LXI.

THE DOCTOR'S VISIT.

SIR JEKYL'S hour was eight o'clock, and punctually his man, Tomlinson, knocked at his door.

'Hollo! Is that Tomlinson?' answered the voice from within.

'Yes, sir, please.'

'See, Tomlinson, I say, it's very ridiculous; but I'm hanged if I can stir, that confounded gout's got hold of my foot again. You'll have to force the door. Send some one down to the town for Doctor Pratt—d'ye see ?—and get me some handkerchiefs, and don't be all day.'

The faithful Tomlinson listening, with a snowy shirt and a pair of socks on his arm and the tips of his fingers fiddling with the door-handle, listening at the other side of the panel, with forehead inclined forward and mouth open, looked, I am sorry to say, a good deal amused, although he answered in a concerned tone; and departed to execute his orders.

'Guv'nor took in toe again,' he murmured, with a solemn leer, as he paused before the butler's broad Marseilles waistcoat.

'As how?' inquired he.

'The gout; can't stir a peg, and he's locked hisself in, as usial, over night.'

'Lawk!' exclaimed the butler, and I dare say both would have liked to laugh, but neither cared to compromise himself.

'Chisel and mallet, Mr. Story, we shall want, if you please, and some one to go at once for the doctor to the town.'

'I know—yes—hinstantly,' ejaculated the butler.

So things proceeded. Pratt, M.D., the medical practitioner of the village, whose yellow hall door and broad brass plate, and shop window round the corner, with the two time-honoured glass jars, one of red the other of green fluid, representing physic in its most attractive hues, were not more widely known than his short, solemn, red face, blue chin, white whiskers, and bald pate, was roused by the messenger's summons, at his toilet, and peeped over his muslin blind to discover the hand that was ringing so furiously among his withered hollyhocks; and at the same time Tomlinson and the butler were working with ripping chisel, mallet, and even a poker, to effect an entrance.

'Ha! Dives,' said the Baronet, as that divine, who had heard the sad news, presented himself at the now open door. 'I sent for you, my dear fellow. A horrid screw in my left toe this time. Such a spoil-sport! curse it, but it won't be anything. I've sent for Pratt, and you'll tell the people at breakfast, you know, that I'm a prisoner; only a trifle though, I hope—down to dinner maybe. There's the gong—run down, like a dear fellow.'

'Not flying—well fixed in the toe, eh?' said Dives, rather anxiously, for he did not like Sir Jekyl's constrained voice and sunken look.

'Quite fixed—blazing away—just the thing Pratt likes—con-

founded pain though.   Now run down, my dear fellow, and make
my excuses, but say I hope to be down to dinner, mind.'

So, with another look, Dives went down, not quite comfortable,
for on the whole he liked Jekyl, who had done a great deal for
him ; he did not like tragedies, he was very comfortable as he
stood, and quite content to await the course of nature.

'Is that d——d doctor *ever* coming ?' asked Sir Jekyl, dismally.

' He'll be he here, sir, please, in five minutes—so he said, sir.'

' I know, but there's been *ten* since, curse him.'

' Shall I send again, sir ?' asked Tomlinson.

' Do ; say I'm in pain, and can't think what the devil's keeping
him.'

Beatrix in a moment more came running up in consternation.

' How do you feel now, papa ?   Gout, is it not ?' she asked,
having obtained leave to come in ; ' not very bad, I hope.'

The Baronet smiled with an effort.

' Gout's never very pleasant, a hot thumbscrew on one's toe,
my dear, but that's all ; it will be nothing.   Pratt's coming, and
he'll get me right in a day or two—only the great toe.   I beg
pardon for naming it so often—very waspish though, that's all.
Don't stay away, or the people will fancy something serious ; and
possibly I may be down, in a slipper though, to dinner.   So run
down, Trixie, darling.'

And Trixie, with the same lingering look that Dives had cast
on him, only more anxious, betook herself to the parlour as he
had desired.

In a little while Doctor Pratt had arrived.   As he toddled
through the hall, he encountered the Rev. Dives on his way to
the breakfast-parlour.   Pratt had suffered some rough handling
and damage at the hands of Time, and Dives was nothing the
better of the sarcastic manipulations of the same ancient god,
since they had last met.   Still they instantly recognised, and
shook hands cordially, and when the salutation was over—

' Well, and what's wrong with the Baronet ?'

' Gout ; he drinks two glasses of port, I've observed, at dinner, and it always disagrees with him. Pray do stop it—the port I mean.'

'Hand or foot?'

'The great toe—the best place, isn't it?'

'No better, sir. There's nothing, nothing of the stomach?—I brought this in *case*,' and he held up a phial.

'No, but I don't like his looks; he looks so haggard and exhausted.'

'H'm, I'd like to see him at once; I don't know his room though.'

So Dives put him in charge of a guide, and they parted.

'Well, Sir Jekyl, how d'ye do, hey? and how's all this? Old enemy, hey—all in the foot—fast in the toe—isn't he?' began the Doctor as he entered the Baronet's room.

'Ay, in the toe. Sit down there, Pratt, beside me.'

'Ah, ha! nervous; you think I'll knock him, eh? Ha, ha, ha! No, no, no! Don't be afraid. Nothing wrong in the stomach—no chill—retching?'

'No.'

'*Head* all right, too; nothing queer there?'

'Nothing.'

'Nothing in the knuckles—old acquaintance, you know, when you meet, sometimes a squeeze by the hand, eh? Ha, ha, ha!'

'No—nothing in the hand,' said the Baronet, a little testily.

'Nor any wandering sensations here, you know, and there, hey?' said the little fellow, sitting down briskly by his patient.

'No; curse it.'

'Troublesome to talk, hey?' asked Pratt, observing that he seemed faint, and talked low and with effort.

'No—yes—that is, *tired*.'

'I see, no pain; all nicely fixed in the toe; *that* could not be better, and what do you refer it to? By Jove, it's eighteen, *nineteen* months since your last! When you came down to Dartbrooke, for the Easter, you know, and wrote to me for the thing with the ether, hey? You've been at that d——d bin, I'm afraid, the forbidden fruit, hey? Egad, sir, I call it fluid gout, and the crust nothing but chalkstone.'

'*No*—I *haven't*,' croaked the Baronet, savagely.

' Ha, ha, ha !' laughed the Doctor, drumming on his fat knee with his stethoscope. ' Won't admit—won't allow, hey ?' As he spoke he was attempting to take him by the wrist.

' Pulse ? How are we there, eh ?'

' Turn that d—d fellow out of the room, and bolt the door, will you ?' muttered Sir Jekyl, impatiently.

' Hey ? I see. How are *you*, Mr. Tomlinson—no return of that bronchial annoyance, eh ? I'll ask you just now—we'll just make Sir Jekyl Marlowe a little more comfortable first, and I've a question or two—we'd be as well alone, you see—and do you mind ? You'll be in the way, you know; we may want you, you know.'

So the docile Tomlinson withdrew with a noiseless alacrity, and Doctor Pratt, in deference to his patron, bolted the mangled door.

' See, Pratt, you're tiring me to death, with your beastly questions. Wait, will you ? Sit down. You'll promise me you won't tell this to anyone.'

' What ?'

' Do hold your tongue, like a dear fellow, and listen. Upon your honour, you don't tell, till I give you leave, what's the matter with me. Come—d——you; yes or no ?'

' Well, you know I must, if you insist; but I'd rayther not.'

' You *must*. On your honour you won't tell, and you'll call it gout ?'

' Why—why, if it *is* not gout, eh ? don't yon see ? it would not *do*.'

' Well, good morning to you, Doctor Pratt, for I'm hanged if you prescribe for me on any other terms.'

' Well, don't you see, I say I must, if you insist, don't you see ; it may be—it may be—egad ! it might be very serious to let you wait.'

' You promise ?'

'Yes, I *do*, *There!*'

'Gout, mind, and nothing else; all gout, upon your honour.'

'Aw, well! *Yes.*'

'Upon your *honour*; why the devil can't you speak?'

'Upon my honour, of course.'

'You kill me, making me talk. Well, 'tisn't in the toe—it's up here,' and he uncovered his right shoulder and chest, showing some handkerchiefs and his night shirt soaked in blood.

'What the devil's all this?' exclaimed the Doctor, rising suddenly, and the ruddy tints of his face fading into a lilac hue. 'Why—why, you're *hurt;* egad, you're hurt. We must examine it. What is it with—how the plague did it all come about?'

'The act of God,' answered Sir Jekyl, with a faint irony in his tone.

'The—ah!—well, I don't understand.'

'I mean the purest accident.'

'Bled a lot, egad! These things seem pretty dry—bleeding away *still?* You must not keep it so hot—the sheet only.'

'I think it's stopped—the things are sticking—I feel them.'

'So much the better; but we must not leave it this way—and —and I daren't disturb it, you know, without help, so we'll have to take Tomlinson into confidence.'

''Gad, you'll do no such thing.'

'But, my dear sir, I *must* tell you, this thing, whatever it is, looks very serious. I can *tell* you, it's not to be trifled with, and this sort of nonsense may be as much as your life's worth, egad.'

'You shan't,' said Sir Jekyl.

'You'll allow me to speak with your brother?'

'No, you shan't.'

'Ho, now, Sir Jekyl, really now'——

'Promised—your honour.'

''Tisn't a fair position,' said the practitioner, shaking his head, with his hands stuffed in his pockets, and staring dismally at the blood-stained linen. 'I'll tell you what we must do—there are two supernumeraries I happen to know at the county hospital, and Hicks is a capital nurse. I'll write a line and they'll send her here. There's a room in there, eh? yes, well, she can be quartered *there*, and talk with no one but you and me; in fact, see no one except in your presence, don't you see? and egad, we *must* have her, or I'll give up the *case*.'

'Well, yes; send for her.'

CHAPTER LXII.

THE PATIENT INTERROGATED.

So Doctor Pratt scribbled a few lines on the back of his card, and Tomlinson was summoned to the door, and told to expedite its despatch, and 'send one of the men in the dogcart as hard as he could peg, and to be sure to see Doctor Hoggins,' who had been an apprentice once of honest Pratt's.

'Tell her not to wait for dressing, or packing, or anything. She'll come just as she is, and we'll send again for her things, d'ye mind? and let him drive quick. It's only two miles, he must not be half an hour about it;' and in a low whisper, with a frown and a nod, he added to Tomlinson on the lobby, 'I *want* her here.'

So he sat down very grave by Sir Jekyl, and took his pulse, very low and inflammatory, he thought.

'You lost a good deal of blood? It is not all here, eh?'

'No; I lost some beside.'

'Mind, now, don't move. You may bring it on again; and you're not in a condition to spare any. How did it happen?'

'A knife, or something.'

'A thrust, eh? Not a *cut*; I mean a *stab*?'

'Yes.'

'About how long ago? What hour?'

Sir Jekyl hesitated.

' Oh ! now come, Sir Jekyl, I beg pardon, but I really must know the *facts*.'

' Remember your promise—awfully tired.'

' Certainly. What o'clock ?'

' Between one and two.'

' You must have some claret;' and he opened the door and issued orders accordingly. The doctor had his fingers on his pulse by this time.

' Give me some water ; I'm dying of thirst,' said the patient.

The Doctor obeyed.

' And there's no gout at all then ?' said he.

' Not a bit,' answered Sir Jekyl, pettishly ; his temper and his breath seemed to be failing him a little.

' Did you feel faint when it happened, or after ?'

' Just for a moment, when it happened, then pretty well; and when I got here, in a little time, worse, very faint ; I think I did faint, but a little blood always does that for me. But it's not deep, I know by the feel—only the muscle.'

' H'm. I sha'n't disturb these things till the nurse comes; glad there's no gout, no complication.'

The claret-jug was soon at the bedside, and the Doctor helped his patient to a few spoonfuls, and felt his pulse again.

I must go home for the things, d'ye see ? I sha'n't be long away though. Here, Tomlinson, you'll give Sir Jekyl a spoonful or a glassful of this claret, d'ye mind, as often as he requires it. About every ten minutes a little to wet his lips : and mind, now, Sir Jekyl, drink any quantity rather than let yourself go down.'

As he went from the room he signed to Tomlinson, who followed him quietly.

' See, now, my good fellow, this is rather a serious case, you understand me ; and he must not be let down. Your master, Sir Jekyl, I say, he must be kept up. Keep a little claret to his lips, and if you see any pallor or moisture in his face, give it him by a glassful at a time ; and go on, do you mind, till he begins to look natural again, for he's in a very critical state ; and if he were to faint, d'ye see, or anything, it might be a very serious thing; and you'd better ring for another bottle or two; but don't leave him on any account.'

They were interrupted here by a tapping in Sir Jekyl's room. Lying on his back, he was rapping with his penknife on the table.

' Why the plague don't you come?' he muttered, as Tomlinson drew near. ' Where's Pratt? tell him I want him.'

' Hey—no—no *pain* ?' asked the Doctor.

' No; I want to know—I want to know what the devil you've been saying to him out there.'

' Nothing; only a direction.'

' Do you think—do you think I'm in *danger* ?' said Sir Jekyl.

' Well, *no*. You needn't be if you mind, but—but don't refuse the claret, mind, and don't be afraid of it if you feel a—a sinking, you know, any quantity; and I'll be back before the nurse comes from the hospital; and—and don't be excited, for you'll do very well if you'll only do as I tell you.'

The Doctor nodded, standing by the bed, but he did not look so cheerfully as he spoke.

' I'll be back in twenty minutes. Don't be fidgety, you know; don't stir, and you'll do very nicely, I say.'

When the Doctor was gone, Sir Jekyl said—

' Tomlinson.'

' Yes, sir, please.'

' Tomlinson, come here; let me see you.

' Yes, Sir Jekyl; sir——'

' I say, Tomlinson, you'll tell the truth, mind.'

' Yes, sir, please.'

' Did that fellow say anything?'

' Yes, sir, please.'

' Out with it.'

' 'Twas claret, Sir Jekyl, please, sir.'

' None of your d——d lies, sir. I heard him say " serious." What *was* it ?'

' Please, sir, he said as how you were to be kep up, sir, which it might be serious if otherwise. So he said, sir, please, it might be serious if you was not properly kep up with claret, please, sir.'

'Come, Tomlinson—see I *must* know. Did he say I was in a bad way—likely to die?—come.' His face was certainly hollow and earthy enough just then to warrant forebodings.

'No, sir; certainly not, sir. No, sir, please, nothing of the kind.'

The Baronet looked immeasurably more like himself.

'Give me some wine—a glass,' said he.

The Doctor, stumping away rapidly to his yellow door, and red and green twin bottles, in the village, was thinking how the deuce this misadventure of Sir Jekyl's had befallen. The Baronet's unlucky character was well known wherever he resided or had property.

'Who the devil did it, I wonder?' conjectured the Doctor. 'Two o'clock at night. Some pretty fury with a scissors, maybe. We'll know time enough; these things always come out—always come out, egad! It's a shame for him getting into scrapes at his time of life.'

In the breakfast-parlour, very merry was the party then assembled, notwithstanding the absence of some of its muster-roll. Lady Jane Lennox, an irregular breakfaster, stood excused. Old Lady Alice was no more expected than the portrait of Lady Mary in her bed-room. General Lennox had business that morning, and was not particularly inquired after. Sir Jekyl, indeed, was missed—bustling, good-natured, lively—his guests asked after him with more than a conventional solicitude.

'Well, and how is papa now?' inquired Sir Paul, who knew what gout was, and being likely to know it again, felt a real interest in the Baronet's case. 'No *acute* pain, I hope?'

'I'm afraid he *is* in pain, more than he admits,' answered Beatrix.

'Tomlinson told me it's all in the—the extremity, though that's well. Intelligent fellow, Tomlinson. Mine is generally what they call atonic, not attended with much pain, you know; and he illustrated his disquisition by tendering his massive mulberry knuckles for the young lady's contemplation, and fondling them with the glazed fingers of the other hand, while his round blue eyes stared, with a slow sort of wonder, in her face, as if he expected a good deal in the way of remark from the young lady to mitigate his astonishment.

Lady Blunket, who was beside her, relieved this embarrassment, and nodding at her ear, said—

'Flannel—*flannel*, chiefly. Sir Paul, there, his medical man, Doctor Duddle, we have great confidence in *him*—relies very much on warmth. My poor father used to take Regent's—Regent's—I forget what—a *bottle*. But Doctor Duddle would not hear of Sir Paul there attempting to put it to his lips. Regent's —*what* is it? I shall forget my own name soon! *Water* is it? At all events he won't hear of it—diet and flannel, that's his method. My poor father, you know, died of gout, quite suddenly, at Brighton. Cucumber, they said.'

And Lady Blunket, overcome by the recollection, touched her eyes with her handkerchief.

'Cucumber and salmon, it was, *I* recollect,' said Sir Paul, with a new accession of intelligence.

'But he passed away most happily, Miss Marlowe,' continued Lady Blunket. 'I have some verses of poor mamma's. *She* was *very* religious, you know; they have been very much admired.'

'Ay—yes,' said Sir Paul, 'he was helped *twice*—very imprudent!'

'I was mentioning dear mamma's verses, you remember.'

Sir Paul not being quite so well up in this aspect of the case, simply grunted and became silent; and indeed I don't think he had been so loquacious upon any other morning or topic since' his arrival at Marlowe.

'They are beautiful,' continued Lady Blunket, 'and so resigned. I was most anxious, my dear, to place a tablet under the monument, you know, at Maisly; a mural tablet, just like the Tuftons,' you know; they are very reasonable, inscribed wlth dear mamma's verses; but I can't persuade Sir Paul, he's so poor, you know; but certainly, some day or other, I'll do it myself.'

The irony about Sir Paul's poverty, though accompanied by a glance from her ladyship's pink eyes, was lost on that excellent man, who was by this time eating some hot broil.

Their judicious conversation was not without an effect commensurate with the rarity of the exertion, for between them they had succeeded in frightening poor Beatrix a good deal.

In other quarters the conversation was proceeding charmingly. Linnett was describing to Miss Blunket the exploits of a terrier of his, among a hundred rats let loose together—a narrative to which she listened with a pretty girlish alternation of terror and interest; while the Rev. Dives Marlowe and old Doocey conversed earnestly on the virtues of colchicum, and exchanged confidences touching their gouty symptoms and affections; and Drayton, assisted by an occasional parenthesis from that prodigious basso, Varbarriere, was haranguing Beatrix and Mrs. Maberly on pictures, music, and the way to give agreeable dinners; and now Beatrix asked old Lady Blunket in what way she would best like to dispose of the day. What to do, where to drive, an inquiry into which the other ladies were drawn, and the debate, assisted by the gentlemen, grew general and animated.

CHAPTER LXIII.

GENERAL LENNOX APPEARS.

IN the midst of this animation the butler whispered in the ear of the Rev. Dives Marlowe, who, with a grave face, but hardly perceived, slid away, and met the Doctor in the hall.

'Aw—*see*—this is a—rather nasty case, I am bound to tell you, Mr. Marlowe; he's in a rather critical state. He'll see you, I dare say, by-and-by, and I hope he'll get on satisfactorily. I hope he'll *do*; but I must tell you, it's a—it's a—serious *case*, sir.'

'Nothing since ?' asked Dives, a good deal shocked.

'Nothing since, sir,' answered the Doctor, with a nod, and his eyebrows raised as he stood ruminating a little, with his fists in his pockets. 'But—but—you'll do *this*, sir, if you please—you'll call in some physician, in whom you have confidence, for I'll tell you frankly, it's not a case in which I'd like to be alone.'

'It's very sudden, sir; whom do you advise ?' said Dives, looking black and pallid.

'Well, you know, it ought to be *soon*. I'd like him at once—you can't send very far. There's Ponder, I would not desire better, if you approve. Send a fellow riding, and don't spare horseflesh, mind, to Slowton. He'll find Ponder there if he's quick, and let him bring him in a chaise and four, and pay the fellows well, and they'll not be long coming. They'd better be quick, for there's something must be done, and I can't undertake it alone.'

Together they walked out to the stable-yard, Dives feeling stunned and odd. The Doctor was reserved, and only waited to see things in train. Almost while Dives pencilled his urgent note on the back of a letter, the groom had saddled one of the hunters and got into his jacket, and was mounted and away.

Dives returned to the house. From the steps he looked with a sinking heart after the man cantering swiftly down the avenue, and saw him in the distance like a dwindling figure in a dream, and somehow it was to him an effort to remember what it was all about. He felt the cold air stirring his dark locks, streaked with silver, and found he had forgot his hat, and so came in.

'You have seen a great deal of art, Monsieur Varbarriere,' said Drayton, accosting that gentleman admiringly, in the outer hall, where they were fitting themselves with their 'wide-awakes' and 'jerries.' 'It is so pleasant to meet anyone who really understands it and has a feeling for it. You seem to me to lean more to painting than to statuary.'

'Painting is the more popular art, because the more literal. The principles of statuary are abstruse. The one, you see, is a repetition—the other a translation. Colour is more than outline,.

and the painter commands it. The man with the chisel has only outline, and must render nature into white stone, with the *natural* condition of being inspected from every point, and the *unnatural* one, in solid anatomy, of immobility. It is a greater triumph, but a less effect.'

Varbarriere was lecturing this morning according to his lights, more copiously and *ex cathedrâ* than usual. Perhaps his declamations and antithesis represented the constraint which he placed on himself, like those mental exercises which sleepless men prescribe to wrest their minds from anxious and exciting preoccupations.

' Do you paint, sir ?' asked Drayton, who was really interested.

' Bah! never. I can make just a little scratching with my pencil, enough to remind. But paint—oh—ha, ha, ha!—no. 'Tis an art I can admire; but should no more think to practise than the dance.'

And the ponderous M. Varbarriere pointed his toe and made a mimic pirouette, snapped his fingers, and shrugged his round shoulders.

' Alas! sir, the more I appreciate the dance, the more I despair of figuring in the ballet, and so with painting. Perhaps, though, *you* paint ?'

' Well, I just draw a little—what you call scratching, and I have tried a little tinting; but I'm sure it's very bad. I don't care about fools, of course, but I should be afraid to show it to anyone who knew anything about it—to you, for instance,' said Drayton, who, though conceited, had sense enough at times to be a little modest.

' What is it ?' said Miss Blunket, skipping into the hall, with a pretty little basket on her arm, and such a coquettish little hat on, looking so naïve and 'girlish, and so remarkably tattooed with wrinkles. ' Shall I run away—is it a secret ?'

' Oh, no ; we have no secrets,' said Drayton.

' No secrets,' echoed Varbarriere.

' And won't you tell ? I'm such a curious, foolish, wretched creature ;' and she dropped her eyes like a flower-girl in a play.

What lessons, if we only could take them, are read us every hour! What a giant among liars is vanity! Here was this withered witch, with her baptismal registry and her looking-glass, dressing herself like a strawberry girl, and fancying herself charming!'

'Only about my drawings—nothing.'

'Ah, I know. Did Mr. Drayton show them to you?'

'No, Mademoiselle; I've not been so fortunate.'

'He showed them to me, though. It's not any harm to tell, is it? and they really *are*—Well, I won't say all I think of them.'

'I was just telling Monsieur Varbarriere. It is not everyone I'd show those drawings to. Was not I, Monsieur?' said Drayton, with a fine irony.

'So he was, upon my honour,' said Varbarriere, gravely.

'He did not mean it, though,' simpered Miss Blunket, 'if *you* can't—*I*'ll try to induce him to show them to you; they are —— Oh! here is Beatrix.'

'How is your papa now, Mademoiselle?' asked Varbarriere, anxious to escape.

'Just as he was, I think, a little low, the Doctor says.'

'Ah!' said Varbarriere, and still his dark eyes looked on hers with grave inquiry.

'He always *is* low for a day or two; but he says this will be nothing. He almost hopes to be down this evening.'

'Ah! Yes. That's very well,' commented Varbarriere, with pauses between, and his steady, clouded gaze unchanged.

'We are going to the garden; are you ready, darling?' said she to Miss Blunket.

'Oh, quite,' and she skipped to the door, smiling, this way and that, as she stood in the sun on the step. 'Sweet day,' and she looked back on Beatrix and the invitation, glanced slightly on Drayton, who looked loweringly after them unmoved, and thought—

'Why the plague does she spoil her walks with that frightful old humbug? There's no escaping that creature.'

We have only conjecture as to which of the young ladies, now running down the steps, Mr. Drayton's pronouns referred to.

'You fish to-day?' asked Varbarriere, on whose 'hands time dragged strangely.

'We were thinking of going down to that pretty place, Gryston. Linnett was there on Saturday morning. It was Linnett's trout you thought so good at luncheon.'

And with such agreeable conversation they loitered a little at the door, and suddenly, with quick steps, there approached, and passed them by, an apparition.

It was old General Lennox. He had been walking in the park —about the grounds—he knew not where, since daybreak. Awfully stern he looked, fatigued, draggled he well might be, gloveless, one hand in his pocket, the other clenched on his thumb like a child's in a convulsion. His thoughts were set on something remote, for he brushed by the gentlemen, and not till he had passed did he seem to hear Drayton's cheery salutation, and stopping and turning towards them suddenly, he said, very grimly—

'Beg your pardon——'

'Nothing, General, only wishing you good-morning,' answered Drayton.

'Yes, charming morning. I've been walking. I've been out —a—thank you,' and that lead-coloured and white General vanished like a wicked ghost.

''Gad, he looks as if he'd got a licking. Did you ever see a fellow look so queer?'

'He's been overworking his mind—business, you know—wants rest, I suspect,' said Varbarriere, with a solemn nod.

'They say fellows make themselves mad that way. I wonder has he had any breakfast; did you see his trowsers all over mud?'

'I half envy your walk to Gryston,' said Varbarriere, glancing up towards the fleecy clouds and blue sky, and down again to the breezy landscape. 'It's worth looking at, a very pretty bit, that steep bridge and glen.'

'No notion of coming; maybe you will?'

Varbarriere smiled and shook his head.

'No angler, sir, never was,' he said.

'A bad day, rather, at all events,' said Drayton; 'a grey day is the thing for us.'

'Ah, yes, a grey day; so my nephew tells me; a pretty good angler, I believe.'

Varbarriere did not hear Drayton's answer, whatever it was; he was thinking of quite other things, and more and more feverishly every minute. The situation was for him all in darkness. But there remained on his mind the impression that something worse even than a guilty discovery had occurred last night, and the spectre that had just crossed them in the hall was not a sight to dissipate those awful shadows.

CHAPTER LXIV.

LADY ALICE REDCLIFFE MAKES GENERAL LENNOX'S ACQUAINT-ANCE.

OLD General Lennox stopped a servant on the stairs, and learned from the staring domestic where Lady Alice Redcliffe then was.

That sad and somewhat virulent old martyr was at that moment in her accustomed haunt, Lady Mary's boudoir, and in her wonted attitude over the fire, pondering in drowsy discontent over her many miseries, when a sharp knock at the door startled her nerves and awakened her temper.

Her 'come in' sounded sharply, and she beheld for the first time in her life, the General, a tall lean old man, with white bristles on brow and cheek, with his toilet disordered by long and rather rapid exercise, and grim and livid with no transient agitation.

'Lady Alice Redcliffe?' inquired he, with a stiff bow, remaining still inclined, his eyes still fixed on her.

'*I* am Lady Alice Redcliffe,' returned that lady, haughtily, having quite forgotten General Lennox and all about him.

'My name is Lennox,' he said.

' Oh, *General* Lennox? I was told you were here last night,' said the old lady, scrutinising him with a sort of surprised frown ; his dress and appearance were a little wild, and not in accordance with her ideas on military precision. ' I am happy, General Lennox, to make your acquaintance. You've just arrived, I dare say ?'

' I arrived yesterday—last night—last night late. I—I'm much obliged. May I say a word ?'

' Certainly, General Lennox,' acquiesced the old lady, looking harder at him—' certainly, but I must remind you that I have been a sad invalid, and therefore very little qualified to discuss or advise ;' and she leaned back with a fatigued air, but a curious look nevertheless.

' I—I—it's about my wife, ma'am. We can—we can't live any longer together.' He was twirling his gold eye-glass with trembling fingers as he spoke.

' You have been quarrelling—h'm ?' said Lady Alice, still staring hard at him, and rising with more agility than one might have expected ; and shutting the door, which the old General had left open, she said, ' Sit down, sir—quarrelling, eh ?'

'A quarrel, madam, that can never be made up—by——, *never*.' The General smote his gouty hand furiously on the chimneypiece as he thus spake.

' Don't General Lennox, *don't*, pray. If you can't command yourself, how can you hope to bear with one another's infirmities ? A quarrel ? H'm.'

' Madam, we've separated. It's worse, ma'am—all over. I thought, Lady—Lady—I thought, madam, I might ask you, as the only early friend—a friend, ma'am, and a kinswoman—to take her with you for a little while, till some home is settled for her ; *here* she can't stay, of course, an hour. That villain ! May —— damn him.'

' Who ?' asked Lady Alice, with a kind of scowl, quite forgetting to rebuke him this time, her face darkening and turning very pale, for she saw it was another great family disgrace.

' Sir Jekyl Marlowe, ma'am, of Marlowe, Baronet, Member of

Parliament, Deputy Lieutenant,' bawled the old General, with shrill and trembling voice. ' I'll drag him through the law courts, and the divorce court, and the House of Lords.' He held his right fist up with its trembling knuckles working, as if he had them in Sir Jekyl's cravat, 'drag him through them all, ma'am, till the dogs would not pick his bones ; and I'll shoot him through the head, by ——, I'll shoot him through the head, and his family ashamed to put his name on his tombstone.'

Lady Alice stood up, with a face so dismal it almost looked wicked.

' I see, sir ; I see there's something very bad ; I'm sorry, sir ; I'm very sorry ; I'm *very* sorry.'

She had a hand of the old General's in each of hers, and was shaking them with a tremulous clasp.

Such as it was, it was the first touch of sympathy he had felt. The old General's grim face quivered and trembled, and he grasped *her* hands too, and then there came those convulsive croupy sobs, so dreadful to hear, and at last tears, and this dried and bleached old soldier wept loud and piteously. Outside the door you would not have known what to make of these cracked, convulsive sounds. You would have stopped in horror, and fancied some one dying. After a while he said—

' Oh ! ma'am, I was very fond of her—I *was*, desperately. If I could know it was all a dream, I'd be content to die. I wish, ma'am, you'd advise me. I'll go back to India, I think ; I could not stay here. You'll know best, madam, what she ought to do. I wish everything the best for her—you'll see, ma'am—you'll know best.'

' Quite—quite ; yes, these things are best settled by men of business. There are papers, I believe, drawn up, arranged by lawyers, and things, and I'm sorry, sir——'

And old Lady Alice suddenly began to sob.

' I'll—I'll do what I can for the poor thing,' she said. ' I'll take her to Wardlock—it's quite solitary—no prying people—and then to—perhaps it's better to go abroad ; and you'll not make it public sooner than it must be ; and it's a great blow to me, sir, a

terrlble blow. I wish she had placed herself more under direction ;
but it's vain looking back—she always refused advice, poor, poor
wretched thing! Poor Jennie! We must be resigned, sir; and
—and, sir, for God's sake, no fighting—no pistoling. That sort
of thing is never heard of now; and if you do, the whole world
will be ringing with it, and the unfortunate creature the gaze of
the public before she need be, and perhaps some great crime
added—some one killed. Do you promise?'

'Ma'am, it's hard to promise.'

'But you *must*, General Lennox, or I'll take measures to stop
it this moment,' cried Lady Alice, drying her eyes and glaring at
him fiercely.

'Stop it! *who'll* stop it?' holloed the General with a stamp.

'*You'll* stop it, General,' exclaimed the old lady; 'your own
common sense; your own compassion; your own self-respect: and
not the less that a poor old woman that sympathises with you
implores it.'

There was here an interval.

'Ma'am, ma'am, it's not easy; but I will—I *will*, ma'am. I'll
go this moment; I will, ma'am; I can't trust myself here. If I
met him, ma'am, by Heaven I *couldn't*.'

'Well, thank you, *thank* you, General Lennox—*do* go; there's
not much chance of meeting, for he's ill; but go, don't stay a
moment, and write to me to Wardlock, and you shall hear everything. There—go. Good-bye.'

So the General was gone, and Lady Alice stood for a while
bewildered, looking at the door through which he had vanished.

It is well when these sudden collapses of the overwrought
nerves occur. More dejected, more broken, perhaps, he looked,
but much more like the General Lennox whom his friends
remembered. Something of the panic and fury of his calamity
had subsided, too; and though the grief must, perhaps, always
remain pretty much unchanged, yet he could now estimate the
situation more justly, and take his measures more like a sane
man.

In this better, if not happier mood, Varbarriere encountered him in that overshadowed back avenue which leads more directly than the main one to the little town of Marlowe.

Varbarriere was approaching the house, and judged, by the General's slower gait, that he was now more himself.

The large gentleman in the Germanesque felt hat raised that grotesque head-gear, French fashion, as Lennox drew nigh.

The General, with two fingers, made him a stern, military salute in reply, and came suddenly to a standstill.

' May I walk a little with you, General Lennox ?' inquired Varbarriere.

' Certainly, sir. *Walk ?* By all means ; I'm going to London,' rejoined the General, without, however, moving from the spot where he had halted.

' Rather a long stretch for me,' thought Varbarriere, with one of those inward thrills of laughter which sometimes surprise us in the gravest moods and in the most unsuitable places. He looked sober enough, however, and merely said—

' You know, General, there's some one ill up there,' and he nodded mysteriously toward the house.

' Is there ? Ay. Well, yes, I dare say,' and he laughed with a sudden quaver. ' I was not sure ; the old woman said something. I'm glad, sir.'

' I—I think I *know* what it is, sir,' said Varbarriere.

' So do I, sir,' said the General, with another short laugh.

' You recollect, General Lennox, what you promised me ?'

' Ay, sir ; how can I help it ?' answered he.

' How can you help it ! I don't quite see your meaning,' replied Varbarriere, slowly. ' I can only observe that it gives me new ideas of a soldier's estimate of his promise.'

' Don't blame me, sir, if I lost my head a little, when I saw that villain there, in *my* room sir, by ——' and the General cursed him here parenthetically through his clenched teeth ; ' I felt, sir, as—as if the sight of him struck me in the face—mad, sir, for a minute—I suppose, *mad*, sir ; and—it occurred. I say, sir, I can't help it—and I could't help it, by —— I couldn't.'

Varbarriere looked down with a peevish sneer on the grass and innocent daisies at his feet, his heel firmly placed, and tapping the sole of his boot from that pivot on the sward, like a man beating time to a slow movement in an overture.

'Very good, sir! It's your own affair. I suppose you've considered consequences, if anything should go wrong?'

And without awaiting an answer, he turned and slowly pursued his route toward the house. I don't suppose, in his then frame of mind, the General saw consequences very clearly, or cared about them, or was capable, when the image of Sir Jekyl presented itself, of any emotions but those of hatred and rage. He had gone now, at all events; the future darkness; the past irrevocable.

CHAPTER LXV.

THE BISHOP SEES THE PATIENT.

In the hall Varbarriere met the Reverend Dives Marlowe.

'Well, sir, how is Sir Jekyl?' asked he.

The parson looked bilious and lowering.

'To say truth, Monsieur, I can't very well make out what the Doctor thinks. I suspect he does not understand very well himself. *Gout*, he says, but in a very sinking state; and we've sent for the physician at Slowton; and altogether, sir, I'm very uneasy.'

I suppose if the blow had fallen, the reverend gentleman would in a little while have become quite resigned, as became him. There were the baronetcy and some land; but on the whole, when Death drew near smirking, and offered on his tray, with a handsome black pall over it, these sparkling relics of the late Sir Jekyl Marlowe, Bart., the Rev. Dives turned away; and though he liked these things well enough, put them aside honestly, and even with a sort of disgust. For Jekyl, as I have said, though the brothers could sometimes exchange a sharp sally, had always been essentially kind to him; and Dives was not married, and, in fact, was funding money, and in no hurry; and those things were sure to come to him if he lived, sooner or later.

'And what, may I ask, do you suppose it *is* ?' inquired Varbarriere.

'Well, *gout*, you know—he's positive; and, poor fellow, he's got it in his foot, and a very nasty thing it is, I know, even *there*. We all of us have it hereditarily—our family.' The apostle and mårtyr did not want him to suppose he had earned it. ' But I am very anxious, sir. Do *you* know anything of gout ? May it be *there* and somewhere else at the same time ? Two members of our family died of it in the stomach, and one in the head. It has been awfully fatal with us.'

Varbarriere shook his head. He had never had a declared attack, and had no light to throw on the sombre prospect. The fact is, if that solemn gentleman had known for certain exactly how matters stood, and had not been expecting the arrival of his contumacious nephew, he would have been many miles on his way to London by this time.

' You know—you know, *sinking* seems very odd as a symptom of common gout in the great toe,' said, Dives, looking in his companion's face, and speaking rather like a man seeking than communicating information. ' We must not frighten the ladies, you know; but I'm very much afraid of something in the stomach, eh ? and possibly the heart.'

' After all, sir,' said Varbarriere, with a brisk effort, ' Doctor— a—what's his name ?—he's but a rural practitioner—an apothecary —is not it so ?'

' The people here say, however, he's a very clever fellow, though,' said Dives, not much comforted.

' We may hear a different story when the Slowton doctor comes. I venture to think we shall. I always fancied when gout was well out in the toe, the internal organs were safe. Oh! there's the Bishop.'

' Just talking about poor Jekyl, my lord,' said Dives, with a sad smile of deference, the best he could command.

'And—and how *is* my poor friend and pupil, Sir Jekyl?—better, I trust,' responded the apostle in gaiters and apron.

'Well, my lord, we hope—I trust everything satisfactory; but the Doctor has been playing the sphinx with us, and I don't know exactly what to make of him.'

'I saw Doctor Pratt for a moment, and expressed my wish to see his patient—my poor pupil—before I go, which must be yes—within an hour,' said the Bishop, consulting his punctual gold watch. 'But he preferred my postponing until Doctor—I forget his name—very much concerned, *indeed*, that a second should be thought necessary—from Slowton—should have arrived. It—it gives me—I—I can't deny, a rather serious idea of it. Has he had many attacks?'

'Yes, my lord, several; never threatened seriously, but once—at Dartbroke, about two years ago—in the stomach.'

'Ah! I forgot it was the stomach. I remember his illness though,' said the Bishop, graciously.

'Not *actually* the stomach—only threatened,' suggested Dives, deferentially. 'I have made acquaintance with it myself, too, slightly; never so sharply as poor Jekyl. I *wish* that other doctor would come! But even at best it's not a pleasant visitor.'

'I dare say—I can well suppose it. *I* have reason to be *very* thankful. I've *never* suffered. My poor *father* knew what it was—suffered horribly. I remember him at Buxton for it—horribly.'

The Bishop was fond of this recollection, people said, and liked it to be understood that there was gout in the family, though he could not show that aristocratic gules himself.

At this moment Tomlinson approached, respectfully—I might even say religiously—and with such a reverence as High-Church-men make at the creed, accosted the prelate, in low tones like distant organ-notes, murmuring Sir Jekyl's compliments to 'his lordship, and would be very 'appy to see his lordship whenever it might be his convenience.' To which his lordship assented, with a grave ' *Now*, certainly, I shall be most happy,' and turning to Dives—

'This, I hope, looks well. I fancy he must feel better. Let us hope;' and with slightly uplifted hand and eyes, the good Bishop followed Tomlinson, feeling so oddly as he threaded the same narrow half-lighted passages, whose corners and panelling came sharply on his memory as he passed them, and ascended the steep back stair with the narrow stained-glass slits, by which he had reached, thirty years ago, the sick-chamber of the dying Sir Harry Marlowe.

The Bishop sighed, looking round him, as he stood on the lobby outside the little ante-room. The light fell through the slim coloured orifice opposite on the oak before him, just as it did on the day he last stood there. The banisters, above and below, looked on him like yesterday's acquaintances; and the thoughtful frown of the heavy oak beams overhead seemed still knit over the same sad problem.

'*Thirty* years ago!' murmured the Bishop, with a sad smile, nodding his silvery head slightly, as his saddened eyes wandered over these things. 'What is man that thou art mindful of him, or the son of man that thou so regardest him?'

Tomlinson, who had knocked at the Baronet's door, returned to say he begged his lordship would step in.

So with another sigh, peeping before him, he passed through the small room that interposed, and entered Sir Jekyl's, and took his hand very kindly and gravely, pressing it, and saying in the low tone which becomes a sick-chamber—

'I trust, my dear Sir Jekyl, you feel better.'

'Thank you, pretty well; very good of you, my lord, to come. It's a long way, from the front of the house—a journey. He told me you were in the hall.'

'Yes, it is a large house; interesting to me, too, from earlier recollections.'

'You were in this room, a great many years ago, with my poor father. He died here, you know.'

'I'm afraid you're distressing yourself speaking. Yes; oddly enough, I recognised the passages and back stairs; the windows, too, are peculiar. The *furniture*, though, that's changed — is not it?'

'So it is. I hated it,' replied Sir Jekyl. 'Balloon-backed blue silk things—faded, you know. It's curious you should remember, after such a devil of a time—such a great number of years, my lord. I hated it. When I had that fever here in this room—thirteen—fourteen years ago—ay, by Jove, it's *fifteen*—they were going to write for *you*.'.

'Excuse me, my dear friend, but it seems to me you *are* exerting yourself too much,' interposed the prelate again.

'Oh dear no! it does me good to talk. I had all sorts of queer visions. People fancy, you know, they see things; and I used to think I saw him—my poor father, I mean—every night. There were six of those confounded blue-backed chairs in this room, and a nasty idea got into my head. I had a servant—poor Lewis—then a very trustworthy fellow, and liked me, I think; and Lewis told me the doctors said there was to be a crisis on the night week of the first consultation—seven days, you know.'

'I really fear, Sir Jekyl, you are distressing yourself,' persisted the Bishop, who did not like the voluble eagerness and the apparent fatigue, nevertheless, with which he spoke.

'Oh! it's only a word more—it doesn't, I assure you—and I perceived he sat on a different chair, d'ye see, every night, and on the fourth night he had got on the fourth chair; and I liked his face less and less every night. You know he hated me about Molly—about *nothing*—he always hated me; and as there were only six chairs, it got into my head that he'd get up on my bed on the seventh, and that I should die in the crisis. So I put all the chairs out of the room. They thought I was raving; but I was quite right, for he did not come again, and here I am;' and with these words there came the rudiments of his accustomed chuckle, which died out in a second or two, seeming to give him pain.

'Now, you'll promise me not to talk so much at a time till you're better. I am glad, sir—very glad, Sir Jekyl, to have enjoyed your hospitality, and to have even this opportunity of thanking you for it. It is very delightful to me occasionally to find myself thus beholden to my old pupils. I have had the pleasure of spending a few days with the Marquis at Queen's Dykely; in fact, I came direct from him to you. You recollect him—Lord Elstowe he was then? You remember Elstowe at school?'

'To be sure; remember him very well. We did not agree, though—always thought him a cur,' acquiesced Sir Jekyl.

The Bishop cleared his voice.]

'He was asking for you, I assure you, very kindly—very kindly indeed, and seems to remember his school-days very affectionately, and—and pleasantly, and quite surprised me with his minute recollections of all the boys.'

'They all hated him,' murmured Sir Jekyl. 'I did, I know.'

'And—and I think we shall have a fine day. I drive always with two windows open—a window in front and one at the side,' said the Bishop, whose mild and dignified eyes glanced at the windows, and the pleasant evidences of sunshine outside, as he spoke. 'I was almost afraid I should have to start without the pleasure of saying good-bye. You remember the graceful farewell in Lucretius? I venture to say your brother does. I made your class recite it, do you remember?'

And the Bishop repeated three or four hexameters with a look of expectation at his old pupil, as if looking to him to take up the recitation.

'Yes, I am sure of it. I think I remember; but, egad! I've quite forgot my Latin, and I knew,' answered the Baronet, who was totally unable to meet the invitation; 'I—I don't know how it is, but I'm sorry you have to go to-day, very sorry!—sorry, of course, any time, but particularly I feel as if I should get well again very soon—that, is, if you were to stay. Do you think you can?'

'Thank you, my dear Marlowe, thank you very much for that feeling,' said the good Bishop, much gratified, and placing his old hand very kindly in that of the patient, just as Sir Jekyl suddenly remembered his doing once at his bedside in the sick-house in younger days, long ago, when he was a school-boy, and the Bishop master; and both paused for a moment in one of those dreams of the past that make us smile so sadly.

CHAPTER LXVI.

IN THE YARD OF THE MARLOWE ARMS.

THE Bishop looked at his watch, and smiled, shaking his head.

'Time flies. I must, I fear, take my leave.'

'Before you go,' said Sir Jekyl, 'I must tell you I've been thinking over my promise about that odious green chamber, and I'll pledge you my honour I'll fulfil it. I'll not leave a stone of it standing; I won't, I assure you. To the letter I'll fulfil it.'

'I never doubted it, my dear Sir Jekyl.'

'And must you really leave me to-day?'

'No choice, I regret.'

'It's very unlucky. You can't think how your going affects me. It seems so odd and unlucky, so depressing just now. I'd have liked to talk to you, though I'm in no danger, and know it. I'd like to hear what's to be said, clergymen are generally so pompous and weak; and to be sure,' he said, suddenly recollecting his brother, 'there's Dives, who is neither—who is a good clergyman, and learned. I say so, of course, my lord, with submission to you; but still it isn't quite the same—you know the early association; and it makes me uncomfortable and out of spirits your going away. You don't think you could possibly postpone?'

'No, my dear friend, quite impossible; but I leave you—tell him I said so—in excellent hands; and I'm glad to add, that so far as I can learn you're by no means in a dying state.'

The Bishop smiled.

'Oh! I know that,' said Sir Jekyl, returning that cheerful expansion; 'I know that very well, my lord: a fellow always knows pretty well when he's in anything of a fix—I mean his life at all in question; it is not the least that, but a sort of feeling or fancy. What does Doctor Pratt say it *is*?'

'Oh! gout, as *I* understand.'

'Ah! yes, I have had a good deal in my day. Do you think

I could tempt you to return, maybe, when your business—this particular business, I mean—is over?'

The Bishop smiled and shook his head.

'I find business—mine at least—a very tropical plant; as fast as I head it down, it throws up a new growth. I was not half so hard worked, I do assure you, when I was better able to work, at the school, long ago. You haven't a notion what it is.'

'Well, but you'll come back some time, not very far away?'

'Who knows?' smiled the Bishop. 'It is always a temptation. I can say that truly. In the meantime, I shall expect to hear that you are much better. Young Marlowe—I mean Dives,' and the Bishop laughed gently at the tenacity of his old school habits, 'will let me hear; and so for the present, my dear Sir Jekyl, with many, many thanks for a very pleasant sojourn, and with all good wishes, I bid you farewell, and may God bless you.'

So having shaken his hand, and kissing his own as he smiled another farewell at the door, the dignified and good prelate disappeared mildly from the room, Jekyl following him with his eyes, and sighing as the door closed on him.

As Sir Jekyl leaned back against his pillows, there arrived a little note, in a tall hand; some of the slim l's, b's, and so on, were a little spiral with the tremor of age.

'Lady Halice Redcliffe, Sir Jekyl, please sir, sends her compliments and hopes you may be able to read it, and will not leave for Warlock earlier than half-past one o'clock.'

'Very well. Get away and wait in the outer room,' said Sir Jekyl, flushing a little, and looking somehow annoyed.

'I hate the sight of her hand. It's sealed, too. I wish that cursed old woman was where she ought to be; and she chooses *now* because she knows I'm ill, and can't bear worry.'

Sir Jekyl twirled the little note round in his fingers and thumb with a pinch. The feverish pain he was suffering did not improve his temper, and he was intemperately disposed to write across the back of the unopened note something to this effect:—'Ill and suffering; the pleasure of your note might be too much for me; pray keep it till to-morrow.'

But curiosity and something of a dread that discovery had occurred prompted him to open it, and he read—

'Having had a most painful interview with unhappy General Lennox, and endured mental agitation and excitement which are too much for my miserable health and nerves, I mean to return to Wardlock as early to-day as my strength will permit, taking with me, at his earnest request, *your victim.*'

'D——n her!' interposed Sir Jekyl through his set teeth.

'I think you will see,' he read on, 'that this house is no longer a befitting residence for your poor innocent girl. As I am charged for a time with the care of the ruined wife of your friend and guest, you will equally see that it is quite impossible to offer my darling Beatrix an asylum at Wardlock. The Fentons, how-ever, will, I am sure, be happy to receive her. She must leave Marlowe, of course, before I do. While here she is under *my care*; but this house is no home for her ; and you can hardly wish that *she* should be *sacrificed* in the ruin of the poor wife whom you have made an *outcast.*'

'Egad! it's the devil sent that fiend to torture me so. It's all about, I suppose,' exclaimed Sir Jekyl, with a gasp. 'Unlucky ! The stupid old fribble, to think of his going off with his story to that Pharisaical old tattler.'

The remainder of the letter was brief.

'I do not say, Jekyl Marlowe, that I regret your illness. You have to thank a merciful providence that it is unattended with danger ; and it affords an opportunity for reflection, which may, if properly improved, lead to some awakening of conscience—to a proper estimate of your past life, and an amendment of the space that remains. I need hardly add, that an amended life involves reparation, so far as practicable, to *all* whom you or, in your interest, *yours* may have injured.

'In deep humiliation and sorrow,

'ALICE REDCLIFFE.'

'I wish you were in a deep pond, you plaguy old witch. That fellow, Herbert Strangways—Varbarriere—he's been talking to her.

I know what she means by all that cant.'

Then he read over again the passages about 'your victim,' and 'General Lennox,' your 'friend and guest.'   And he knocked on the table, and called as well as he could—'Tomlinson,' who entered.

'Where's General Lennox ?'

'Can't say, Sir Jekyl, please, sir—'avn't saw him to-day.'

'Just see, please, if he's in the house, and let him know that I'm ill, but very anxious to see him.   You may say *very* ill, do you mind, and only wish a word or two.'

Tomlinson bowed and disappeared.

'Don't care if he strikes me again.   I've a word to say, and he *must* hear it,' thought Sir Jekyl.

But Tomlinson returned with the intelligence that General Lennox had gone down to the town, and was going to Slowton station ; and his man, with some of his things, followed him to the Marlowe Arms, in the town close by.

In a little while he called for paper, pen, and ink, and with some trouble wrote an odd note to old General Lennox.

'GENERAL LENNOX,

'You must hear me.   By ——,' and here followed an oath and an imprecation quite unnecessary to transcribe.   'Your wife is innocent as an angel! I have been the fiend who would, if he could, have ruined her peace and yours.   From your hand I have met my deserts.   I lie now, I believe, on my death-bed.   I wish you knew the whole story.   The truth will deify her and make you happy.   I am past the age of romance, though not of vice.   I speak now as a dying man.   I would not go out of the world with a perjury on my soul ; and, by ——, I swear your wife is as guiltless as an angel.   I am ill able to speak, but will see and satisfy you.   Bring a Bible and a pistol with you—let me swear to every answer I make you ; and if I have not convinced you before you leave, I promise to shoot myself through the head, and save you from all further trouble on account of

'JEKYL MARLOWE.'

'Now see, Tomlinson, don't lose a moment. Send a fellow running, do you mind, and let him tell General Lennox I'm in pain—*very* ill—mind—and—and all that; and get me an answer; and he'll put this in *his* hand.'

Sir Jekyl was the sort of master who is obeyed. The town was hardly three-quarters of a mile away. His messenger accom· plished the distance as if for a wager.

The waiter flourished his napkin in the hall of the Marlowe Arms, and told him—

'No General, *nothing* was there, as he heerd.'

'Who do you want?' said the fat proprietress, with a red face and small eyes and a cap and satin bow, emerging from a side door, and superseding the waiter, who said—

'A hofficer, isn't it?' as he went aside.

'Oh! from the Manor,' continued the proprietress in a conciliatory strain, recognising the Marlowe button, though she did not know the man. 'Can I do anything?'

And she instinctively dropped a courtesy—a deference to the far-off Baronet; and then indemnifying herself by a loftier tone to the menial.

'A note for General Lennox, ma'am.'

'General Lennox?—I know, I think, a millentery man, white-'aired and spare?'

'I must give it 'im myself, ma'am, thankee,' said he, declining the fat finger and thumb of the curious hostess, who tossed her false ringlets with a little fat frown, and whiffled—

'Here, tell him where's the tall, thin gemm'n, with white mistashes, that's ordered the hosses—that'll be him, I dessay,' she said to the waiter, reinstated, and waddled away with a jingle of keys in her great pocket. So to the back yard they went, the thin, little, elderly waiter skipping in front, with a jerk or two of his napkin.

'Thankee, that's him,' said the messenger.

CHAPTER LXVII.

ABOUT LADY JANE.

THE General was walking up and down the jolty pavement with a speed that seemed to have no object but to tire himself, his walking-stick very tightly grasped, his lips occasionally contracting, and his hat now and then making a vicious wag as he traversed his beat.

'Hollo!' said the General, drawing up suddenly, as the man stood before him with the letter, accosting him with his hand to his cap. 'Hey! *well*, sir?'

'Letter, please, sir.'

The General took it, stared at the man, I think, without seeing him, for a while, and then resumed his march, with his cane, sword-fashion, over his shoulder. The messenger waited, a little perplexed. It was not until he had made a third turn that the General, again observing the letter in his hand, looked at it, and again at the messenger, who was touching his cap, and stopping short, said—

'Well—ay! *This?*—aw—you *brought* it, didn't you?'

So the General broke it open—he had not his glasses with him—and, holding it far away, read a few lines with a dreadful glare, and then bursting all on a sudden into such a storm of oaths and curses as scared the sober walls of that unmilitary hostelry, he whirled his walking-stick in the air, with the fluttering letter extended toward the face of the astounded messenger, as if in another second he would sweep his head off.

At the sound of this hoarse screech the kitchen-wench looked open-mouthed out of the scullery-window with a plate dripping in her hand. 'Boots,' with his fist in a 'Wellington,' held his blacking-brush poised in air, and gazed also; and the hostler held the horse he was leading into the stable by the halter, and stood at the door gaping over his shoulder.

'Tell your master I said he may go to *hell*, sir,' said the General, scrunching the letter like a snowball in his fist, and stamping in his fury.

What more he said I know not. The man withdrew, and, once or twice, turned about, sulkily, half puzzled and half angered, perhaps not quite sure whether he ought not to 'lick' him.

'What'll be the matter now?' demanded the proprietress, looking from under her balustrade of brown ringlets from the back door.

'Drat me if I know; he's a rum un, that he be,' replied the man with the Marlowe button. 'When master hears it he'll lay his whip across that old cove's shouthers, I'm thinking.'

'I doubt he's not right in his head; he's bin a-walkin' up an' down the same way ever since he ordered the chaise, like a man beside himself. *Will* ye put *them* horses to?' she continued, raising her voice; 'why, the 'arniss is on 'em this half-hour. Will ye put 'em to or *no?*' and so, in something of an angry panic, she urged on the preparations, and in a few minutes more General Lennox was clattering through the long street of the town, on his way to Slowton, and the London horrors of legal consultations, and the torture of the Slow processes by which those whom God hath joined together are sundered.

'Send Donica Gwynn to me,' said Lady Alice to the servant whom her bell had summoned to Lady Mary's boudoir.

When Donica arrived—

'Shut the door, Donica Gwynn,' said she, 'and listen. Come a little nearer, please. Sir Jekyl Marlowe is ill, and, of course, we cannot all stay here.' Lady Alice looked at her dubiously.

'Fit o' the gout, my lady, I'm told.'

'Yes, an attack of gout.'

'It does not hold long with him, not like his poor father, Sir Harry, that would lie six months at a time in flannel. Sir Jekyl, law bless you, my lady! He's often had his toe as red as fire overnight, and before supper to-morrow walking about the house. He says, Tomlinson tells me, this will be nothink at all; an' it might fret him sore, my lady, and bring on a worse fit, to see you all go away.'

'Yes, very true, Gwynn; but there's something more at present,' observed Lady Alice, demurely.

Donica folded her hands, and with curious eyes awaited her mistress's pleasure.

Lady Alice continued in a slightly altered tone

'It's not altogether *that*. In fact, Gwynn, there has been— you're not to talk, d'ye see,—I know you *don't* talk; but there has been—there has been a *something*—a *quarrel*—between Lady Jane and her husband, the General; and for a time, at least, she will remain with me at Wardlock, and I may possibly go abroad with her for a little.'

Donica Gwynn's pale sharp face grew paler and sharper, as during this announcement she eyed her mistress askance from her place near the door; and as Lady Alice concluded, Donica dropped her eyes to the Turkey carpet, and seemed to read uncomfortable mysteries in its blurred pattern. Then Donica looked up sharply, and asked—

'And, please, my lady, what is your ladyship's orders?'

'Well, Gwynn, you must get a "fly" now from the town, and go on before us to Wardlock. We shall leave this probably in little more than an hour, in the carriage. Tell Lady Jane, with my compliments, that I hope she will be ready by that time—or no, you may give her my love—don't say compliments—and say, I will either go and see her in her room, or if she prefer, I will see her here, or anywhere else; and you can ask her what room at Wardlock she would like best—do you mind? Whatever room she would like best she shall have, except *mine*, of course, and the moment you get there you'll set about it.'

'Yes, ma'am, please, my lady.'

Donica looked at her mistress as if expecting something more; and her mistress looked away darkly, and said nothing.

'I'll return, my lady, I suppose, and tell you what Miss Jane says, ma'am?'

'Do,' answered Lady Alice, and, closing her eyes, she made a sharp nod, which Donica knew was a signal of dismissal.

Old Gwynn, mounting the stairs, met Mrs. Sinnott with those keys of office which she had herself borne for so many years.

'Well, Mrs. Sinnott, ma'am, how's the master now?' she inquired.

'Doctor's not bin yet from Slowton, Mrs. Gwynn; we don't know nothink only just what you heard this morning from Mr. Tomlinson.'

'Old Pratt, baint *he* here neither?'

'No, but the nurse be come.'

'Oh! *respeckable*, I hope? But no ways, Mrs. Sinnott, ma'am, take my advice, and on no account don't you give her her will o' the bottle; there's none o' them hospital people but likes it—jest what's enough, and no more, I would say.'

'Oh! no! no!' answered Mrs. Sinnott scornfully. 'I knows somethink of them sort, too—leave 'em to me.'

'Lady Alice going away this afternoon.'

'And what for, Mrs. Gwynn?' asked the housekeeper.

'Sir Jekyl's gout.'

'Fidgets! Tiresome old lass, baint she? law,' said Mrs. Sinnott, who loved her not.

'She don't know Sir Jekyl's constitution like I does. Them little attacks o' gout, why he makes nothink o' them, and they goes and comes quite 'armless. I'm a-going back to Wardlock, Mrs. Sinnott, this morning, and many thanks for all civilities while 'ere, lest I should not see you when a leavin'.'

So with the housekeeper's smiles, and conventional courtesies, and shaking of hands, these ladies parted, and Mrs. Gwynn went on to the green chamber.

As she passed through the Window dressing-room her heart sank. She knew, as we are aware, a good deal about that green chamber, more than she had fancied Lady Jane suspected. She blamed herself for not having talked frankly of it last night. But Lady Jane's *éclat* of passion at one period of their interview had checked her upon any such theme; and after all, what could the green chamber have to do with it? Had not the General arrived express very late last night? It was some London story that sent him down from town in that hurry, and Sir Jekyl laid up in gout too. Some o' them jealous stories, and a quarrel over it. It will sure be made up again—ay, ay.'

And so thinking, she knocked, and receiving no answer, she opened the door and peeped in. There was but a narrow strip of one shutter open.

'Miss Jennie, dear,' she called. Still no answer. 'Miss Jennie, darling.' No answer still. She understood those sulky taciturnities well, in which feminine tempest sometimes subsides, and was not at all uneasy. On the floor, near the foot of the bed, lay the General's felt hat and travelling coat. Standing there, she drew the curtain and saw Lady Jane, her face buried in the pillow, and her long hair lying wildly on the coverlet and hanging over the bedside.

'Miss Jennie, dear—Miss Jennie, darling; it's me—old Donnie, miss. Won't you speak to me?'

Still no answer, and Donica went round, beginning to feel uneasy, to the side where she lay.

CHAPTER LXVIII.

LADY JANE'S TOILET.

'MISS JENNIE, *darling*, it's *me*,' she repeated, and placed her fingers on the young lady's shoulder. It was with an odd sense of relief she saw the young lady turn her face away.

'Miss Jennie, dear; it's me—old Donnie—don't you know me?' cried Donica once more. 'Miss, dear, my lady, what's the matter you should take on so!—only a few wry words—it will all be made up, dear.'

'Who told you—who says it will be made up?' said Lady Jane, raising her head slowly, very pale, and, it seemed to old Gwynn, grown so thin in that one night. Don't mind—it will *never* be made up—no, Donnie, never; it oughtn't. Is my—is General Lennox in the house?'

'Gone down to the town, miss, I'm told, in a bit of a tantrum

—going off to Lunnon. It's the way wi' them all—off at a word; and then cools, and back again same as ever.'

Lady Jane's fingers were picking at the bed-clothes, and her features were sunk and peaked as those of a fever-stricken girl.

'The door is shut to—outer darkness. I asked your God for mercy last night, and see what he has done for me!'

'Come, Miss Jennie, dear, you'll be happy yet. Will ye come with me to Wardlock?'

'That I will, Donnie,' she answered, with a sad alacrity, like a child's.

'I'll be going, then, in half an hour, and you'll come with me.'

Lady Jane's tired wild eyes glanced on the gleam of light in the half-open shutter with the wavering despair of a captive.

'I wish we were there. I wish we were—you and I, Donnie—just you and I.'

'Well, then, what's to hinder? My missus sends her love by me, to ask you to go there, till things be smooth again 'twixt you and your old man, which it won't be long, Miss Jennie, dear.'

'I'll go,' said Lady Jane, gliding out of her bed toward the toilet, fluttering along in her bare feet and night-dress. 'Donnie, I'll go.'

'That water's cold, miss; shall I fetch hot?'

'Don't mind—no; very nice. Oh, Donnie, Donnie, Donnie! my heart, my heart! what is it?'

'Nothink, my dear—nothink, darlin'.'

'I wish it was dark again.'

'Time enough, miss.'

'That great sun shining! They'll all be staring. Well, *let* them.'

'Won't you get your things on, darling? I'll dress you. You'll take cold.'

'Oh, Donnie! I wish I could cry. My head! I don't know what it is. If I could cry I think I should be better. I must see him, Donnie.'

'But he's gone away, miss.'

'*Gone! Is* he?'

'Ay, sure I told ye so, dear, only this minute. To Lunnon, I hear say.'

'Oh! yes, I forgot; yes, I'll dress. Let us make haste. I wish I knew. Oh! Donnie, Donnie! oh! my heart, Donnie, Donnie—my heart's breaking.'

'There, miss, dear, don't take on so; you'll be better when we gets into the air, you will. What will ye put on?—here's a purple mornin' silk.'

'Yes: very nice. Thank you. Oh! Donnie, I wish we were away.'

'So we shall, miss, presently, please God. Them's precious bad pins—Binney and Clew—bends like lead; *there's* two on 'em. Thompson's mixed shillin' boxes—them's the best. Miss Trixie allays has 'em. Your hair's beautiful, miss, allays was; but dearie me! what a lot you've got! and so beautiful fine! I take it in handfuls—floss silk—and the weight of it! Beautiful hair, miss. Dearie me, what some 'd give for that!'

Thus old Gwynn ran on; but fixed, pale, and wild was the face which would once have kindled in the conscious pride of beauty at the honest admiration of old Donnie, who did not rise into raptures for everyone and on all themes, and whose eulogy was therefore valuable.

'I see, Donnie—nothing bad has happened?' said Lady Jane, with a scared glance at her face.

'Bad? Nonsense! I told you, Miss Jennie, 'twould all be made up, and so it will, please God, miss.

But Lady Jane seemed in no wise cheered by her promises, and after a silence of some minutes, she asked suddenly, with the same painful look—

'Donnie, tell me the truth, for God's sake; how is he?'

Donica looked at her with dark inquiry.

'The General is gone, you know, ma'am.'

'*Stop*—you *know*,' cried Lady Jane, seizing her fiercely by the arm, with a wild fixed stare in her face.

'Who?' said Donica.

'Not he. I mean——'

'Who?' repeated Gwynn.

'How is Sir Jekyl?'

It seemed as if old Donica's breath was suspended. Shade after shade her face darkened, as with wide eyes she stared in the gazing face of Lady Jane, who cried, with a strange laugh of rage—

'Yes—Sir Jekyl—how *is* he?'

'Oh, Miss Jane!—oh, Miss Jane!—oh, Miss Jane!—and is *that* it?'

Lady Jane's face was dark with other fiercer passions.

'Can't you answer, and not talk?' said she.

Donica's eyes wandered to the far end of the room to the fatal recess, and she was shaking her head, as if over a tale of horror.

'Yes, I see, you know it all, and you'll *hate* me now, as the others will, and I don't care.'

Suspicions are one thing—faint, phantasmal; certainties quite another. Donica Gwynn looked appalled.

'Oh! poor Miss Jennie!' she cried at last, and burst into tears. Before this old domestic Lady Jane was standing—a statue of shame, of defiance—the fallen angelic.

'You're doing that to make me mad.'

'Oh! no, miss; I'm sorry.'

There was silence for a good while.

'The curse of God's upon this room,' said Donica, fiercely, drying her eyes. 'I wish you had never set foot in it. Come away, my lady. I'll go and send at once for a carriage to the town, and we'll go together, ma'am, to Wardlock. Shall I, ma'am?'

'Yes, I'll go,' said Lady Jane. 'Let us go, you and I. I won't go with Lady Alice. I won't go with her.'

'Good-bye, my lady; good-bye, Miss Jennie dear; I'll be here again presently.'

Dressed for the journey, with her cloak on and bonnet, Lady Jane sat in an arm-chair, haggard, listless, watching the slow shuffling of her own foot upon the floor, while Donica departed to complete the arrangements for their journey.

CHAPTER LXIX.

THE TWO DOCTORS CONSULT.

THE doctor from Slowton had arrived at last. The horses, all smoking with the break-neck speed at which they had been driven, stood at the hall-door steps. The doctor himself, with Pratt and the nurse, were up-stairs in the patient's room. The Rev. Dives Marlowe, looking uncomfortable and bilious, hovered about the back stairs that led to Sir Jekyl's apartment, to waylay the doctors on their way down, and listened for the sound of their voices, to gather from their tones something of their spirits and opinions respecting his brother, about whose attack he had instinctive misgivings. The interview was a long one. Before it was over, Dives had gradually ascended to the room outside the Baronet's, and was looking out of the window on the prospect below with the countenance with which one might look on a bad balance-sheet.

The door opened, the doctors emerged—the Slowton man first, Pratt following, both looking grave as men returning from the sacrament.

'Oh! Mr. Dives Marlowe—the Rev. Dives Marlowe,' murmured Pratt as the door was shut.

The lean practitioner from Slowton bowed low, and the ceremony over—

'Well, gentlemen?' inquired the Rev. Dives Marlowe.

'We are about to compare notes, and discuss the case a little—Doctor Pratt and I—and we shall then, sir, be in a position to say something a—a—definite, we hope.'

So the Rev. Dives withdrew to the stair-head, exchanging bows with the priests of Æsculapius, and there awaited the opening of the doors. When that event came, and the Rev. Dives entered—

'Well, Mr. Marlowe,' murmured the Slowton doctor, a slight

and dismal man of five-and-fifty — 'we think, sir, that your brother, Sir Jekyl Marlowe, is not in immediate danger; but it would not be right or fair to conceal the fact that he is in a very critical state—highly so, in fact; and we think it better on the whole that some member of his family should advise him, if he has anything to arrange—a—a will, or any particular business, that he should see to it; and we think that—we are quite agreed upon this, Doctor Pratt?'

Pratt bowed assent, forgetful that he had not yet heard what they were agreed on.

'We think he should be kept very quiet; he's very low, and must have claret. We have told the nurse in what quantities to administer it, and some other things; she's a very intelligent woman, and your servants can take their directions from her.'

Dives felt very oddly. We talk of Death all our lives, but know nothing about him until he stands in our safe homesteads suddenly before us, face to face. He is a much grizzlier object than we had fancied when busied with a brother or a child. What he is when he comes for ourselves, the few who have seen him waiting behind the doctor and live can vaguely remember.

'Good Lord, sir!' said Dives, 'is he really in that state? I had no idea.'

'Don't mis-*take* us, sir. We don't say he may not, if everything goes right, do very well. Only the case is critical, and we should deceive you if we shrank from telling you so; is not that your view, Doctor—Dr. Pratt?'

Dr. Pratt was of course quite clear on the point.

'And you are in very able hands here,' and the Slowton doctor waved his yellow fingers and vouchsafed a grave smile and nod of approbation toward Pratt, who wished to look indifferent under the compliment, but simpered a little in spite of himself.

The Rev. Dives Marlowe accompanied the two doctors downstairs, looking like a man going to execution.

'You need not be afraid, sir,' said Dives, laying his hand on the Slowton leech's sleeve. The grave gentleman stopped and inclined his ear to listen, and the three stood huddled together on the small landing, Dives' nervous fingers in the banister.

' I don't quite see, sir,' observed the doctor.

' I give him up, sir; you need not be afraid to tell me.'

'You are right, perhaps, to give him up; but I always say exactly what I think. Doctor—a—*Pratt* and I—we tell you frankly—we think him in a very critical state; but it's quite on the cards he may recover; and we have given very full directions to the nurse, who appears to be a very intelligent person; and don't let him shift his attitude unnecessarily, it may prejudice him, and be in fact attended with danger—very *serious* danger; and Doctor Pratt shall look in at five o'clock—you were so good as to say, Doctor Pratt, you would look in at five. Doctor Pratt will look in *then*, and do anything that may be necessary; and if there should be the slightest symptom of hæmorrhage, send for him instantly, and the nurse knows what to do; and I think—I think I have said everything now.'

' Hæmorrhage, sir! But *what* hæmorrhage? Why, what hæmorrhage is apprehended?' asked Dives, amazed.

'Internal or external it may occur,' said the doctor; and Pratt, coughing and shaking his chops, interposed hurriedly and said—

' Yes, there may be a bleeding, it may come to that.'

' He has bled a great deal already, you are aware,' resumed the Slowton doctor, ' and in his exhausted state a return of that might of course be very bad.'

' But I don't understand,' persisted Dives. ' I beg pardon, but I really must. What *is* this hæmorrhage? it is not connected with gout, is it?'

' Gout, sir! no; who said gout? A bad wound that seems to run toward the lung,' answered the Slowton man.

' Wound! how's this? I did not hear,' and Dives looked frightened, and inquiringly on Pratt, who said—

' Not hear, didn't you? Why, Sir Jekyl undertook to tell you, and would not let me. He took me in for a while, poor fellow, quite, and said 'twas gout, that's all. I'm surprised he did not tell you.'

'No—*no*—not a word; and—and you think, sir, it may begin bleeding afresh?'

'That's what we chiefly apprehend. Farewell, sir. I find I have not a moment. I must be at Todmore in three quarters of an hour. A sad case that at Todmore; only a question of a few days, I'm afraid; and a very fine young fellow.'

'Yes,' said Dives—'I—I—it takes me by surprise. Pray, Dr. Pratt, don't go for a moment,' and he placed his hand on his arm.

'Farewell, sir,' said the Slowton doctor, and putting up his large gold watch, and bowing gravely, he ran at a quiet trot down the stairs, and jumped into his chaise at the back entrance, and vanished.

'You did not tell me,' began Dives.

'No,' said Pratt, promptly, 'he said he'd tell *himself*, and did not choose me.'

'And you think—you think it's very bad?'

'Very bad, sir.'

'And you think he'll not get over it?'

'He may not, sir.'

'It's frightful, Doctor, frightful. And how was it, do you know?'

'No more than the man in the moon. You must not tease him with questions, mind, to-day. In a day or two you may ask him. But he said, upon his honour, no one was to blame but himself.'

'Merciful Heavens! sir. To think of his going this way!'

'Very sad, sir. But we'll do all we can, and possibly may pull him through.'

With slow steps Dives began to ascend the stairs toward his brother's room. He recollected that he had not bid Pratt goodbye, and gave him his adieux over the banister; and then, with slow and creaking steps, mounted, and paused on the lobby, to let his head clear and to think how he should accost him.

Dives was not a Churchman to pester people impertinently

about their sins; and out of the pulpit, where he lashed the vice
but spared the man, he was a well-bred divine, and could talk of
sheep, and even of horses, and read everything from St. Paul to Paul
de Köck; and had ridden till lately after the hounds, and gave
recherché little dinners, such as the New Testament character
whose name, with a difference in pronunciation, he inherited, might
have praised, and well-iced champagne, which, in his present uncomfortable state, that fallen gentleman would have relished.
And now he stood in a sombre mood, with something of panic at
the bottom of it, frightened that the ice upon which men held
Vanity Fair, and roasted oxen, and piped and danced, and
gamed, should prove so thin; and amazed to see his brother
drowning among the fragments in that black pool, and no one
minding, and he unable to help him.

And it came to him like a blow and a spasm. 'The special
minister of Christ!—am I what I'm sworn to be? Can I go in
and talk to him of those things that concern eternity with any
effect? Will he mind me? Can I even now feel the hope, and
lead the prayer as I ought to do?'

And Dives, in a sort of horror, as from the pit, lifted up his
eyes, and prayed 'have mercy on me!' and saw a misspent hollow
life behind, and judgment before him; and blamed himself, too,
for poor Jekyl, and felt something of the anguish of his namesake
in the parable, and yearned for the safety of his brother.

Dives, in fact, was frightened for himself and for Jekyl, and
in those few moments, on the lobby, his sins looked gigantic and
the vast future all dismay; and he felt that, bad as poor Jekyl
might be, *he* was worse—a false soldier—a Simon Magus—chaff,
to be burnt up with unquenchable fire!

'I wish to God the Bishop had stayed over this night,' said
Dives, with clasped hands, and again turning his eyes upward.
'We must send after him. I'll write to implore of him. Oh, yes,
he'll come.'

Even in this was a sense of relief; and treading more carefully,
he softly turned the handle of the outer door, and listened, and
heard Jekyl's cheerful voice say a few words to the nurse. He

sighed with a sense of relief, and calling up a sunnier look, he knocked at Jekyl's half-open door, and stepped to his bed-side.

~~~~~~~~~~

CHAPTER LXX.

VARBARRIERE IN THE SICK ROOM.

'WELL, Jekyl, my dear fellow—and how do you feel now? There, don't; you must not move, they told me,' said Dives, taking his brother's hand, and looking with very anxious eyes in his face, while he managed his best smile.

'Pretty well—nothing. Have they been talking? What do they say?' asked Sir Jekyl.

'Say? Well, not much; those fellows never do; but they expect to have you all right again, if you'll just do what you're bid, in a week or two.'

'Pratt's coming at five,' he said. 'What is it now?'

Dives held his watch to Jekyl, who nodded.

'Do you think I'll get over it, Dives?' he asked at length, rather ruefully.

'Get over? To be sure you will,' answered Dives, doing his best. 'It might be better for you, my dear Jekyl, if it *were* a little more serious. We all need to be pulled up a little now and then. And there's nothing like an alarm of—of that kind for making a man think a little; for, after all, health is only a long day, and a recovery but a reprieve. The sentence stands against us, and we must, sooner or later, submit.'

'Yes, to be sure. We're all mortal, Dives—is not that your discovery?' said Sir Jekyl.

'A discovery it is. my dear fellow, smile as we may—a dis-covery to me, and to you, and to all—whenever the truth, in its full force, opens on our minds.'

'That's when we're going to die, I suppose,' said Sir Jekyl.

' *Then*, of course; but often, in the mercy of God, long before it. That, in fact, is what we call people's growing serious, or religious; their perceiving, as a fact, that they a*re* mortal, and resolving to make the best preparation they can for the journey.'

' Come, Dives, haven't those fellows been talking of me—eh?— as if I were worse than you say?' asked the Baronet, oddly.

' The doctors, you mean? They said exactly what I told you. But it is, not, my dear Jekyl, when we are sick and frightened, and maybe despairing, that these things are best thought on ; but when we are, like you and me, likely to live and enjoy life—*then* is the time. I've been thinking, myself, my dear Jekyl, a good deal for some time past. I have been living too much in the spirit of the world ; but I hope to do better.'

' To do better—to be sure. You've always been hoping to do better ; and I've given you a lift or two,' said the Baronet, who, in truth, never much affected his brother's pulpit-talk, as he called it, and was falling into his old cynical vein.

' But, seriously, my dear fellow, I do. My mind has been troubled thinking how unworthy I have been of my calling, and how fruitless have been my opportunities, my dear brother, with you. I've never improved them ; and I'd be so glad—now we are likely to have a few quiet days—if you'll let me read a little with you.'

' Sermons, do you mean?' interposed the Baronet.

' Well, what's better ?—a little of the Bible ?'

' Come now, Dives, those doctors *have* been shaking their heads over me. I say, you must tell me. Do they say I'm in a bad way ?'

' They think you'll recover.'

' Did they tell you what it is ?'

' Yes. A wound.'

' They had no business, d—— them,' said Sir Jekyl, flushing.

' Don't, don't, my dear Jekyl; they could not help it. I pressed that doctor—I forget his name—and he really could not help saying.'

' Well, well, it doesn't much signify ; I'd have told you myself by-and-by. But you must not tell—I've a reason—you must not tell anyone, mind. It was my fault, and I'm greatly to blame ; and I'll tell you in a little while—a day or two—all about it.'

'Yes, so you can. But, my dear Jekyl, you look much fatigued ; you are exerting yourself.'

Here the nurse interposed with the claret-jug, and intimated that the Rev. Dives was making her patient feverish, and indeed there was an unpleasantly hot hectic in each cheek. But the Baronet had no notion of putting himself under the command of the supernumerary, and being a contumacious and troublesome patient, told her to sit in the study and leave him alone.

'I've a word to say, Dives. I must see that fellow Herbert Strangways.'

' *Who* ?' said Dives, a good deal alarmed, for he feared that his brother's mind was wandering.

'Herbert—that fellow Varbarriere. I forgot I had not told you. Herbert Strangways, you remember ; they're the same. And I want to see him. Better now than to-morrow. I may be feverish then.'

'By Jove ! It's very surprising. Do you really mean——'

'Yes ; he is. I do ; they are the same. You remember Herbert, of course—Herbert Strangways—the fellow I had that long chase after all over Europe. He has things to complain of, you know, and we might as well square the account in a friendlier way, eh ?—don't you think ?'

' And was it he—was there any altercation ?' stammered Dives.

'That did *this*, you mean,' said Sir Jekyl, moving his hand toward the wound. ' Not a bit—no. He seems reasonable ; and I should like — you know they are very old blood, and there's nothing against it—that all should be made up. And if that young fellow and Beatrix—don't you see ? Is Tomlinson there?'

' In the outer room,' said Dives.

' Call him. Tomlinson, I say, you take my compliments to Monsieur Varbarriere, and say, if he has no objection to see me for a few minutes here, I should be very happy. Try and make him out, and bring me word.'

So Tomlinson disappeared.

'And, Dives, it tires me;—so will you—I'm sure you will—see Pelter, after we've spoken with that fellow Herbert, and consult what we had best do, you know. I dare say the young people would come to like one another—he's a fine young fellow; and that, you know, would be the natural way of settling it—better than law or fighting.'

'A great deal—a great deal, certainly.'

'And you may tell him I have that thing—the deed, you know —my poor father——'

'I—I always told you, my dear Jekyl, I'd rather know nothing of all that—in fact, I *do* know nothing; and I should not like to speak to Pelter on that subject. You can, another time, you know,' said Dives.

'Well, it's in the red trunk in there.'

'Pray, dear Jekyl, don't—I assure you I'd rather know nothing —I—I can't; and Pelter will understand you better when he sees you. But I'll talk to him with pleasure about the other thing, and I quite agree with you that any reasonable arrangement is better than litigation.'

'Very well, be it so,' said Sir Jekyl, very tired.

'I'm always drinking claret now—give me some—the only quick way of making blood—I've lost a lot.'

'And you must not talk so much, Jekyl,' said Dives, as he placed the glass at his lips; 'you'll wear yourself out.'

'Yes, I *am* tired,' said the Baronet; 'I'll rest till Strangways comes.'

And he closed his eyes, and was quiet for a time. And Dives, leaning back in his chair at the bedside, felt better assured of Jekyl's recovery, and his thoughts began to return to their wonted channel, and he entertained himself with listlessly reading and half understanding a tedious sculling match in a very old copy of 'Bell's Life,' which happened to lie near him.

A tap at the outer door called up Dives from Sandy Dick's sweep round a corner, and Jekyl said—

'Tell him to come in—and stay—you're not to say I'm hurt—do you mind?'

'My dear Jekyl, I—I sha'n't say anything. There he's knocking again.'

'Well, tell him—come in!'

'Come in!' echoed Dives, in a louder key.

And Monsieur Varbarriere entered with that mysterious countenance and cautious shuffle with which men enter a sick-chamber.

'Very sorry to hear you've been suffering,' began Varbarriere, in a low tone.

'Thanks—you're very good, I'm sure,' said Sir Jekyl, with a faint smile. 'I—I wished very much to see you. I expect to be better very soon, and I thought I might have a word, as you are so good, in the meantime.'

'Very happy, indeed—most happy, as long as you please; but you must not try too much. You know they say you may disturb gout if you try too much, particularly at first,' said Varbarriere, knowing very well how little gout really had to do with it.

'Oh! no danger—doing very nicely,' said Sir Jekyl.

'That's well—that's very good,' said Varbarriere, with a leisurely sympathy, looking on him all the time, and calling to mind how the Comte de Vigny looked after he received the sword-thrust of which he died in Varbarriere's house, to which he had been carried after his duel with young D'Harnois. And he came to the conclusion that Sir Jekyl looked a great deal better than the Comte had done—and, in fact, that he would do very well.

CHAPTER LXXI.

GUY DEVERELL ARRIVES.

'SIT down, Herbert, I sha'n't keep you long. *There*, I've just been saying to Dives I think it's a pity we should quarrel any more—that is, if we can help it; and I don't see why we should not be friendly—I mean more friendly, than, in fact, we have ever been—I don't; do you?'

'Why, I see no reason—none; that is, of course, with the reservations that are—that are always assumed—I don't see any.'

Varbarriere was answering plausibly, politely, smiling. But it was not like last night, when for a few transient moments he had seemed moved from his equilibrium. There was no emotion now. It was diplomatic benignity. Still it was something. Here was his foe willing to hear reason.

'It was just in my mind—Dives and I talking—I think I've seen some signs of liking between the young people—I mean your nephew and Beatrix.'

'Indeed!' interrupted Varbarriere, prolonging the last syllable after his wont, and raising his thick eyebrows in very naturally acted wonder.

'Well, yes—only a sort of conjecture, you know—haven't you?'

'Well, I—ha, ha! If I ever observed anything, it hasn't remained in my mind. But she is so lovely—Miss Marlowe—that I should not wonder. And you think——'

'I think,' said Sir Jekyl, supplying the pause, 'if it be so, we ought not to stand in the way; and here's Dives, who thinks so too.'

'I—in fact, my brother, Jekyl, mentioned it, of course, to me—it would be a very happy mode of—of making matters—a—*happy;* and—and that, I think, was all that passed,' said Dives, thus unexpectedly called into the debate.

'This view comes on me quite by surprise. That the young fellow should adore at such a shrine is but to suppose him mortal,' said Varbarriere, with something of his French air. 'But—but you know the young lady—that's quite another thing—quite. Young ladies, you know, are not won all in a moment.'

'No, of course. We are so far all in the clouds. But I wished to say so much' to you; and I prefer talking face to face, in a friendly way, to sending messages through an attorney.'

'A thousand thanks. I value the confidence, I assure you— yes, much better—quite right. And—and I shall be taking my leave to-morrow morning—business, my dear Sir Jekyl—and *greatly* regret it; but I've outstayed my time very considerably.'

'Very sorry too—and only too happy if you could prolong it a little. *Could* you, do you think?'

Varbarriere shook his head, and thanked him with a grave smile again—but it was impossible.

'It is a matter—such an arrangement, should it turn out practicable—on which we should reflect and perhaps consult a little. It sounds not unpromisingly, however; we can talk again perhaps, if you allow it, before I go.'

'So we can—you won't forget, and I shall expect to see you often and soon, mind.'

And so for the present they parted, Dives politely seeing him to the head of the stairs.

'I think he entertains it,' said Sir Jekyl to his brother.

'Yes, certainly, he does—yes, he entertains it. But I suspect he's a cunning fellow; and you'll want all the help you can get Jekyl, if it comes to settling a bargain.'

'I dare say,' said Sir Jekyl, very tired.

Meanwhile our friend Varbarriere was passing through the conservatory, the outer door of which stood open ever so little, tempering the warmth of its artificial atmosphere. He stopped before a file of late exotics, looking at them with a grave meaning smile, and smelling at them abstractedly.

'Can the Ethiopian change his skin, or the leopard his spots? Selfish rogue! Could it be? A wedding, in which Guy, the son of that murdered friend, should act bridegroom, and the daughter of his murderer, bride; while he, the murderer, stood by smiling, and I, the witness, cried 'amen' to the blessing! *Disgusting!* Never, *never*—bah! The proposition shows weakness. Good— *very* good! A come-down for you, Master Jekyl, when you sue for an alliance with Herbert Strangways! Oh! ho! ho! *Never!*'

A little while later, Varbarriere, who was standing at the hall-door steps, saw a chaise approaching. He felt a presentiment of what was coming. It pulled up at the door.

'No melodrama—no *fracas*—no foolery. Those young turkeys, my faith! they will be turkeys still. Here he comes, the hero of the piece! Well, what does it matter?' This was not articulated, spoken only in thought, and aloud he said—

'Ha!—Guy?'

And the young man was on the ground in a moment, pale and sad, and hesitated deferentially, not knowing how his uncle might receive him.

'So, here you are,' said Varbarriere, coolly but not ill-humouredly. 'Those rambles of yours are not much to the purpose, my friend, and cost some money—don't you see?'

Guy bowed sadly, and looked, Varbarriere saw, really distressed.

'Well, never mind—the expense need not trouble us,' said Varbarriere, carelessly extending his hand, which Guy took. 'We may be very good friends in a moderate way; and I'm not sorry you came, on the whole. Don't mind going in for a few minutes—you're very well—and let us come this way for a little.'

So side by side they turned the corner of the house, and paced up and down the broad quiet walk under the windows.

'We must leave this immediately, Guy; Sir Jekyl is ill—more seriously, I believe, than they fancy; not dangerously, but still a tedious thing. They call it gout, but I believe there is something more.'

'Indeed! How sudden!' exclaimed Guy. And to do him justice, he seemed both shocked and sad, although perhaps all his sorrow was not on Sir Jekyl's account.

'And I'll be frank with you, Guy,' continued Varbarriere. 'I think I can see plainly, maybe, what has drawn you here. It is not I—it is not business—it is not Sir Jekyl. Who or what can it be?'

'I—I thought, sir, my letter had explained.'

'And I am going away in the morning—and some of the party probably to-day; for there's no chance of Sir Jekyl's coming down for some time,' continued Varbarriere, not seeming to hear Guy's interruptions.

'*Very* sorry!' said Guy, sincerely, and his eyes glanced along the empty windows.

'And so, you see, this visit here leads pretty much to nothing,' continued Varbarriere. 'And it might be best to keep that carriage for a few minutes—eh?—and get into it, and drive back again to Slowton.'

'Immediately, sir?'

'Immediately—yes. I'll join you there in the morning, and we can talk over your plans then. I do not know exactly—we must consider. I don't want to part in unkindness. I wish to give you a lift, Guy, if you'll let me.' So said Varbarriere in his off-hand way.

Guy bowed deferentially.

'And see, nephew; there's a thing—*attend*, if you please,' said Varbarriere, lowering his voice.

'I attend, sir.'

'See—you answer upon your honour—do you hear?'

'I do, sir. You hear nothing but truth from me.'

'Well, yes—very good. Is there—have you any correspondence in this house?' demanded the ponderous uncle, and his full dark eyes turned suddenly on the young man.

'No, sir, no correspondence.'

'No one writes to you?'

'No, sir.'

'Nor you to anyone?'

'No, sir.'

'There must be no nonsense of that kind, Guy—I've told you so before—put it quite out of your head. You need not speak—I am merely discussing a hypothesis—quite out of your head. Nothing could ever come of it but annoyance. You know, of course, to whom all this relates; and I tell you it can't be. There are reasons you shall hear elsewhere, which are final.'

What Guy might have answered does not appear, for at that moment old Doocey joined them.

'Oh! come back—how d'ye do?—going to break up here, I fancy;' this was to Varbarriere; 'Sir Jekyl's in for a regular fit of it evidently. Old Sir Paul Blunket was talking to Pratt, their doctor here—and old fellows, you know, go into particulars' (Doocey, of course, was rather a young fellow), 'and generally know more about things of this sort—and he says Dr. Pratt thinks he'll not be on his legs for a month, egad. So he says he's going either to-night or to-morrow—and I'm off this evening; so is Linnett. Can I do anything for you at Llandudno? Going there first, and I want to see a little of North Wales before the season grows too late.'

Varbarriere was grateful, but had nothing to transmit to Llandudno.

'And—and Drayton—*he's* going to stay,' and he looked very sly. 'An attraction, you know, *there*; besides, I believe he's related—is not he?—and, of course, old Lady Alice Redcliffe stays for chaperon. A great chance for Drayton.'

There was a young man at his elbow who thought Doocey the greatest coxcomb and fool on earth, except, perhaps, Drayton, and who suffered acutely and in silence under his talk.

'Drayton's very spooney on her—eh?—the young lady, Miss Marlowe—haven't you observed?' murmured old Doocey, with a sly smile, to Varbarriere.

'Very suitable it would be—fine estate, I'm told,' answered Varbarriere; 'and a good-looking young fellow too.'

'A—*rather*,' acquiesced Doocey. 'The kind of fellow that pays very well in a ball-room; he's got a lot to say for himself.'

'And good family,' contributed Varbarriere, who was not sorry that old Doocey should go on lowering his extinguisher on Guy's foolish flame.

'Well—well—*family*, you know—there's nothing very much of that—they—they there was—it's not the family name, you know. But no one minds family now—all money—*we*'re a devilish deal better family, and so is Mr. Strangways here—all to nothing. I was telling him the other day who the Draytons are.'

Precisely at this moment, through a half-open upper window, there issued a sudden cry, followed by sobs and women's gabble.

All stopped short—silent, and looking up—

Some one crying,' exclaimed Doocey, in an under-key.

And they listened again.

'Nothing bad, I hope,' muttered Varbarriere, anxiously looking up like the rest.

A maid came to the window to raise the sash higher, but paused, seeing them.

'Come away, I say—hadn't we better?' whispered Doocey.

'Let's go in and ask how he is,' suggested Varbarriere suddenly, and toward the hall door they walked.

Was it something in the tone and cadence of this cry that made each in that party of three feel that a dreadful tragedy was consummated? I can't say—only they walked faster than usual, and in silence, like men anticipating evil news and hastening to a revelation.

CHAPTER LXXII.

I AM THINE AND THOU ART MINE, BODY AND SOUL, FOR EVER.

IN order to understand the meaning of this cry, it will be necessary to mention that so soon as the corpulent and sombre visitor had left the bed-room of Sir Jekyl Marlowe, Dives lent his reverend aid to the nurse in adjusting his brother more comfortably in his

bed; and he, like Varbarriere, took instinctively a comfortable
and confident view of Sir Jekyl's case, so that when the officious
handmaid of Æsculapius assumed her airs of direction he put
aside her interference rather shortly. At all events, there was
abundance of time to grow alarmed in, and certainly no need for
panic just now. So Dives took his leave for the present, the
Baronet having agreed with him that his visitors had better be
allowed to disperse to their own homes, a disposition to do so having
manifested itself here and there among them.

Sir Jekyl, a little more easy in consequence of these manipulations, was lying back on pillows, with that pleasant confidence in
his case at which a sanguine man so easily arrives, and already
beginning to amuse himself with pictures in the uncertain future.
The hospital nurse, sitting by a fire in that dim and faded study
which opened from the sick room, now and then rose, and with
soundless steps drew near the half-open door, and sometimes
peeped, and sometimes only listened. The patient was quiet. The
woman sat down in that drowsy light, and ruminated, looking into
the fire, with her feet on the fender, and a good deal of stocking
disclosed; when, all on a sudden, she heard a rustling of a loose
dress near her, and looking over her shoulder, surprised, still more
so, saw a pale and handsome lady cross the floor from near the
window to the door of Sir Jekyl's room, which she closed as she
entered it.

With her mouth open, the nurse stood up and gazed in the
direction in which she had disappeared. Sir Jekyl, on the other
hand, witnessed her entrance with a silent amazement, scarcely
less than the nurse's. A few hurried steps brought her to his bedside, and looking down upon him with great agony, and her hands
clasped together, she said, with a kind of sob—

' Thank God, thank God!—alive, alive! Oh, Jekyl, what hours
of torture!'

' Alive! to be sure I'm alive, little fool!' said the Baronet, with
an effort, smiling uncomfortably. 'They have not been telling
you it's anything serious?'

' They told me nothing. I've heard nothing. I've seen no one but Gwynn. Oh, Jekyl! tell me the truth; what do they say?—there's so much blood on the floor.'

' Why, my precious child, don't worry yourself about it; they evidently think it's nothing at all. I know it's nothing, only what they call, just, the muscles—you know—a little sore. I'll be on my legs again in a week.'

'I'm going to Wardlock, Jekyl; you'll hear news of me from there.'

Had the tone or the look something ineffably ominous? I know not.

'Come, Jennie, none of that,' he answered. 'No folly. I've behaved very badly. *I've* been to blame; altogether *my* fault. Don't tease yourself about what can't be helped. We must not do anything foolish, though. I'm tired of the world; so are you, Jennie; we are both sick of it. If we choose to live out of it, what the plague do we really lose?'

At this moment the nurse, slowly opening the door a little, said, with a look of quiet authority—

' Please, sir, the doctor said particularly you were not to talk, sir.'

' D——n you and the doctor—get out of that, and shut the door!' cried the Baronet; and the woman vanished, scared.

'Give me your hand, Jennie darling, and don't look as if the sky had fallen. I'm not going to make my bow yet, I promise you.'

' And then, I suppose, a duel,' said Lady Jane, wringing her hands in an agony.

'Duel, you little fool! Why, there's no such thing now, that is, in these countries. Put fighting quite out of your head, and listen to me. You're right to keep quiet for a little time, and Wardlock is as good a place as any. I shall be all right again in a few days.'

' I can look no one in the face; no—never again—and Beatrix; and—oh, Jekyl, how will it be? I am half wild.'

' To be sure, everyone's half wild when an accident happens, till they find it really does not signify two pence. Can't you listen to

me, and not run from one thing to another ?' and I'll tell you
everything.'

With a trembling hand he poured some claret into a tumbler
and drank it off, and was stronger.

'He'll take steps, you know, and I'll help all I can ; and when
you're at liberty, by —— I'll marry you, Jane, if you'll accept me.
Upon my honour and soul, Jennie, I'll do exactly whatever you
like. *Don't* look so. *What* frightens you ?   I tell you we'll be
happier than you can think or imagine.'

Lady Jane was crying wildly and bitterly.

' Fifty times happier than ever we could have been if this—this
annoyance had not happened.   We'll travel.   I'll lay myself out
to please you, every way, and make you happy ; upon my soul I
will, Jennie.   I owe you everything I can do.   We'll travel.
We'll not try Pharisaical England, but abroad, where people have
common sense.   Don't, don't go on crying, darling, that way ; you
can't hear me ; and there's really nothing to tease yourself about
—quite the contrary, you'll see ; you'll like the people abroad
much better than here—more common sense and good nature ;
positively better people, and a devilish deal more agreeable and—
and cleverer.   And why do you go on crying, Jennie ?   You must
not ; hang it ; you'll put me in the dumps.   You don't seem to
hear me.'

' Yes, I do, I do ; but it's all over, Jekyl, and I've come to bid
you farewell, and on earth we'll never meet again,' said Lady
Jane, still weeping violently.

' Come, little Jennie, you sha'n't talk like a fool.   I've heard you
long enough ; you must listen to me—I have more to say.'

' Jekyl, Jekyl.   I am sorry—oh !   I'm sorry, for your sake, and
for mine, I ever saw your face, and sorrier that I am to see you no
more ; but I've made up my mind—nothing shall change me—
nothing—never.   Good-bye, Jekyl.   God forgive us.   God bless you.'

' Come, Jane, I say, don't talk that way.   What do you
mean ?' said the Baronet, holding her hand fast in his, and
with his other hand encircling her wrist.   ' If you really do want
to make me ill, Jennie, you'll talk in that strain.   I know, of

course, I've been very much to blame. It was all my fault, I said —I *say*—everything; but now you will be free, Jennie. I wish I had been worthy of you; I wish I had. No, you must not go. Wait a moment. I say, Jennie, I wish to heaven I had made you marry me when you might; but I'll not let you go now; by Heaven, I'll never run a risk of losing you again.'

'No, Jekyl, no, I've made up my mind; it is all no use, I'll go. It is all over—quite over, for ever. Good-bye, Jekyl. God bless you. You'll be happier when we have parted—in a few days—a great deal happier; and as for me, I think I'm broken-hearted.'

'By ——, Jennie, you sha'n't go. I'll make you swear; you shall be my wife—by Heaven, you shall; we'll live and die together. You'll be happier than ever you were; we have years of happiness. I'll be whatever you like. I'll go to church—I'll be a Puseyite, or a Papist, or anything you like best. I'll—I'll——'

And with these words Sir Jekyl let go her hand suddenly, and with a groping motion in the air, dropped back on the pillows. Lady Jane cried wildly for help, and tried to raise him. The nurse was at her side, she knew not how. In ran Tomlinson, who, without waiting for directions, dashed water in his face. Sir Jekyl lay still, with waxen face, and a fixed deepening stare.

'Looks awful bad!' said Tomlinson, gazing down upon him.

'The wine—the claret!' cried the woman, as she propped him under the head.

'My God! what is it?' said Lady Jane, with white lips.

The woman made no answer, but rather shouldered her, as she herself held the decanter to his mouth; and they could hear the glass clinking on his teeth as her hand trembled, and the claret flowed over his still lips and down upon his throat.

'Lower his head,' said the nurse; and she wiped his shining forehead with his handkerchief; and all three stared in his face, pale and stern.

'Call the doctor,' at last exclaimed the nurse. 'He's not right.'

'Doctor's gone, I think,' said Tomlinson, still gaping on his master.

'*Send* for him, *man!* I tell ye,' cried the nurse, scarce taking her eyes from the Baronet.

Tomlinson disappeared.

'Is he better?' asked Lady Jane, with a gasp.

'He'll never be better; I'm 'feared he's gone, ma'am,' answered the nurse, grimly, looking on his open mouth, and wiping away the claret from his chin.

'It can't be, my good Lord! it can't—quite well this minute—talking—why, it can't—it's only weakness, nurse! for God's sake, he's not—it is not—it can't be,' almost screamed Lady Jane.

The nurse only nodded her head sternly, with her eyes still riveted on the face before her.

'He ought 'a bin let alone—the talkin's done it,' said the woman in a savage undertone.

In fact, she had her own notions about this handsome young person who had intruded herself into Sir Jekyl's sick-room. She knew Beatrix, and that this was not she, and she did not like or encourage the visitor, and was disposed to be sharp, rude, and high with her.

Lady Jane sat down, with her fingers to her temple, and the nurse thought she was on the point of fainting, and did not care.

Donica Gwynn entered, scared by a word and a look from Tomlinson as he passed her on the stair. She and the nurse, leaning over Sir, Jekyl, whispered for a while, and the latter said—

'Quite easy—off like a child—all in a minute;' and she took Sir Jekyl's hand, the fingers of which were touching the table, and laid it gently beside him on the coverlet.

Donica Gwynn began to cry quietly, looking on the familiar face, thinking of presents of ribbons long ago, and school-boy days, and many small good-natured remembrances.

CHAPTER LXXIII.

IN THE CHAISE.

HEARING steps approaching, Donica recollected herself, and said, locking the room door—

'Don't let them in for a minute.'

'Who is she?' inquired the nurse, following Donica's glance.

'Lady Jane Lennox.'

The woman looked at her with awe and a little involuntary courtesy, which Lady Jane did not see.

'A relation—a—a sort of a niece like of the poor master—a'most a daughter like, allays.'

'Didn't know,' whispered the woman, with another faint courtesy; 'but she's better owt o' this, don't you think, ma'am?'

'Drink a little wine, Miss Jennie, dear,' said Donica, holding the glass to her lips. 'Won't you, darling?'

She pushed it away gently, and got up, and looked at Sir Jekyl in silence.

'Come away, Miss Jennie, darling, come away, dear, there's people at the door. It's no place for you,' said Donica, gently placing her hand under her arm, and drawing her toward the study door. 'Come in here, for a minute, with old Donnie.'

Lady Jane did go out unresisting, hurriedly, and weeping bitterly.

Old Donica glanced almost guiltily over her shoulder; the nurse was hastening to the outer door. 'Say nothing of us,' she whispered, and shut the study door.

'Come, Miss Jennie, darling; do as I tell you. They must not know.'

They crossed the floor; at her touch the false door with its front of fraudulent books opened. They were now in a dark passage, lighted only by the reflection admitted through two or three narrow lights near the ceiling, concealed effectually on the outside.

The reader will understand that I am here describing the architectural arrangements, which I myself have seen and examined. At the farther end of this room, which is about twenty-three feet long, is a niche, in which stands a sort of cupboard. This swings upon hinges, secretly contrived, and you enter another chamber of about the same length. This room is almost as ill-lighted as the first, and was then stored with dusty old furniture, piled along both sides, the lumber of fifty years ago. From the side of this room a door opens upon the gallery, which door has been locked for half a century, and I believe could hardly be opened from without.

At the other end of this dismal room is a recess, in one side of which is fixed an open press, with shelves in it; and this unsuspected press revolves on hinges also, shutting with a concealed bolt, and is, in fact, a door admitting to the green chamber.

It is about five years since I explored, under the guidance of the architect employed to remove this part of the building, this mysterious suite of rooms; and knowing, as I fancied, thoroughly the geography of the house, I found myself with a shock of incredulity thus suddenly in the green chamber, which I fancied still far distant. Looking to my diary, in which I that day entered the figures copied from the ground plan of the house, I find a little column which explains how the distance from front to rear, amounting to one hundred and seventy-three feet, is disposed of.

Measuring from the western front of the house, with which the front of the Window dressing-room stands upon a level, that of the green chamber receding about twelve feet :—

	ft.	in.
Window dressing-room or hexagon	12	0
Green chamber	38	0
Recess	2	0
First dark room	23	0
Recess	1	6
Second dark room	23	0
Recess	1	6
Study	25	0
Wall	1	0
Sir Jekyl's bed-room	27	0
Ante-room	10	0
Stair, bow-window of which forms part of the eastern front	9	0
	173	0

I never spoke to anyone who had made the same exploration who was not as much surprised as I at the unexpected solution of a problem which seemed to have proposed bringing the front and rear of this ancient house, by a ' devilish cantrip slight,' a hundred feet at least nearer to one another than stone mason and foot-rule had ordained.

The rearward march from the Window dressing-room to the foot of the back stair, which ascends by the eastern wall of the house, hardly spares you a step of the full distance of one hundred and seventy-three feet, and thus impresses you with an idea of complete separation, which is enhanced by the remote ascent and descent. When you enter Sir Jekyl's room, you quite forget that its great window looking rearward is in reality nineteen feet nearer the front than the general line of the rear; and when you stand in that moderately proportioned room, his study, which appears to have no door but that which opens into his bed-room, you could not believe without the evidence of these figures, that there intervened but two rooms of three-and-twenty feet in length each, between you and that green chamber, whose bow-window ranks with the front of the house.

Now Lady Jane sat in that hated room once more, a room henceforward loathed and feared in memory, as if it had been the abode of an evil spirit. Here, gradually it seemed, opened upon her the direful vista of the future; and as happens in tales of magic mirrors, when she looked into it her spirit sank and she fainted.

When she recovered consciousness—the window open—eau de cologne, sal volatile, and all the rest around her, with cloaks about her knees, and a shawl over her shoulders, she sat and gazed in dark apathy on the floor for a time. It was the first time in her life she had experienced the supernatural panic of death.

Where was Jekyl now? All irrevocable! Nothing in this moment's state changeable for ever, and ever, and ever.

This gigantic and inflexible terror the human brain can hardly apprehend or endure; and, oh! when it concerns one for whom you would have almost died yourself!

'Where is he? How can I reach him, even with the tip of my finger, to convey that one drop of water for which he moans now and now, and through all futurity?' Vain your wild entreaties. Can the dumb earth answer, or the empty air hear you? As the roar of the wild beast dies in solitude, as the foam beats in vain the blind cold precipice, so everywhere apathy receives your frantic adjuration—no sigh, no answer.

Now, when Donica returned and roused Lady Jane from her panic, she passed into a frantic state—the wildest self-upbraidings; things that made old Gwynn beat her lean hand in despair on the cover of her Bible.

As soon as this frenzy a little subsided, Donica laid her hand firmly on the young lady's arm.

'Come, Lady Jane, you must stop that,' she said, sternly. 'What *I* hear matters nothing, but there's others that must not. The house full o' servants; *think*, my darling, and don't let yourself *down*. Come away with me to Wardlock—this is no place any longer for you—and let your maid follow. Come along, Miss Jennie; come, darling. Come by the glass door, there is no one

there, and the chaise waiting outside. Come, miss, you must
not lower yourself before the like o' them that's about the
house.'

It was an accident; but this appeal did touch her pride.

'Well, Donnie, I will. It matters little who now knows everything. Wait one moment—my face. Give me a towel.'

And with feminine precaution she hastily bathed her eyes and
face, looking into the glass, and adjusted her hair.

'A thick veil, Donnie.'

Old Gwynn adjusted it, and Lady Jane gathered in its folds in
her hand; and behind this mask, with old Donnie near her, she
glided down stairs without encountering anyone, and entered the
carriage, and lay back in one of its corners, leaving to Gwynn, who
followed, to give the driver his directions.

When they had driven about a mile, Lady Jane became strangely
excited.

'I must see him again—I *must* see him. Stop it. I *will*. Stop
it.' She was tugging at the window, which was stiff. 'Stop him,
Gwynn. Stop him, woman, and turn back.'

'Don't, Miss Jennie; don't, darling. Ye could not, miss. Ye
would not face all them strangers, ma'am.'

'Face them! What do you mean? *Face* them! How dare
they? I despise them—I *defy* them! What is their staring and
whispering to me? I'll go back. I'll return. I *will* see him
again.'

'Well, Miss Jennie, where's the good. He's cold by this
time.'

'I must see him again, Donnie—I *must.*'

'You'll only see what will frighten you. You never saw a
corpse, miss.'

'Oh! Donnie, Donnie, Donnie, don't—you mustn't. Oh!
Donnie, yes, he's gone, he is—he's *gone,* Donnie, and *I*'ve been
his ruin. I—I—my wicked, wretched, vanity. He's gone, lost
for ever, and it's *I* who've done it all. It's *I,* Donnie. I've
destroyed him.'

It was well that they were driving in a lonely place, over a rough way, and at a noisy pace, for in sheer distraction Lady Jane screamed these wild words of unavailing remorse.

'Ah! my dear,' expostulated Donica Gwynn. ' *You*, indeed! Put that nonsense out of your head. *I* know all about him, poor master Jekyl; a wild poor fellow he was always. *You*, indeed! Ah! it's little you know.'

Lady Jane was now crying bitterly into her handkerchief, held up to her face with both hands, and Donica was glad that her frantic fancy of returning had passed.

' Donnie,' she sobbed at last—' Donnie, you must never leave me. Come with me everywhere.'

'Better for you, ma'am, stay with Lady Alice,' replied old Donnie, with a slight shake of her head.

' I—I'd rather die. She always hated him, and hated me. I tell you, Gwynn, I'd swallow poison first,' said Lady Jane, glaring and flushing fiercely.

' Odd ways, Miss Jane, but means kindly. We must a-bear with one another,' said Gwynn.

' I hate her. She has brought this about, the dreadful old woman. Yes, she always hated me, and now she's happy, for she has ruined me—quite ruined—for nothing—all for nothing—the cruel, dreadful old woman. Oh, Gwynn, is it all true? My God! is it true, or am I mad?'

' Come, my lady, you must not take on so,' said old Gwynn. ' 'Tisn't nothing, arter all, to talk so wild on. Doesn't matter here, shut up wi' me, where no one 'ears ye but old Gwynn, but ye must not talk at that gate before others, mind; there's no one talking o' ye yet—not a soul at Marlowe; no one knows nor guesses nothing, only you be ruled by me; you *know* right well they can't guess nothink; and you must not be a fool and put things in people's heads, d'ye *see*?'

Donica Gwynn spoke this peroration with a low, stern emphasis, holding the young lady's hand in hers, and looking rather grimly into her eyes.

This lecture of Donica's seemed to awaken her to reflection, and she looked for a while into her companion's face without speaking, then lowered her eyes and turned another way, and shook old Gwynn's hand, and pressed it, and held it still.

So they drove on for a good while in silence.

'Well, then, I don't care for one night—just one—and to-morrow I'll go, and you with me ; we'll go to-morrow.'

'But, my lady, mistress, *she* won't like that, mayhap.'

'Then *I*'ll go alone, that's all ; for another night I'll not stay under her roof; and I think if I were like myself nothing could bring me there even for an hour ; but I am not. I am quite worn out.'

Here was another long silence, and before it was broken they were among the hedgerows of Wardlock; and the once familiar landscape was around her, and the old piers by the roadside, and the florid iron gate, and the quaint and staid old manor-house rose before her like the scenery of a sick dream.

The journey was over, and in a few minutes more she was sitting in her temporary room, leaning on her hand, and still cloaked and bonneted, appearing to look out upon the antique garden, with its overgrown standard pear and cherry trees, but, in truth, seeing nothing but the sharp face that had gazed so awfully into space that day from the pillow in Sir Jekyl's bed-room.

CHAPTER LXXIV.

OLD LADY ALICE TALKS WITH GUY.

As Varbarriere, followed by Doocey and Guy, entered the hall, they saw Dives cross hurriedly to the library and shut the door. Varbarriere followed and knocked. Dives, very pallid, opened it, and looked hesitatingly in his face for a moment, and then said—

'Come in, come in, pray, and shut the door. You'll be—you'll be shocked, sir. He's gone—gone. Poor Jekyl! It's a terrible thing. He's gone, sir, quite suddenly.'

His puffy, bilious hand was on Varbarriere's arm with a shifting pressure, and Varbarriere made no answer, but looked in his face sternly and earnestly.

'There's that poor girl, you know—my niece. And—and all so unexpected. It's awful, sir.'

'I'm very much shocked, sir. I had not an idea there was any danger. I thought him looking very far from actual danger. I'm *very* much shocked.'

'And—and things a good deal at sixes and sevens, I'm afraid,' said Dives—'law business, you know.'

'Perhaps it would be well to detain Mr. Pelter, who is, I believe, still here,' suggested Varbarriere.

'Yes, certainly; thank you,' answered Dives, eagerly ringing the bell.

'And I've a chaise at the door,' said Varbarriere, appropriating Guy's vehicle. 'A melancholy parting, sir; but in circumstances so sad, the only kindness we can show is to withdraw the restraint of our presence, and to respect the sanctity of affliction.'

With which little speech, in the artificial style which he had contracted in France, he made his solemn bow, and, for the last time for a good while, shook the Rev. Dives, now Sir Dives Marlowe, by the hand.

When our friend the butler entered, it was a comfort to see one countenance on which was no trace of flurry. *Nil admirari*—his manner was a philosophy, and the convivial undertaker had acquired a grave suavity of demeanour and countenance, which answered all occasions—imperturbable during the comic stories of an after-dinner sederunt—imperturbable now on hearing the other sort of story, known already, which the Rev. Dives Marlowe recounted, and offered, with a respectful inclination, his deferential but very short condolences.

Varbarriere in the meanwhile looked through the hall vestibule and from the steps, in vain, for his nephew! He encountered Jacques, however, but he had not seen Guy, which when Varbarriere, who was in one of his deep-seated fusses, heard, he made a few *sotto voce* ejaculations.

'Tell that fellow—he's in the stable yard, I dare say—who drove Mr. Guy from Slowton, to bring his chaise round this moment; we shall return. If his horses want rest, they can have it in the town, Marlowe, close by; I shall send a carriage up for you; and you follow, with all our things, immediately for Slowton.'

So Jacques departed, and Varbarriere did not care to go up stairs to his room. He did not like meeting people; he did not like the chance of hearing Beatrix cry again; he wished to be away, and his temper was savage. He could have struck his nephew over the head with his cane for detaining him.

But Guy had been summoned elsewhere. As he walked list-lessly before the house, a sudden knocking from the great window of Lady Mary's boudoir caused him to raise his eyes, and he saw the grim apparition of old Lady Alice beckoning to him. As he raised his hat, she nodded at him, pale, scowling like an evil genius, and beckoned him fiercely up with her crooked fingers.

Another bow, and he entered the house, ascended the great stair, and knocked at the door of the boudoir. Old Lady Alice's thin hand opened it. She nodded in the same inauspicious way, pointed to a seat, and shut the door before she spoke.

Then, he still standing, she took his hand, and said, in tones unexpectedly soft and fond—

'Well, dear, how have you been? It seems a long time, although it's really nothing. Quite well, I hope?'

Guy answered, and inquired according to usage; and the old lady said—

'Don't ask for me; never ask. I'm *never* well—always the same, dear, and I hate to think of myself. You've heard the dreadful intelligence—the frightful event. What *will* become of my poor niece? Everything in distraction. But Heaven's will be done. I sha'n't last long if this sort of thing is to continue—quite impossible. There—don't speak to me for a moment. I wanted to tell you, you must come to me; I have a great deal to say,' she resumed, having smelt a little at her vinaigrette; 'but not just now. I'm not equal to all this. You know how I've been tried and shattered.'

Guy was too well accustomed to be more than politely alarmed by those preparations for swooning which Lady Alice occasionally saw fit to make; and in a little while she resumed—

'Sir Jekyl has been taken from us—he's gone—awfully suddenly. I wish he had had a little time for preparation. Ho, dear! *poor* Jekyl! Awful! But we all bow to the will of Providence. I fear there has been some dreadful mismanagement. I always said and knew that Pratt was a quack—positive infatuation. But there's no good in looking to secondary causes. Won't you sit down?'

Guy preferred standing. The hysterical ramblings of this selfish old woman did not weary or disgust him. Quite the contrary; he would have prolonged them. Was she not related to Beatrix, and did not this kindred soften, beautify, glorify that shrivelled relic of another generation, and make him listen to her in a second-hand fascination?'

'You're to come to me—d'ye see?—but not immediately. There's a—there's some one there at present, and I possibly sha'n't be at home. I must remain with poor dear Beatrix a little. She'll probably go to Dartbroke, you know; yes, *that* would not be a bad plan, and I of course must consider her, poor thing. When you grow a little older you'll find you must often sacrifice yourself, my dear. I've served a long apprenticeship to that kind of thing. You must come to Wardlock, to my house; I have a great deal to say and tell you, and you can spend a week or so there very pleasantly. There are some pictures and books, and some walks, and everybody looks at the monuments in the church. There are two of them—the Chief Justice of Chester and Hugo de Redcliffe—in the "Gentleman's Magazine." I'll show it to you when you come, and you can have the carriage, provided you don't tire the horses; but you must come. I'm your kinswoman —I'm your relation—I've found it all out—very near—your poor dear father.'

Here Lady Alice dried her eyes.

'Well, it's time enough. You see how shattered I am, and so pray don't urge me to talk any more just now. I'll write to you, perhaps, if I find myself able ; and *you* write to *me*, mind, directly, and address to Wardlock Manor, Wardlock. Write it in your pocket-book or you'll forget it, and put " to be forwarded " on it. Old Donica will see to it. She's very careful, I *think;* and you promise you'll come ?'

Guy did promise ; so she said—

'Well, dear, till we meet, good-bye ; *there*, God bless you, dear.'

And she drew his hand toward her, and he felt the loose soft leather of her old cheek on his as she kissed him, and her dark old eyes looked for a moment in his, and then she dismissed him with—

'There, dear, I can't talk any more at present ; there, farewell. God bless you.'

Down through that changed, mysterious house, through which people now trod softly, and looked demure, and spoke little on stair or lobby, and that in whispers, went Guy Deverell, and glanced upward, involuntarily, as he descended, hoping that he might see the beloved shadow of Beatrix on the wall, or even the hem of her garment ; but all was silent and empty, and in a few seconds more he was again in the chaise, sitting by old Varbarriere, who was taciturn and ill-tempered all the way to Slowton.

By that evening all the visitors but the Rev. Dives Marlowe and old Lady Alice, who remained with Beatrix, had taken flight. Even Pelter, after a brief consultation with Dives, had fled Londonwards, and the shadow and silence of the chamber of death stole out under the door and pervaded all the mansion.

That evening Lady Alice recovered sufficient strength to write a note to Lady Jane, telling her that in consequence of the death of Sir Jekyl, it became her duty to remain with her niece for the present at Marlowe. It superadded many religious reflections thereupon ; and offering to her visitor at Wardlock the use of that asylum, and the society and attendance of Donica Gwynn, it

concluded with many wholesome wishes for the spiritual improvement of Lady Jane Lennox.

Strangely enough, these did not produce the soothing and ele-
vating effect that might have been expected; for when Lady
Jane read the letter she tore it into strips and then into small
squares, and stamped upon the fragments more like her fierce old
self than she had appeared for the previous four-and-twenty
hours.

'Come, Donica, you write to say I leave this to-morrow, and
that you come with me. You said you'd wish it—you must not
draw back. You would not desert me?'

I fancy her measures were not quite so precipitate, for some arrangements were indispensable before starting for a long sojourn
on the Continent. Lady Jane remained at Wardlock, I believe,
for more than a week; and Donica, who took matters more peaceably in her dry way, obtained, without a row, the permission
of Lady Alice to accompany the forlorn young wife on her journey.

CHAPTER LXXV.

SOMETHING MORE OF LADY JANE LENNOX.

'SEE, Doctor Pratt—how do you do? — you've been up-stairs.
I—I was anxious to see you—most anxious—this shocking, dreadful occurrence,' said the Reverend Dives Marlowe, who waylaid
the Doctor as he came down, and was now very pale, hurrying
him into the library as he spoke, and shutting the door. 'The
nurse is gone, you know, and all quiet; and—and the quieter
the better, because, you know, that poor girl Beatrix my niece,
she has not a notion there was any hurt—a wound, you see, and
knows nothing in fact. I'll go over and see that Slowton doctor
—a—a gentleman. I forget his name. There's no need—I've
considered it—none in the world—of a—a—that miserable ceremony, you know.'

'I don't quite follow you, sir,' observed Doctor Pratt, looking puzzled.

'I mean—I mean a—a—coroner—that a'——

'Oh! I see—I—I see,' answered Pratt.

'And I went up, poor fellow; there's no blood—nothing. It may have been apoplexy, or any natural cause, for anything I know.'

'Internal hæmorrhage—an abrasion, probably, of one of the great vessels; and gave way, you see, in consequence of his over-exerting himself.'

'Exactly; a blood-vessel has given way—I see,' said the Reverend Dives; 'internal hæmorrhage. I see, exactly; and I—I know that Slowton doctor won't speak any more than you, my dear Pratt, but I may as well see him, don't you think? And—and there's really no need for all that terrible misery of an inquest.'

'Well, you know, it's not for me; the—family would act naturally.'

'The family! why, look at that poor girl, my niece, in hysterics! I would not stake that—that *hat* there, I protest, on her preserving her wits, if all that misery were to be gone through.'

'Does Lady Alice know anything of it?'

'Lady Alice Redcliffe? Quite right, sir—very natural inquiry; —not a syllable. She's, you know, not a—a person to conceal things; but she knows and suspects nothing; and no one—that nurse, you told me, thought the hurt was an operation—not a soul suspects.'

And thus the Reverend Dives agreed with himself that the scandal might be avoided; and thus it came to pass that the county paper, with a border of black round the paragraph, announced the death of Sir Jekyl Marlowe, Baronet, at the family residence of Marlowe Manor, in this county, the immediate cause of his death being the rupture of a blood-vessel in the lungs, attended by internal hæmorrhage. By the death of Sir Jekyl Marlowe, it further stated, 'a seat in Parliament and a deputy lieutenancy for thi county become vacant.' Then came a graceful tribute to Sir Jekyl's value as a country gentleman, followed by the usual summary from the 'Peerage,' and the fact that, leaving no male issue, he would be succeeded in his title and the bulk of his estates by his brother, the Rev. Dives Marlowe.

So in due course this brother figured as the Reverend Sir Dives Marlowe, and became proprietor of Marlowe Manor, where, however, he does not reside, preferring his sacred vocation, and the chance of preferment—for he has grown, they say, very fond of money—to the worldly life and expensive liabilities of a country gentleman.

The Rev. Sir Dives Marlowe, Bart., is still unmarried. It is said, however, that he was twice pretty near making the harbour of matrimony. Lady Bateman, the relict of Sir Thomas, was his first object, and matters went on satisfactorily until the stage of business was arrived at; when unexpectedly the lovers on both sides were pulled up and thrown on their haunches by a clause in Sir Thomas's will, the spirit of which is contained in the Latin words, *durante viduitate*. Over this they pondered, recovered their senses, shook hands, and in the name of prudence parted good friends, which they still are.

The second was the beautiful and accomplished Miss D'Acre. In earlier days the Reverend Dives would not have dreamed of anything so imprudent. Time, however, which notoriously does so much for us, if he makes us sages in some particulars, in others, makes us spoonies. It is hard to say what might have happened if a more eligible bridegroom had not turned up in George St. George Lighton, of Seymour Park, Esq. So that Dives' love passages have led to nothing, and of late years he has attempted no further explorations in those intricate ways.

I may as well here mention all I know further about Lady Jane Lennox. I cannot say exactly how soon she left Wardlock, but she did not await Lady Alice's return, and, I think, has never met her since.

Sir Jekyl Marlowe's death was, I suppose, the cause of the abandonment of General Lennox's resolution to proceed for a divorce. He remained in England for fully four months after the Baronet's death, evidently awaiting any proceedings which the family might institute, in consequence, against him. Upon this point he was fiercely obstinate, and his respectable solicitor even fancied him 'cracked.' With as little *fracas* as possible, a separation was arranged—no difficult matter—for the General was open-handed, and the lady impatient only to be gone. It was a well-kept secret; the separation, of course, a scandal, but its exact cause enveloped in doubt. A desperate quarrel, it was known, had followed the General's return from town, but which of the younger gentlemen, then guests at Marlowe, was the hero of the suspicion, was variously conjectured. The evidence of sojourners in the house only deepened the mystery. Lady Jane had not shown the least liking for anyone there. It was thought by most to have a reference to those old London stories which had never been quite proved. A few even went the length of conjecturing that something had turned up about the old General, which had caused the explosion.

With an elderly female cousin, Donica Gwynn, and her maid, she went abroad, where she has continued nearly ever since, living rather solitarily, but not an outcast—a woman who had been talked about unpleasantly, but never convicted—perhaps quite blameless, and therefore by no means excluded.

But a secret sorrow always sat at her heart. The last look of that bad man, who, she believed, had loved her truly though guiltily—summoned as he talked with her—irrevocably gone. Where was he now? How was it with him?

'Oh, Jekyl! Jekyl! If I could only know if we are ever to meet again—forgiven!'

With fingers clasped together under her cloak, and eyes up-turned to the stars in the beautiful Italian skies, she used, as she walked to and fro alone on the terrace of her villa, to murmur these agonised invocations. The heedless air received them; the silent stars shone cold above, inexorably bright. But Time, who dims the pictures, as well as heals the wounds of the past, spread his shadows and mildews over these ghastly images; and as her unselfish sorrow subsided, the sense of her irrevocable forfeiture threw its ever-lengthening shadow over her mind.

' I see how people think—some wonder at me, some accept me, some flatter me—all suspect me.'

So thought she, with a sense of sometimes nearly insupportable loneliness, of resentment she could not express, and of restlessness —dissatisfied with the present, hopeless of the future. It was a life without an object, without a retrospect—no technical compromise, but somehow a fall—a fall in which she bitterly acquiesced, yet which she fiercely resented.

I don't know that her Bible has yet stood her in stead much. She has practised vagaries—Tractarian sometimes, and sometimes Methodist. But there is a yearning, I am sure, which will some day lead her to hope and serenity.

It is about a year since I saw the death of General Lennox in the 'Times,' an event which took place rather suddenly at Vichy. I am told that his will contains no allusion to Lady Jane. This, however, was to have been expected, for the deed of separation had amply provided for her; so now she is free. But I have lately heard from old Lady Alice, who keeps her memory and activity wonderfully, and maintains a correspondence with old Donnie Gwynn, that she shows no symptom of a disposition to avail herself of her liberty. I have lived long enough to be surprised at nothing, and therefore should not wonder if hereafter she should do so.

CHAPTER LXXVI.

THE LAST.

OLD Lady Alice, who liked writing and reading letters, kept up an active correspondence with her grandson, and that dutiful young gentleman received them with an interest, and answered them with a punctuality that did him honour.

Shortly after Lady Jane Lennox's departure from Wardlock, Lady Alice Redcliffe and her fair young charge, Beatrix, arrived at that discreet old dower house. Old Lady Alice, who, when moved, could do a good-natured thing, pitying the solitariness of her pretty guest, so soon as she thought her spirits would bear it, invited first the Miss Radlowes, and afterwards the Miss Wynkletons—lively young ladies of Beatrix's time of life—who helped to make Wardlock less depressing. These hospitalities led to 'invites;' and so the time passed over without the tedium that might have been looked for, until the period drew near when Beatrix was to make the Italian tour she had arranged with that respectable and by no means disagreeable family, the Fentons of Appleby. A rumour reached Guy that Drayton was to be one of the party. This certainly was not pleasant. He alluded to it in his next letter, but Lady Alice chose to pass the subject by.

There had been no step actually taken in the threatened lawsuit since the death of Sir Jekyl. But there were unpleasant rumours, and Pelter and Crowe were in communication with the Rev. Sir Dives Marlowe on the subject, and he occasionally communicated his peevish sense of poor Jekyl's unreasonableness in having died just when everything was at sixes and sevens, and the unfairness of his having all the trouble and so little of the estates.

Varbarriere, I suppose, was on good terms once more with his nephew. There was no more talk of Algeria, and they were now again in London. That corpulent old gentlemen used to smile with an unctuous scorn over the long letters with which Lady Alice occasionally favoured him.

'My faith! she must suppose I have fine leisure, good eyes also, to read all that. I wish, Guy, she would distinguish only you with her correspondence. I suppose if I answer her never, she will cease some time.'

He had a letter from her while in London, on which he discoursed in the above vein. I doubt that he ever read it through.

Guy received one by the same post, in the conclusion of which she said—

'Beatrix Marlowe goes in a few days, with the Fentons, to Paris, and thence to Italy. My house will then be a desert, and I miserably solitary, unless you and your uncle will come to me,

as you long since promised, and as you well know there is nothing
to prevent. I have written to him, naming Wednesday week. I
shall then have rooms in which to place you, and you positively
must not refuse.'

Under this hospitable pressure, Varbarriere resolved to make
the visit to Wardlock—a flying visit of a day and night—rather
to hear what she might have to say than to enjoy the excellent
lady's society. From Slowton, having there got rid of their railway dust and vapour, the gentlemen reached Wardlock at the approach of evening. In the hall they found old Lady Alice, her
thin stooping figure cloaked and shawled for a walk, and her close
bonnet shading her hollow and wrinkled face.

Hospitable in her way, and really glad to see her guests, was
the crone. She would have dismantled and unbonneted, and
called for luncheon, and would have led the way into the parlour;
but they would not hear of such things, having refreshed at
Slowton, and insisted instead on joining the old lady in her
walk.

There is a tall glass door in the back hall, which opens on the
shorn grass, and through it they passed into the circumscribed but
pretty pleasure-ground, a quadrangle, of which the old house,
overgrown with jessamine and woodbine, formed nearly one side;
the opposite garden wall, overtopped with ancient fruit-trees,
another; and screens of tall-stemmed birch and ash, and an un-
derwood of juniper and evergreens, the others; beds of brilliant
verbena here and there patterned the green sod; and the whole
had an air so quaint and cloister-like, as drew forth some honest
sentences of admiration from old Varbarriere.

They strolled among these flowers in this pleasant seclusion for
a time, until Lady Alice pronounced herself fatigued, and sat
down upon a rustic seat, with due ceremony of adjustment and
assistance.

'Sit down by me, Mr. Strangways. Which am I to call you,
by-the-bye?'

'Which you please, madam,' answered Varbarriere, with the
kind of smile he used with her—deferential, with, nevertheless, a

suspicion of the scornful and amused in it, and as he spoke he was seated.

'As for you, grandson,' she continued, 'you had better take a walk in the garden—you'll find the door open;' she pointed with her parasol to the old-fashioned fluted doorcase of Caen stone in the garden wall; 'and I want to talk a little to my friend, M. de Varbarriere—Mr. Strangways, as I remember him.' And turning to that sage, she said—

'You got my letter, and have well considered it, I trust?'

'I never fail to consider well anything that falls from Lady Alice Redcliffe.'

'Well, sir, I must tell you——'

These were the last words that Guy heard as he departed, according to orders, to visit her ladyship's old-fashioned garden. Could a young fellow fancy a duller entertainment? Yet to Guy Deverell it was not dull. Everything he looked on here was beautified and saddened by the influence that had been there so recently and was gone.

Those same roses, whose leaves were dropping to the earth, she had seen but a day or two ago in their melancholy clusters; under these tall trees she had walked, here on this rustic seat she had rested; and Guy, like a reverent worshipper of relics, sat him down in the same seat, and, with a strange thrill, fancied he saw a pencilled word or two on the arm of it. But no, it was nothing, only the veining of the wood. Why do ladies use their pencils so much less than we men, and so seldom (those I mean whose relics are precious) trace a line by chance, and throw this bread upon the waters, where we poor devils pull cheerless against wind and tide?

Here were flowers, too, tied up on tall sticks. He wondered whether Beatrix ever tended these with her delicate fingers, and he rose and looked at the bass-mat with inexpressible feeling.

Then, on a sudden, he stopped by a little circle of annuals, overgrown, run into pod, all draggled, but in the centre a split stick and a piece of bleached paper folded and stuck across it. Had she written the name of the flower, which perhaps she sowed?

and he plucked the stick from the earth, and with tender fingers
unfolded the record. In a hideous scrawl, evidently the seeds-
man's, ' Lupines' sprawled across the weather-beaten brown
paper.

He raised his eyes with a sigh, and perceived that the respectable
gardener, in a blue body-coat with brass buttons, was at hand,
and eyed him with a rather stern inquisitiveness. Guy threw the
stick down carelessly, feeling a little foolish, and walked on with
more swagger than usual.

And now he had entered that distant part of the garden where
dark and stately yew hedges, cut here and there in arches, form a
meditative maze. With the melancholy yearnings of a lover he
gazed on these, no doubt the recent haunts of that beautiful creature who was his day-dream. With a friendly feeling he looked
on the dark wall of yew on either side; and from this solemn walk
he turned into another, and—saw Beatrix !

More beautiful than ever he thought her—her features a little
saddened. Each gazed on the other, as the old stories truly say
in such cases, with changing colour. Each had imagined the
other more than a hundred miles away. Neither had fancied a
meeting likely, perhaps possible. The matter hung upon the wills
of others, who might never consent until too late. A few days
would see Beatrix on her way to Italy with the Fentons ; and yet
here were she and Guy Deverell, by the sleight of that not ill-
natured witch, old Lady Alice, face to face.

I don't know exactly what Guy said. I don't know what she
answered. The rhetoric was chiefly his ; but he held her hand in
his, and from time to time pleaded, not quite in vain, for a word
from the goddess with glowing cheeks and downcast eyes, by
whose side he walked. Low were those tones, and few those words,
that answered his impetuous periods; yet there was a magic in
them that made him prouder and more blessed than ever his hopes
had dared to promise.

Sometimes they stopped, sometimes they walked slowly on,
quite unconscious whether they moved or paused—whether the

birds sang or were silent—of all things but their love—in a beautiful dream.

They had surprised one another, and now in turn both were surprised by others; for under one of those airy arches cut so sharply in the yew hedge, on a sudden, stood old Lady Alice and Monsieur Varbarriere—the Enchanter and the Fairy at the close of a tale.

Indulgently, benevolently, the superior powers looked on. The young people paused, abashed. A sharp little nod from Lady Alice told them they were understood. Varbarriere came forward, and took the young lady's hand very kindly, and held it very long, and at the close of his salutation, stooping towards her pretty ear, murmured something, smiling, which made her drop her eyes again.

'I think you both might have waited until I had spoken; to you; however, it does not signify much. I don't expect to be of any great consequence, or in any great request henceforward.'

Her grandson hastened to plead his excuses, which were received, I must allow, with a good grace.

In matters of true love, I have observed, where not only Cupid applauds, but Plutus smiles, Hymen seldom makes much pother about his share in the business. Beatrix did *not* make that tour with the Fentons. They, on the contrary, delayed their departure for rather more than a month; and I find Miss Fenton and Miss Arabella Fenton among the bridesmaids. Drayton did not attend the wedding, and oddly enough, was married only about three weeks after to Lady Justina Flynston, who was not pretty, and had but little money; and they say 'he has turned out rather cross, and hates the French and all their products, as 'utter rot.'

Varbarriere has established two great silk-factories, and lives in France, where they say gold pours in upon him in streams before which the last editor of ' Aladdin' and Mr. Kightley of the ' Ancient Mythology' hang their heads. His chief 'object' is the eldest son of the happy union which we have seen celebrated a few lines back. They would have called the boy Herbert, but Varbarriere would not hear of anything but Guy. They say that he is a prodigy of beauty and cleverness. Of course, we hear accounts of infant phenomena with allowance. All I can say is, ' If he's not handsome it's very odd, and he has at least as good a right to be clever as most boys going.' And as in these pages we have heard something of a father, a son, and a grandson, each bearing the same name, I think I can't do better than call this tale after them—GUY DEVERELL.

THE END.

A CATALOGUE OF SELECTED DOVER BOOKS
IN ALL FIELDS OF INTEREST

A CATALOGUE OF SELECTED DOVER
BOOKS IN ALL FIELDS OF INTEREST

CELESTIAL OBJECTS FOR COMMON TELESCOPES, T. W. Webb. The most used book in amateur astronomy: inestimable aid for locating and identifying nearly 4,000 celestial objects. Edited, updated by Margaret W. Mayall. 77 illustrations. Total of 645pp. 5⅜ x 8½.
20917-2, 20918-0 Pa., Two-vol. set $9.00

HISTORICAL STUDIES IN THE LANGUAGE OF CHEMISTRY, M. P. Crosland. The important part language has played in the development of chemistry from the symbolism of alchemy to the adoption of systematic nomenclature in 1892. ". . . wholeheartedly recommended,"—Science. 15 illustrations. 416pp. of text. 5⅝ x 8¼. 63702-6 Pa. $6.00

BURNHAM'S CELESTIAL HANDBOOK, Robert Burnham, Jr. Thorough, readable guide to the stars beyond our solar system. Exhaustive treatment, fully illustrated. Breakdown is alphabetical by constellation: Andromeda to Cetus in Vol. 1; Chamaeleon to Orion in Vol. 2; and Pavo to Vulpecula in Vol. 3. Hundreds of illustrations. Total of about 2000pp. 6⅛ x 9¼.
23567-X, 23568-8, 23673-0 Pa., Three-vol. set $27.85

THEORY OF WING SECTIONS: INCLUDING A SUMMARY OF AIR-FOIL DATA, Ira H. Abbott and A. E. von Doenhoff. Concise compilation of subatomic aerodynamic characteristics of modern NASA wing sections, plus description of theory. 350pp. of tables. 693pp. 5⅜ x 8½.
60586-8 Pa. $8.50

DE RE METALLICA, Georgius Agricola. Translated by Herbert C. Hoover and Lou H. Hoover. The famous Hoover translation of greatest treatise on technological chemistry, engineering, geology, mining of early modern times (1556). All 289 original woodcuts. 638pp. 6¾ x 11.
60006-8 Clothbd. $17.95

THE ORIGIN OF CONTINENTS AND OCEANS, Alfred Wegener. One of the most influential, most controversial books in science, the classic statement for continental drift. Full 1966 translation of Wegener's final (1929) version. 64 illustrations. 246pp. 5⅜ x 8½. 61708-4 Pa. $4.50

THE PRINCIPLES OF PSYCHOLOGY, William James. Famous long course complete, unabridged. Stream of thought, time perception, memory, experimental methods; great work decades ahead of its time. Still valid, useful; read in many classes. 94 figures. Total of 1391pp. 5⅜ x 8½.
20381-6, 20382-4 Pa., Two-vol. set $13.00

DRAWINGS OF WILLIAM BLAKE, William Blake. 92 plates from Book of Job, *Divine Comedy, Paradise Lost,* visionary heads, mythological figures, Laocoon, etc. Selection, introduction, commentary by Sir Geoffrey Keynes. 178pp. 8⅛ x 11. 22303-5 Pa. $4.00

ENGRAVINGS OF HOGARTH, William Hogarth. 101 of Hogarth's greatest works: *Rake's Progress, Harlot's Progress, Illustrations for Hudibras, Before and After, Beer Street and Gin Lane,* many more. Full commentary. 256pp. 11 x 13¾. 22479-1 Pa. $12.95

DAUMIER: 120 GREAT LITHOGRAPHS, Honore Daumier. Wide-ranging collection of lithographs by the greatest caricaturist of the 19th century. Concentrates on eternally popular series on lawyers, on married life, on liberated women, etc. Selection, introduction, and notes on plates by Charles F. Ramus. Total of 158pp. 9⅜ x 12¼. 23512-2 Pa. $6.00

DRAWINGS OF MUCHA, Alphonse Maria Mucha. Work reveals draftsman of highest caliber: studies for famous posters and paintings, renderings for book illustrations and ads, etc. 70 works, 9 in color; including 6 items not drawings. Introduction. List of illustrations. 72pp. 9⅜ x 12¼. (Available in U.S. only) 23672-2 Pa. $4.00

GIOVANNI BATTISTA PIRANESI: DRAWINGS IN THE PIERPONT MORGAN LIBRARY, Giovanni Battista Piranesi. For first time ever all of Morgan Library's collection, world's largest. 167 illustrations of rare Piranesi drawings—archeological, architectural, decorative and visionary. Essay, detailed list of drawings, chronology, captions. Edited by Felice Stampfle. 144pp. 9⅜ x 12¼. 23714-1 Pa. $7.50

NEW YORK ETCHINGS (1905-1949), John Sloan. All of important American artist's N.Y. life etchings. 67 works include some of his best art; also lively historical record—Greenwich Village, tenement scenes. Edited by Sloan's widow. Introduction and captions. 79pp. 8⅜ x 11¼. 23651-X Pa. $4.00

CHINESE PAINTING AND CALLIGRAPHY: A PICTORIAL SURVEY, Wan-go Weng. 69 fine examples from John M. Crawford's matchless private collection: landscapes, birds, flowers, human figures, etc., plus calligraphy. Every basic form included: hanging scrolls, handscrolls, album leaves, fans, etc. 109 illustrations. Introduction. Captions. 192pp. 8⅞ x 11¾. 23707-9 Pa. $7.95

DRAWINGS OF REMBRANDT, edited by Seymour Slive. Updated Lippmann, Hofstede de Groot edition, with definitive scholarly apparatus. All portraits, biblical sketches, landscapes, nudes, Oriental figures, classical studies, together with selection of work by followers. 550 illustrations. Total of 630pp. 9⅛ x 12¼. 21485-0, 21486-9 Pa., Two-vol. set $15.00

THE DISASTERS OF WAR, Francisco Goya. 83 etchings record horrors of Napoleonic wars in Spain and war in general. Reprint of 1st edition, plus 3 additional plates. Introduction by Philip Hofer. 97pp. 9⅜ x 8¼. 21872-4 Pa. $4.00

THE COMPLETE BOOK OF DOLL MAKING AND COLLECTING, Catherine Christopher. Instructions, patterns for dozens of dolls, from rag doll on up to elaborate, historically accurate figures. Mould faces, sew clothing, make doll houses, etc. Also collecting information. Many illustrations. 288pp. 6 x 9. 22066-4 Pa. $4.50

THE DAGUERREOTYPE IN AMERICA, Beaumont Newhall. Wonderful portraits, 1850's townscapes, landscapes; full text plus 104 photographs. The basic book. Enlarged 1976 edition. 272pp. 8¼ x 11¼. 23322-7 Pa. $7.95

CRAFTSMAN HOMES, Gustav Stickley. 296 architectural drawings, floor plans, and photographs illustrate 40 different kinds of "Mission-style" homes from The Craftsman (1901-16), voice of American style of simplicity and organic harmony. Thorough coverage of Craftsman idea in text and picture, now collector's item. 224pp. 8⅛ x 11. 23791-5 Pa. $6.00

PEWTER-WORKING: INSTRUCTIONS AND PROJECTS, Burl N. Osborn. & Gordon O. Wilber. Introduction to pewter-working for amateur craftsman. History and characteristics of pewter; tools, materials, step-by-step instructions. Photos, line drawings, diagrams. Total of 160pp. 7⅞ x 10¾. 23786-9 Pa. $3.50

THE GREAT CHICAGO FIRE, edited by David Lowe. 10 dramatic, eyewitness accounts of the 1871 disaster, including one of the aftermath and rebuilding, plus 70 contemporary photographs and illustrations of the ruins—courthouse, Palmer House, Great Central Depot, etc. Introduction by David Lowe. 87pp. 8¼ x 11. 23771-0 Pa. $4.00

SILHOUETTES: A PICTORIAL ARCHIVE OF VARIED ILLUSTRATIONS, edited by Carol Belanger Grafton. Over 600 silhouettes from the 18th to 20th centuries include profiles and full figures of men and women, children, birds and animals, groups and scenes, nature, ships, an alphabet. Dozens of uses for commercial artists and craftspeople. 144pp. 8⅜ x 11¼. 23781-8 Pa. $4.50

ANIMALS: 1,419 COPYRIGHT-FREE ILLUSTRATIONS OF MAMMALS, BIRDS, FISH, INSECTS, ETC., edited by Jim Harter. Clear wood engravings present, in extremely lifelike poses, over 1,000 species of animals. One of the most extensive copyright-free pictorial sourcebooks of its kind. Captions. Index. 284pp. 9 x 12. 23766-4 Pa. $8.95

INDIAN DESIGNS FROM ANCIENT ECUADOR, Frederick W. Shaffer. 282 original designs by pre-Columbian Indians of Ecuador (500-1500 A.D.). Designs include people, mammals, birds, reptiles, fish, plants, heads, geometric designs. Use as is or alter for advertising, textiles, leathercraft, etc. Introduction. 95pp. 8¾ x 11¼. 23764-8 Pa. $3.50

SZIGETI ON THE VIOLIN, Joseph Szigeti. Genial, loosely structured tour by premier violinist, featuring a pleasant mixture of reminiscenes, insights into great music and musicians, innumerable tips for practicing violinists. 385 musical passages. 256pp. 5⅝ x 8¼. 23763-X Pa. $4.00

HISTORY OF BACTERIOLOGY, William Bulloch. The only comprehensive history of bacteriology from the beginnings through the 19th century. Special emphasis is given to biography-Leeuwenhoek, etc. Brief accounts of 350 bacteriologists form a separate section. No clearer, fuller study, suitable to scientists and general readers, has yet been written. 52 illustrations. 448pp. 5⅝ x 8¼. 23761-3 Pa. $6.50

THE COMPLETE NONSENSE OF EDWARD LEAR, Edward Lear. All nonsense limericks, zany alphabets, Owl and Pussycat, songs, nonsense botany, etc., illustrated by Lear. Total of 321pp. 5⅜ x 8½. (Available in U.S. only) 20167-8 Pa. $3.95

INGENIOUS MATHEMATICAL PROBLEMS AND METHODS, Louis A. Graham. Sophisticated material from Graham *Dial*, applied and pure; stresses solution methods. Logic, number theory, networks, inversions, etc. 237pp. 5⅜ x 8½. 20545-2 Pa. $4.50

BEST MATHEMATICAL PUZZLES OF SAM LOYD, edited by Martin Gardner. Bizarre, original, whimsical puzzles by America's greatest puzzler. From fabulously rare *Cyclopedia,* including famous 14-15 puzzles, the Horse of a Different Color, 115 more. Elementary math. 150 illustrations. 167pp. 5⅜ x 8½. 20498-7 Pa. $2.75

THE BASIS OF COMBINATION IN CHESS, J. du Mont. Easy-to-follow, instructive book on elements of combination play, with chapters on each piece and every powerful combination team—two knights, bishop and knight, rook and bishop, etc. 250 diagrams. 218pp. 5⅜ x 8½. (Available in U.S. only) 23644-7 Pa. $3.50

MODERN CHESS STRATEGY, Ludek Pachman. The use of the queen, the active king, exchanges, pawn play, the center, weak squares, etc. Section on rook alone worth price of the book. Stress on the moderns. Often considered the most important book on strategy. 314pp. 5⅜ x 8½. 20290-9 Pa. $4.50

LASKER'S MANUAL OF CHESS, Dr. Emanuel Lasker. Great world champion offers very thorough coverage of all aspects of chess. Combinations, position play, openings, end game, aesthetics of chess, philosophy of struggle, much more. Filled with analyzed games. 390pp. 5⅜ x 8½. 20640-8 Pa. $5.00

500 MASTER GAMES OF CHESS, S. Tartakower, J. du Mont. Vast collection of great chess games from 1798-1938, with much material nowhere else readily available. Fully annotated, arranged by opening for easier study. 664pp. 5⅜ x 8½. 23208-5 Pa. $7.50

A GUIDE TO CHESS ENDINGS, Dr. Max Euwe, David Hooper. One of the finest modern works on chess endings. Thorough analysis of the most frequently encountered endings by former world champion. 331 examples, each with diagram. 248pp. 5⅜ x 8½. 23332-4 Pa. $3.75

SECOND PIATIGORSKY CUP, edited by Isaac Kashdan. One of the greatest tournament books ever produced in the English language. All 90 games of the 1966 tournament, annotated by players, most annotated by both players. Features Petrosian, Spassky, Fischer, Larsen, six others. 228pp. 5⅜ x 8½.   23572-6 Pa. $3.50

ENCYCLOPEDIA OF CARD TRICKS, revised and edited by Jean Hugard. How to perform over 600 card tricks, devised by the world's greatest magicians: impromptus, spelling tricks, key cards, using special packs, much, much more. Additional chapter on card technique. 66 illustrations. 402pp. 5⅜ x 8½. (Available in U.S. only)   21252-1 Pa. $4.95

MAGIC: STAGE ILLUSIONS, SPECIAL EFFECTS AND TRICK PHOTOGRAPHY, Albert A. Hopkins, Henry R. Evans. One of the great classics; fullest, most authorative explanation of vanishing lady, levitations, scores of other great stage effects. Also small magic, automata, stunts. 446 illustrations. 556pp. 5⅜ x 8½.   23344-8 Pa. $6.95

THE SECRETS OF HOUDINI, J. C. Cannell. Classic study of Houdini's incredible magic, exposing closely-kept professional secrets and revealing, in general terms, the whole art of stage magic. 67 illustrations. 279pp. 5⅜ x 8½.   22913-0 Pa. $4.00

HOFFMANN'S MODERN MAGIC, Professor Hoffmann. One of the best, and best-known, magicians' manuals of the past century. Hundreds of tricks from card tricks and simple sleight of hand to elaborate illusions involving construction of complicated machinery. 332 illustrations. 563pp. 5⅜ x 8½.   23623-4 Pa. $6.00

MADAME PRUNIER'S FISH COOKERY BOOK, Mme. S. B. Prunier. More than 1000 recipes from world famous Prunier's of Paris and London, specially adapted here for American kitchen. Grilled tournedos with anchovy butter, Lobster a la Bordelaise, Prunier's prized desserts, more. Glossary. 340pp. 5⅜ x 8½. (Available in U.S. only)   22679-4 Pa. $3.00

FRENCH COUNTRY COOKING FOR AMERICANS, Louis Diat. 500 easy-to-make, authentic provincial recipes compiled by former head chef at New York's Fitz-Carlton Hotel: onion soup, lamb stew, potato pie, more. 309pp. 5⅜ x 8½.   23665-X Pa. $3.95

SAUCES, FRENCH AND FAMOUS, Louis Diat. Complete book gives over 200 specific recipes: bechamel, Bordelaise, hollandaise, Cumberland, apricot, etc. Author was one of this century's finest chefs, originator of vichyssoise and many other dishes. Index. 156pp. 5⅜ x 8.
23663-3 Pa. $2.75

TOLL HOUSE TRIED AND TRUE RECIPES, Ruth Graves Wakefield. Authentic recipes from the famous Mass. restaurant: popovers, veal and ham loaf, Toll House baked beans, chocolate cake crumb pudding, much more. Many helpful hints. Nearly 700 recipes. Index. 376pp. 5⅜ x 8½.
23560-2 Pa. $4.50

THE CURVES OF LIFE, Theodore A. Cook. Examination of shells, leaves, horns, human body, art, etc., in *"the* classic reference on how the golden ratio applies to spirals and helices in nature . . . . "—Martin Gardner. 426 illustrations. Total of 512pp. 5⅜ x 8½.   23701-X Pa. $5.95

AN ILLUSTRATED FLORA OF THE NORTHERN UNITED STATES AND CANADA, Nathaniel L. Britton, Addison Brown. Encyclopedic work covers 4666 species, ferns on up. Everything. Full botanical information, illustration for each. This earlier edition is preferred by many to more recent revisions. 1913 edition. Over 4000 illustrations, total of 2087pp. 6⅛ x 9¼.   22642-5, 22643-3, 22644-1 Pa., Three-vol. set $25.50

MANUAL OF THE GRASSES OF THE UNITED STATES, A. S. Hitchcock, U.S. Dept. of Agriculture. The basic study of American grasses, both indigenous and escapes, cultivated and wild. Over 1400 species. Full descriptions, information. Over 1100 maps, illustrations. Total of 1051pp. 5⅜ x 8½.   22717-0, 22718-9 Pa., Two-vol. set $15.00

THE CACTACEAE,, Nathaniel L. Britton, John N. Rose. Exhaustive, definitive. Every cactus in the world. Full botanical descriptions. Thorough statement of nomenclatures, habitat, detailed finding keys. The one book needed by every cactus enthusiast. Over 1275 illustrations. Total of 1080pp. 8 x 10¼.   21191-6, 21192-4 Clothbd., Two-vol. set $35.00

AMERICAN MEDICINAL PLANTS, Charles F. Millspaugh. Full descriptions, 180 plants covered: history; physical description; methods of preparation with all chemical constituents extracted; all claimed curative or adverse effects. 180 full-page plates. Classification table. 804pp. 6½ x 9¼.   23034-1 Pa. $12.95

A MODERN HERBAL, Margaret Grieve. Much the fullest, most exact, most useful compilation of herbal material. Gigantic alphabetical encyclopedia, from aconite to zedoary, gives botanical information, medical properties, folklore, economic uses, and much else. Indispensable to serious reader. 161 illustrations. 888pp. 6½ x 9¼. (Available in U.S. only)   22798-7, 22799-5 Pa., Two-vol. set $13.00

THE HERBAL or GENERAL HISTORY OF PLANTS, John Gerard. The 1633 edition revised and enlarged by Thomas Johnson. Containing almost 2850 plant descriptions and 2705 superb illustrations, Gerard's *Herbal* is a monumental work, the book all modern English herbals are derived from, the one herbal every serious enthusiast should have in its entirety. Original editions are worth perhaps $750. 1678pp. 8½ x 12¼.   23147-X Clothbd. $50.00

MANUAL OF THE TREES OF NORTH AMERICA, Charles S. Sargent. The basic survey of every native tree and tree-like shrub, 717 species in all. Extremely full descriptions, information on habitat, growth, locales, economics, etc. Necessary to every serious tree lover. Over 100 finding keys. 783 illustrations. Total of 986pp. 5⅜ x 8½.   20277-1, 20278-X Pa., Two-vol. set $11.00

AMERICAN BIRD ENGRAVINGS, Alexander Wilson et al. All 76 plates. from Wilson's *American Ornithology* (1808-14), most important ornithological work before Audubon, plus 27 plates from the supplement (1825-33) by Charles Bonaparte. Over 250 birds portrayed. 8 plates also reproduced in full color. 111pp. 9⅜ x 12½. 23195-X Pa. $6.00

CRUICKSHANK'S PHOTOGRAPHS OF BIRDS OF AMERICA, Allan D. Cruickshank. Great ornithologist, photographer presents 177 closeups, groupings, panoramas, flightings, etc., of about 150 different birds. Expanded *Wings in the Wilderness*. Introduction by Helen G. Cruickshank. 191pp. 8¼ x 11. 23497-5 Pa. $6.00

AMERICAN WILDLIFE AND PLANTS, A. C. Martin, et al. Describes food habits of more than 1000 species of mammals, birds, fish. Special treatment of important food plants. Over 300 illustrations. 500pp. 5⅜ x 8½. 20793-5 Pa. $4.95

THE PEOPLE CALLED SHAKERS, Edward D. Andrews. Lifetime of research, definitive study of Shakers: origins, beliefs, practices, dances, social organization, furniture and crafts, impact on 19th-century USA, present heritage. Indispensable to student of American history, collector. 33 illustrations. 351pp. 5⅜ x 8½. 21081-2 Pa. $4.50

OLD NEW YORK IN EARLY PHOTOGRAPHS, Mary Black. New York City as it was in 1853-1901, through 196 wonderful photographs from N.-Y. Historical Society. Great Blizzard, Lincoln's funeral procession, great buildings. 228pp. 9 x 12. 22907-6 Pa. $8.95

MR. LINCOLN'S CAMERA MAN: MATHEW BRADY, Roy Meredith. Over 300 Brady photos reproduced directly from original negatives, photos. Jackson, Webster, Grant, Lee, Carnegie, Barnum; Lincoln; Battle Smoke, Death of Rebel Sniper, Atlanta Just After Capture. Lively commentary. 368pp. 8⅜ x 11¼. 23021-X Pa. $8.95

TRAVELS OF WILLIAM BARTRAM, William Bartram. From 1773-8, Bartram explored Northern Florida, Georgia, Carolinas, and reported on wild life, plants, Indians, early settlers. Basic account for period, entertaining reading. Edited by Mark Van Doren. 13 illustrations. 141pp. 5⅜ x 8½. 20013-2 Pa. $5.00

THE GENTLEMAN AND CABINET MAKER'S DIRECTOR, Thomas Chippendale. Full reprint, 1762 style book, most influential of all time; chairs, tables, sofas, mirrors, cabinets, etc. 200 plates, plus 24 photographs of surviving pieces. 249pp. 9⅞ x 12¾. 21601-2 Pa. $7.95

AMERICAN CARRIAGES, SLEIGHS, SULKIES AND CARTS, edited by Don H. Berkebile. 168 Victorian illustrations from catalogues, trade journals, fully captioned. Useful for artists. Author is Assoc. Curator, Div. of Transportation of Smithsonian Institution. 168pp. 8½ x 9½. 23328-6 Pa. $5.00

YUCATAN BEFORE AND AFTER THE CONQUEST, Diego de Landa. First English translation of basic book in Maya studies, the only significant account of Yucatan written in the early post-Conquest era. Translated by distinguished Maya scholar William Gates. Appendices, introduction, 4 maps and over 120 illustrations added by translator. 162pp. 5⅜ x 8½.
23622-6 Pa. $3.00

THE MALAY ARCHIPELAGO, Alfred R. Wallace. Spirited travel account by one of founders of modern biology. Touches on zoology, botany, ethnography, geography, and geology. 62 illustrations, maps. 515pp. 5⅜ x 8½.
20187-2 Pa. $6.95

THE DISCOVERY OF THE TOMB OF TUTANKHAMEN, Howard Carter, A. C. Mace. Accompany Carter in the thrill of discovery, as ruined passage suddenly reveals unique, untouched, fabulously rich tomb. Fascinating account, with 106 illustrations. New introduction by J. M. White. Total of 382pp. 5⅜ x 8½. (Available in U.S. only) 23500-9 Pa. $4.00

THE WORLD'S GREATEST SPEECHES, edited by Lewis Copeland and Lawrence W. Lamm. Vast collection of 278 speeches from Greeks up to present. Powerful and effective models; unique look at history. Revised to 1970. Indices. 842pp. 5⅜ x 8½.
20468-5 Pa. $8.95

THE 100 GREATEST ADVERTISEMENTS, Julian Watkins. The priceless ingredient; His master's voice; 99 44/100% pure; over 100 others. How they were written, their impact, etc. Remarkable record. 130 illustrations. 233pp. 7⅞ x 10 3/5.
20540-1 Pa. $5.95

CRUICKSHANK PRINTS FOR HAND COLORING, George Cruickshank. 18 illustrations, one side of a page, on fine-quality paper suitable for watercolors. Caricatures of people in society (c. 1820) full of trenchant wit. Very large format. 32pp. 11 x 16.
23684-6 Pa. $5.00

THIRTY-TWO COLOR POSTCARDS OF TWENTIETH-CENTURY AMERICAN ART, Whitney Museum of American Art. Reproduced in full color in postcard form are 31 art works and one shot of the museum. Calder, Hopper, Rauschenberg, others. Detachable. 16pp. 8¼ x 11.
23629-3 Pa. $3.00

MUSIC OF THE SPHERES: THE MATERIAL UNIVERSE FROM ATOM TO QUASAR SIMPLY EXPLAINED, Guy Murchie. Planets, stars, geology, atoms, radiation, relativity, quantum theory, light, antimatter, similar topics. 319 figures. 664pp. 5⅜ x 8½.
21809-0, 21810-4 Pa., Two-vol. set $11.00

EINSTEIN'S THEORY OF RELATIVITY, Max Born. Finest semi-technical account; covers Einstein, Lorentz, Minkowski, and others, with much detail, much explanation of ideas and math not readily available elsewhere on this level. For student, non-specialist. 376pp. 5⅜ x 8½.
60769-0 Pa. $4.50

THE EARLY WORK OF AUBREY BEARDSLEY, Aubrey Beardsley. 157 plates, 2 in color: *Manon Lescaut, Madame Bovary, Morte Darthur, Salome,* other. Introduction by H. Marillier. 182pp. 8⅛ x 11. 21816-3 Pa. $4.50

THE LATER WORK OF AUBREY BEARDSLEY, Aubrey Beardsley. Exotic masterpieces of full maturity: *Venus and Tannhauser, Lysistrata, Rape of the Lock, Volpone,* Savoy material, etc. 174 plates, 2 in color. 186pp. 8⅛ x 11. 21817-1 Pa. $5.95

THOMAS NAST'S CHRISTMAS DRAWINGS, Thomas Nast. Almost all Christmas drawings by creator of image of Santa Claus as we know it, and one of America's foremost illustrators and political cartoonists. 66 illustrations. 3 illustrations in color on covers. 96pp. 8⅜ x 11¼. 23660-9 Pa. $3.50

THE DORÉ ILLUSTRATIONS FOR DANTE'S DIVINE COMEDY, Gustave Doré. All 135 plates from Inferno, Purgatory, Paradise; fantastic tortures, infernal landscapes, celestial wonders. Each plate with appropriate (translated) verses. 141pp. 9 x 12. 23231-X Pa. $4.50

DORÉ'S ILLUSTRATIONS FOR RABELAIS, Gustave Doré. 252 striking illustrations of *Gargantua and Pantagruel* books by foremost 19th-century illustrator. Including 60 plates, 192 delightful smaller illustrations. 153pp. 9 x 12. 23656-0 Pa. $5.00

LONDON: A PILGRIMAGE, Gustave Doré, Blanchard Jerrold. Squalor, riches, misery, beauty of mid-Victorian metropolis; 55 wonderful plates, 125 other illustrations, full social, cultural text by Jerrold. 191pp. of text. 9⅜ x 12¼. 22306-X Pa. $7.00

THE RIME OF THE ANCIENT MARINER, Gustave Doré, S. T. Coleridge. Dore's finest work, 34 plates capture moods, subtleties of poem. Full text. Introduction by Millicent Rose. 77pp. 9¼ x 12. 22305-1 Pa. $3.50

THE DORE BIBLE ILLUSTRATIONS, Gustave Doré. All wonderful, detailed plates: Adam and Eve, Flood, Babylon, Life of Jesus, etc. Brief King James text with each plate. Introduction by Millicent Rose. 241 plates. 241pp. 9 x 12. 23004-X Pa. $6.00

THE COMPLETE ENGRAVINGS, ETCHINGS AND DRYPOINTS OF ALBRECHT DURER. "Knight, Death and Devil"; "Melencolia," and more—all Dürer's known works in all three media, including 6 works formerly attributed to him. 120 plates. 235pp. 8⅜ x 11¼. 22851-7 Pa. $6.50

MECHANICK EXERCISES ON THE WHOLE ART OF PRINTING, Joseph Moxon. First complete book (1683-4) ever written about typography, a compendium of everything known about printing at the latter part of 17th century. Reprint of 2nd (1962) Oxford Univ. Press edition. 74 illustrations. Total of 550pp. 6⅛ x 9¼. 23617-X Pa. $7.95

THE COMPLETE WOODCUTS OF ALBRECHT DURER, edited by Dr. W. Kurth. 346 in all: "Old Testament," "St. Jerome," "Passion," "Life of Virgin," Apocalypse," many others. Introduction by Campbell Dodgson. 285pp. 8½ x 12¼. 21097-9 Pa. $7.50

DRAWINGS OF ALBRECHT DURER, edited by Heinrich Wolfflin. 81 plates show development from youth to full style. Many favorites; many new. Introduction by Alfred Werner. 96pp. 8⅛ x 11. 22352-3 Pa. $5.00

THE HUMAN FIGURE, Albrecht Dürer. Experiments in various techniques—stereometric, progressive proportional, and others. Also life studies that rank among finest ever done. Complete reprinting of *Dresden Sketchbook*. 170 plates. 355pp. 8⅜ x 11¼. 21042-1 Pa. $7.95

OF THE JUST SHAPING OF LETTERS, Albrecht Dürer. Renaissance artist explains design of Roman majuscules by geometry, also Gothic lower and capitals. Grolier Club edition. 43pp. 7⅞ x 10¾ 21306-4 Pa. $3.00

TEN BOOKS ON ARCHITECTURE, Vitruvius. The most important book ever written on architecture. Early Roman aesthetics, technology, classical orders, site selection, all other aspects. Stands behind everything since. Morgan translation. 331pp. 5⅜ x 8½. 20645-9 Pa. $4.50

THE FOUR BOOKS OF ARCHITECTURE, Andrea Palladio. 16th-century classic responsible for Palladian movement and style. Covers classical architectural remains, Renaissance revivals, classical orders, etc. 1738 Ware English edition. Introduction by A. Placzek. 216 plates. 110pp. of text. 9½ x 12¾. 21308-0 Pa. $10.00

HORIZONS, Norman Bel Geddes. Great industrialist stage designer, "father of streamlining," on application of aesthetics to transportation, amusement, architecture, etc. 1932 prophetic account; function, theory, specific projects. 222 illustrations. 312pp. 7⅞ x 10¾. 23514-9 Pa. $6.95

FRANK LLOYD WRIGHT'S FALLINGWATER, Donald Hoffmann. Full, illustrated story of conception and building of Wright's masterwork at Bear Run, Pa. 100 photographs of site, construction, and details of completed structure. 112pp. 9¼ x 10. 23671-4 Pa. $5.50

THE ELEMENTS OF DRAWING, John Ruskin. Timeless classic by great Viltorian; starts with basic ideas, works through more difficult. Many practical exercises. 48 illustrations. Introduction by Lawrence Campbell. 228pp. 5⅜ x 8½. 22730-8 Pa. $3.75

GIST OF ART, John Sloan. Greatest modern American teacher, Art Students League, offers innumerable hints, instructions, guided comments to help you in painting. Not a formal course. 46 illustrations. Introduction by Helen Sloan. 200pp. 5⅜ x 8½. 23435-5 Pa. $4.00

ART FORMS IN NATURE, Ernst Haeckel. Multitude of strangely beautiful natural forms: Radiolaria, Foraminifera, jellyfishes, fungi, turtles, bats, etc. All 100 plates of the 19th-century evolutionist's *Kunstformen der Natur* (1904). 100pp. 9⅜ x 12¼. 22987-4 Pa. $5.00

CHILDREN: A PICTORIAL ARCHIVE FROM NINETEENTH-CENTURY SOURCES, edited by Carol Belanger Grafton. 242 rare, copyright-free wood engravings for artists and designers. Widest such selection available. All illustrations in line. 119pp. 8⅜ x 11¼. 23694-3 Pa. $4.00

WOMEN: A PICTORIAL ARCHIVE FROM NINETEENTH-CENTURY SOURCES, edited by Jim Harter. 391 copyright-free wood engravings for artists and designers selected from rare periodicals. Most extensive such collection available. All illustrations in line. 128pp. 9 x 12. 23703-6 Pa. $4.50

ARABIC ART IN COLOR, Prisse d'Avennes. From the greatest ornamentalists of all time—50 plates in color, rarely seen outside the Near East, rich in suggestion and stimulus. Includes 4 plates on covers. 46pp. 9⅜ x 12¼. 23658-7 Pa. $6.00

AUTHENTIC ALGERIAN CARPET DESIGNS AND MOTIFS, edited by June Beveridge. Algerian carpets are world famous. Dozens of geometrical motifs are charted on grids, color-coded, for weavers, needleworkers, craftsmen, designers. 53 illustrations plus 4 in color. 48pp. 8¼ x 11. (Available in U.S. only) 23650-1 Pa. $1.75

DICTIONARY OF AMERICAN PORTRAITS, edited by Hayward and Blanche Cirker. 4000 important Americans, earliest times to 1905, mostly in clear line. Politicians, writers, soldiers, scientists, inventors, industrialists, Indians, Blacks, women, outlaws, etc. Identificatory information. 756pp. 9¼ x 12¾. 21823-6 Clothbd. $40.00

HOW THE OTHER HALF LIVES, Jacob A. Riis. Journalistic record of filth, degradation, upward drive in New York immigrant slums, shops, around 1900. New edition includes 100 original Riis photos, monuments of early photography. 233pp. 10 x 7⅞. 22012-5 Pa. $7.00

NEW YORK IN THE THIRTIES, Berenice Abbott. Noted photographer's fascinating study of city shows new buildings that have become famous and old sights that have disappeared forever. Insightful commentary. 97 photographs. 97pp. 11⅜ x 10. 22967-X Pa. $5.00

MEN AT WORK, Lewis W. Hine. Famous photographic studies of construction workers, railroad men, factory workers and coal miners. New supplement of 18 photos on Empire State building construction. New introduction by Jonathan L. Doherty. Total of 69 photos. 63pp. 8 x 10¾. 23475-4 Pa. $3.00

THE DEPRESSION YEARS AS PHOTOGRAPHED BY ARTHUR ROTH-STEIN, Arthur Rothstein. First collection devoted entirely to the work of outstanding 1930s photographer: famous dust storm photo, ragged children, unemployed, etc. 120 photographs. Captions. 119pp. 9¼ x 10¾.
23590-4 Pa. $5.00

CAMERA WORK: A PICTORIAL GUIDE, Alfred Stieglitz. All 559 illustrations and plates from the most important periodical in the history of art photography, Camera Work (1903-17). Presented four to a page, reduced in size but still clear, in strict chronological order, with complete captions. Three indexes. Glossary. Bibliography. 176pp. 8⅜ x 11¼.
23591-2 Pa. $6.95

ALVIN LANGDON COBURN, PHOTOGRAPHER, Alvin L. Coburn. Revealing autobiography by one of greatest photographers of 20th century gives insider's version of Photo-Secession, plus comments on his own work. 77 photographs by Coburn. Edited by Helmut and Alison Gernsheim. 160pp. 8⅛ x 11.
23685-4 Pa. $6.00

NEW YORK IN THE FORTIES, Andreas Feininger. 162 brilliant photographs by the well-known photographer, formerly with Life magazine, show commuters, shoppers, Times Square at night, Harlem nightclub, Lower East Side, etc. Introduction and full captions by John von Hartz. 181pp. 9¼ x 10¾.
23585-8 Pa. $6.95

GREAT NEWS PHOTOS AND THE STORIES BEHIND THEM, John Faber. Dramatic volume of 140 great news photos, 1855 through 1976, and revealing stories behind them, with both historical and technical information. Hindenburg disaster, shooting of Oswald, nomination of Jimmy Carter, etc. 160pp. 8¼ x 11.
23667-6 Pa. $5.00

THE ART OF THE CINEMATOGRAPHER, Leonard Maltin. Survey of American cinematography history and anecdotal interviews with 5 masters—Arthur Miller, Hal Mohr, Hal Rosson, Lucien Ballard, and Conrad Hall. Very large selection of behind-the-scenes production photos. 105 photographs. Filmographies. Index. Originally Behind the Camera. 144pp. 8¼ x 11.
23686-2 Pa. $5.00

DESIGNS FOR THE THREE-CORNERED HAT (LE TRICORNE), Pablo Picasso. 32 fabulously rare drawings—including 31 color illustrations of costumes and accessories—for 1919 production of famous ballet. Edited by Parmenia Migel, who has written new introduction. 48pp. 9⅜ x 12¼.
(Available in U.S. only)
23709-5 Pa. $5.00

NOTES OF A FILM DIRECTOR, Sergei Eisenstein. Greatest Russian filmmaker explains montage, making of Alexander Nevsky, aesthetics; comments on self, associates, great rivals (Chaplin), similar material. 78 illustrations. 240pp. 5⅜ x 8½.
22392-2 Pa. $4.50

HOLLYWOOD GLAMOUR PORTRAITS, edited by John Kobal. 145 photos capture the stars from 1926-49, the high point in portrait photography. Gable, Harlow, Bogart, Bacall, Hedy Lamarr, Marlene Dietrich, Robert Montgomery, Marlon Brando, Veronica Lake; 94 stars in all. Full background on photographers, technical aspects, much more. Total of 160pp. 8⅜ x 11¼.   23352-9 Pa. $6.00

THE NEW YORK STAGE: FAMOUS PRODUCTIONS IN PHOTO-GRAPHS, edited by Stanley Appelbaum. 148 photographs from Museum of City of New York show 142 plays, 1883-1939. *Peter Pan, The Front Page, Dead End, Our Town*, O'Neill, hundreds of actors and actresses, etc. Full indexes. 154pp. 9½ x 10.   23241-7 Pa. $6.00

DIALOGUES CONCERNING TWO NEW SCIENCES, Galileo Galilei. Encompassing 30 years of experiment and thought, these dialogues deal with geometric demonstrations of fracture of solid bodies, cohesion, leverage, speed of light and sound, pendulums, falling bodies, accelerated motion, etc. 300pp. 5⅜ x 8½.   60099-8 Pa. $4.00

THE GREAT OPERA STARS IN HISTORIC PHOTOGRAPHS, edited by James Camner. 343 portraits from the 1850s to the 1940s: Tamburini, Mario, Caliapin, Jeritza, Melchior, Melba, Patti, Pinza, Schipa, Caruso, Farrar, Steber, Gobbi, and many more—270 performers in all. Index. 199pp. 8⅜ x 11¼.   23575-0 Pa. $7.50

J. S. BACH, Albert Schweitzer. Great full-length study of Bach, life, background to music, music, by foremost modern scholar. Ernest Newman translation. 650 musical examples. Total of 928pp. 5⅜ x 8½. (Available in U.S. only)   21631-4, 21632-2 Pa., Two-vol. set $11.00

COMPLETE PIANO SONATAS, Ludwig van Beethoven. All sonatas in the fine Schenker edition, with fingering, analytical material. One of best modern editions. Total of 615pp. 9 x 12. (Available in U.S. only)
                                23134-8, 23135-6 Pa., Two-vol. set $15.50

KEYBOARD MUSIC, J. S. Bach. Bach-Gesellschaft edition. For harpsichord, piano, other keyboard instruments. English Suites, French Suites, Six Partitas, Goldberg Variations, Two-Part Inventions, Three-Part Sinfonias. 312pp. 8⅛ x 11. (Available in U.S. only)   22360-4 Pa. $6.95

FOUR SYMPHONIES IN FULL SCORE, Franz Schubert. Schubert's four most popular symphonies: No. 4 in C Minor ("Tragic"); No. 5 in B-flat Major; No. 8 in B Minor ("Unfinished"); No. 9 in C Major ("Great"). Breitkopf & Hartel edition. Study score. 261pp. 9⅜ x 12¼.
                                                        23681-1 Pa. $6.50

THE AUTHENTIC GILBERT & SULLIVAN SONGBOOK, W. S. Gilbert, A. S. Sullivan. Largest selection available; 92 songs, uncut, original keys, in piano rendering approved by Sullivan. Favorites and lesser-known fine numbers. Edited with plot synopses by James Spero. 3 illustrations. 399pp. 9 x 12.   23482-7 Pa. $9.95

A MAYA GRAMMAR, Alfred M. Tozzer. Practical, useful English-language grammar by the Harvard anthropologist who was one of the three greatest American scholars in the area of Maya culture. Phonetics, grammatical processes, syntax, more. 301pp. 5⅜ x 8½.　　　　23465-7 Pa. $4.00

THE JOURNAL OF HENRY D. THOREAU, edited by Bradford Torrey, F. H. Allen. Complete reprinting of 14 volumes, 1837-61, over two million words; the sourcebooks for *Walden*, etc. Definitive. All original sketches, plus 75 photographs. Introduction by Walter Harding. Total of 1804pp. 8½ x 12¼.　　　　20312-3, 20313-1 Clothbd., Two-vol. set $70.00

CLASSIC GHOST STORIES, Charles Dickens and others. 18 wonderful stories you've wanted to reread: "The Monkey's Paw," "The House and the Brain," "The Upper Berth," "The Signalman," "Dracula's Guest," "The Tapestried Chamber," etc. Dickens, Scott, Mary Shelley, Stoker, etc. 330pp. 5⅜ x 8½.　　　　20735-8 Pa. $4.50

SEVEN SCIENCE FICTION NOVELS, H. G. Wells. Full novels. *First Men in the Moon, Island of Dr. Moreau, War of the Worlds, Food of the Gods, Invisible Man, Time Machine, In the Days of the Comet.* A basic science-fiction library. 1015pp. 5⅜ x 8½. (Available in U.S. only)
　　　　20264-X Clothbd. $8.95

ARMADALE, Wilkie Collins. Third great mystery novel by the author of *The Woman in White* and *The Moonstone*. Ingeniously plotted narrative shows an exceptional command of character, incident and mood. Original magazine version with 40 illustrations. 597pp. 5⅜ x 8½.
　　　　23429-0 Pa. $6.00

MASTERS OF MYSTERY, H. Douglas Thomson. The first book in English (1931) devoted to history and aesthetics of detective story. Poe, Doyle, LeFanu, Dickens, many others, up to 1930. New introduction and notes by E. F. Bleiler. 288pp. 5⅜ x 8½. (Available in U.S. only)
　　　　23606-4 Pa. $4.00

FLATLAND, E. A. Abbott. Science-fiction classic explores life of 2-D being in 3-D world. Read also as introduction to thought about hyperspace. Introduction by Banesh Hoffmann. 16 illustrations. 103pp. 5⅜ x 8½.
　　　　20001-9 Pa. $2.00

THREE SUPERNATURAL NOVELS OF THE VICTORIAN PERIOD, edited, with an introduction, by E. F. Bleiler. Reprinted complete and unabridged, three great classics of the supernatural: *The Haunted Hotel* by Wilkie Collins, *The Haunted House at Latchford* by Mrs. J. H. Riddell, and *The Lost Stradivarius* by J. Meade Falkner. 325pp. 5⅜ x 8½.
　　　　22571-2 Pa. $4.00

AYESHA: THE RETURN OF "SHE," H. Rider Haggard. Virtuoso sequel featuring the great mythic creation, Ayesha, in an adventure that is fully as good as the first book, *She*. Original magazine version, with 47 original illustrations by Maurice Greiffenhagen. 189pp. 6½ x 9¼.
　　　　23649-8 Pa. $3.50

UNCLE SILAS, J. Sheridan LeFanu. Victorian Gothic mystery novel, considered by many best of period, even better than Collins or Dickens. Wonderful psychological terror. Introduction by Frederick Shroyer. 436pp. 5⅜ x 8½. 21715-9 Pa. $6.00

JURGEN, James Branch Cabell. The great erotic fantasy of the 1920's that delighted thousands, shocked thousands more. Full final text, Lane edition with 13 plates by Frank Pape. 346pp. 5⅜ x 8½. 23507-6 Pa. $4.50

THE CLAVERINGS, Anthony Trollope. Major novel, chronicling aspects of British Victorian society, personalities. Reprint of Cornhill serialization, 16 plates by M. Edwards; first reprint of full text. Introduction by Norman Donaldson. 412pp. 5⅜ x 8½. 23464-9 Pa. $5.00

KEPT IN THE DARK, Anthony Trollope. Unusual short novel about Victorian morality and abnormal psychology by the great English author. Probably the first American publication. Frontispiece by Sir John Millais. 92pp. 6½ x 9¼. 23609-9 Pa. $2.50

RALPH THE HEIR, Anthony Trollope. Forgotten tale of illegitimacy, inheritance. Master novel of Trollope's later years. Victorian country estates, clubs, Parliament, fox hunting, world of fully realized characters. Reprint of 1871 edition. 12 illustrations by F. A. Faser. 434pp. of text. 5⅜ x 8½. 23642-0 Pa. $5.00

YEKL and THE IMPORTED BRIDEGROOM AND OTHER STORIES OF THE NEW YORK GHETTO, Abraham Cahan. Film *Hester Street* based on *Yekl* (1896). Novel, other stories among first about Jewish immigrants of N.Y.'s East Side. Highly praised by W. D. Howells—Cahan "a new star of realism." New introduction by Bernard G. Richards. 240pp. 5⅜ x 8½. 22427-9 Pa. $3.50

THE HIGH PLACE, James Branch Cabell. Great fantasy writer's enchanting comedy of disenchantment set in 18th-century France. Considered by some critics to be even better than his famous *Jurgen*. 10 illustrations and numerous vignettes by noted fantasy artist Frank C. Pape. 320pp. 5⅜ x 8½. 23670-6 Pa. $4.00

ALICE'S ADVENTURES UNDER GROUND, Lewis Carroll. Facsimile of ms. Carroll gave Alice Liddell in 1864. Different in many ways from final Alice. Handlettered, illustrated by Carroll. Introduction by Martin Gardner. 128pp. 5⅜ x 8½. 21482-6 Pa. $2.50

FAVORITE ANDREW LANG FAIRY TALE BOOKS IN MANY COLORS, Andrew Lang. The four Lang favorites in a boxed set—the complete *Red, Green, Yellow* and *Blue* Fairy Books. 164 stories; 439 illustrations by Lancelot Speed, Henry Ford and G. P. Jacomb Hood. Total of about 1500pp. 5⅜ x 8½. 23407-X Boxed set, Pa. $15.95

AMERICAN ANTIQUE FURNITURE, Edgar G. Miller, Jr. The basic coverage of all American furniture before 1840: chapters per item chronologically cover all types of furniture, with more than 2100 photos. Total of 1106pp. 7⅞ x 10¾.　　　　21599-7, 21600-4 Pa., Two-vol. set $17.90

ILLUSTRATED GUIDE TO SHAKER FURNITURE, Robert Meader. Director, Shaker Museum, Old Chatham, presents up-to-date coverage of all furniture and appurtenances, with much on local styles not available elsewhere. 235 photos. 146pp. 9 x 12.　　　　22819-3 Pa. $6.00

ORIENTAL RUGS, ANTIQUE AND MODERN, Walter A. Hawley. Persia, Turkey, Caucasus, Central Asia, China, other traditions. Best general survey of all aspects: styles and periods, manufacture, uses, symbols and their interpretation, and identification. 96 illustrations, 11 in color. 320pp. 6⅛ x 9¼.　　　　22366-3 Pa. $6.95

CHINESE POTTERY AND PORCELAIN, R. L. Hobson. Detailed descriptions and analyses by former Keeper of the Department of Oriental Antiquities and Ethnography at the British Museum. Covers hundreds of pieces from primitive times to 1915. Still the standard text for most periods. 136 plates, 40 in full color. Total of 750pp. 5⅜ x 8½.
23253-0 Pa. $10.00

THE WARES OF THE MING DYNASTY, R. L. Hobson. Foremost scholar examines and illustrates many varieties of Ming (1368-1644). Famous blue and white, polychrome, lesser-known styles and shapes. 117 illustrations, 9 full color, of outstanding pieces. Total of 263pp. 6⅛ x 9¼. (Available in U.S. only)　　　　23652-8 Pa. $6.00

Prices subject to change without notice.

Available at your book dealer or write for free catalogue to Dept. GI, Dover Publications, Inc., 31 East Second Street, Mineola, N.Y. 11501. Dover publishes more than 175 books each year on science, elementary and advanced mathematics, biology, music, art, literary history, social sciences and other areas.